More Praise fc

"Waights Taylor has been writing
time, and it shows. If you have been like me and have read ... s
drafts you will know that the novel has steadily improved. At this point it's hard to imagine how it might be revised for the better. The characters are finely drawn, the dialogue is crisp, the plot moves along and the dramatic conflicts enhance the suspense. Then, too, there's the Alabama setting. As a son of the Yellowhammer State, which is also referred to as the Heart of Dixie and the Cotton State, Taylor knows 'Bama as only a true Southerner can know it. In Nevermore he creates compelling Black characters and compelling white characters and conjures the ambiance of the Deep South. He also digs deeply into Black history and provides information about Black historical figures that are largely unknown today and that are well worth remembering. With the title 'Nevermore' you can bet that Edgar Allan Poe—the author of the poem "The Raven"and its infamous bird—show up. Shakespeare is also here and so is Southern Gothic. The novel can be read and enjoyed by young adults and by their parents. It cuts across generations and across the seemingly endless American racial divide. Oh, I forgot to say that members of the Ku Klux Klan with their torches, guns and ugliness also feature in the narrative. The Klan did many atrocities, killing twenty-five Blacks and burning down many Black houses and warehouses. It is hard to imagine the atrocities, but it's as true today as it was when Waights was a boy growing up in Alabama."

JONAH RASKIN, author of the novel, *Beat Blues San Francisco 1955*

"Nevermore is a startling story set in the segregated South of 1949 Alabama, which the author knows well, with its ramifications still deeply felt over fifty years later by the protagonist Steve. He learned, as a young white teenager, the realities of the deep Black/white cultural prejudice and separation built into his world and the whole town's everyday life. The awful events he witnessed on the night of terror ultimately made him stronger, and able to withstand the incredulity and disbelief of the adult world when he told his truth, putting himself and his family at risk. Waights brings the reader into this dystopian world and of its conflicted people, with chilling echoes to our present-day cultural and political divisiveness."

Arnold Levine, author of a memoir, *Banned by the BBC*

NEVERMORE

Bubba,

As always I thank you for all the help you've given me, and thanks for the great blurb.

Your friend,

[illegible]

NEVERMORE

Waights Taylor Jr.

McCaa Books • Santa Rosa

McCaa Books
684 Benicia Drive #50
Santa Rosa, CA 95409

ISBN 978-1-7378683-5-4
Library of Congress Control Number 2023906563

First published in 2023 by McCaa Books,
an imprint of McCaa Publications.

Printed in the United States of America
Typeset in Minion Pro

www.mccaabooks.com

Dedicated

to

Sarah Martin and George Martin

"The past is never dead. It's not even past"

William Faulkner—*Requiem for a Nun*

Part I

Delphi, Alabama—2001

"Let my heart be still a moment and this mystery explore;
—'Tis the wind and nothing more!"

Edgar Allan Poe—*The Raven*

1

The Birds

Tuesday—March 13, 2001

A MURDER OF CROWS APPEARED, cawing and flying in circles around the cabin, as the morning sun struggled to be recognized amongst the threatening clouds. Steve sat on the porch, sipping coffee and staring in fascination. The birds continued this ritual for a while until a few flew away, and shortly thereafter, in what seemed to be a choreographed winged dance, the others followed.

Raindrops started falling on the cabin's tin roof when another black bird came out of nowhere, perched on a tree limb in front of the cabin, and stared relentlessly at Steve.

He blurted out, "Why are you here again? Why do you keep haunting me?"

The raven remained silent, yet Steve couldn't help but dread that the bird would call out, *Nevermore.* Steve was about to yell at the raven again when he flew away.

Steve repressed the pain that roiled up in his gut. Suddenly the only thing he heard was the increasing spattering of raindrops on the roof as if a snare drummer were directing a faster tempo.

Delphi was Steve's childhood hometown and many of his adult trips to the small town were uneventful, even though thoughts of the past always lurked in his mind. Presently living in Durham, North Carolina, he tried to visit Delphi and the cabin at least once a year. He was a Professor of English Literature at Duke University and Spring break was a good getaway opportunity. Since both of his parents had died, he wondered if the visits were a penance. "Stop bashing yourself, Steve," he said aloud, "it's over and been over for years."

Trying to regain his composure, he stood up and looked around to ensure the raven was gone. He checked his watch and realized he soon had to pick up Nick McAdams at Montgomery's airport. He and Nick had become friends in college and had remained so since.

As he got in the car, his cell phone chimed. "Hi, I'm just leaving to pick up Nick. I'll call when I have a chance." After a pause, he added, "Thanks, I love you too. G'bye."

Steve's mood improved as he drove. He tuned the car radio to a classical music station. It happened to be playing one of his parents' favorite pieces: Beethoven's Ninth Symphony and, lo and behold, "Ode to Joy" had just begun. He smiled, thinking about his mother and father who were originally from Montgomery. Until he left for college, they often visited his grandparents there.

Nick had lived in Philadelphia all his life. He had visited his daughter in Atlanta before flying to Montgomery to visit Steve. She worked as a lawyer in a prestigious bi-racial law firm representing poor Black and white people who couldn't get fair trials in the South.

Although Nick had been to the South many times on business and to visit his daughter, he had never been to Alabama, much less Delphi.

As Steve thought about these things, he realized for the first time that "delphi" was embedded in "Philadelphia." *What does that mean if anything?* he thought.

Delphi, the county seat of Allen County, twenty-five miles west of Montgomery, was four miles from the Alabama River. During Steve's childhood, the town had about 3,000 people, most of whom worked for either the paper mill on the river or one of several logging companies that satisfied the mill's insatiable appetite for pine and fir wood. The county courthouse sat in the center of the town square. On one corner sat a small pavilion with a water fountain that offered the most God-awful tasting and smelling mineral water one could imagine. On another corner was a Confederate statue, a quintessential feature in most southern towns. On the third corner was the police station, and on the final corner was the library. The town's main business district surrounded the square's four sides and included a bank, a Winn-Dixie grocery store, a movie theater, and lots of smaller stores for drugs, clothing, laundry, books, and offices of doctors, accountants, and lawyers.

Before Steve was born, his father had purchased the county's newspaper, then named the *Delphi Delta*, and although he disliked the name, the owner had stipulated that the name could not be changed. Steve's dad finally convinced the owner to let him rename it *Delphi Delta News* and the sale was completed. The family's house was two blocks west of the square, and his parents always described it as *faux-antebellum*. The newspaper's office was next door, where, as a kid, Steve learned to set type, making an inky mess of himself.

As Steve approached Montgomery, he thought about his relationship with Nick, one of his best friends. They first met in 1953, soon after enrolling as freshmen at Dartmouth College in New Hampshire. Nick's father was a Dartmouth grad, which helped Nick get admitted, while most knew it was his basketball skills that interested the school.

Steve's path to Dartmouth was not as straightforward. His parents wanted him to attend an Ivy League school and initially thought he should apply at Princeton. When they learned that Princeton was noted for accepting students from southern states, his parents decided Steve should apply to Dartmouth to broaden his cultural experiences beyond his southern upbringing. So it was Dartmouth. The college got a bright young man and, unbeknown to them, another good basketball player.

At the end of the first day of freshman class orientation, the Associate Dean of Residential Life asked Nick and Steve to join him in his office for a private chat.

Steve, who had a habit of sizing-up people he met, was amused by the dean's appearance. He had developed the trait when he was seven or eight years old as a form of self-interest and self-protection. He realized he might sometimes be wrong in his assessment, but he felt these insights assisted him in better understanding people.

Steve tried not to smile as he observed the dean, a short, squirrelly-looking man, his eyes constantly darting around as if he were unsure of himself. He had a high-pitched voice, which Steve thought matched his demeanor. However, he did dress well and wore a natty bowtie.

Steve had never seen a man, Black or white, as handsome as Nick. He had no idea what the proportions for a perfect face were, but he figured Nick's were a good model. His eyes were blue, his nose almost aquiline, and he had a strong chin. His hair had a slight tinge of red in it. Well over six feet tall, maybe six-four, his skin was light brown, as if he were a bronzed Adonis. Steve laughed quietly to himself. *I guess you could call Nick colored, but aren't we all?*

The dean opened the meeting very carefully by saying, "Gentlemen, welcome to Dartmouth, and I hope your years with us will be enjoyable and productive for you both. We pride ourselves on being a progressive college, and since you both had excellent high school academic records, I would like to propose a residential housing arrangement for you."

Nick and Steve looked at one another quizzically, Then Nick winked at him and smiled. Steve smiled back.

The dean cleared his throat to get their attention, and continued, "What I'm about to propose is in no way mandatory as I know you two have already specified your housing choices. I'd like you to consider sharing a room in Allen Hall. Are you comfortable with that?"

I get it, Steve thought, *he's using us as guinea pigs in his housing experiment.*

Nick asked, "Where are you from, Steve?"

When Steve responded, "Delphi, Alabama," Nick laughed, and soon the dean and Steve joined him.

"Well, hot damn, I'm in." Nick said. "How about you Steve? I'm from Philadelphia."

Steve felt cornered, but he didn't want to get started on the wrong foot, so he replied emphatically, "Damn right, I'm in."

The dean smiled, "Gentlemen, I think you two will set a fine example for our students. Please go to Allan Hall where the staff will take care of you. By the way, Mr. McAdams, your new roommate said on his application that he was a basketball player."

Some of Steve's classmates wondered how he could be so comfortable living with a Black student. He ignored their concerns and questions, knowing they wouldn't understand his liberal parents and others that influenced his early years.

Both men earned bachelor's degrees with honors at Dartmouth—Steve in English literature and Nick in business administration. Steve later earned a Masters and a Ph.D. in English literature at Duke University, and accepted a professorship at the school where he was still employed. Nick remained at Dartmouth and earned an MBA, establishing what became a successful private investment firm in Philadelphia.

Without warning, Steve's mood shifted to the present, and he thought of the raven and his penetrating stare. What was the bird trying to tell him? Something to do with Nick?

2

Mood Swings

Tuesday—March 13, 2001

NICK STOOD AT THE AIRPORT'S CURBSIDE holding his bag. Steve hadn't seen Nick in five years, but noted that he was still drop-dead handsome. Men and women, especially *women*, were always turning to stare at him.

Steve jumped out and gave him a big hug, pushed him back and said, "Welcome to Alabama, Nick, but damn it, you're still several inches taller than I am. You're supposed to shrink when you get older."

They laughed, and Nick responded, "Well, Shorty, I'm glad to be in 'bama. Can't wait to see Delphi. And don't forget, you could nail long shots from the back court and were often the team's top scorer."

"Yeah, but you were the slam dunk king. Let's get in the car before we get any wetter." Driving toward Delphi, Steve said, "I'm glad you'll be here three days so I can show you around my hometown and Montgomery."

"Yeah…that was the plan, but something came up at work and I have to leave day after tomorrow on a flight at 3:30. Didn't you ever have to cut one of your visits to Delphi short and go back to Durham?"

Steve smiled wanly, trying not to appear disappointed. "Yes, it happens, but I bet you have to get back to Philadelphia and make another gazillion bucks at your brokerage firm."

Nick guffawed, and then grinned. "You'd lose that bet. Yes, my company's doing all right, but I think you have an inflated opinion about my success."

"Probably, but you should try making it on a college professor's salary. We're almost to Delphi. I'll park on the town square. Don't get too excited, it's a small town. I hope you enjoy yourself and that nothing crazy happens."

"I get your drift, Steve," Nick said, "I've experienced all the crazy things Black men must endure—like cop pullovers for no specific reason, constant racial slurs from the right and left. I wanted to join the Black crowd that protested Philadelphia's police brutality in 1964. The establishment called it a race riot. I was twenty-eight and just getting my new business started. When I told Mom and Dad what I was going to do, Mom called me. I'll never forget what she said as only a Black woman could, 'Nick, please don't get involved in the protests. I know you want to, but you might get your head bashed in by a cop's billy club and get arrested. You must get your business started because your success might help the Black community. Don't be a martyr.' Of course, I didn't say *No* to Mom, although I still wish I had participated in the protests in at least a small way. The last thing I'll tell you about is how to create dead silence. As I got more successful with my business, I would often meet with a group of investors, mostly white men who didn't know me. I would purposely arrive a bit late, and when I opened the door and stepped into the conference room all the idle chatter came to an abrupt end. I liked doing it, so I doubt Delphi can raise my hackles. Sorry for the lecture."

Steve smiled. "You're something else, Mr. Nick, welcome to Delphi."

The rain had subsided, so people were out and about on the square and sidewalks. Steve played square tour guide, explaining the fountain, the buildings, and most of the statues on the square.

Nick listened and studied everything carefully and said, "That statue looks like a young kid." He walked up to the plinth and read aloud, "Marvin Gibbs." Then Nick looked at the library which was on the square and read aloud, "Moses Douglas Public Library." Who are Marvin and Moses, Steve?"

Steve tried to look nonchalant and said, "Oh, their stories are for another day. C'mon, we gotta go over to the fountain."

Nick nodded as they started walking toward the fountain. "I think you told me years ago, but why was the town named Delphi? This sure as hell isn't Greece."

Steve tried to sound smug, "You're walking right at what became the inspiration for Delphi's name."

"I'm not feeling inspired." Nick said, "You'll have to tell me again. He appeared stoic.

"Well, not inspired, it's a funny story my Dad told me when I was a kid. When the town was established in the 1840s, one of the city founders came up with the idea of Delphi. Soon after that, the fountain was first drilled and started flowing, and he sold the idea to the city fathers with an embellishment. He said they could tout the water as having special healing powers. Another guy, who apparently knew his ancient Greek history, chimed in and added that they could hire a young lady to dress as Pythia, who was the Oracle of Delphi, and for a few bucks, she would sniff the noxious odors of the mineral water and spout gibberish that could be interpreted in any number of ways. Another young lady would act as an acolyte to Pythia and suggest interpretations."

Nick couldn't stop laughing. "Well, I'll give it to the town's founders for their chutzpah. Did it work?"

Steve was having fun with this. "Depends on which version of the story you believe. Some still think it worked for about fifteen years until the Civil War started. Others, including my father, preferred to think it stopped after two years, when one of the young Pythias was assaulted."

"Wow, that's a doozy. Are there any books or historical records from that period?" Nick asked.

"Not that I know of. Dad thought most people just wanted to forget the whole debacle and move on. Maybe the Pythia part of the story is pure fantasy."

Nick held his nose and grinned, "I guess I have to drink the water and see what I think. Want to join me?"

"No, thanks. I've had enough. Be my guest."

They noticed a group of people, both Black and white, staring at them. Nick turned to Steve, and said, "Do you think they're going to give me a hard time?"

Steve shook his head, pointed at the fountain, nodding at Nick, hoping that he was right.

Nick took a swig and froze, still leaning over the fountain. For a moment, Steve thought Nick was going to spit it out as he swished it around in his month. Instead, he bent his head backwards and gargled the water before he swallowed it.

People stared at him in amazement, and Nick threw up his arms and shouted, "Wow, that's invigorating. My throat never felt so good. Mighty fine stuff, folks."

To Steve's surprise and delight, the gathered audience laughed and clapped. "Now you've got them in your hip pocket," Steve whispered. "What did you really think of the water?"

Nick whispered back with a straight face, "It tastes and smells like shit, but my throat does feel good."

"C'mon, let's go to the cabin. It's peaceful there, and we've got a lot to talk about."

As Steve drove out of Delphi, Nick cleared his throat and said, "I know I made your father's funeral service ten years ago, but I'm still sorry I didn't make your mother's service in 1993. You remember, I was in Hawaii with my family when I heard the news and didn't have time to get here." Nick paused, staring out the window. "Nice countryside. There's one thing for sure. When I met your parents at our commencement ceremonies in '57, I knew immediately that if all southerns were like your parents, things would be better."

Steve tried to hide it, but his eyes were a bit misty. "I know when you're an only child and have older parents, you must endure losing them earlier than most. You're lucky both of your parents are still alive."

"Well, an old Scotsman like my Dad won't give up easily and Mom is just as tough."

Steve reached over and tapped Nick on the hand. "Good genes."

As Steve drove to the cabin, the rain stopped, the dark clouds quickly changing to cumulus clouds scattered about a blue sky, a startling transformation. Nick was duly impressed and said, "This is gorgeous. All the greenery and trees highlighted by the sky. Does the weather change that often here?"

"Spring's a'coming, Nick. The change of seasons can be dramatic and quick. It'll get warmer soon, maybe even hot and humid. One dramatic change we don't want is tornadoes, but we get our fair share. Here's the turn to the cabin. You can see it on that rise ahead. It's close to a creek that flows into the Alabama River, but thanks to the rise, the cabin has never flooded."

Steve showed Nick to his room. "When you're ready, I'll be on the porch."

"Which side?" Nick asked.

"Good question. The west porch. Mom and Dad designed the cabin based on one they saw on a Caribbean island before I was born. They liked the idea of being able to view the rising and setting sun. Want a beer?"

"Hell, yes! I thought you'd never ask. Where's your southern manners?"

"Since Mom always said I lost them when I went to Dartmouth, then it must be your fault."

Nick shrugged. "So be it. Can't second guess your mother."

THEY SAT ON THE PORCH DRINKING BEER, and Nick said, "It still grieves me that you and Barbara divorced in 1972. I liked her, but I know all couples handle things differently. It must have been tough for your kids, Alice and Daniel. Rebecca and I had a tough patch years ago. Counseling, listening to each other, and perseverance got us through it. Do you ever see Barbara?"

Steve was reticent to talk about her, but he answered politely, "Of course, we saw each other at important family events, like birthdays and school graduations. But the last few years of our marriage were not good years which led to our divorce...Unfortunately, Barbara died three years ago and our extended family had to go through another ordeal."

"I'm so sorry to hear all that. I can't imagine how tough it must have been," Nick said.

Steve felt forlorn and lost, and said, "Thanks, Nick." *Maybe the raven is somehow involved in all this.*

"Well, you were certainly a hot catch for another women, but I guess you never took the bait."

"How's that? Where did that curve ball come from?" Steve asked.

"Simple. Over the years you've established quite a resume. You're considered one of the prominent professors of English literature in the country. You've written several books on literature and Shakespeare. You started acting in plays when you were in college. What's a lady to not like?"

"You make me sound better than I am, but thanks anyway. If it hadn't been for Duke's generous tuition program for kids of faculty members and other staff members, we wouldn't have been able to pay for our kids' education."

Nick grinned in what appeared to be a questioning stare, and said, "You didn't answer my question. Oh, what the hell, I propose a toast to our kids who have done well and have good jobs." They tapped beer bottles and repeated, "To our kids."

"We're lucky guys, Steve. Look at that marvelous sunset you ordered up. Thank you."

Steve was glad he had moved off the subjects of his marriage to Barbara. "I aim to please. As Prospero, I can conjure up a storm and then make it subside. It's all magic, you know."

"Well, Prospero, done any part-time acting lately? I know you enjoy it."

Steve nodded and smiled. "I still do some at Duke and other local theaters around the South. Roles are harder to find now, unless they're looking for an older guy. Okay, enough nostalgia. Let's rustle up some grub."

In the small kitchen Steve said, "You always did a good steak. I've got two rib eyes in the fridge. You have at 'em, but give me a few minutes head start with the potatoes and vegetables. And I've got a great bottle of Cabernet Sauvignon to share with you."

"Can't wait," Nick said. "I'll get right on it, Chef."

Their second bottle was nearly gone when Nick said, "Enough. Great meal. Great wine, but my head's starting to spin."

"Coffee?"

"No, thanks. Let's wash the dishes, and then I'm hitting the sack."

Twenty minutes later, Nick said, "Good night."

The raven reappeared in Steve's mind just before he said, "Good night."

Nick looked worried, "You all right, Steve?"

"Sure, see you in the morning."

In bed, he felt the raven's presence and said quietly, "I know why you're here. Please, please don't make it happen again."

3

Nightmares

Wednesday—March 14, 2001

STEVE'S NIGHT WAS A MESS. The raven ignored his plea. He tossed and turned all night. And when he did fall asleep for short periods, he soon awoke in a sweat, fighting off frightening thoughts and images spinning in his head. At dawn he gave up trying to sleep. He fixed a pot of coffee and took a cup to the east porch just as the sun peeked over the horizon. A few moments later, Nick joined him with cup in hand.

"Good morning, Steve."

"Mornin', Nick. How'd you sleep?"

"Well enough, but you don't look too rested."

Nick was right. Steve had dared to peek at himself in the bathroom mirror and saw the face of a haggard man. "Oh, I'm not as bad as I look. Just had a night filled with dreams. Sometimes dreams can be weird, huh? Do you have nights like that?"

"Sure, I've had weird dreams. Steve, tell me if this is none of my business, but as your good friend, I can't ignore what I heard last night."

"Don't worry. I'm fine. Just some nightmares. What did you hear?"

"Must've been really bad. You screamed three times last night. First you yelled 'Joshua' and later 'Moses.' I couldn't understand what you said the third time. You sounded frightened. No, no, it was more like you were terrorized. Who are Joshua and Moses, Steve?"

Steve looked at the branch the raven had been on, fully expecting to see the bird, but he wasn't there. Steve crossed his arms and leaned over, trying to relive the pain he felt in his gut. The raven had completed his task. His past had found him. He didn't answer Nick.

Nick put his coffee cup down and folded his hands in his lap, making himself look like a yogi. "There's one other thing I need to tell you that happened in our freshman year at Dartmouth. In December, a few days before we went home for the holiday break, you had a night similar to last night. You woke up twice, screaming out the names *Joshua* and *Moses*. I've remembered Moses all these years but had forgotten Joshua's name until last night. I want to help you, Steve, so please tell me who Joshua and Moses are other than Hebrew prophets."

Steve rocked back and forth a few times, struggling to remain calm. Unable to, he looked straight at Nick, and said angrily, "Why didn't you tell me this then?"

Nick stiffened up. "I didn't know you that well."

"Damn you, Nick, the yogi, do you think you can bug me about it after all these years?"

Nick remained in his yoga-like position, smiling. He said, "No, but I have to add that I never heard you say those names again until last night. It must be more than weird dreams."

Steve felt the anger drain out of his body like a maple tree giving up its sap. "Sorry, I didn't mean to snap at you. I didn't hear their names again in college. Hell, I don't know why. After the holiday break, I guess college stimulated and excited me and absorbed my thoughts. But after Dartmouth, I started hearing them again."

Nick nodded. "Okay. But who are Joshua and Moses?"

Rubbing his jaw as if it pained him to speak, Steve said, "When I was a kid, Joshua Marshall was the only Black doctor in Delphi. He graduated from Fisk University in Nashville with a BS and earned his MD at Ohio State University. He had his medical office in a room at his house in the Black part of town called Westtown, which wasn't officially a part of Delphi. Moses Douglas earned a Masters's degree in English at Morehead College in Atlanta. He was Delphi's librarian in the small Black library that abutted the white library. Moses and Joshua lived in the same house."

While I was sure who the third voice was, I didn't tell Nick who it was.

"I didn't know there were libraries for Black people in Alabama back then," Nick said.

"My father told me the white librarian in Delphi had suggested it before I was born, and the city agreed. Dad laughed when he added that the townspeople went around congratulating themselves on being so progressive."

Nick appeared stunned. "Incredible. How well did you know Joshua and Moses?"

"Very well for a white kid." Steve stopped talking.

Nick's face said he was still confused, searching for something to say. He finally said, "That can't be all. There must be more."

"There is. Way too much more."

"C'mon, Steve. We've been friends too long not to share. Maybe, just maybe, I can help you."

"It'll take too long. You're leaving tomorrow."

"Just a minute, I've got to make a phone call. Is cell phone service reliable here?"

Steve answered, "It's okay, but it can be spotty at times."

"Good. I'll hope for the best. I'll go into cabin to make the call."

As Nick went inside, Steve saw Nick pull out his cell phone and punch in a number. Intentionally or not, Nick spoke loudly enough so Steve could hear his side of the conversation.

> "It's Nick. I'm glad you're in early."
>
> "Yeah, I'm having a good time with Steve. I need you to change my return flight from Montgomery to Philadelphia to Saturday, March 17. I'd prefer a flight late in the afternoon, say 3:30, if possible."
>
> "I know he wants me at the meeting Friday morning. That's why I was coming back tomorrow."
>
> "Yes, yes, the investors are expecting me. You tell him I have every confidence in him. Hell, I'm just the window dressing. He can tell the investors I have to help a family member."

"No, it's not serious, but it needs my attention."

"Thanks for your concern, and tell him I'll call him tomorrow or Friday."

"Yep, that's it. Thanks."

Nick came back onto the porch, and Steve said, "I heard what you said."

Nick shrugged.

"You didn't need to do that."

"Yes, I did, Steve. And you are like family."

"You're too much. Let's have breakfast, then we can talk more."

After breakfast, Steve said, "I need to tell you about yesterday morning before you got here. It involves crows and a raven."

Nick, who had been sipping a coffee, almost inhaled his sip, gasping. He said, "You gotta be kidding me. What's next, condors and vultures?"

Steve grimaced. "Very funny."

"Sorry. Bad joke. What happened?"

Steve thought Nick might think he was nuts, but he continued, "Early yesterday morning, I was having coffee on the east porch when a murder of crows flew around the cabin making their usual god-awful racket. Right after they flew away a single raven appeared. It was almost as if the crows had escorted the raven to the cabin. The raven stared at me so intensely that it spooked me. I thought he might say 'Nevermore.' Of course, the bird didn't say anything, but he sure scared the shit out of me."

Steve sat silently for several minutes until Nick said, "Steve, I don't know where this is going. No doubt, you're terrorized or haunted by something, but it is fascinating. Have the birds visited you in person before?"

"Funny you should ask. Damn, what a foolish expression. Of course, it's not funny, it's serious." *Why did I go off on a tangent*? Steve thought. *Maybe I'm trying to stall.*

"Well, you've still got your sense of humor, professor. But what about the birds?"

"Right…the birds," Steve mumbled. "I've come to Delphi on visits almost every year since I started college, maybe forty times or so. Often, I would work on writing and editing one of my books unless my parents or guests were with me. The birds started appearing when I was alone right after my Mom's death. Why then, you ask? I have no idea, but I can't get the raven out of my mind. Do you think I'm hallucinating?"

"Do *you*?"

"No, the raven's too damn real."

"I believe you," Nick said. "Is there much more to the story? Is Marvin Gibbs a part of this story?"

Steve blinked. "Yes, to both questions."

"Well, tell me the whole story. And why are you so distraught?"

Steve sighed and took a deep breath. "Even though I was there, I don't think I can. Memory is elusive. Sometimes you're sure something is true when it's a figment of your imagination or perverted by dreams. In *Hamlet*, Ophelia says, *'Tis in my memory lock'd, and you yourself shall keep the key of it.'* While Ophelia was speaking to her brother, Laertes, I struggle with who best keeps my key."

Steve faltered momentarily, but then added, "I doubt you'll understand this, but the person who keeps my key, and knows the whole story is the person who experienced it at that time, and that's soon to be fourteen-year-old Steve."

Nick was obviously perplexed. He said, "Excuse my bluntness. The Ophelia quote is your Shakespearean way of expressing it, but how the hell can you disassociate yourself from young Steve?"

"Fair enough, Nick. Here's another way to think of things. Looking back through the house of mirrors that is memory, sometimes we question the truth of what we believed happened because years of remembering and re-imagining, and the influence of dreams and nightmares have blurred the events." Steve paused, feeling stiff and frightened, and said, "Yes, it's been haunting at times. Now, the raven has appeared as a symbol, taunting me. That bird's trying to egg me on, to push me back into the miasma of these horrid memories. These hauntings are all mine now, but a young Steve dealt with his youthful trauma in 1949, including a court case. One last Shakespearean reference, on which I will rest my case, is from *Richard III* when George Plantagenet, the Duke of Clarence, says to his jailer *'O, I have passed a miserable night, So full of ugly dreams, of ugly sights,...'*"

Nick shook his head, still confused. "So, who will be telling the story?"

Steve wryly smiled at Nick, finally saying, "I don't know. Since my explanations are anything but perfect, I'll guess we'll have to *see*."

Part II
The Good Times—1949

"Time doth transfix the flourish set on youth
And delves the parallels in beauty's brow."

William Shakespeare—*Sonnet 60*

4

Edgar Allan Poe

Thursday—February 3, 1949

I WAS READING A BOOK IN BED when I felt a chill in the air. Although it was winter, the chill was different. I looked around the bedroom, not sure what was going on, but it was sure weird. After a few moments, it seemed to pass, and I shrugged my shoulders and continued to read the book aloud, quietly.

> Now, as the owner came to our door, we were both wondering if that man would, as Dupin guessed, be a sailor.
>
> He was a large man, and strong. He carried a big, heavy piece of wood, but no gun. He said to us, in French: "Good evening."
>
> "Sit down, my friend. I suppose you have come to ask about the orangutan. A very fine animal. I have no doubt that it is a very valuable animal. How old do you think it may be?"

My mother opened the bedroom door, grimaced, and said, "I thought I heard your voice. Steve Andrew Thompson, I told you earlier to get to sleep. Turn out that light right now!"

I liked my mother a lot, but sometimes she really bugged me, so I pleaded with her in the snarky manner of most thirteen-year-old boys, "But, Mom, I just read Poe's poem 'The Raven,' I've got three pages left to read in his short story 'The Murders in the Rue Morgue.' It's really exciting."

Unable to suppress a grin, she said, "I'm glad you like to read, but you need your sleep. It's cold. Use both of your blankets. Good night." She turned out the light.

"Yes, ma'am." I sighed and nestled under the covers, knowing I had lost, when I heard her say, "Andy, he's reading that Poe anthology you gave him. He'll probably have nightmares now."

5

Trot Line

Saturday—February 5, 1949

I WAS IN MANY WAYS LIKE ALL THE BOYS I KNEW. We fished, played football, basketball, and baseball, and all of us played with colored boys who were our age. However, I was different in several noticeable ways. I was an insatiable reader, always asking my parents for books or going to the library to look for something new. Some said I was curious and observant beyond my years. I was unusually polite for a thirteen-year-old, as my parents had strictly framed my attitudes and manners and interests. More than once they reminded me, "Steve, you will always respect and address Negroes as you would any white person."

I would later learn a harsh fact of southern life that all white boys were expected to accept. When we were young, Negro and white boys played together and were friends as if it would last forever. Forever ended when a white boy started high school, and the dark door of segregation slammed shut on black boys, and the joyful childhood age of innocence ended.

After school got out on Friday, I was ready for the weekend. I went home, and had a glass of milk and a cookie, but I didn't tell mother I had finished the Poe story while at school.

"Thanks for the treat, Mom. Tomorrow, I'm going to meet Billy and Marvin at the creek around noon. We're gonna set a new trot line. Of course, we'll have to check it often to see if we caught any fish."

I expected she would object. She proved me right when she said, "Why do you boys insist on going to the creek this time of year? It's early February. It's still cold, and it might rain."

"Mom, it's not that bad. We're always careful, and maybe we'll have a few catfish in a day or two."

"That would be nice," Mom said, softening her objection. "But wear your warm jacket and hurry home if it starts raining."

"Yes, ma'am. It won't take us long to set the trot line."

"And Steve, you be sure to invite Billy and Marvin to come home with you. I've got two fresh apple pies working in the oven."

"Yes, ma'am, I sure will. They always love your pies."

Billy and Marvin had been my friends for about three years, and I thought it was just natural that it happened. A couple of "Heys," and a few "Whatcha doin's?" seemed to close the deal. They lived in the part of Delphi called Westtown, where colored people lived. Oops, I should have said, where Negro people live.

I had always sized up other kids by their height and other physical characteristics, and my new friends had gotten a full appraisal.

Billy had a husky body but was shorter than me by a few inches. He had black hair, dark black skin, and a round face.

Marvin was taller than me by a couple of inches, and his fuzzy hair seemed to match his brown skin. Nonetheless, his long, thin face confused me. Assessing it, I figured Marvin was either a deep thinker or afraid of something.

After I had known Billy and Marvin for a while, I also picked up on the way they looked when thinking hard, before they spoke. Of course, they didn't do it all the time, but Marvin's head would twitch a little when he was thinking, while Billy would tilt his head to the right. I reckon I did something like that, but I really can't say. Maybe I should have looked in a mirror more often.

I ran most of the way to the creek, only half a mile from my house. When I saw Billy and Marvin, I called out, "Hey, I'm here."

Marvin turned and saw me, calling out, "Well, 'bout time, Steve. We just laid out the long line. You start and tie and bait the short lines. You need the practice." Marvin and Billy laughed.

I ignored their laughter, and said, "I'll give it a go. But it's the only thing you two dimwits can do better than me."

"Well, hoot, hoot, listen to the smarty-pants white boy," Marvin said. "Okay, show us your stuff."

I clenched my jaw and tied the twelve short lines every foot or so to the longer twenty-foot line. When I started baiting hooks, my fingers got real slippery, and I couldn't finish them all.

"Shit…y'all gonna have to help me bait the trot line," I said. "I just can't get the hang of it."

"Dammit, Steve, move over," Billy said. "We done told you enough times how to do it. Watch." Billy and Marvin deftly attached pieces of bait to each hook.

"How about that, Steve," Marvin said. "You done such a good job, we gonna let you throw the line in the creek." Marvin and Billy laughed, and I blushed, knowing I had been joshed. *What else is new?* I thought.

Okay, here goes. I tied one end of the long line to a tree stump next to the creek. Then I checked to make sure the heavy weight was securely tied to the other end of the long line. I had never been able to do the throw very well. It had to be thrown in one motion into the center of the creek downstream from where I stood.

I laid the first eight-feet of the long line on the ground downstream of where it was tied to the stump. Then I looped the remaining twelve feet of the long line upstream on the ground and closer to the creek, so that four feet of the long line was upstream of the stump. A good throw required the thrower to judge how hard to throw the line, to estimate the height for the throw, to pick an aiming point about twenty feet or so downstream, and then pray it would land in the middle of the creek. I picked up the weighted end of the line, did my estimate, and threw it, hoping it would work.

"Well, sweet Jesus, he done it right," Billy yelled.

We ran together, hugged, and jumped up and down. I got cocky and stepped back from the scrum, and said pretentiously, "Piece a cake."

Billy and Marvin started punching me softly, not hurting me. Then we fell on the ground and lay quietly for a while.

I broke whatever private reverie each of us was enjoying when I said, "Hey, you guys ever read Edgar Allan Poe?"

Billy tilted his head and said, "Huh?"

Marvin added, "Maybe."

I wasn't sure I should go on because I didn't want to embarrass my friends, but I decided they might like the stories. "Poe wrote short stories and poems. He died a hundred years ago in Baltimore."

"Whoa," Marvin said, "I got an auntie that lives in Baltimore. Mama took me to see her two years ago. It was some big city. Auntie was a smart lady and read a lot. She told Mama that a famous writer named Poe had lived in Baltimore years ago. I don't know if he was white or colored?"

"White, I said. "And get this, he wrote short stories that were mysteries. Some of them are scary as hell. I just finished one called 'The Murders in the Rue Morgue.' Want me to tell you the story? It's weird—murders, a wild animal, a smart detective, and dumb cops."

Billy shook his head hard. "No way, Steve. I don't like ghost stories. They too scary."

Marvin sneered, turned to Billy, and said, "Billy, you're a sissy. Besides, Steve didn't say it was a ghost story. I wanna hear it."

"You okay, Billy?" I asked.

"Yeah, go ahead. Tell the story," Billy said, and then he glared at Marvin, and shouted, "I ain't no sissy."

I realized I had opened a hornet's nest. "Calm down guys. Just sit back and listen. The story's set in Paris, France, in 1840. That's over 100 years ago. The main character is Auguste Dupin. He kinda works like a detective. An old woman and her daughter live on the fourth floor of an old building in the Rue Morgue and no one else lives in the building."

"What's that Rue Morgue mean, Steve," Billy asked.

"I don't know. Anyway, in the middle of the night, people hear awful screams, and when a policemen and others finally get to that apartment on the fourth floor, they find the front door locked from the inside. After they smash the front door open, they find a terrible scene. The room's a mess. There's blood everywhere." I paused, thinking to myself, *Hey, I'm enjoying telling this story.* "There is a knife on the floor along with valuable objects like jewelry and gold. Then they find the daughter's body stuffed up into the fireplace's chimney. She had been strangled to death. The old woman's body is found on the ground behind the building. Her throat had been cut, and when they pick up the body, her head falls off."

"Oh, God," Billy yelled. "This an awful story."

"Billy, that's the worst part. I'll jump to the end where Dupin solves the murders. Even though the apartment door is locked from the inside, the police think the murderer is a bank employee who knows the old lady has money, so they arrest him. Dupin figures out several things the police overlooked or ignored. You two know how the cops are. Dupin knows there was no way in or out of the apartment except through one of two windows, since the front door is locked from the inside. From the windows, it is a four-story drop. He finds some orange hair under the fingernails of the old woman. The two women are so badly mutilated that it would have taken great strength to do it. Okay, so far?"

Billy sounded calmer, "Yeah, I get it. Dupin is a smart fella."

Marvin nodded.

"Dupin has an idea who the murderer might be. He has to test his idea, so he put an ad in a Paris newspaper saying something like 'An orangutan has been caught. The owner is a sailor. He can have the animal back if he can prove it is his.' Pretty good, huh?" I asked.

"I reckon," Billy said. "What's an orang…How do you say it?"

"Orangutan. I'll tell you more in a minute. Last part of story. A sailor comes to Dupin's room. It's his animal. The sailor goes on a sea voyage to Borneo where orangutans live. He and a friend catch the animal and the sailor keeps it. The animal escapes from his home, climbs into the women's apartment, and kills the two women. Dupin tells the cops they have to release the banker guy. It seems the cops are pissed that Dupin solves the crime. That's about it in a nutshell. I hope y'all like the story. It's okay to not like it. I'm not a teacher."

I paused. Billy and Marvin were leaning on their elbows staring at me. I couldn't tell if they were angry or interested.

"Well," I said, "I gotta tell you, Billy, what I know about orangutans. They're apes. You know, like gorillas. They grow up to about 200 pounds, four to five feet tall, has reddish fur, and long arms. They're supposed to be one of the smartest animals. And Borneo is on the other side of the world. It's on the equator. It's a jungle and hot as hell. That's where orangutans live. Well, that's about it."

Marvin's head twitched, as if he wasn't sure. "How the hell you know all that stuff about orangutans and Borneo, Steve. I know you smart, but you ain't that smart."

"You're right. I made a quick stop at the library and looked things up."

"I'm goin' to the colored library and talk to Mr. Douglas. I'll find out if you tellin' it straight," Marvin said, adding, "You wanna go, Billy?"

"Nah, you the smart one, Marvin. I'll just git more confused."

"Billy, you should go with Marvin," I said. "You can always learn something."

Billy tilted his head. "I'll think 'bout it."

I nodded. "Good. Marvin, is Mr. Douglas the man I see downtown who is always dressed so well?"

"You bet he is. You oughta meet him. You'd like him."

"I can't go in the colored library. The door says *Colored Only*."

"That's the front door, stupid. Don't you know 'bout the door between the colored library and white library?"

I scratched my head a moment. "I suppose it's the door by the wall next to the colored library. I never thought much about it."

Marvin laughed at me, wagging his finger. "You gotta think harder. One time, Mr. Douglas opened it so I could peek in the white side. You white folks sure got a bigger library with lotsa books."

I nodded but what could I say. Knowing Marvin was right, I changed the subject, "We better get going. We can check the trot line tomorrow. Mom wants you to come to our house. She made two apples pies to share."

"Well, shit, Steve, you shoulda said so earlier," Billy said. "I love your Mama's pies."

I opened the front door, and led Billy and Marvin into the house and called out, "Hey, Mom, we're here. Billy and Marvin can't wait for some apple pie."

Unlike most white people in Delphi who wanted colored people to come into their home through the back door, my parents told me to always bring Negroes in through the front door.

"C'mon in the kitchen," Mom said. "Hey, Billy and Marvin, y'all doing okay?"

"Yes, Miss Lillis, be jus' fine," Marvin said.

"And you, Billy?" Mom asked.

"Doing fine, ma'am, 'cepting my Mama a bit under the weather."

"Oh, I'm sorry to hear that, Billy. You tell her if she needs anything to let me know, and I'll be right over. Y'all sit down. I'm gonna cut three pieces of one of the pies for you to eat now along with some milk to wash it down. I'll cut the other pie in two large pieces and wrap them, so you can take them home to your families."

We ate our pies as if we were afraid the pies might disappear any moment. When we finished, Marvin said, "I reckon we better get goin', Miss Lillis. Thank you for the pie, ma'am."

"You're both welcome. Here's the wrapped pies. Now y'all be good," Mom said, laughing.

After Billy and Marvin left, I asked Mom, "Do you know the colored man that works at the colored library? His name's Mr. Douglas."

"Steve, I've told you a number of times not to use the word 'colored.' It's Negro."

"Yes, ma'am." I said, knowing it would do no good to tell her again that everybody, white and Negro alike, used the word *colored*.

Mom rested her chin in her hand as her little finger gently scratched her upper lip. I had no idea what she was thinking. "Yes, I know Mr. Moses Douglas quite well, and he doesn't just *work* at the library, he is the librarian of the Negro Library. He's a fine man, well educated, and he helps the Negro people in the area immensely. He goes to Negro elementary and high schools and talks about books and poems. Some of the high school kids work at the library and get hands-on training about library business and books—"

Just then we heard the front screen door slam shut, and in walked my father. "Brrr, it's cold. Hey, Lillis. Hey, Steve. Well, what are you two cooking up?"

"You're home early, Andy. Everything all right?" Mom said.

"Yeah, the layout work went faster than usual. How did your day go, Steve?"

"Fine, Dad. I went down to the creek with Billy and Marvin to help set a trot line."

"Steve, did you forgot something? Mom said. "I just told him about Moses Douglas."

"A fine man, son," Dad said. "You should meet him. You should also meet Dr. Joshua Marshall. Do you know who he is?"

I shook my head. "I don't think so."

Dad sat down and pulled his chair closer to me. "Well, young man, it's time you came to better understand your little town. Dr. Marshall is a well-trained medical doctor, and the only Negro doctor in this area. If he wasn't here, Negros would have to go to Montgomery for proper medical attention."

I squirmed in my chair, trying to process all that had happened today. "I guess Dr. Marshall and Mr. Douglas are friends?" I mumbled as more of a question than a statement.

Dad sat up, laughed, and said, "They're brothers."

"Oh," I said, now completely confused, "but they don't have the same last name."

"Dr. Marshall explained it to me years ago, and it's really simple. Dr. Marshall's father died soon after he was born. His mother remarried, and Mr. Douglas' father's last name was Douglas. *Voila*, they are brothers. Well, one should really say they're half-brothers. They own and live in a very nice house in Westtown. Dr. Marshall's medical office is in the house."

I turned my head to the right and stared blankly at the wall, saying nothing.

"Steve, I know you had a good time with Billy and Marvin. They're nice boys. I think that's enough town history for one day," Mom said, and she added, laughing. "Please go wash up and change clothes. You're a mess. And Andy, you've got ink on your hands".

When I got in bed, I didn't even consider reading another Poe story. As I snuggled under my blanket, my mind was awash with thoughts of Mr. Douglas and Dr. Marshall. I drifted off to sleep, and one central thought drifted off with me. *What a strange town. What other secrets don't I know?*

6

Laissez les Bon Temps Rouler

Tuesday—March 1, 1949

As far back as I could remember, I had always enjoyed the city's celebration of Mardi Gras, a much smaller version of the famous carnivals in New Orleans and Mobile. Dad had told me Alabamians were proud of Mobile's Mardi Gras because it was said to have started before the famous one in New Orleans. However, he added that people in New Orleans did not agree one damn bit, or for that matter, Alabamians didn't pay much attention to Delphi's celebration.

Mom opened the front door and called out, "Steve, the parade starts in two hours. I know Dad is working with you and Jack on the float, but where are Billy and Marvin? They've got to help you. I do like your float idea. I think it might be a winner."

"Mom, I'm sure they'll be here soon. The four of us came up with the idea together."

Jack, one of my best friends in the fifth grade, was a nice-looking kid about my size with blonde hair, but it seemed to me that he was not the brightest kid in the class. I figured that Billy and Marvin were brighter than Jack.

Dad put down the screwdriver and said, "Don't worry, Mom just wants your float to be a success. What do you think of the airplane model you built?"

"Looks damned fine, Mr. Andy," Billy called out as he and Marvin arrived. "I think everybody will recognize it as a C-47."

"Dumbo, you bet they will," Marvin said. "It's got C-47 written on both its sides."

Everybody laughed, and I said, "Don't forget, Marvin, it was Billy who first came up with the Berlin Airlift idea when we were trying to think of something."

"Golly gee," Jack said. "The model looks great, but how come Delphi does a Mardi Gras?"

I knew what was coming. Dad loved to tell stories, and Jack had opened the door. I couldn't resist saying, "Dad, I think you know the answer to Jack's question."

Dad ignored my joke, and said, "Well, I reckon I do. You see, Jack, Delphi prides itself on being fair to everyone who lives here, including Negros. About twenty years ago, the city decided to build the Negro Library that's on the Square. Then city hall folks came up with the idea to sponsor a Mardi Gras parade. They hoped it would attract a lot of visitors, but it hasn't. Doesn't matter, the locals continue to love it. So, here we are in a C-47."

Marvin twitched, and I knew that meant Marvin had something on his mind.

"Mr. Andy, I don't mean no disrespect," Marvin said, "but there's a Ku Klux Klan here."

"Marvin you can say anything to me," Dad said, "and you're right about the Klan, but they've been behaving themselves for quite a while. In fact, the Klan has been on the decline for years. Can't promise it'll continue. I wrote an editorial for the newspaper last year blasting the Dixiecrat Party, because I'm a staunch supporter of the Democratic Party. I got a bunch of both nice and nasty letters about it, and the Klan threatened to burn a cross in our yard, but it didn't happen. We just have to be alert."

"Yes, sir," Marvin said. "I will."

"Good," Dad said. "Kids, get to work. You have to finish the decorations around the float and the two signs y'all did saying, 'In Honor of the Berlin Airlift Pilots.' A nice touch, guys. I have to join Lillis and get in our costumes. We'll walk in the parade."

The centerpiece of our float, the ten-foot C-47 model, was secured to a four-foot pedestal. Marvin and I dressed as American and French pilots, and stood in the front of the float holding American and French flags. Billy and Jack dressed as American and British pilots, and stood in the rear of the float holding American and British flags.

Each of our mothers had hand sewn our uniforms using wartime photos for patterns. Dad had found four pairs of pilot leather hats with goggles, even though many of the pilots flew wearing baseball-style hats. Dad told us the leather hats were more dramatic.

"Ready to go kids?" Fred Watson, who worked for Dad as a typesetter, asked as he looked back at us in our positions on the float.

I called out, "Yes, sir, Mr. Fred. Marvin and I are ready to take-off."

Billy chimed in, "Roger, Mr. Fred. Jack and I reportin' for duty."

My curiosity, along with Dad's input, had taught me a lot about our parade. Townspeople created all kinds of floats: the paper mill float threw rolls of toilet paper to the crowd, the grocery store float threw candy bars, and many people just walked the procession in outlandish costumes, generally making fools of themselves.

Unlike New Orleans's social clubs which gave their Mardi Gras parade krewes strange names like Mystick Krewe of Comus and Zulu, Delphi's social clubs kept parade names simple, like Delphi Darlings or Negro Nightingales.

The supposedly secret social clubs were a joke since everyone in Delphi knew who was in each one, even though the members wore masks when on a float. Their common denominators were a king and queen of that Mardi Gras Day—and that most participants drank too much.

As the floats progressed along the ten-block parade route, people cheered for our float and called out for beads.

A cute, little girl from my class yelled, "Hey, Steve, some beads, some beads."

I blushed and obliged, saying, "Here you go, Betty."

Unbeknown to us and the parade organizers, three young white men, all in their twenties, had slipped into the back of the parade, and slowly worked their way toward our float as if they knew about it. They wore red pullover shirts with the letters "KKK" inscribed on them and red hats, featuring the Blood Drop Cross symbol.

One of the men walked up beside Marvin and said, "Hey, colored boy. You ain't no goddamn American pilot. Ya bettah watch yourself." He then gave Marvin the finger.

Fred heard it all, stopped the tractor, and walked up to the young man. "Jimmy, you get the hell outta here. We don't cotton to your kind."

"Ya a white piece of nigger-loving shit, Fred. Ya bettah—"

Several parade organizers along with Dad started escorting the three men well off the parade route, when Jimmy yelled back at Marvin, "Boy, I'm gonna keep my eye on you."

But for the brief, if intense, disturbance, the parade was a rousing success. The judges awarded our float first place in the younger kid category, but to our surprise and delight, we also won second place in the open float category.

Back at my house, Marvin **said**, "Well, I reckon the Klan still alive here, Mr. Andy."

Dad scratched his head as if were trying to decide what to say. "It seems so, Marvin. But I know those three guys. The guy that insulted you is Jimmy Jackson. None of them are worth much. They live on nearby farms and work at the paper mill and are angry about everything. Like I said, we have to be alert."

I put my arm around Marvin's shoulder. "Don't worry, Jack and I and are right here for you and Billy," I said, having no idea what I really meant. "Now, y'all c'mon inside. I hear tell Mom's got a key lime pie waiting for us."

After we ate our pies, I walked outside with my friends as they headed home. Billy nudged me, asking, "Why the hell ain't Mardi Gras on the same date every year? You know, like this year, March first."

Jack piped in and added, "Yeah, Steve, Billy's right. It don't make any sense."

I knew the answer didn't make sense, so I asked. "It's complicated. Y'all sure you want to know?"

Marvin, a glint in his eyes, said, "You bet." Jack and Billy nodded.

"Well, to get to the Mardi Gras date, you have to know when Easter is since it changes every year. I don't know the background too good. Dad told me the date for Easter was set way back when. Hold on to your hats. Easter happens on the first Sunday after the first full moon after the Spring equinox. I had to memorize that. Get it?"

Billy said, "Huh?"

"Yep, it a huh," I said. "Try this one. Mardi Gras always takes place forty-seven days before Easter."

Billy threw his baseball cap on the ground. "Crap, sorry I asked. Musta been some smart idiot to dream all that up."

Jack shook his head, as if confused, but said nothing.

I grinned, and said, "Well, y'all asked."

"I get it," Marvin said, smiling. "I'll check it out with Mr. Douglas tomorrow."

"Well, I reckon I'm gonna go the library with Marvin," Billy said. "Somebody's gotta make sure he understands what Mr. Douglas tells him."

I smiled, glad that Billy decided to go to the library, but I didn't say anything.

7

The Library

Wednesday—March 2, 1949

I REMEMBER WHEN I FIRST VISITED the Delphi Library with Dad. I was eight-years old. Dad wanted to introduce me the to the chief librarian, Kathryn Davis.

Entering the library, Dad said, "Good morning, Kathryn. I'd like you to meet my son, Steve."

"Good morning, Steve. I'm glad to meet you."

I said nothing as I was looking at the murals on the library's walls. Dad nudged me, and I spoke up, "Good morning, Miss Kathryn. I'm glad to meet you."

"You appear to be admiring the murals. Can I explain them to you?"

"Yes, ma'am, I'd like that."

Dad beamed with pleasure as Miss Kathryn began, "Well, a little history first, Steve. This library was designed and furnished by a man from Birmingham named James Head. He and his company have furnished most of the libraries in Alabama, and he used only the best products. He even hired a noted artist named Ezra Winter to do the murals you're looking at. Outstanding, aren't they?"

I was still staring at the walls. I said offhandedly, "Yes, ma'am. But how did the artist paint the walls? They're so big."

Miss Kathryn ignored my rudeness and smiled. "A good question, but the answer is a lengthy one. I'll just explain a little bit today. Mr. White's studio was in New York where he painted the murals on large canvases using oils. Then, best of all, he came to little, old Delphi to supervise the installation of the murals. They were affixed to the walls using white lead. The different figures you see represent the history of literature. More on that at your next library visit. Now let's fill out a library card for you."

Miss Kathryn handed the card to me. "What book would you like to check out today?"

I turned to Dad, but he said nothing. Miss Kathryn apparently knew exactly what to do. "Steve, I have a recommendation. A French author named Jules Verne wrote a great story that I'm sure you'll enjoy. His book is entitled *Twenty Thousand Leagues Under the Sea*. Remember your first book and all the others that you read later. You'll meet many real and fictional characters with strange names and many with simple names. It's likely that you'll remember many of them forever."

I left the library, proudly holding the book, still looking at the cover, which intrigued me. It was my first library book.

Yesterday, when Billy and Marvin said they were going to the library to see Mr. Douglas, I decided I would go since I hadn't been there in several weeks. But I admitted to myself, *Okay, I'm worried that Mr. Douglas might say my explanations about Easter and Mardi Gras are hogwash*.

"Mornin', Miss Kathryn," I said the day after the parade. "I've got three books to return." I placed the books on the return shelf.

"Which one did you enjoy the most, Steve?" Miss Kathryn asked.

"Well, I liked them all, but I liked Jack London's *Call of the Wild* best."

"Why?"

"Because of Buck, the hero of the story. He was a brave dog who endured all kinds of terrible things during the gold rush. But he finally yielded to the call of the wild and became free."

Miss Kathryn nodded and said, "Excellent summary, Steve. Are you going to read more Jack London?"

"Yes, ma'am, I'll look around now."

I browsed the shelves for thirty minutes, and choose two books: London's *White Fang* and John Steinbeck's *The Grapes of Wrath*. I checked them out, said goodbye to Miss Kathryn. Outside, I waited near the front door to the Negro Library in hopes of seeing Marvin and Billy.

After five or ten minutes of *White Fang*, which seemed like an eternity to me, I decided it was time to go. Besides, I thought, if Marvin and Billy can't go into the white library, I suppose I can't go into the Negro Library. Feeling rather smug about my logic, it would be several years before I understood that both whites and blacks were being denied equal access.

I walked across the square toward my house when I heard Billy's voice, "Hey, Steve, wait up."

I spun around, grinned, and said, "Well I'll be damn. There you two are. Were you in the library?"

"Yes. We told you yesterday we were going to see Mr. Douglas and ask him about Easter and Mardi Gras."

"What did he say?"

"Mr. Douglas said you got it right. He also told us other stuff about Easter. Mardi Gras means 'Fat Tuesday.' How do you like that?"

"That's funny, but why is it called Fat Tuesday?"

Marvin interrupted Billy, adding, "That's the last day you can have fun and eat and drink all you want because the next day is 'Ash Wednesday' which is the start of Lent. So, today's the first day of Lent. Wanna pray?"

"No, I don't wanna pray, smart aleck," I said. "And yeah, I've heard of Lent, but I don't know much about it."

Marvin smiled benignly, seemingly because he was enjoying teaching me things. "Well, you see here, Steve, Lent goes on for forty days until just before Easter. Catholics and others are 'posed to repent their sins, beg forgiveness, not have fun, and some even fast. That means they don't eat very much."

I smirked. "I know what *fast* means. Did Mr. Douglas tell you all this?"

"He sure did. He's a smart guy and he's okay. You gotta meet him."

I tried to regain my lost ground. "I reckon he's okay, but maybe I will, or maybe I won't. I'll have to think about it."

Marvin laughed, knowing me only too well. "That's right. You think about it." Marvin changed the subject by saying, "Whatcha reading? I see you got two books."

I handed them to Marvin.

Marvin glanced at *White Fang*, but spent more time reading the back cover of *The Grapes of Wrath* and thumbing through a few pages. He said, "I've read two Jack London books. Liked them a lot. I ain't read *The Grapes of Wrath*, but it sounds interesting. White folks getting mistreated by other whites. I think if you read it, Steve, maybe you'll understand how colored people feel." He handed the books back to me.

At that moment, I came to realize how smart Marvin was. "Does Mr. Douglas suggest books for you to read?"

"Yep, all the time. And he explains them to me if I get confused about what it means. Billy, show Steve what you checked out. He got a library card, and this is his first book."

Billy handed me *Twenty Thousand Leagues Under the Sea*, and I said, "This was my first library book. It's a good story. You'll like it."

Billy looked pleased with himself, saying, "Mr. Douglas recommended it. He's a good guy."

"That's nice," I said. "Miss Kathryn does the same for me."

"Mr. Douglas introduced me to her once," Marvin said. "I like her. We gotta get going."

I watched them until they disappeared around a corner, and said to no one in particular, "*Whew!*"

8

Presbyterians & Lent

Friday—April 15, 1949

I LIKED TO QUOTE FROM Poe's poem, "the Raven." I decided to *ponder weak and weary* over Lent and other religious questions the next few days. I didn't know much about this stuff. I figured I better be prepared since my conversation with Marvin and Billy had captured my imagination about Lent. My parents and grandparents were Presbyterians, so I hadn't heard much talk about Lent, even at church.

As I mulled things over, one thought kept bugging me. The Presbyterian faith believed in predestination, and to me that meant when you were born, God pegged you as either *Chosen or Damned.* Dad had told me it was more complicated than that, but I couldn't help wondering, *Which I am? Chosen or Damned? Why can't I change it? If you can't, you might as well forget it.*

I had asked Dad once why we went to church so often since he'd made it clear that religion was each person's private business.

Dad had put his fingers tips together and held them under his chin, finally saying, "Well, Steve, religion should be private. Your mother and I believe that quite seriously. However—and it's a big *however*—in a small town like Delphi, religion is an important issue and everybody knows your faith and business. As a newspaper owner and publisher, if Mom and I didn't go to church, people would start talking about us behind our backs, and might even stop reading the paper and stores might stop buying ads." Dad put his hands down, smiled, and added, "I know it's self-serving, but don't forget, Mom and I want to put you through college."

"I know, Dad, but dang, all this religious stuff is awfully complicated."

He laughed, and said, "Amen to that, son."

ON FRIDAY, WE WENT TO GOOD FRIDAY services at the First Presbyterian Church. The service started at two o'clock in the afternoon, and the church was packed.

I tried to pay attention, but my mind kept wandering, even when I heard the minister say something about Lent. As usual, it didn't make sense. It sounded like we should observe Lent, but I didn't think the minister's heart was in the message. *Maybe he'll mention the Chosen and Damned.* When he didn't, I almost laughed. *Oh, what the Hell...that's probably where I'm headed.*

After the service, I wanted to run off and find Marvin and Billy, but I had to stand in line with my parents, so we could be greeted by the minister at the front door. I shook his hand and mumbled, "Thank you, sir."

The minister smiled at me and said in his best ministerial voice, "Young Steve, did you enjoy today's message about Lent?"

I put one hand behind my back and crossed my fingers. "Yes, sir. It was great. I learned a lot."

The minister beamed rather sanctimoniously, and replied, "I am so glad." He then turned to the next couple in line.

I looked back and recognized a man, and he smiled and winked at me. I knew he was joshing me about my crossed fingers. *Damn adults*, I thought, *they're always spying on us kids.*

9

Moses Douglas

Saturday—April 16, 1949

I ROLLED THROUGH LENT AND GOOD FRIDAY, and went to the library early Saturday morning, before the library got crowded. "G'day, Miss Kathryn," I said as I placed my two books on the return table.

"G'day? Where did you hear that, Steve?" Miss Kathryn grinned.

I smiled meekly. "I heard it on the radio. It's what Aussies say to each other. I thought it was neat."

"Ah, Aussies and G'day…neat indeed. What did you think of the books, Steve?"

I liked it when she asked me questions since she always seemed to be interested in what I read. "Well, tell you the truth, ma'am, *White Fang* is kinda like *Call of the Wild*. I mean it's okay, but it's another story set in Alaska that has an animal who is a hero in it."

Miss Kathryn smiled. "That's correct, but you will soon learn that many authors write stories in similar styles. Perhaps, they do it because their books sell well, or maybe, because that's the limit of their writing ability. Other great authors don't appear to labor under those constraints."

I sorta understood what she meant, and asked, "Who are some great authors, Miss Kathryn?"

"A difficult question to answer. Each person likely has favorites. Four of mine are Jane Austin, Leo Tolstoy, F. Scott Fitzgerald, and William Faulkner. Oh, and let me add John Steinbeck. What did you think of *The Grapes of Wrath*?"

I perked up, saying, "I really liked it. I'm not sure if it's my favorite, but the story was about how..." I paused, realizing I was going to repeat what Marvin had said when he briefly thumbed through the book, "white folks mistreated other whites, and it makes you understand how Negro people around here feel." I hoped I hadn't said the wrong thing, but I'm sure I committed plagiarism.

"You know more than you think, Steve. That's also correct, but you won't get many white people to agree with you."

"No, ma'am, I guess not. Miss Kathryn, do you know Moses Douglas?"

Miss Kathryn looked surprised at my question, but she recovered quickly. "Of course, I know him, Steve. He's just on the other side of that door," she said, pointing. "Would you like to meet him?"

All of a sudden, I felt squeamish, not sure I wanted to go on, having no idea where this might lead, but I replied, "Yes, ma'am."

So she led me to the door, knocked, and called out, "Moses, are you there?"

As Miss Kathryn lifted her hand to knock again, the door slowly opened. There stood Moses Douglas.

What happened next led to one of those experiences in life when the world becomes a different place, offering new and different meanings.

Before I could think of anything to say, Mr. Douglas said, "Good morning, Miss Kathryn, and good morning, young Steve. I know your parents well. It's nice to finally meet you in person. How are you doing today?"

I felt dumbstruck, which is probably an understatement. I stared at Mr. Douglas, deciding to size him up, thinking, *Why am I doing this?* I couldn't tell how tall he was because all adults looked tall. He was a bit on the heavy side but not fat, with dark-black skin, a squarish face featuring a trim beard, and fuzzy dark hair. He was well dressed in tan slacks, a darker tan jacket, and a colorful tie with hints of red, brown, and orange.

"Cat got your tongue, young Steve?" Moses asked.

God, I'm nervous, I thought. "Uh, no, sir, just thinking," I said as I spouted out a lot of things on my mind. "Miss Kathryn and I were just talking about writers we like. She likes Leo Tolstoy and F. Scott Fitzgerald and Jane Austin and William Faulkner. I like John Steinbeck. I also like Edgar Allen Poe. I know Billy and Marvin. We set trot lines a lot. Marvin and Billy told me they asked you about Mardi Gras and Easter, and they said you told them some things about it I didn't know. Marvin and Billy say you're very smart. Marvin, Billy, Jack, and I built a float for our Mardi Gras parade called *In Honor of the Berlin Airlift Pilots*. Our float won two awards. Three Ku Klux Klan guys came up to our float. One of them called Marvin a nigger." Steve looked down. "I'm sorry I used that word. I don't like it."

Miss Kathryn and Mr. Douglas turned to each other and smiled.

I paid no attention to them, just kept talking, "The guy also gave Marvin the…uh, finger." I blushed and continued. "Dad and some other guys came up and hustled the three KKK guys off. One of them was Jimmy Jackson. I don't know where they went. We were all upset. I'm a Presbyterian, and I don't know if I'm going to heaven or hell. That's about it."

Mr. Douglas stroked his beard, and said, "Well, young Steve that was quite a recitation. Do you think you left anything out?"

"Probably, but I can't remember right now."

"Would you like to come in and see the Negro Library?"

I felt nervous, as if I was stepping through the door into something I knew nothing about, and shyly asked, Miss Kathryn, "Is it okay?"

Miss Kathryn must have sensed my hesitation. She patted me on the shoulder. "Of course, we share visitors in our two libraries often. Mr. Douglas is a fine man, and I think he knows more about authors and their books than I do."

I was still nervous, but Mr. Douglas tried to calm me down by saying, "Follow me, young Steve, into my world of books." He led me through the door, and added, "Welcome to the Delphi Negro Library. I have to close the door now. That's the rules. We can come and go through it, but it has to be closed most of the time. You are my special and honored guest now. Please, take a look around."

I had already been peering around, and, nodding, I continued to do so. The library was really small. It was darker than the white library although the reading tables were well lit. There were no windows and no murals or other paintings on the walls. In fact, all the walls were covered with bookcases and books. Several ladders leaned against the shelves. I figured they were needed to get to the books on the top shelves.

"It's pretty small, and you have no murals," I said.

"Had to do it that way, young Steve. There wasn't money available for murals for our library. That's just the way it is. I do love the murals in the white library, but I love books more, so I insisted the bookcases be floor to ceiling on the four walls. That's the only way I could accommodate all the books I wanted. But even so, there are many titles I wish I had space for. There is a warehouse in Westtown where I store books. The young Negro kids who work here part-time, including Marvin, help me shuffle books to and from the library and warehouse, so we can find space for new titles. An endless task. Any more questions or observation, young Steve?"

"Yes, sir, Mr. Douglas. How do you keep track of all the books in the library and warehouse? Many are so hard to get to. And please, just call me Steve."

"Well, Steve, first off I want to tell you that you are a very polite young man. Most white people call me Moses and would never think to call me Mr. Douglas. Now to the book tracking problem. You know what the Dewey Decimal System is, don't you?"

I nodded. "Yes, sir. I use it in the white library."

"Good. We use the same system in our library, but as I'm sure you observed, we need several movable ladders to get to many books, but we do know right where to go for them. For the warehouse, I developed a modified Dewey Decimal System. There we have shelves that don't require ladders, so we can get to books quickly. It does take time to keep two systems up-to-date but until improved library technology comes along, that's where we are. Now let's talk books. I know you like to read, and I know what you read lately. Any other books you've read that you haven't mentioned?"

Oh, boy, I wish he hadn't asked me that. I can't think fast enough. So I said the first thing that came to my mind, "Jules Verne's *Twenty*

Thousand Leagues Under the Sea, *From the Earth to the Moon*, *Around the World in Eighty Days*, and *Journey to the Center of the Earth*."

"A quite impressive set, Steve. What's remarkable is that Jules Verne wrote his science fiction books well before the events in them actually came to pass. Now we have submarines, airplanes, and rockets, and who knows, maybe soon we will go to the moon. I recommended a Jules Verne book to your friend Billy. Now, let's turn to another well-known writer. Have you read anything written by William Shakespeare?"

Yikes, what am I getting into? I thought. "No, sir, not really. Mom and Dad like him a lot, especially Mom. Sometimes, she reads a short passage to me. I don't quite understand the way he writes. I know it's English, but I don't get it."

Mr. Douglas seemed to know that would be my reaction, so he said, "Yes, Mr. Shakespeare can be hard on the ear at first. He wrote his plays and poems about 350 years ago. And English was different then. We have to work to tune our ears to Shakespeare's poetic style. I have introduced a number of students to Shakespeare, including Marvin, and they all get the gist sooner or later. Let me read you the opening passage from—"

The main door to the Negro Library opened and a girl walked in, a few books in her hand. She said, "Hello, Mr. Douglas, I'm returning—"

When she glanced up and saw me, a white boy with red hair and freckles, she had no idea what was going on. I stared at her and went into my size-em up mode. I thought she was about my age. She was about my height, but it was her skin color that stopped me. It wasn't dark black or light brown. It was golden bronze-like and seemed to have a radiant glow. My mouth was wide open.

Mr. Douglas smiled as we stared at one another. "Nancy, I'd like you to meet Steve. He likes to read as much as you do. And Steve, I'd like you to meet Nancy. She studies Shakespeare with me. Maybe Nancy will join us in a brief discussion about the first passages of *Romeo and Juliet*." Mr. Douglas stopped talking. I thought he was waiting for one of us say something.

It was quiet for a few moments. I couldn't believe what my eyes were seeing. I had seldom spoken to a young Negro girl but I finally broke the ice. "Hey, Nancy."

She replied, timidly, "Hey, Steve."

Mr. Douglas, trying not to smile, must have felt our discomfort, so he picked up the copy of *Romeo and Juliet* he had intended to have me read from, and said, "Nancy, please be so kind as to read the first eight lines in *Romeo and Juliet's* Prologue." He handed the book to Nancy.

She accepted it as if it were sacred. "Yes, sir, Mr. Douglas." She fumbled to find the prologue, but momentarily began reading.

> Two households, both alike in dignity
> In fair Verona, where we lay our scene,
> From ancient grudge break to new mutiny,
> Where civil blood makes civil hands unclean.
> From forth the fatal loins of these two foes
> A pair of star-crossed lovers take their life,
> Whose misadventured piteous overthrows
> Doth with their death bury their parents' strife.

I was mesmerized. I couldn't believe that Nancy had read the passage with such ease and clarity. She had a lovely voice and was cute.

Mr. Douglas, not surprised at Nancy's reading, sensed my mood, saying, "Well done, Nancy. Now let's go through each line and dissect it."

We went through the first five lines, and they explained the meanings to me. I would then either nod my head at each line's explanation or ask a question.

At the sixth line, Mr. Douglas asked me, "Steve, this line reads 'A pair of star-crossed lovers take their life.' What do you think 'star-crossed lovers' means?"

I responded with the only meaning I could imagine. "I think it means their love was blessed by the stars."

Nancy snickered at my answer.

Mr. Douglas coughed, and said, "Now Nancy, that was impolite. Please tell Steve what 'star-crossed lovers' means."

I saw her blush and was surprised a Negro could blush.

"Yes, sir. I'm sorry, Steve....Back in Shakespeare's time, people believed the stars controlled people's destiny. So, if two stars were crossed, the lovers were doomed."

"Thank you, Nancy. Quite correct."

Suddenly Nancy said, "I have to go, Mr. Douglas. My mama will wonder where I am. I'll leave these two books here."

"Don't you want to check a couple more out, Nancy?"

"No, sir. I'll get some next time." She was ready to walk out the door when she turned around and said, "Bye, Steve."

I smiled, hoping she wouldn't leave. "Bye, Nancy."

After she left, I turned to Mr. Douglas, saying, "She's knows a lot."

"She sure does, Steve. She's a freshman in high school and an honors student."

I wasn't going to be out-aged, and said, "Well, she must be fourteen. But I'll be fourteen on June sixteenth. I'll be a freshman in high school in September."

"Ah, that's important, but I think you might be interested to know that Nancy's only thirteen. She skipped a grade in elementary school. She not only helps me in the library, but she's also quite a good actress for her age. She acts in some plays we put on. Have you been in a play, Steve?"

Oh boy, a chance to show off, I thought. "Yes, sir, I was in *A Christmas Carol* last December at my elementary school."

"An excellent play for grade schoolers," Mr. Douglas said. "What part did you play? I dare say it wasn't Tiny Tim. You're too old for that part."

I tried not to sound too cocky. "A boy in the second grade played Tiny Tim. I had two parts. I was Jacob Marley, and I sang in the chorus."

Mr. Douglas grinned. "Splendid parts. You must sell the audience on the agonies Marley has suffered, and I assume you have a good singing voice as well. Did you enjoy being in a play?"

"It was okay. Mr. Hart teaches drama at the high school, and he helps us with our plays."

"I know Mr. Hart. Fine man. Do you think you'll be in some plays in high school?"

"I don't know, sir. I'll have to think about it."

"Well, please do. You'll learn a lot from Mr. Hart."

I nodded and asked, "Does Marvin act?"

Mr. Douglas paused, not wanting to answer my question, but I felt sure he would be honest. "No. Alas, I have a hard time getting young, Negro males to participate on the stage. It seems they think it's unmanly, and I'm sorry to say, many of them can't read and write very well. While our stage is not segregated, their schools are, as I'm sure you know."

"Yes, sir, I do. Where is your stage?"

"It's a small theater within the warehouse. Maybe you could come and see one of our plays?"

I felt confused, like I was in another world rather than Delphi. "Thank you."

Mr. Douglas, always perceptive, said, "Bring your parents. Other white families come to see our plays. Miss Kathryn has the schedule of our upcoming plays. I'm sure she'll let you see it. Now let's finish the last three lines of the prologue."

After we finished, Mr. Moses said, "See, Steve, it's not too hard to understand Shakespeare. You just have to work at it a bit."

"Yes, sir. I guess you're right. I have to go now. Thanks for the help."

"Before you go, would you like to check out a book? I have one in mind."

"Isn't my card just good in the white library?"

"Aha, so it is. But I'll issue you a one-time dispensation. I'm sure Miss Kathryn won't mind."

"What's a dispensation, Mr. Douglas?"

"I like it that you ask when you don't understand something. A dispensation is granted as an exception to a rule. So, here's what I propose. I'd like you to take this copy of *Romeo and Juliet* home and read it slowly and carefully with your mother. Perhaps, she has her own copy. She can help explain the language. Will you do that?"

"Yes, sir, but I know it'll take me longer than two weeks to read it."

Mr. Douglas laughed. "Not to worry. The dispensation has no time limit."

"Oh, that's good," I said. I picked up the book and asked, "Which door should I use, Mr. Douglas?"

"Alas, Steve. I think it best you use the door that goes into the white library. I'll open it a bit and make sure no one is nearby. And, Steve, when you return *Romeo and Juliet*, I hope we can discuss it."

"Yes, sir, me too."

Mr. Douglas opened the door. It appeared clear. I walked back into the white library, and said over my shoulder, "Thanks again, Mr. Douglas."

Miss Kathryn saw me as I walked toward the front door, and said, "Steve, did you enjoy the Negro Library and Mr. Douglas."

"Yes, ma'am. We talked a lot about Shakespeare." I held up the copy of *Romeo and Juliet* for her to see.

Miss Kathryn smiled broadly. "That's good. Did he tell you about his theater?"

"Yes, ma'am."

She reached under the counter and handed me a piece of paper. "This is the theater's schedule through the coming summer. Show it to your parents. White people go there often, including me."

"Thank you. Mr. Douglas seems to know a lot about Shakespeare."

"It's more than seems, Steve. I don't know anyone in Delphi who knows as much as he does. He studied English Literature in college. I consider him a Shakespearean scholar."

"Oh, I guess that's good. I gotta go, Miss Kathryn."

"Hope to see you soon, Steve."

As I walked home, my head kept spinning like a movie reel. First, there was Mr. Douglas explaining Shakespeare in perfect English with his soft Southern accent. And then the image changed to Nancy as she read *Romeo and Juliet's* prologue in English as perfect as Mr. Douglas had. The image that seemed to freeze in my head was the one when Nancy kept repeating "star-crossed lovers." I shook my head, and the image disappeared. *This is crazy*, I thought. *What's going on?*

10

Supper Time

Saturday—April 16, 1949

AT THE DINNER TABLE, I ASKED, "Did you have to work today, Dad?"

"Yep, afraid so, son," Dad said, grabbing his forehead. "Oh, woe is me, a newspaperman is always on the job."

Mom and I smirked at Dad as if to say: *You should have it so bad.* I stopped mulling over what to tell my parents about my day because I knew it would be the next question.

On cue, Dad asked, "And how did your day go, Steve? Check your trot line?"

"No, sir, I think Billy did it today." I thought for a few seconds about what to say, then said simply, "I did go to the library."

"That's nice," Mom said. "Did you talk to Miss Kathryn?"

"Yes, ma'am." Then I told Mom and Dad about my visit to the Negro Library and how much I liked Mr. Douglas. I didn't mention Nancy, so I decided to show off, "Dad, did you know Mr. Douglas has a theater in the warehouse where he has extra books?"

"Yes, I do, son."

"My, my, young man," Mom said, "it sounds like you had a fine day with Mr. Douglas. Do you think you'll see him again?"

"Yes, ma'am, I hope so." I reached under my chair for the *Romeo and Juliet* book and held it up. I told my parents what Mr. Douglas had said about reading it together.

Mom was pleased and said, "I also have a copy, but let me see yours." She opened my copy, found the Prologue, read it aloud, and asked, "Steve, do you know what 'star-crossed lovers,' means."

I pinched my nose, trying to keep from laughing. "Yes, Mom," I answered as I decided not to cross my fingers since Mom hadn't asked me who told me what it meant, so I told Mom what Nancy had said while not mentioning her name.

Dad, smiling, leaned back in his chair and listened to us talk about Shakespeare.

Mom clapped her hands in delight. "Well, Mr. Douglas has given you an excellent start on the play. I'd love to read it together with you. Shall we start tonight?"

"Sure, Mom, but let's go slow. Mr. Douglas thinks I understand it better than I do. He said we can take as much time as we need."

"Good. He's very accommodating. Dad and I have been to several of his plays. The last one was *A Midsummer's Night Dream* a few years ago. Although it's a good play for young people, we decided you weren't quite old enough for it. Now, you can go with us. Mr. Douglas frequently presents abbreviated versions of Shakespeare's plays. One of them, *Hamlet*, is four hours long."

"Wow, that's something. Miss Kathryn gave me this. I'd sure like to see one," I said, handing the play schedule to Mom.

She took a quick look at the schedule, and said, "Well, they're doing *The Tempest* next week on Friday and Saturday nights at six o'clock. Tomorrow is Easter Sunday. Monday, I'll check with Kathryn and Mr. Douglas about tickets. What do you think, Andy?"

"Absolutely, you know I love to write theatrical reviews, but I'll need your help. You're the Shakespeare expert in the family. You still raring to go, Steve?"

"Yes, sir, you bet," I answered, smiling, knowing my parents had no idea why I was really smiling.

11

The Play

Saturday—April 23, 1949

I HAD NEVER HAD SO MANY THINGS to think about at once. I was excited about going to the play and was glad Mom and I read *The Tempest* together. It was hard, but I understood most of it. Mom said that Mr. Douglas would appreciate that I had read *The Tempest* before the play.

And then there was Nancy. I was excited about seeing her again, but I knew I had a big problem. If she just walked up to me and said, "Hey, Steve," what should I do? I figured people would stare at me, wondering why a Negro girl would talk to me. If any of my white buddies were there, they would ask me what was up and tease the hell out of me. *I could say, I'm sorry, but I don't know you.* I decided that was a bad idea but couldn't come up with anything else.

One other thing really bugged me. Why had I reacted to Nancy like this? It had never happened to me before. Girls were a pain that boys had to deal with. They did things like giggling all the time and pointing at boys and talking about them, most of the time behind their backs. I figured Betty, who was in my class, had a crush on me, but I ignored her.

As for tonight, I decided to wait and see what happened. I also might have to cross my fingers behind my back at some point, knowing this was serious business, especially this girl stuff.

At the foot of the stairs to the second floor, Mom called out, "Andy, Steve, it's time to go to the play. We don't want to be late."

As Dad drove us toward Westtown and the warehouse, he said, "Steve, you're in for a big evening. Besides the play, you'll probably meet a lot of people you don't know, both black and white. Be polite to everybody and enjoy the experience."

"Yes, sir," I said, all my concerns roiling around in my head. Another question that had been bothering me. "Dad, if Negros and whites have to go to separate schools, why can Negros and whites get together at Mr. Douglas' theater?"

I think Dad turned to Mom for help, but she offered none. "Good question, Steve. That bothers me and your mother too. You know we've talked about this sort of thing before. While Delphi considers itself progressive, there are still separate libraries, neighborhoods, restaurants, water fountains, bathrooms, and more. Negroes can participate in the Mardi Gras parade, but they have separate clubs and parties. Mr. Douglas' plays are—"

"Excuse me, Andy, let me explain this."

"Sure," Dad said, smiling as if he were glad to be off the hook.

"Mr. Douglas created the only live theater in Westtown, although there is one in Delphi's white high school. He has been doing plays for years. Some are amateurish, but overall, they are well done with Negro actors who have reasonable skills. When whites expressed an interest in seeing his plays, they went to the Delphi City Council and asked them to grant the theater an exemption from laws affecting Westtown. The council argued about it for a while, and finally agreed to allow whites to attend with the stipulation that seating had to be segregated. Whites and Negroes could not sit together. Mr. Douglas had to provide a separate set of seats for whites and a separate set for Negroes."

"Huh? How'd he do that?" I asked, scrunching my face to try and understand.

"It's crazy, but the seats are split into three sections separated by two aisles. Whites sit in the center section, and Negros sit in the right- and left-hand sections."

I realized I had to add another item to my list of things to think about. *This is getting pretty heavy*, I thought.

"That's enough about that," Dad said. "Let's try and enjoy the evening."

I tried to relax in the back seat. Of course, I had been in Westtown before, mostly with Marvin or Billy but only in the daytime. My parents wanted me at home before dark. Dad drove through a part of Westtown I didn't recognize, the houses were much nicer than Billy's and Marvin's.

It was still daylight, but the warehouse was well-lit outside. I was surprised it was so big. We walked in and I saw lots of bookshelves full of books. On the other side where the curtains were closed across the stage, Mom explained, "The theater and the actors' dressing rooms are inside the curtains. Women dress on the right and men on the left. You'll understand it better when we go in."

There were a number of people, both white and Negro, standing around in the lobby talking. Dad got in line for tickets, and I stayed with him, not wanting to miss a thing.

When Dad's turn came, he said to an older woman, "Good evening, I'm Andy Thompson. I have three tickets in will call."

"Good evening, Mr. Thompson," the woman said in a pleasant voice. She reached into the will call box, found the tickets, handed them to Dad, and said, "Here you are, sir, enjoy the play."

"Thank you, I'm sure we will."

I couldn't resist and added, "Thank you, ma'am."

The box office woman, smiled, and said, "You're welcome, young man."

As we waited to go into the theater, Mom and Dad pointed out Delphi's mayor, a few members of the city council, two white doctors, and Fred who worked for Dad, and a few Negro men Dad knew.

Dad turned to me and said, "I think you know that Westtown is not within Delphi's city limits. Westtown takes care of itself, but is still under the thumb of Delphi's and Alabama's segregation laws."

"That doesn't sound fair," Steve said.

"Of course it isn't. Let's hope it changes soon."

A tall, well-dressed man walked up to me, and said, "You're Steve Thompson, aren't you?"

I wasn't sure who he was, so I asked politely, "Yes, sir, how did you know my name?"

"Moses told me all about you. I'm his brother, Joshua Marshall."

I was stunned. Dr. Marshall looked different than Mr. Douglas. Besides being much taller and in really good shape, he had light-brown skin, a thinner face, no beard, and graying hair, whereas Mr. Douglas was a bit heavy, with dark-black skin, a squarish face, a trim beard, and fuzzy dark hair. I thought of Marvin, imagining he might look like Dr. Marshall when he got older.

"Oh," was all I said.

My parents joined us, and Dad said, "Well, Steve, I see you've met Joshua. And how are you, Joshua? Busy as a bee as usual?"

"Of course. Unfortunately, a doctor never wants for business, Andy. And how are you, Lillis? Moses was quite impressed with your son."

They're using first names. What's going on? Rules were being broken. It just wasn't done publicly.

"Moses has enticed another youngster to read Shakespeare, and we are delighted," Mom said. The lights in the lobby flashed off and on. I guessed it was time to take our seats.

"Let's meet in the lobby after the play," Dr. Marshall said. "Moses will want to talk to Steve and get his opinion of the performance."

As we entered the theater, a lady handed us programs and offered to show us to our seats. She led us down the aisle, and pointed them out.

I was impressed and asked, "Dad, does everybody have a reserved seat?"

"Absolutely, son. Moses's theater is first class. He would have it no other way. And I can see the wheels spinning in your mind. Moses insists that everyone be on a first name basis while they're in here. So, besides what Mom said earlier, he does have his way with a number of things. Okay, settle down and look around. The play will start soon."

Not bothering to look at the program, I saw that the theater was nearly full and couldn't resist asking, "Dad, how many seats in here?"

"About 250."

The stage was really interesting. It was on a platform, maybe four or five feet high. The front of the platform was arched, but I couldn't be sure because a few feet behind the arched part was the curtain. I started trying to figure how big it was, when it got dark.

The curtain opened, the whole stage appeared, and then there were sounds of thunder and lightning as the Shipmaster and Boatswain entered and spoke. From that moment on, I was in the clutches of my first Shakespeare play.

When the second scene started, Prospero appeared with his daughter, Miranda. I was excited and whispered to Dad, "It's Mr. Douglas."

He whispered back, "Yes, he acts in all his plays. We have to be quiet."

Later in the second scene, Ariel came on stage and spoke her first lines.

> All hail, great master, grave sir, hail, I come
> To answer thy best pleasure.

My jaw dropped when I realized what I was seeing. *Oh my God, Nancy is Ariel, my favorite character in the play.* I was entering my own brave new world.

At intermission, Mom asked, "What do you think, Steve? Can you follow it?"

"Yeah, it's great. I'm following it pretty good."

"Who's your favorite character?" she asked.

I thought about crossing my fingers, but choose not to, and said, "Ariel."

"One of my favorites too. I think Nancy Dawson is doing an excellent job."

How does Mom know her name?

The house lights flickered, and we sat down for the second part of the play. I looked at the program's cast of characters and realized how Mom knew Nancy's name. *Whoa, that was a close call.*

The second half of the play kept me on pins and needles as I struggled to focus on each scene, but what I waited for anxiously were the scenes with Ariel in them. Even then, I tried to act cool when she was on stage, hoping not to attract my parents' attention.

I really got excited when Act 5 started. That's when Prospero pardoned Caliban and others, set Ariel free, and released his control of the story and the characters in the last two lines of the play by asking the audience to pardon him.

> As you from crimes would pardoned be,
> Let your indulgence set me free.

As soon as Prospero's last lines were spoken, I leapt up and applauded vigorously. Mr. Douglas, Prospero, bowed toward me as my parents and others around me, smiled at my enthusiasm, and joined in, clapping and cheering.

I watched the actors as they came on stage and kept bowing because the applause continued. I thought I had been fair and applauded equally for all the actors, including Nancy.

I realized that was not so when Mom asked, "You really like Ariel, don't you?"

"Yes, ma'am, great character," I answered, hoping that would take the spot light off of Nancy.

Finally, Mr. Douglas came on center stage, and said, "Thank you for coming tonight, and I want you to know how much all the actors appreciate your response to our play." He then joined the actors, held hands with Miranda and Ariel, while the entire casts bowed to the audience one last time.

In the lobby, my head was still buzzing from all the excitement when I saw Mr. Douglas, Dr. Marshall, and Nancy coming toward me. *Oh boy*, I thought, *and crossed my fingers for good luck.*

Mr. Douglas said, "I hope y'all enjoyed the play. I'd like to introduce the young lady who played Ariel, Miss Nancy Dawson. Nancy, this is Mr. Andy Thompson, Mrs. Lillis Thompson, and their son, Steve Thompson."

I squeezed my fingers together as tight as I could, having no idea what Nancy might say.

Nancy was polite as she spoke to Mom and Dad. Then she turned to me and said, "It's nice to meet you, Steve."

Sighing, I relaxed my fingers, and said, "Nice to meet you, Nancy. I really liked the play." I said no more, realizing that Mr. Douglas was Prospero-like and must have planned our meeting tonight, so that neither Nancy nor I would be embarrassed.

Mom spoke up and said, "Moses, I'm always amazed at the excellent performances you get out of your actors. I also think this play is your best production."

"Thank you, Lillis, but the credit goes to the actors, all of whom work tirelessly to not only memorize their lines but to deliver them with correct elocution and dramatic effect."

"Moses, what's up next?" Dad asked, always playing the reporter.

"Aha, good that you ask. In mid-July, we'll do *Romeo and Juliet*. We haven't done it for several years. And guess who will play Juliet?"

Everybody looked at Nancy. I thought for sure that she blushed and quietly protested, "Mr. Douglas, you're embarrassing me."

"No, my dear Juliet," Mr. Douglas said, "as you said of yourself, 'What's in a name? That which we call a rose by any other name would smell as sweet.' "

"Brother," Dr. Marshall said, "I think it's time you and Nancy retired to the dressings rooms, and then went home."

"Quite right, Joshua. Nancy and I bid you adieu."

As Nancy and Mr. Douglas walked away, Dr. Marshall said, "Forgive Moses please, he gets carried away with things Shakespearian.... Steve, I hope you'll visit his library soon. I know he'd like to see you."

Hoping for a little less attention, I said, "Yes, sir, I plan to."

"Good. And perhaps, if your parents agree, you could visit us at our house nearby. In addition to Shakespeare, we could discuss medicine and other things."

Mom said, "I'm sure we could arrange something, Joshua."

"But Dr. Marshall," I said, "I don't know anything about medicine."

" 'Ay there's the rub', Steve. It's a problem to be solved." Dr. Marshall winked at me. "And don't worry, there won't be any exams. I'll say good night."

As we drove home, Dad said, "Well, Steve, I suspect you got a lot more than you bargained for tonight."

"I don't know what that means, Dad, but I sure have a lot of stuff to think about."

Mom asked me, "Do you know where the saying 'Ay there's the rub' comes from?"

"No, ma'am."

"Shakespeare's play *Hamlet*. Most consider it his greatest play."

"Mom, can we stop talking about Shakespeare for a while?"

"Of course, I know you're tired. But tomorrow, we start reading *Romeo and Juliet*."

I crawled into bed, and even though I was tired, my only thought was of Nancy as Ariel. Or was I thinking of Ariel as Nancy? I wasn't sure. I wasn't sure of anything.

12

The Haunted House

Sunday—April 24, 1949

SUNDAY MORNING AFTER CHURCH, I was getting ready to skedaddle in hopes of finding Marvin and Billy, when I heard Billy shout, "Hey, Steve, wanna go to a new creek?"

I opened the front door, saw them standing in the yard, and said, "Why didn't you knock on the door? You know my parents don't care."

Marvin snickered and said, "Oh, it's just Billy. He says he wants to be polite. I say he just plain afraid."

Marvin usually got away with teasing Billy, but sometimes Billy blew his stack. I figured trouble was brewing.

And sure enough, Billy said, "Marvin, you full of shit. Next time you say that I'll bash you're head in." But then he changed his tone some. "Okay, I got it. We gotta go through Westtown to get to the creek. Let's show Steve the haunted house."

"Billy, I've told you a hundred times that house ain't haunted. But let's do this. We'll go by it, take a look, and let Steve decide if it's haunted. You game, Steve?"

Damn, I didn't like being between a rock and a hard place, but I decided to adhere to rule number one—don't ever appear chicken in front of your buddies. So, I said like I didn't care, "Sure. But I still want to go to the new creek."

AS WE WALKED TOWARD WESTTOWN, which most people called colored town, I could tell we weren't headed toward the warehouse, so I didn't say anything about being there last night. Just to be friendly, I said, "Isn't your house around here, Billy?"

He still appeared angry. "Yep, it's around the corner over yonder," Billy said, pointing, and then added to my surprise, "It ain't much to look at. Marvin's house is close by, too."

Hoping to make Billy feel better, I said, "I've been in Marvin's house. I liked it."

When Marvin spoke, I hoped he would cheer Billy up, "Billy, your house is like mine. You heard what Steve said."

Billy replied simply, "Yeah I heard....The haunted house is just around the corner."

We stood and stared at it, and I had to admit that if any house was haunted, this one sure fit the bill. There was an old picket fence in front of the yard. It looked like hell, as did the yard, which was overgrown with weeds and ivies wrapping the trees. It hadn't been painted in years. Its outstanding feature were two spires that looked like they might fall over any minute. *Was it kinda Gothic? I didn't know.*

I was still staring at it when an old colored man came out the front door with a baseball bat. I was ready to run, but didn't since Billy and Marvin stood still.

The old man roared like a lion, "I done told you two to leave me alone. Now you done brought a whitey."

"This whitey was at the warehouse last night when Mr. Douglas put on one of his plays," Marvin said.

I didn't tell him, so how did Marvin know I was there?

"The old man roared again, "I don't give a shit what Moses and his so-called brother are doing. Now, git outta here."

He walked down the stairs of the porch waving the bat. All three of us ran like hell until we were well out of sight.

When I caught my breath, I said, "Marvin, were you at the warehouse last night?"

He answered sheepishly, "Yep, I work back stage. I do sounds and anything else Mr. Douglas wants me to do. I saw you when you were the first one to start applauding. You liked it, huh?"

"You bet. It was great," I said. But I wondered something, and added, "I asked Mr. Douglas if you acted in his plays. He said no. Why did he lie to me?"

Marvin laughed at me. "Sometimes you ain't too smart, Steve. If he said no, that was the truth. He didn't lie."

Marvin had me there, so I let it be. "Are we close to the creek yet?"

"Almost there," Billy said. "Well, Steve, do you think the house is haunted?"

"Can't say for sure. It looks like it could be haunted, but the old man didn't look like a ghost. Has he chased you two off before?"

"Yep, but I think we better leave the old man alone. What you think, Marvin?"

"I'm with you, Billy. The old man's a pain in the ass, but who knows, he might just lay that bat on somebody's head someday, and I don't want it to be mine."

When we got to the creek, it wasn't as nice as the other one we often visited, so I asked, "You got a trot line set here?"

"Nope," Marvin said. "Billy and I talked about it. Maybe we oughta try. What do you think, Steve?"

"I'm game," I said.

I heard some sparrows singing to us. Nice voices. It was a warm day, not too hot, puffy clouds all around, and no signs of rain.

"Let's sit down for a minute," I said, "I've got something to tell you."

"What's up, Steve? You gonna tell me a big secret?" Marvin asked.

I thought for a minute about how much I wanted to tell them and decided to keep it simple. "A week ago, yesterday, I met Mr. Douglas for the first time in the Negro Library. Miss Kathryn introduced me. He's a nice man, and we talked about books and Shakespeare. That's about it. I wanted you to know." I really wanted to ask about Nancy but didn't.

Marvin appeared quizzical, but said nothing.

Billy stepped right in, "Well, ain't you something. You can use both libraries, and we can't. What about that?"

"You're right, Billy, it's not fair. I can't fix it. What am I supposed to do?"

Marvin finally spoke up, "Nothing. Just don't make it worse."

They stared hard at me. I guessed I never understood how close to the edge friendships could be. I kept thinking, *What can I say? What can I say?*

My Dad always told me that when all else fails, drop back ten and punt. So, I punted and changed the subject, saying, "Why did the old man say something like, 'Moses and his *so-called* brother?' Aren't they brothers?"

I think we all calmed down, because Marvin smiled and said, "I believe they're brothers. You can't believe anything that old man says. He's nutty as a fruitcake. Besides he hates everybody, coloreds and whites."

"Yeah, Marvin's right," Billy said. "Don't worry about him. We just gotta leave him alone."

"Okay, back to the play," Marvin said. "What did you like most about it, Steve."

Uh oh, I felt the edge coming up again. "I liked it all. And I really liked Prospero's final speech when he asked the audience to forgive him."

Billy tilted his head and said, "Damn, I wish I knew what y'all were talking about. Never heard of no Prospero."

"Well, Billy," Marvin said, "maybe, if you saw a few plays, you'd get the hang of it." Marvin then asked me the question I didn't want to hear. "Steve, who were your favorite actors?"

I hemmed and hawed a bit. "Oh, let me think.... Uh, of course, Mr. Douglas as Prospero, and...I can't remember her name, but the lady that played Miranda. That's about it."

"Miranda was played by Ruth Wilson," Marvin said.

"Right, now I remember her."

"How did you like Nancy Dawson, the girl who played Ariel?"

The guillotine had dropped. I tried to act normal. "Yeah, she was really good."

Marvin smiled. "She a cute kid, but Nancy's too young for me. I've got my eyes on Ruth."

"Isn't she older than you, Marvin?"

"Oh, c'mon on Steve. She's only fifteen. I'm thirteen, going on fourteen. Things will work out later."

I nodded. "Hope they do."

"Well, if you come to see *Romeo and Juliet* in July, you'll see Nancy as Juliet. I know Ruth was disappointed, but she does play two characters, a young man and an older woman."

I didn't respond because I didn't want to tell Marvin that I already knew about Nancy.

"Let's go," Billy said, "I gotta go home. I'm tired of listenin' to you two."

In Westtown, Billy said goodbye when we got to his house. Damn, I thought, I wish he was more like Marvin, even though I knew it wasn't my place to tell him what to do. But I was glad he had finally gone to the library and had a book to read.

As we walked toward Marvin's house, I asked, "Y'all go to the same school, right?"

"For crying out loud, Steve, you must know there's only one colored school in Westtown. Hell, everybody we've talked about tonight goes there. I'll tell you a secret if you can keep it."

"I can. What?"

"Billy's got a crush on Nancy. She pays him no mind."

At first his words felt like a gut punch, but I waved my hand like I didn't care. "Good for Billy. She seems to be a nice girl."

Marvin grinned at me as if he knew. I grinned back.

At Marvin's house, his father, Zeke came out. I had seen him only a couple of times. He was a tall man and always a bit grumpy. Marvin had said he was okay.

Mr. Zeke said, "Hey, Steve, you doin' good?"

"Yes, sir, I be doin' fine."

He nodded and said, "Marvin, you come inside in a few minutes. Mama needs some help."

"Yes, sir."

Mr. Zeke went inside without a goodbye.

Before Marvin went in, he said, "Don't worry, Steve, Dad only talks tough. You gonna be okay walking home alone?"

Trying to sound tough, I said, "No problem. I come out here to see you and Billy a lot."

"Not exactly what I meant. Something's bugging you. What is it? Are you still mad at Billy for what he said about the two libraries?"

Maybe, I was a little, but I said, "No, I get it. I think we're okay."

Marvin twitched as if he weren't convinced. "Sure, we're okay. I still think you're holding out on me. Something else is under your skin."

I wanted to tell him, but I just couldn't do it. "Nope, that's it. I gotta go. See you later."

As I walked home, I don't know why, but I decided to have a conversation with myself out loud.

"Self, what's going on in Steve's head about Nancy?"

"Well, since you asked, it seems it's pretty simple to me. I've got a crush on Nancy."

"You're right, Self, but why do I have a hard time admitting it?"

"Steve, what do you think the consequences will be if you admit it?"

"None, Self, if I just admit it to myself, but I'm afraid of what might happen if I tell anybody."

"Why is that, Steve?"

"Self, you're smarter than that. You know why."

"No, I don't, Steve."

"Self, Nancy is colored. I'm white."

"Interesting, Steve. Now what?"

"Self, all hell will break loose."

I laughed, even though it wasn't funny, and said goodbye to *Self*. But I was still in a pickle and didn't know which way to turn.

When I got home Mom said, "Did you have fun with Billy and Marvin?"

I answered, "Yes, ma'am. It's a nice creek. We might set a new trot line there."

13

The Library

Saturday—April 30, 1949

MOM REALLY PUSHED HARD to get us through our reading of *Romeo and Juliet* this week. It took us five days. We read every night, and Mom always explained things to me. I think I got most of it.

When we closed the book on Friday night, Mom said, "I think you're ready to talk to Mr. Douglas. Why don't you go to the library tomorrow morning and see if he's available?"

"Yes, ma'am, I will."

I took the copy of *Romeo and Juliet* that Mr. Douglas had lent me, and asked Miss Kathryn if Mr. Douglas was here.

"I think so," she said. "Let's see."

She knocked on the door, and somehow like magic, the door opened and there he was. Of course, to me, he was Prospero, the magician.

"Well, come in, Steve. I've been expecting you although I thought you and your mother might require more time."

"We finished last night, Mr. Douglas. Mom thought it best that I talk to you now while everything was fresh in my mind."

"Sit down, Steve. Your Mom was quite right, but I have no doubt that you have a retentive memory. Shall we discuss the play?"

"Yes, sir," I said, handing him the book.

Mr. Douglas read passages from the play and asked me to explain them. Mostly he just nodded and said nothing, but a few times, he offered different interpretations of a passage although he always qualified it by saying, "Your interpretation was correct, but remember there are cases where others can be appropriate."

We talked for over an hour, and several times someone came into the library to return or check out books. Each time I heard the door open, I looked in hopes that it was Nancy, but it never was. Mr. Douglas always introduced me to the new visitors, who were very nice to me.

"Well, Steve, you are now prepared to see our upcoming production of *Romeo and Juliet*. I assure you that you will enjoy and understand it better than many in the audience. Will you attend?"

"Oh, yes, sir, Mom and Dad will come too."

"I'm sure," Mr. Douglas said. Pausing, he rolled his heard around as if his neck were sore, and said, "As you know, Nancy will play Juliet....You like her, don't you?"

I opened my mouth, and nothing came out as I blushed and looked around for help, but then I finally admitted, "Yes, sir, I do."

He smiled and said, ever so quietly, "Quite understandable. She is an attractive young lady. She and her family live in a house at the other end of this block. Her father is the only mortician in Westtown. Her mother is a *Creole* lady from New Orleans, and she's very beautiful. Do you know what Creole means?"

"No, sir."

"It can be confusing. Most simply, it means white Europeans born on one of the Caribbean islands, or a person born to a white European and a Negro. I'm sure Mrs. Dawson is in the latter category."

I nodded, and said, "Yes, sir, it sure is confusing. Does that mean Nancy's Creole?"

"My, that's a good question. I'm not sure how to explain it. Let's just say that Nancy inherited her mother's lovey skin color. But there are other things to consider."

'Ay there's the rub,' immediately popped into my mind. "Yes, sir, I know. What should I do?"

"You mean, what should both of you do. I have no perfect answer. What I can say is that you should quietly enjoy your feelings. But you must be cognizant of the fact that Delphi and Westtown are two disparate communities. Each has its own value systems and opinions."

"What does disparate mean, sir?"

"Most simply, it means different, like apples and oranges. But disparate also implies two things that may be intractably different, like the North and South during the Civil War, or like today, the Negroes in Westtown and the white folks in Delphi. Understand?"

Since I had a retentive memory, I reminded myself to look up the word intractably. "Mr. Douglas, please don't tell anyone I told you this, but why do I find Negroes much easier to deal with than white folks?"

"Good question and suggestion. How about we agree not to tell anyone what we talk about? Deal?"

I smiled because he liked my idea. "Yes, sir, deal."

"As to your question, Negroes mostly have a mask on when they associate with whites. But I can tell you this, in Westtown we often get angry at each other. And even worse, we can treat some people very badly if we disagree with them, especially on religious and political issues, or matters of the heart."

I nodded, thinking I got his message. "You mean like people would feel about me if they knew I liked Nancy."

"Yes, you do get it, and of course, vice-versa. Let's change the subject. Joshua and I would like you to visit us soon. Your mother seemed to agree it would be all right. Perhaps, next week on Friday at five o'clock. We'll have a nice dinner, talk a while, and ensure you get home by eight."

"Sure, I'd like that as long as I don't have to take a medical exam."

Mr. Douglas laughed and said, "I'll remind Joshua. I also plan to invite Marvin."

I may have furrowed my brow, because I could tell that Mr. Douglas sensed I was surprised. "Why didn't you tell me that Marvin worked on your plays? He's my friend."

"As he is mine, but you are right, I was remiss in not telling you when you asked about him the first time we met. Please, forgive me."

I was impressed when Mr. Douglas fessed up. I wished all my buddies were like that. But I felt silly when I said to Mr. Douglas, an adult, "Thank you, sir. That's all right."

"And thank you. Now, shall we invite Marvin?"

I grinned, thinking I was in control. "Yes, sir, of course."

Mr. Douglas grabbed my hand and shook it. "Well, then we have another deal. *Jolly good* as the British say."

I had no idea what that meant, but I laughed along with Mr. Douglas.

He looked at his watch, and said, "Alas, Steve, I have another appointment in a few minutes. You or your mother can let me or Joshua know about our dinner engagement."

"Yes, sir, I will," I said. But I was thinking, *What's a dinner engagement?*

14

Dinner Engagement

Friday—May 6, 1949

Mom insisted on driving me to Mr. Douglas' house, and she said that Dad would pick me no later than eight o'clock. I tried to talk her out of it, but I knew before I started that she wouldn't change her mind. Sure, I was excited about going, but at the same time, I was antsy, kind of like the first time I met Mr. Douglas. I just hoped I wouldn't say anything stupid or embarrassing. While Mom parked the car, I looked up and down the block, hoping to figure out where Nancy's house was.

I really got ticked off when Mom went to their front door with me. I kept my mouth shut, but it made me feel even younger.

Dr. Marshall opened the door and welcomed us, "Good evening, Steve and Lillis, I'm glad to see you. Please come in."

"Thank you, Joshua. I can only stay a minute. Steve, don't forget that Dad will pick you up at eight o'clock."

I ignored Mom and said, "Hi, Dr. Marshall,"

The adults talked, and I listened, while I checked out the house. The front of the house had a nice lawn, and it looked like it had been recently mowed. But what immediately blew me away was the inside. I couldn't see all of the rooms, but what I saw was incredible. The entryway had dark hardwood floors that shined as if they were a quietly flowing river stream. I could see into the living room on the right and a dining room on the left, and many of the pieces of furniture were antiques. On the floors were oriental rugs. I was sure about this because my grandmother in Montgomery collected and sold antiques and oriental rugs. The dining room table was set with finery that was fit for a king, not for boys. There were elegant oil paintings on the walls. I knew nothing about art, but I figured this had to be good stuff. I also knew that Billy and Marvin lived in the poorer part of Westtown in small houses. I had never seen a house in Delphi as fine as this, including our house. *I better not tell my parents this.*

"Fortunately for me, Moses does most of our cooking. He's always been the best cook in our family. He's in the kitchen preparing a meal that I think the boys will like."

"That's nice," Mom said, adding, "Steve, are you paying attention?"

Another oops. "Yes, ma'am," I said as I saw Mr. Douglas approaching us, wearing an apron and a white hat.

"Did someone mention my name?" he said, laughing. "You caught me in my cooking apparel," He turned and called out, "Marvin, come out and join us."

"Hello, Marvin," Mom said. "I didn't know you'd be here."

"Hey, Miss Lillis," Marvin said, "I'm helping Mr. Douglas fix supper."

"I didn't know you could cook?"

"Yes, ma'am. I help my Mom at home. I'm not very good, but I like it."

"My, my, what a surprise. I knew you assisted Moses backstage in his plays."

"Yes, ma'am, I like that too. For *The Tempest*, I pounded on metal drums to create the thunder, and I switched the wind machine off and on. The light guy created the lightning."

Why does everybody know things I don't know?

"I have to be going," Mom said. "You boys be good and have a fun time."

"Well, young men, let's have a fun time," Dr. Marshall said. "And don't pay any attention to the apron and toque Moses is wearing. By the way, a toque is French for a chef's hat, and Moses is always on stage."

Mr. Douglas grinned, threw his head back, and placed his hand on his forehead, and said, "'O, what a rogue and peasant slave am I.' *Hamlet*, Act 2, Scene 2. Forgive my indulgences, lads. A thespian can be a bore at times. Now, house rule number one. We are on a first name basis while in our house. Call us Moses and Joshua, please. House rule two is...hmm, there are no other rules."

My head was spinning again. One moment Moses is serious and the next, he's funny. I'll have to size up Joshua more to get a handle on him.

"Let's repair to the kitchen," Moses said. "We have a few things to complete. Then to the den for a few hors d'oeuvres, and a bit of chit chat."

I was so proud because I knew what 'hors d'oeuvres' meant. Mom used it often. But I made a mental note to look up *repair* as Moses used it.

But I couldn't wait, so as we walked toward the kitchen, I whispered to Marvin, "Moses said *repair to the kitchen*. Is something broken?"

I could tell that Marvin wanted to laugh, but he didn't, and whispered, "His repair means going somewhere. Get used to it. These guys use a lot of words I don't get."

After Moses and Marvin stirred a few pots and checked something in the oven, we repaired to the den. I chuckled to myself for having used the word. The den was off the kitchen and was decorated much like the other rooms. Oh, I forgot, the kitchen was large with shiny appliances like a refrigerator and stove. *Wow, Moses and Joshua must have lots of money.*

In the den, Moses served us sweet iced tea. "Steve and Marvin, you see before you three hors d'oeuvres." And pointing with his usual flair, said, "First, we have bacon wrapped dates with almonds, a very tasty treat. Second, there are deviled eggs, a favorite of mine. Finally, southern pimento cheese dip. Just dip a cracker in the cheese and enjoy. I suggest no more than two of each hors d'oeuvre as we have a salad, an entrée with accompaniments, and a dessert to be served in the den. Please enjoy, our young friends."

That was like saying, "Ready-set-go," to us and go we did. Moses was right, they were all great. I had never had the bacon wrap before, but now it was my favorite of the three, and I cheated and had three of them. I think Marvin did, too.

"Boys, I don't need to ask if you enjoyed the hors d'oeuvres," Moses said. "But as is my wont, I have hogged the stage for too long. So, brother, it's your turn."

Joshua grinned and said, "Well, Moses, I know how hard it is for you to step out of the limelight, but I shall do my best."

Damn, I thought, *two sentences and two new words: wont and limelight*.

"Steve, I told you that we might talk medicine," Joshua said, "but I've decided to keep it short tonight. Quite simply, I consider medicine a noble profession and becoming a doctor is the noblest of all. Of course, I'm biased. Have you ever thought about becoming a doctor?"

"No, sir," I said, but trying to say something knowledgeable, I added, "My Dad told me you were the only Negro doctor in Delphi, and if it weren't for you, Negroes would have to drive to Montgomery for a doctor."

"Yes, that is true, Steve. However, the Delphi white clinic will accept Negroes for emergencies, but they will send them to me as soon as possible. That's not as bad as it sounds because it is also about money. The white clinic charges more than I do and many of my patients have limited financial resources."

"Can all your patients pay you?" I asked, hoping it wouldn't insult Joshua.

"Aha, Moses told me you asked good questions. The answer is no, but they repay me in many ways by providing us goods and services. Some of them have small farms and provide us vegetables they've grown and meat from their pigs and heifers and steers. Some give us building materials if we need them. Some even do work for us like tend the yard and garden or do housework or rebuild and repair things. Best of all, it gives Moses and me a sense of being part of the community."

I don't know why I thought of this or why I asked, but I did. "Do you know the old man who lives nearby? His house looks haunted, but I don't think it is. Does he do things for you?"

Joshua shook his head, looking concerned. "The old man you're referring to is named Zach. His house is not haunted, but he is. You boys should leave him alone. I rather not talk about—"

Moses cut in, "Time for the main meal. Marvin and I will serve it. Joshua, you and Steve go into the dining room. And Joshua, please put on some quiet classical music as background for our dinner. As I am expert in books and Shakespeare, Joshua is an expert in classical music and opera. He has a large record collection. *Tally ho.*"

We all laughed, but it seemed to me that Joshua didn't want to talk about Zach. I shrugged that off, and said, "Moses, can I help you and Marvin?"

"Of course, into the kitchen."

After Moses finished the salad, he sliced the roast beef while Marvin and I prepared bowls of mashed potatoes and vegetables and rolls.

I whispered to Marvin, "Are these the accompaniments?"

He giggled, and said, "Yep, fancy word for sides."

Just then we heard someone playing the piano. It sounded nice. I guessed it was classical music.

Moses answered my question before I asked it. "Boys, that is a record of a famous pianist named Artur Schnabel playing Beethoven's sonatas. Don't think too hard about it. Just enjoy the music. Now, we must perform as waiters and put the food on the dining room table."

Moses led our performance with the salad and roast beef, I followed with the mashed potatoes, and Marvin with the vegetables and rolls.

We ate with gusto, but Marvin and I did pretty good on the manners thing and watched Moses and Joshua for cues to what was proper. They asked us a lot of questions about what we liked to do. I didn't know about Marvin, but for me this was an experience.

After we finished eating, we cleared the table, and Moses said, "We'll have dessert shortly. Let's go into the den, and Joshua can tell you about music and opera."

We *repaired* to the den. I couldn't stop using that word. It made me feel good.

Joshua placed another record on the turntable and turned up the volume, saying nothing. After a couple of minutes, I think he saw that Marvin and I were looking at each other as if to say: *What is this?* He turned the volume down.

Joshua asked us, "What did this music say to you?"

Marvin spoke first and answered, "It was exciting. I liked the rhythms."

Not to be outdone, I added, "I might be wrong, but I think the music wants to tell a story."

"You're both right. This in the overture from *The Marriage of Figaro*, a comic opera by an Austrian composer named Wolfgang Amadeus Mozart. An overture is like an introduction or preface in a book. It uses a summary of the opera's tunes which will tell the story. It's best not to try and wrap your head around opera in one gulp. Like Shakespeare, I think it takes time to understand and appreciate opera. Let's leave it there for now. Perhaps, when you come to join us again, we can listen to the first act of *The Marriage of Figaro*. It really is a funny story."

We both nodded yes, and Marvin asked, "Joshua, operas have words in them, don't they?"

"They sure do, Marvin. However, the words in *The Marriage of Figaro* are sung in Italian."

I had to step in. "Joshua, what comes first in opera, the words or the music?"

"Boys, you keep asking good questions. Steve, most simply, it is a collaboration between the words written by a poet and the composer of the music, but I prefer to give the music the first position. If you try to imagine opera without music, a reading of the poet's words, while wonderful in themselves, would not achieve the soaring inspiration and drama the music facilitates. Now, that's enough opera for tonight."

"I really enjoyed it, Joshua. Thank you," I said, finally getting ahead of Marvin.

Joshua bowed his head as if we were royalty. "Now, my young friends, we must balance the scales. I want to play you one other short piece by a composer named Joseph Boulogne. He lived in Paris in the 18th century, and as a young man became such an extraordinary fencer that Louis XV, the king of France, knighted him with the name Chevalier de Saint-Georges. Saint-Georges became an excellent classical music composer. And here's the surprise, he was a Negro, and I doubt many people have heard of him."

Joshua paused. Marvin and I stared at him in wonder. I waited for Marvin to speak, and he sure did.

"Joshua, how come he's so unheard of?"

"Several reasons. First, he was a Negro, and you know how most people around here feel about us. Second, he was a fencer and that's not a popular sport here. Third, he composed his important works almost 200 years ago. Fourth, recordings of his music are hard to find. It took me several years to get the record I want to play for you. Enough about the reasons. Steve, what do you think?"

Yikes, the hot seat again, I thought. "Seems fair to me. He sounds great. What did the French people think about Mr. Chevalier?"

"Interesting question. Our second president, John Adams, knew of him and admired him. It is said that Saint-Georges met Mozart when he was in Paris. However, the hard shoe of racism dropped on Saint-Georges when he was offered a prestigious musical position. Some French musicians and performers in the group objected to taking orders from a Negro, and he was denied the position. Now, I'll play you part of the opening movement of one of our Negro maestro's better compositions. Based on your observations about the Mozart piece, I think you'll enjoy this."

Marvin and I listened carefully, nodding our heads and tapping our feet to the music's rhythm. As Joshua removed the record from the turntable, I leaned over and whispered to Marvin, "I want dessert."

He replied, "Me too. I've had enough music."

As if he heard us, Joshua said, "Let's have dessert, boys. Moses has baked a wonderful pecan pie."

The evening came to a close precisely at eight o'clock when Dad arrived to take me home. He offered to drive Marvin home, but he said he'd prefer to walk.

Marvin tapped on the window and said, "Steve, you wanna go to a new creek with Billy and me tomorrow and set a trot line?"

I looked at Dad. He nodded, so I said, "Sure. I'll be at you house at ten o'clock."

"See you then," Marvin said.

15

Nancy's House

Saturday—May 7, 1949

SATURDAY MORNING, I RAN over to Marvin's house and saw Billy and Marvin in the front yard putting together the lines and hooks we'd need to set the new trot line.

"Hey, guys," I said. "Let's get going."

Just then Marvin's mother, Mabel Gibbs, opened the front door and said, "Marvin, now you be sure and be back by two o'clock. You gotta go to town with me to help with shopping. Hey, Steve, how you doin'?"

"I'm doin' fine, Miss Mabel. You okay?"

"Can't complain. You gotta come over to eat some of my fried chicken. I know you like it."

"Yes, ma'am. I sure do."

"You boys behave," she said as she went back inside the house.

"Ain't you the mama's boy?" Billy said, poking me in the ribs.

"Well, she didn't invite you, smart ass," I said, poking back.

Billy tilted his head as he often did when he was thinking. "Got an idea. Let's walk by Nancy's house on the way to the creek. Maybe, I'll get a chance to see her."

Here she comes again. I'll just have to be cool. But I couldn't resist and said, "Maybe, all three of us will see her."

Billy's head snapped back, and it almost sounded like he barked, "You know Nancy, Steve?"

"I told you that I saw and met her at Mr. Douglas' play. Sometimes, you act like a birdbrain, Billy."

Now Billy seemed to be pouting. "Oh yeah, I forgot. Let's go."

Billy led the way, as if he thought Marvin and I didn't know where we were going. Billy carried the bait and Marvin the trot lines. When we got to Mr. Douglas' neighborhood, Billy marched right by his house to the end of the block and stopped.

He announced in a formal manner, "This is Nancy's house."

Like all the houses in this neighborhood, it was nice with a neatly trimmed front yard, and while I couldn't see the inside, I imagined it was elegant. *I don't know, sometimes I think I overdo it when describing things.*

We stared at the house, and Billy said something to Marvin when I saw Nancy looking at us from a front window. Without thinking, I waved at her. She waved back, and a moment later, she came out the front door. I thought I was going to freak out, but I just stood there and looked at her.

She walked a few steps toward us and stopped, and said, "Hey, y'all. I'm getting ready to go to the first rehearsal of *Romeo and Juliet*. Where are y'all going?"

None of us said anything until Billy finally spoke up, "Hey, Nancy ...Uh,...we're going to a creek over yonder...we're going to set a trot line. I got the bait."

I felt like she kept looking at me. I sure hoped she was.

"That sounds like fun. We're doing our first reading of the play this afternoon, as each actor reads their part aloud to get a sense of how it sounds."

I was staring at my feet, feeling silly, and unable to think of anything to say. I finally lifted my head and said, "How do you memorize all those lines? It seems impossible to me."

Nancy laughed, and I knew for sure she was laughing at me. "Well, silly, I kinda just told you one thing when each actor reads their parts in order. Want to know more?"

How does she know how I feel? Now, I was determined. I started this, and I had to finish it. "Of course."

"Okay. Here's a few others. Mr. Douglas has each of us write our parts in longhand on paper. Then we run our lines with an actor. Like I'll run mine with George who is playing Romeo. That's it.... Oh, I forgot, we also memorize cue lines. That's the lines that lead into mine. Sounds easy, but it's not. Lots of memorizing and lots of rehearsals."

Holy mackerel, Nancy amazes me. How does she do all that?

"What do you think, Marvin?" Nancy asked. "You've been to lots of rehearsals."

Marvin nodded and looked as if he was glad to finally be on stage. "The backstage boys and girls aren't required for most of what you just said. But you know that. I'm a sound guy and we come to the rehearsals just before the play opens. But maybe someday I'll try out for a part in a play. Maybe I could play Othello."

"And I could play Desdemona. That would be fun. Well, not really fun because you have to kill me before you kill yourself." She laughed and added, "Of course, it's just a play."

Billy's head was tilted. I figured he was itching to get back into the conservation.

"Nancy, I checked my first book out of the library," Billy said. "Mr. Douglas suggested I read *Twenty Thousand Leagues Under the Sea*. I'm almost finished reading it. I like the story. Have you read it?"

Oops, I thought, *wrong question, Billy*.

"Yes, I have, Billy. I've read most of Jules Verne's books. They're nice, but I'm well beyond them now. You should try Shakespeare."

Billy appeared like he wanted to slink away slowly, but he recovered well enough, and said, "Yeah. Well, we gotta go to the creek. Goodbye."

We followed Billy, but I looked back briefly and Nancy smiled and waved at me. I floated the rest of the way to the creek.

While Billy moped around, Marvin and I arranged the trot lines at the edge of the creek.

Billy kept staring at us as if we were crazy. Finally, he said, "What the hell, let's go home. This ain't worth the effort. And you can't be late, Marvin. Your Mom would be pissed." Billy dumped the bait in the creek.

Marvin and I didn't say anything as we followed Billy's lead and wrapped the trot lines up for later use.

Billy led the way back, and he avoided going anywhere near Nancy's house. It felt like a forced march. When we got to his house, he turned and glared at Marvin and me as he slammed his front door shut.

As we walked toward Marvin's house, he said, "I'll tell you who's pissed. Billy's pissed at all three of us. He's pissed at himself because Nancy talked down to him. And he's pissed at you and me since she treated us okay. You agree?"

"I reckon you're right. But if he has a crush on her, I can understand how he feels."

"Why?"

Damn it. I walked right into that one. I decided to punt, and said, "Well, you have a crush on Ruth. You'd be pissed if she dumped you."

"Ruth hasn't dumped me. She doesn't know I have a crush on her.…But I can tell that you have a crush on Nancy. What you got to say about that?"

I shook my head and decided to pivot away again. "Well, even if I do, she doesn't know it."

I hoped Marvin would let go of it. But he chose not to, and said, "I'll tell you what I think. You've got a serious crush on Nancy. Hell, every time her name comes up, you try to hide by saying something silly. You can't fool me, Steve. And she knows, because I saw her smile and wave at you when we left her house."

Marvin didn't miss anything. *Damn.* "You're not going to tell Billy or Nancy what you think, are you?"

Marvin laughed, but it sounded more like a siren blowing in my ears. "I ain't no snitch, Steve. But you gotta know that you'll be in real hot water if you become really good friends with Nancy."

I knew he was right, but I kept pushing back. "Why?"

"Get real, Steve. If a white man gets close to a colored woman, nothing happens to the white man. And it started during slavery, and it ain't never stopped. You can bet your sweet ass, if a colored man gets close to a white woman, he's a dead man."

Why do I refuse to keep pushing? I ought to start answering my own questions, but I said, "Yeah, I get it. But I haven't heard of any problems around here. Have you?"

"No. But you and I haven't lived that long. As I told your daddy, the KKK is still on the prowl. And listen, if you and Nancy got serious, you know all hell would break loose."

We had been so intent in our conversation, we didn't realize we were at Marvin's house until we heard Miss Mabel call out, "Hey, you boys are home early. Did you have fun?"

"Yes, ma'am," Marvin said.

"How about you, Steve?" she asked.

"Yes, Miss Mabel. I have to go home now. Bye, Marvin. Bye, Miss Mabel."

Miss Mabel called out to me, "Now don't forget to come over for some fried chicken, you hear?"

"Yes, ma'am," I answered over my shoulder.

16

The Rehearsal

Monday—May 23, 1949

SCHOOL GOT OUT for the summer break last Friday. I had focused on my studies the last two weeks of school. It paid off. When I got my report card, I was happy to see that I got all As. Mom and Dad were pleased as punch. That made me feel good. Now on to the summer break with lots of time to hang out with Marvin and Billy and others.

I had four books I needed to return to the library. Three were required reading for the last few weeks of school. Thank goodness they weren't very big.

"Hi, Miss Kathryn," I said as I put the books in the return area.

"Hey, Steve. I hear you got all As. Well done."

"How do you know my grades, Miss Kathryn?"

She actually giggled. I had never seen her giggle. "I have my sources young man, and I have promised never to reveal them."

"Like a mystery, huh?"

"Yes, like a mystery. I'm glad you came by today. Haven't seen you in over two weeks. Mr. Douglas asked me to let him know the next time you were here. He'd like to see you."

I think I squinted my eyes when I asked, "Oh, am I in trouble?"

"I can't imagine Mr. Douglas thinks you're in trouble. He's here now. Let's knock on the door."

I still got anxious every time we knocked on his door. It seemed kind of mysterious, and I never knew what might happen.

As always, Mr. Douglas opened the door and said, "Hello, Steve. I'm glad to see you. Thank you, Miss Kathryn. Come in, Steve, and have a seat."

I did as he asked. "Good morning, Mr. Douglas."

He smiled as always. "I hear you got all As this school year. Excellent. Marvin and Nancy did as well, and Billy had a good year. I think he has more potential than he thinks. One has to shed self-doubt and learn to trust in themselves and what they can achieve. I hope you have lofty goals, Steve."

Gees, there he goes again with an important message. "Yes, sir, I'll do the best I can."

"I know you will. Now, why did I want to see you? Nancy asked me to invite you to some of the rehearsals for our upcoming play, *Romeo and Juliet*."

My jaw dropped. I couldn't believe it. "Uh, yes, sir, I suppose so. Do white people come to the rehearsals?"

"Good question. Yes, they do, but by invitation only, although there are some town bigwigs who are always welcome."

I regained my composure, and said, "What would I do?"

"Observe. You'll likely learn something. I sense a fine actor lurking in the weeds. Steve, do you want to come to a rehearsal? It's all right to say no."

How the hell do I get in these situations? He's got me cornered. "Sure, I'll come," I said, wondering what was next.

"Since school is out, we have the luxury of being able to rehearse more often. We'll have rehearsals on Monday, Wednesday, and Friday each week until just before the opening. You can come to one or all of them if you wish. While I know this is short notice, today is the first rehearsal, and if you don't enjoy it, you can stop coming. I must tell you that it can be a bit boring for observers at times. Often, there is lots of starting and stopping when I have to explain to actors how and why I want them to speak their lines in a certain way. But there are entertaining moments, especially when an actor suggests that I'm wrong, as I often am. We start promptly at two o'clock and finish no later than five. You'll have plenty of time to get home for supper."

"Yes, sir, good idea. I'll come today if it's okay with my parents."

"Of course, your parents must agree. "

"Yes, sir. Well, I have to go. Thank you."

"Thank you, Steve. I'll show you to the door."

I told Mom about my invitation to attend the rehearsals at Mr. Douglas's theater. She was delighted.

Mom had said, "I think it'll be a wonderful experience for you, Steve. You may find that you become interested in acting. I'll call your Dad and see what he thinks."

Mom called Dad, but I couldn't hear the conversation, but I sure tried.

Mom said to me, "Dad had some misgivings, but he agreed with me that you could go. He said to mind your P's and Q's, as it may surprise you to know that as popular as Mr. Douglas is, there are Negroes and whites in our community who are jealous of him."

That really bothered me, but I didn't ask why. I just wanted a chance to see Nancy.

I arrived fifteen minutes early and sat in one of the back rows. No one seemed to notice me. There were several people sitting in the first three rows, including a white man. I couldn't tell who it was. And there were more people on the stage holding papers. I assumed they were scripts. I didn't see Nancy.

Mr. Douglas walked on stage, clapped his hands, and called out, "Okay, actors, let's get started. We'll start with Act 1. You can use your scripts as your personal cue cards, but I'd like you to speak as many lines from memory as possible. While we haven't blocked any scenes yet, I want you to walk around the stage in a manner that you think the character requires. Before we start, I 'd like to recognize our visitors. Of course, you all know Mr. Graves. He's sitting up front near the stage." Pointing at me, he said, "Please welcome a new visitor, Steve Thompson. His father owns the *Delphi Delta News* newspaper."

Most of the actors waved at me and one called out, "Are you gonna write an article about us for your Dad's newspaper?"

I wanted to crawl under the seat. I must have blushed. "Uh, no. I'm going to just watch."

Nancy stepped onto the stage and said, "Welcome, Steve."

I could have flipped, but I just nodded. The actors started reading lines while they moved around the stage. Mr. Douglas stopped them a few times to make some suggestions. The actors were into Act 1 when the white man sat next to me.

He spoke to me quietly, "Hi, Steve. Enjoying yourself."

"Yes, sir, Mr. Graves." He was a high up boss man at the paper mill, but that's all I knew. I figured he was one of the white people Mr. Douglas mentioned who could come to rehearsals whenever they wanted to.

"Do you know this play very well?"

"Yes, sir, I read it carefully with both my mother and Mr. Douglas."

"My goodness, how nice. Steve, do you come here often?"

"No, sir, this is my first rehearsal. I did see the last play, *The Tempest*. I liked it."

"Well, Shakespeare certainly has another admirer," Mr. Graves said. Then he looked around as if to see who might be listening, and said to me in an even quieter voice, "Steve, let me give you some advice. Enjoy today, but in the future, stay away from here. Things are not as they appear...I have to be going."

He stood up and abruptly walked out of the theater. *What the hell was that all abou*t.

I tried to focus, but I couldn't keep my mind on the actors. Was Mr. Graves threatening me, or was he mad at me because I knew Mr. Douglas? Nothing made sense. Finally, I let it go for now and watched the actors. Soon after that, Mr. Douglas gave everybody a fifteen-minute break.

I supposed that meant me too, so, I walked down nearer to the stage. A couple of boys came up to me and chatted. Mostly, they wondered why I was here. I'm sure I didn't answer their questions very well.

With five minutes left in the break, I walked back to my seat when Nancy touched my shoulder, "Hey, Steve. I'm glad you could come. Enjoying the rehearsal."

Trying not to act like a tongue-tied idiot, I immediately said, "Oh, very much. You have the Juliet part down pat. Are you satisfied?"

"I'm making progress, but I must do better."

Neither of us said anything. We just stared at each other as if transfixed for what seemed like forever. Then we grinned and continued gazing at each other.

Finally, Nancy said, "Steve, I like you."

"Nancy, I like you too."

As soon as I said it, Mr. Douglas clapped his hands. Startled, we looked around as Mr. Douglas said, "Back to work actors."

"Will I see you Wednesday, Steve?"

"Yes," I said while Mr. Graves comment came into my mind, but I didn't tell Nancy that.

She smiled and walked toward the stage. A boy older than me approached. I could hear what he said.

"Nancy, what you doin' talking to that white boy?"

"It's none of your damn business. He's a friend of Mr. Douglas, and he likes Shakespeare. That's enough for me."

When the rehearsal ended, I headed for home. So much to think about—I ran most of the way. I was running by the town square when I saw five white guys. Three of them were the guys who hassled Marvin on our Mardi Gras float. Now they were dressed in white shirts and pants, not the KKK stuff they wore then.

The one named Jimmy Jackson saw me and yelled, "Hey, pipsqueak, I know you. You were on the float with the colored boy what acted like he was an American pilot. You tell him that I'm gonna whup his ass and maybe worse next time I see him, you hear?"

One of the other guys shouted, "I'll scare the shit out of him."

"Oh, shut up," Jimmy barked. "I can handle the pipsqueak."

I veered around them and said, "Yes, sirs. I gotta get home."

I was glad to be home. It was almost six o'clock.

When I walked into the kitchen, Mom smiled and said, "Hi, Steve. Dad's working late tonight. You and I are going to eat now. If it's not too late when he gets home, we'll join him while he eats."

"Yes, ma'am."

At supper, I told Mom about the rehearsal, but I didn't mention either Nancy or Mr. Graves. Hoping Dad would be home soon, I read a book until a little after nine o'clock, when I got tired and decided to go to bed. Just then, Dad came home. He looked tired and worried.

Mom came out of the kitchen, and said, "Andy, I've got a plate of food waiting for you."

"Thanks, honey, I need a drink. Let's sit in the living room and talk for a bit."

Dad fixed his favorite drink, a Scotch and soda. We joined him in the living room, and he asked me about the rehearsal.

I hurried the telling and asked, "Dad, do you know Mr. Graves, the bigwig at the paper mill?"

Dad laughed. "Sure do, but Bob Graves is not a bigwig. He'd like to be. He's a supervisor. He probably has four small groups of workers reporting to him. Why do you ask?"

I told Mom and Dad everything I could remember about Mr. Graves and what he said to me.

Mom looked worried.

Dad said, "That son of a bitch..." Dad paused, then continued, "I think it best you follow his advice. It was certainly a veiled threat. Things are a bit tense around here now."

"What's going on, Dad?" I asked.

"Not absolutely sure, but there have been some labor issues at the paper mill recently. Hopefully it'll blow over. It usually does. Steve, I think you should go to bed now. You've had a long day."

"Okay, but you've had a long day too, Dad."

"Thanks, son," he said as he kissed me on the forehead.

I kissed Mom and went to bed.

It's funny, but usually after a busy day, I stay awake for a while in bed, thinking about all that's happened. That night I was in never-never land in a moment and the next thing I knew, it was morning.

Part III
The Night of Terror—1949

"We make trifles of terrors, Ensconcing ourselves into seeming knowledge, When we should submit ourselves to an unknown fear."

William Shakespeare—*All's Well That Ends Well*

17

Morning

Tuesday—May 24, 1949

I GOT UP EARLY TUESDAY MORNING and looked out my window to check on the weather. It looked okay, but the real test came when I went out the front door. The last few days had been hot and humid. I hated days like this.

At breakfast, we were all quiet except for Mom commenting about what she had cooked—which wasn't necessary because she usually cooked the same things. She seemed jittery. So did Dad.

Dad finally put his fork down next to his unfinished scrambled eggs, and said, "Steve, I want to tell you more about what's going on at the paper mill. The owners live in New York City, a much more liberal place than Delphi. Apparently, they have asked the mill's manager to make some changes that have a lot of the white workers quite upset." Dad sighed, as if he didn't really want to go on, and so for a moment I said nothing.

But I had to know, and I asked, "What are they upset about?"

"The Negro workers at the mill are currently supervised by white men and always have been. The owners want Negro supervisors to oversee all Negro work teams. The white supervisors are upset, to put it mildly, as are the white rank and file workers. Bottom line is that several white supervisors will have to go back to rank and file positions to make room for the Negro supervisors." Dad paused again.

"Dad, rank and file workers are regular workers, right?"

"Yes, that's right. They have no authority and have to do what they're told."

"Dad, did Mr. Graves start in the rank and file at the mill?"

"That's what Mr. Graves will become if this policy is instituted, and he's not happy. He was born here. His Dad worked in the mill and later became a supervisor. Mr. Graves went to Huntingdon College in Montgomery, but he quit school in the middle of his senior year. No one knows why, and the family never talks about it. One thing Mr. Graves enjoyed at college was Shakespeare. As soon as Mr. Douglas was allowed to have whites attend his plays, Mr. Graves was one of the first to attend."

I was getting the picture, but I had to ask, "Do you think Mr. Graves was warning me because of the mess at the mill?"

"Hard to see it any other way, Steve. That's why you should not go to any more rehearsals. Sorry to have to say that, but it's the safest thing to do. Now, I have to go. I'm working with some city council members to try and broker a peace treaty with all the parties. You behave yourself and be safe."

Dad kissed Mom and patted my forehead and left.

Mom appeared as if she might cry. I sure felt like I would, and I didn't know which way to turn. *Punt, Steve, punt.*

"Mom, when the library opens, I have to return a book that's overdue."

Mom smiled a weak reassurance, and said, "Steve, I think the library is your sanctuary. If there are any problems, stay in the library, or if you're outside, come straight home."

"Yes, ma'am, I will."

I lied to Mom. I didn't have an overdue book, so I left the house with one of my books.

I got to the library a little before it opened. As I looked around the square and the nearby shops, I saw a handful of people, mostly white. It was weird. It was usually busy by now with both white and Negro people.

"Hi, Miss Kathryn," I said when I entered, "looks pretty quiet downtown."

"Hi, Steve, glad to see you. Yes, it is quiet."

I wasn't sure, but she seemed concerned. "Any idea why?" I asked.

She shook her head, and I thought she grimaced. “I wish I knew for sure, Steve. All I’ve heard is that there’s some labor problems at the paper mill.”

“Yes, ma’am, my Dad told me about that. Is Mr. Douglas here today?”

She actually smiled. “Ah, you and Mr. Douglas. I’m so glad he introduced you to Shakespeare. You’ll love his works the rest of your life.”

That’s all she said, so I had to ask again, “Is Mr. Douglas here?”

“Oh, silly me,” she said, giggling. “I haven’t heard his voice today. Let’s go knock on his door.”

Mr. Douglas opened the door so quickly that I thought it was like he knew I was coming. “Good morning Miss Kathryn and to you too, Steve. I was hoping you might pay me a visit today. I’d like to hear your impression of the rehearsal yesterday. Come in and sit down, please.”

We sat and Mr. Douglas said, “Well, your thoughts, young man. Did we seem to be making progress in the play?”

Jeez, he always ask me tough questions. “Uh…Yes, sir, I think so. But I’m not sure I understood it all.”

“Can you be more specific. What didn’t you understand?”

I wished I hadn’t been so upset by Mr. Graves that I tuned out for a while. I didn’t want to mention Mr. Graves, so I said, “I didn’t get all the starts and stops. Was it necessary?”

“Absolutely, actors need coaching and encouragement. One actor who needs little help is Nancy. I saw you and her talking at the break.” He smiled and waited for me say something.

I hemmed and hawed and finally said, “She’s a good actor and a nice girl.”

“Yes, she is,” he said. I thought I was off the hook, but then he said, “I also saw you talking to Mr. Graves. He has been a longtime supporter of our theater. He acted in some Shakespeare plays when he was in college. A few white people have been in our plays, so some years ago, I asked Mr. Graves to join us, but he declined. Why do you suppose he did that?”

Always the tough questions, but I answered, "Maybe because he thought his white friends wouldn't like it?"

"My thoughts at the time also. What did you and Mr. Graves talk about?"

"Oh, just about Shakespeare," I said.

"I'll wager you impressed him."

"I wouldn't make that bet, Mr. Douglas." *He must think I'm a know-it-all.*.

"As the saying goes, Steve, we'll have to let the chips fall where they may."

"Yes, sir," I said, and having no idea what he meant, I punted. "Not very busy here today."

"Alas, Steve, 'once more unto the breach,' Henry V." Mr. Douglas paused.

I sat quietly, and then he said, "Well, to cheerier thoughts. I hope you come to the rehearsal tomorrow. I know Nancy likes you to come."

Now, he had me in a corner, so I lied, "Yes, sir, I plan to be there." Then I thought as if to protect myself, *Damn, at least I said 'I plan' to Mr. Douglas*, so I asked him. "Have you heard about any trouble brewing in the town?"

"Like what kind of trouble?"

"I'm not sure, something about the paper mill."

He shook his head as if to say no. "Steve, Negroes are always alert to trouble. As you say, it always seems to be *brewing*. But usually it amounts to nothing. Are you worried?"

"I try not to be. I think I better go now."

"Let me walk you to the door. Ah, this door is a portal between two worlds. What do you make of that, Steve?"

"I just wish the door was always open, sir. Goodbye."

As I walked home, I had no idea what I would do tomorrow, but I knew I had to talk to Marvin today. When I got home, I had a quick lunch. Mom, as usual, peppered me with all kinds of questions, ones mostly about Mr. Douglas. I didn't lie, but I didn't tell her everything. Then I told her I was going over to Marvin's house.

"Steve, Dad told you not to go in that part of town."

"No, ma'am, he said I shouldn't go to the rehearsal tomorrow night. Marvin and I, and maybe Billy, will just mess around. Probably check out our trot line. I'll be home before supper time."

Still not happy, Mom said, "Young man, I'm sure your Dad meant more than that. Please be careful."

I wasn't sure what to say to Marvin. I thought about it as I walked to his house. Ideas rambled through my head from tell him everything I had heard and seen to tell him very little. *Why would you even consider that last idea, Steve? Are you nuts?*

At Marvin's house, I looked around and didn't see him. I knocked and heard someone shuffling toward the door.

Miss Mabel opened the door just a bit and peeked out. "For gosh sakes, Steve, what you doin' here? Ain't you heard about all the troubles?"

"Yes, ma'am, if you mean what's going on at the paper mill."

"Well, yes, that's where it started," she said, looking kind of out of sorts. "But I'll tell you this, it ain't gonna stop there. There's trouble comin'. I can feel it in my bones. Now, what you want?"

"Is Marvin here?"

"No. He left about an hour ago. I don't know where he is. I'm worried about him."

"Yes, ma'am, I'll try to find him and make sure he comes home."

I decided to go to Billy's house, hoping he was home. This whole mess was driving me crazy. *Do this. Do that. Do nothing. What the hell, just do something.* Since Billy didn't want me to come into his house, I stood in the street and yelled, "Hey, Billy, you home?" a few times.

Finally, he opened the front door and yelled back, "What the hell you doin' here, Steve?" He looked scared.

Why does everybody keep asking me that? I thought. "I'm looking for Marvin. Do you know where he is?"

"No. Is he in trouble?"

"Don't think so. But there's someone who might cause him trouble. The KKK guy, Jimmy Jackson, told me yesterday that if he sees Marvin, he's gonna whup his ass."

"I don't know nothing 'bout that. What you gonna do?"

Billy hit the nail on the head. What was I gonna do? I answered, "I reckon I'll go check the trot line and see if Marvin's there. Wanna come?"

Billy drooped his head and sagged his shoulder. I was sure he'd say no. He lifted his head and stared at me. "Yeah, I reckon I will. I'll tell Ma where I'm goin' and be right with you. I got some bait if we need to add it to the hooks"

When we got to the creek, Marvin wasn't there. So, we pulled the trot line in and there were three medium-size catfish on it. Billy put them in a bag he had, and we added bait to the hooks, and tossed the trot line back into the creek.

As we walked back to Billy's house, I asked him, "Billy, if you see Marvin, please tell him about Jimmy Jackson. He sure as hell wasn't kidding."

"Okay. You want one of these catfish?"

"No, thanks. I'll go by Marvin's house and see if he's home. See you later."

I knocked on the door, and Miss Mabel said, "Who's that?"

"It's Steve, Miss Mabel. Is Marvin home?"

She opened the door slightly, and said, "Come in, Steve," closing the door as soon as I was inside. "Marvin's not here. Troublesome times, Steve. You better go home and stay there."

"Yes, ma'am, I will. If I see Marvin, I'll tell him you're worried about him and he should go straight home."

"You do that, Steve. Thank you. Now, git on home."

"Yes, ma'am." I felt awful. I was really worried about Marvin.

When Dad came home, I had never seen him so dejected. He said nothing to Mom or me as he threw his sport jacket toward the coat rack, and when it fell to the floor, he didn't bother to pick it up. Instead, he went straight to the whiskey cabinet to pour himself a drink.

Then he asked Mom, "You want a drink, Lillis?"

"Yes. Thank you, I'll have what you're having."

"Steve, do you want a Coke?"

"Yes. Thanks, Dad."

Dad handed us our drinks and sat in his big leather chair facing us on the sofa. He didn't say anything.

Mom asked him, "Honey, how did the meeting go?"

He finally said, "At best, we won a Pyrrhic victory. Hell, it probably wasn't even that good."

"Well, what happened, Dad?" I asked, feeling something bad was going to happen.

Dad shook his head as if it were a bad dream. "Always questions, Steve. The mill manager, Winston Drake, was at the meeting. We've known him for years, and he's a good, honest man. I'm confident he's trying to calm everybody down. But he said he wasn't sure he could keep the white men under control. To use his words, he said, 'The colored men are scared shitless, and the white men are mad as hell.' After throwing a lot of ideas around that didn't go anywhere, Winston said he was willing to call the owners in New York City and ask them to withdraw the order. He asked the mayor to join him on the call, and they went into the mayor's private office."

Dad finished his drink and refilled his glass, took two big swigs, and continued. "They returned to our meeting in about twenty-five minutes. Winston said that at first the owners were not interested in his request, but he convinced them to give it serous thought. He added that there was talk among the white men about taking care of the Negroes, emphasizing that could lead to a lot of trouble. The owners agreed to consider Winston's request and told him they would call him Thursday or Friday with their decision. That was it. The phone call was over. Winston left the meeting and went back to the mill to tell the men what the owners had agreed to do. The meeting was over."

I didn't understand what all this meant. "Will the owners agree?"

"It's in the lap of the gods, Steve, and that means we don't know, but must hope and pray the owners agree."

"And if they don't agree, Dad?"

"We'll have to wait and see, but all hell might descend on us."

Mom finally spoke up and said, "Andy, don't be so pedantic with your references to the *Iliad* and the Bible. Answer Steve's questions directly."

Dad blushed. “Right. Steve, we just don’t know how things will come out, but we must hope for the best.”

“Does that mean I can go to the rehearsal tomorrow night?”

“Everything’s a tough call. No, you can’t go.”

Mom broke the tension, “Enough of all that. Dinner is almost ready.”

18

Morning

Wednesday—May 25, 1949

DAD HAD LEFT THE HOUSE when I got up Wednesday morning. After I got dressed, I went to the kitchen. Mom was seated at the kitchen table, drinking a cup of coffee.

"Good morning, Mom. Dad left early today."

"Morning, Steve. Yes, he said he had to write an editorial for a special edition he wants to publish this morning. Would you like some scrambled eggs?"

"No, ma'am. I'll just have cereal. I bet I know what Dad's going to write. And Mom, I've heard of the *Iliad*. I haven't read it, but our English teacher told us it was written by a Greek poet named Homer."

Even though it was morning, Mom was pensive and appeared weary. "That's good. I'm sure you're right about Dad's editorial. Don't worry, Steve. When Dad gets on his high-horse when explaining things, he's not being pompous. That's just the way he is."

"Yes, ma'am, I know. Don't tell him, but sometimes I kinda laugh behind his back when he gets really riled up."

She gave me a big grin. "Okay, it'll be our little secret because I also laugh behind Dad's back."

I grinned and said, "Wow!....Mom, can I go to the library?"

"Only if you promise you won't go to Westtown."

"Yes, ma'am, I promise." I meant it. I didn't cross my fingers.

When I got to the library at ten-thirty, Miss Kathryn was the only person there.

"Hi, Miss Kathryn."

"Hi, Steve, as you can see, you're my first customer today. Have you seen your father's special edition newspaper? It's only one page, the front page, and the only article is an editorial by your father. It's extraordinary. Let me read you the opening paragraph.

> Citizens of Delphi and Allen County, lend me your ears. I come not to bury the paper mill, but to extol the virtues of its leaders as they seek to find a compromise to the issue of changes in important positions at the mill. You and I and the leaders must be very deliberate so that a dark veil of misunderstanding does not engulf our neighborhoods. Please heed my call for tolerance so that our county can continue as one prosperous community, both economically and culturally.

"And that's just the first paragraph. It goes on for most of the front page. Your father is an excellent writer and brave man."

"Why is he a brave man, Miss Kathryn?"

"Many in the county will not take kindly to his words. You must be very proud of him. You can have this copy. I have several."

I stared at it as if I were looking at the Magna Carta or the Declaration of Independence. Dad was my hero, but I was worried a crazy nut might kill him.

After I finished reading Dad's editorial, I asked, "Miss Kathryn, is Mr. Douglas here today?"

"I don't think so. Go knock on the door and see if anyone answers."

I knocked several times and there was no answer.

I left the white library and walked to the front door of the Negro Library. There was a sign on the door that read CLOSED UNTIL FURTHER NOTICE. *On my gosh, Mr. Douglas is taking this seriously!*

I went home, had lunch, and read a book I had checked out at the library. It was the *Iliad*. I had to ask Mom several times to explain what was going on. As always, she explained it so clearly that I was able to sorta understand the poem. I mean it was kinda simple. It was an adventure story, and I love adventures.

19

Evening

Wednesday—May 25, 1949

I READ THE *ILIAD* UNTIL DINNER TIME, but Dad was still not home, so Mom said we'd wait for him. As it started to get dark, he finally arrived at seven o'clock and we sat down to eat.

"I read your editorial, Dad. It was really good."

"Thanks, Steve. That makes me feel good."

"How was it received, Andy?" Mom asked, smiling, as she handed a bowl of mashed potatoes to Dad.

Dad grimaced. "I wish I could say it had been received well. You know, the expected. I got lots of pats on the back and job-well-done accolades. But at best it was fifty-fifty from the phone calls. And some of the calls were nasty, a few even making threats."

Mom groaned and rubbed her forehead. "What kind of threats, Andy?"

I could see that Mom and Dad were very concerned. I was too, and I wanted to help. But I didn't know what to do.

"Oh, the usual Klan crap. We'll burn a cross in your yard, or we've got you in our cross hairs. I went to the cafe for lunch. I counted twelve people. They all stared at me. At first, only two said something nice. One guy I didn't know said to me as he passed behind me, 'You'll get yours, you son of a bitch.' At least at that moment the others in the cafe and the owner came over and were more supportive. We're going to have to be careful and alert for the next few days. Hopefully, by then things will have calmed down."

Dad turned to me, "You okay, son?"

"Yes, sir. But I worry about Marvin and Billy, and Mr. Douglas and Dr. Marshall. Do you think we should call the police?"

"Perhaps, but not now. Truth is, son, we don't know whom we can trust. And I do worry about our Negro friends. Yes, yes, these are troubled times. Oh hell, forgive me for that stupid statement."

Mom got up and took plates into the kitchen. She came back with dessert: peach pie with vanilla ice cream on top. "Boys, here's something you can trust and enjoy."

"Thanks, Mom," I said as I took a bite. "Wow. This is great."

"Ditto," said Dad.

"So, Dad, maybe we have a one-or-two-day period of grace before anything crazy happens, right?"

Dad smiled. "Grace. I like your use of that word, Steve. I'm tired. I'm going to bed. I have to get an early start tomorrow morning. And, Steve, I want you to stay close to the house until this mess is over." He gave me a stern look and I got his meaning. Then he turned and kissed me on my head. "Good night, Steve."

Dad went upstairs, and Mom and I cleared the table and washed the dishes.

"Steve, I'm going to read in the living room for a while. Want to join me?"

"Thanks to you, Mom, I'm really enjoying the *Iliad*. I'll read it in my room before I go to sleep."

"Well, sweet dreams, honey, as hard as that might sound tonight, and remember what Dad said."

20

Night

Wednesday—May 25, 1949

I WAS READING WHEN MOM CLOSED her bedroom door. I got in bed, but had a hard time falling asleep. I must have dozed off because I woke up with a start when I heard something like a gunshot or a car backfiring. I peered out my window where I had a partial view of the square, and I saw something burning. Dad was right, it looked like the troubled time had arrived.

I sat in my desk chair, pondering what I should do. After a few minutes, I realized I didn't have to ponder anymore. I said to myself, *Damn it, Steve. You know what you have to do. You have to find Marvin and warn him.* I got dressed and peeked out my door toward my parent's bedroom. I didn't hear anything. Since their bedroom didn't face the square, maybe they didn't hear the sound. Even though I knew they'd be really pissed at me, I quietly crept downstairs, opened the front door, and slipped out. The stifling heat and humidity from the recent heat wave still hung in the air.

I walked only a short distance toward the square when I saw a burning cross and lots of men in Klan robes and hoods. It was the scariest thing I had ever seen. I headed the other direction toward Westtown, hoping no Klansmen saw me. It was pitch black dark, no moonlight. Some houses in Delphi were still lit, but as I approached Westtown, all the houses were dark. I moved cautiously toward Marvin's house because Westtown didn't have many street lights.

I passed the haunted house on my way to Marvin's and just as I got to it, I heard guns firing and men shouting. The commotion sounded close to me, so I hid in the bushes across the street from the house. Then I saw Klansmen approaching with torches and guns.

They stopped in front of the house, and the one man wearing a red hood shouted, "Let's torch this old house. It looks like shit and the old man that lives here is crazy."

The guy's voice sounded familiar, but I couldn't put my finger on it. I didn't have time to think much about the voice because a Negro man came out of the haunted house. I couldn't believe it. It was old man Zach. *The Klan will probably kill him*, I thought, feeling sorry for Zach.

Zach walked right up to the Klansman and said, "Ya don't want me. Ya want the queers, the doctor and that Shakespeare guy."

A few of the Klansmen stepped toward Zach, when the red-hooded man held up his hands and said, "Hold off, men."

"What the fuck is wrong with you, Graves? Let's get him," a youngish Klan guy said.

Oh my god, the red-hooded man is Mr. Graves. By now I was scared, and I got even lower behind the bushes.

Mr. Graves shoved the man back saying, "Back off, I said. And don't ever use our names when we're in Klan garb. Do it again and you might be history."

Mr. Graves turned to Zach, and said, "Do you mean Joshua Marshall and Moses Douglas?"

"Well, hell yes. Who'd ya think?"

"I thought they were brothers."

"Shit! That's what they tell everybody, but I knows it ain't true."

"How come it ain't true?"

"Because, I'm from the same town as Joshua. He had a sister, but I swear he didn't have no brother. His Papa and Mama raised him 'til he went to college. I 'pose that's where he met Moses. I'm sure they's queers."

I couldn't understand everything Zach was saying, but it didn't sound good. I figured Joshua might know him.

Mr. Graves must have read my mind because he asked Zach, "Well, Joshua must know you live here now. He must talk to you every now and then."

"No, sir, he never knowed me. Ya see, I was what ya might call poor black trash. He was too uppity and rich to pay me no mind."

The youngish guy butted in again. "Damn it, Grand Turk, sorry about blurting out your name, but when you gonna stop talkin' to this nigger, so we can look for the queers."

Since Mr. Graves was obviously the Grand Turk and leader, that's why he had the red hood. I had no idea what all that meant, but it sounded and looked like trouble. Now I know why Mr. Graves had told me to stay away from the rehearsals in Westtown. And I figured Zach was trying to save his bacon.

The Grand Turk said, "Okay." Turning back to Zach, he said, "Old man, get your butt in the house. Keep the lights out and pay no attention to what's going on, you hear me?"

"Yes, sir, I goes right in. Sure glad ya gonna take care of those queers."

"Who said anything about that. Now get." Then the Grand Turk yelled to his men, "Let's move out. I know exactly where we're going. Where the hell do you suppose the other men are?"

"Sir," another Klansman said, "I see torches down the road. Must be the Grand Monk with about twenty guys. A few are supposed to be on horseback."

"Good," the Grand Turk said, "Follow me."

Where the hell does the Klan get those weird names. They're like kids' summer camp stuff. I knew exactly where they were going, but I had to stay hidden until the next group was well past me. I moved behind a big tree. I figured if there were guys on horses, they might be able to look down on me. I was scared and started to wonder if I had made a big mistake coming over here.

I huddled behind the tree and peeked around it a few times while the Grand Monk's group went by. I saw six or eight men on horseback. I waited a few minutes before I came out of hiding. As I walked toward Marvin's house, I stayed on the side of the road where there was some cover if I had to hide quickly. When I got to Marvin's, I went around the house to the backdoor. I knocked softly a few times. No answer. So, I said only as loud as I thought necessary, "Marvin. It's, Steve."

The second time I said it, Marvin looked out of the window next to the door and saw me. He opened the door a bit and said, "Steve, what you doin' here? You crazy? Ain't you seen the Klan?"

"Marvin, we need to talk. And, no, I'm not crazy. I've seen about forty Klansmen, some on horses. Can I come in?"

He let me in. I told him what I had heard and seen at the old man's haunted house.

Marvin shook his head as if he didn't believe me. "Shit, that's crazy. Moses and Joshua aren't like that, but even if it's true, I still like them."

"Me too," I said, knowing that Marvin had beat me to the punch on what was right.

Marvin beat me to the punch again when he said, "Good, but we gotta hurry over to their house and warn them."

"Yeah, but the Klan's already headed that way."

"Don't matter. Gotta try. I know a way through some alleys and paths. Let's go."

"Ain't you gonna tell your Mom and Dad?"

"Shit, Steve, Mama and Daddy are asleep. They could sleep through almost anything. Besides, Daddy don't work at the paper mill. Did you tell your Mom and Dad you were coming over here?"

He had nailed me again. "No," I said, drooping my head.

"C'mon, let's go."

Just before Marvin opened the back door, Miss Mabel came into the room. "Marvin, what are you and Steve doing? And Steve, why ain't you home, like I told you yesterday?"

I looked at Marvin, waiting to hear what he would say.

"Mama, we gotta go and check on Joshua and Moses. They might be in trouble."

Miss Mabel stared at Marvin. "You stay right here , Marvin. You might git kilt."

"Goodnight, Mama. Sorry, but we gotta do this."

Marvin grabbed my hand and pulled me out the back door and shut it tight in his Mama's face.

"Marvin, your Mama's going to be some pissed."

"That ain't nothing new. Follow me."

He led me down an alley behind his house and it felt even darker than the street. We went around so many twists and turns, I wasn't sure where we were. My eyes got more used to the darkness, but I still had to ask Marvin to slow down so I could catch up. We could see some light above the tree tops ahead of us. I assumed it was the Klan's torches.

I whispered to Marvin, "Are we almost there?"

"Yep. In two blocks, we'll use the alley behind Nancy's house, and then we're almost there."

Just *then* we heard a lot of gun fire and saw a big plume of flames and smoke rising into the air.

"Shit, Marvin. Do you think that's Moses' and Joshua's house?"

"Yeah, dammit, could be. Stay low and be ready to hide if we have to." Marvin kept going for half a block, "That's the back of Nancy's house," he said, pointing it out. "The house looks okay. Her Daddy owns this huge lot in back of the house. It's got a small rise on it. We call it Westtown Mountain. Lets' crawl to the top and see what we can see."

Wasn't much of a crawl, but we did get a view, and it's one I wish I had never seen. The house was aflame and spitting sparks in the air, and Joshua and Moses were stumbling out of their house with their hands in the air. A few Klansmen started beating on them. Somebody yelled out, "String 'em up." Another yelled, "Cut off their peckers."

Marvin and I stared in horror. What could we do? We didn't say anything, but I knew there was nothing to be done.

While we could hear shouting, we weren't close enough to hear much of what the Klansmen were saying. After about a minute, the Grand Turk walked over and got the men who were beating Joshua and Moses to step aside. The Grand Turk pulled out a pistol, and after shooting Joshua and Moses in both legs, he made a throwing motion toward the burning house. I could hear voices screaming. I was pretty sure it was Moses and Joshua. I turned to Marvin and said, "I hate Mr. Graves. He's the Grand Turk."

Four men threw Moses and Joshua into the inferno, as other men fired their guns in the air and cheered. The riders mounted their horses and headed in the direction of the warehouse.

"You think they're gonna burn the warehouse, Marvin?"

"Shit, Steve, when you gonna get it? They gonna burn and kill whatever they want to."

I couldn't stand it anymore, and I laid my head on Marvin's shoulder and cried, "How could they do that, Marvin? Joshua and Moses were alive, and now they're burning to death!"

Marvin patted me on the head like an older brother, and said, "I don't know. But I do know they will soon be in heaven and have some eternal peace."

It was strange, but what Marvin said calmed me. I pulled away from him and said, "Marvin, you sound like a preacher."

Marvin smiled, but I saw tears in his eyes as he said, "I ain't no preacher-man, Steve. I'm just another nigger the Klan wants to kill."

I had to tell him. Why did I wait this long? "Marvin, I saw Jimmy Jackson downtown last Monday. You remember him, right?"

Marvin's stare felt like it was boring a hole in my head. "For Christ sake, Steve, how could I forget him after he shouted at me on the Mardi Gras float. So, what about him?"

"Jimmy said he's gonna whup your ass and maybe something worse next time he sees you. He might be here tonight."

"Probably is. C'mon, I know a back way to the warehouse."

I followed Marvin through another maze of paths and twist toward the backside of the warehouse. I couldn't believe how brave Marvin was. He acted like Jimmy Jackson didn't matter. I was scared to death, shaking inside and out, my head twisting and turning in fear we'd be spotted.

We hid behind some trees and bushes, and saw the Klansmen near the warehouse throwing flaming torches on it. A couple of guys threw large cans of something into the building. A few minutes later we realized it must have been gasoline cans because a huge explosion took place and the entire warehouse burst into flames.

The fire increased in intensity and the night sky brightened around the warehouse. We slithered back behind more bushes, hoping the Klansmen wouldn't see us.

I felt so angry and I wanted to help and said, "Marvin, they're crazy. What are we gonna do?"

"Well, we sure as hell can't put out the fire."

"Where's the fire department and police? Maybe, we can call them."

"Steve, you're the crazy one now. Some of the Klansmen you're looking at are probably police and firemen. The firemen are volunteers. I seen the police out here a few times when they wanna arrest a colored man. I ain't never seen the Delphi Fire Department out here. And I'll bet some of the volunteers work at the paper mill."

Damn, he's sharp. "How do you know all that, Marvin? I know the fire department has a lot of volunteers, but I never put two and two together about some of them working at the mill. Makes sense though."

"Damn right it does, Steve. That's all the people in Westtown have been talking about since the problem with colored workers at the mill came up."

"What's next?" I asked. "You've got all the answers."

"I wish. But I do know we gotta get outta here before the Klan starts heading back to Delphi."

"Where we going?"

"I'm going home, and you should get your white ass home. C'mon, follow me."

My head was buzzing so bad about all the awful things we had seen that I couldn't think straight. I followed Marvin blindly, completely lost.

He said only one thing. "Steve, if I motion right or left, jump behind the trees and bushes, 'cause it means I see trouble coming."

I was getting tired, but I kept going. Then I heard horses running somewhere behind us. Marvin pointed to the right and we jumped. I didn't realize how close we were to the road to Marvin's house.

The horses stopped close to where we lay in the bushes. The horses snorted as if they had been running a while.

One of the riders clearly called out to us, "Git out here, you two. We saw you and know you're in there. Move it or we'll start shooting, or maybe, we'll burn you out."

Marvin stood up and walked toward the men. I followed Marvin and saw three riders in white hoods.

The same voice that told us to come out, said, "Fellas, lookie what we got here. The nigger-boy Marvin who thinks he's an American pilot. And his nigger-loving friend Steve, who ain't worth a piece of shit. He ain't nothing but a pipsqueak. What you think we oughta do to them?"

"I reckon we oughta go easy on the white boy," another voice cautioned.

The first voice shouted, "Bubba, you're a pussy. I'll take care of things."

I was sure the first voice was Jackson, so I spoke up, "Jimmy, we ain't done you no harm. Leave us alone."

Jimmy made his horse rear up in front of us as he said, "Mind your manners, Steve. You speak again, and it'll be your last words."

Marvin stepped in front of me and said, "Mr. Jackson, I'm the one you're mad at. Leave Steve out of this."

"My, my, now Marvin wants to be brave," Jimmy said, "so he can save Steve. Ain't that nice. Tell you what, I'll be nice too. Steve, if I killed a white boy whose daddy was the newspaper owner, I'd be in the electric chair in a flash. You run on home now like a good little boy."

Trying to act as if I were brave, I said, "I ain't going nowhere without Marvin."

"You get going, Steve," Marvin said, pushing me in the direction I had to run. "These guys aren't kidding."

Jimmy fired his rifle in the air, and said, "You better do as Marvin tells ya, or I'm gonna change my mind about killing your white ass." Jimmy paused and pointed at his two Klan buddies and said, "We'll fire our rifles three more times. If you ain't running home by then, you're done."

They fired the first shot. I looked at Marvin. He shoved me toward home again, and said, "Run, Steve. Run."

They fired the second shot. I stood still. Marvin shoved me again, and cried out at me, "For Christ's sake, Steve, run like hell."

The third shot was fired, and I started running. The Klan guys were laughing and firing their rifles in the air.

I heard Jimmy Jackson shout at Marvin, "Okay, nigger, let's see how fast you can run."

Then I heard Marvin yell for the last time, "Keep running, Steve. Don't stop."

I ran as shots seemed to come from everywhere. I looked back and saw the men shooting at Marvin. I couldn't tell who shot him. As Marvin staggered, I thought he was the bravest person I had ever met.

Then one of the men saw me and pointed his rifle at me. I thought he was going to shoot me, but then he lowered his rifle. He didn't shoot. Feeling like the coward I was, I ran as fast as I could, while I kept repeating in my head, and sometimes shouting out loud, "Keep running, Steve," until I got home.

The lights were on in our house. I opened the front door, and Dad was standing there, and Mom stood behind him. They grabbed me, squeezing me. Mom was weeping.

Dad nearly shouted, "Steve, where the hell have you been?"

I stumbled in babbling like a baby. The story of the evening came out of me like rushing water tumbling over rocks. When I stopped talking, I collapsed on the floor. I wasn't even sure what I said, and as I cried inconsolably, my body shook as if I had epilepsy. I think I heard Mom say, "I'll call Dr. Thatcher."

Nick

Wednesday—March 14, 2001

Nick knew he shouldn't interrupt young Steve's childhood story, but he felt compelled to do so. He was having a hard time processing all that he had heard.

"Sorry to interrupt, Steve, but I had no idea of what you went through. No wonder you've had bad dreams most of your life. How do you keep all those horrors so bottled up?"

"I don't know, Nick," Steve said shaking his head. "I guess *bottled up* is the right phrase. I just try to keep this story to myself because I didn't want to bother other people."

"Steve, that's not a good recipe for healing. Anyway, who do think was the Klansman that threatened to shoot you, but then lowered his rifle?"

"I'm pretty sure it was Bubba, and you'll hear a lot more about him later."

"One last question. Were any of the Klan guys like Jimmy and Mr. Graves ever brought to justice?"

"Well, I reckon, Nick, that I'm not going to answer that question."

"Well…okay Steve. I think that's my cue. Let's get back to the story."

21

Morning

Thursday—May 26, 1949

When I got out of bed, I was confused. The only thing I remembered from last night was falling down on the floor and trembling. I didn't feel dizzy, but I had a mild headache. The sun shone through the window. I checked my watch: 7:35. I opened the window and felt a cool breeze blowing in my face. It seemed the heat wave was over. I brushed my teeth, got dressed, and went downstairs, expecting Mom and Dad to be mad at me.

In the kitchen, Mom gave me a cautious smile. "Good morning, Steve. How do you feel?"

I wasn't sure how to answer. "Did I tell you last night where I had been and what Marvin and I saw?"

Mom said, "Yes, but Dad and I had a hard time understanding anything you said. I'm sure it was awful, but let's talk about other things right now. I don't want to upset you again."

"Where's Dad? Has he heard anything about Marvin?"

"Dad left early this morning for Westtown. You know how conscientious he is about reporting the news. I haven' heard anything about Marvin."

I felt ignored and said, "Yes, ma'am. But darn it, I wish Dad had taken me with him. I could've showed him what happened."

"Steve, you're still upset, and it's best you stay home and rest. When Dad gets home, I'm sure he'll have answers to a lot of your questions."

I knew Mom wouldn't change her mind, so I let it go. As much as I tried to rest, it didn't work. All I felt was restlessness. I wanted to see the library. I asked Mom if I could go the town square. She agreed after I promised to be home in twenty minutes or so, and I intended to keep that promise.

When I got to the square, I saw two men removing what was left of the burning cross. One of them knew me and waved and said, "Nasty night, Steve."

I waved back and said, "Yes, sir," wanting to add, *You have no idea how nasty.*

I walked across the street toward the library. I wasn't sure what I would do, and then I saw Miss Kathryn coming around from the back side of the library.

I said, "Good morning, Miss Kathryn."

She appeared surprised to see me. Her eyes were red and puffy. And she looked tired. "Oh, hi, Steve. How are you this morning?"

"Okay, I guess. How are you?"

"I've been better. Some awful things happened in Westtown last night. A man just told me that Mr. Douglas and Dr. Marshall are dead." She started crying. "I just checked the Negro Library. Nothing was destroyed. It's fine."

I wanted to tell her everything, but I didn't. How could I? I hardly knew what was real and what was nightmare. "That's good, Miss Kathryn. Are you going to check the white library?"

She wiped her eyes. "Yes."

"Can I help?"

At first, I thought she was going to say no, but she said. "Thank you, a little company would be nice. It won't take long."

I followed her into the library. Everything seemed to be in order, so I offered, "Looks good to me, Miss Kathryn. What do you think?"

"You're right, Steve. Now I can go home and try to get some sleep."

Although I wanted to tell her that rest and sleep were hard to come by, I simply said, "Good idea, Miss Kathryn."

She actually smiled. "Yes, a good idea, and I think you should do the same."

"Yes, ma'am." I looked at my watch. She was right. It was time for me to go home.

As I turned to go, Miss Kathryn said, "Steve, Mr. Douglas loved you."

"Yes, ma'am, and I loved him and Dr. Marshall." I held back my tears.

Mom was pleased to see me come home as I promised. The remainder of the day was hopeless, as I tried to stay busy. I mostly moped around the house and occasionally read the *Iliad*, but it was hard to focus. Mom fixed me a nice lunch, a chicken salad sandwich and iced tea. I pecked at the sandwich, but drank all the iced tea. I kept wishing Dad would come home.

Dad finally got home late in the afternoon. He stumbled in the doorway, and his face was ashen as if he had seen the devil. He nodded at Mom and me, said nothing, and went straight to his wet bar and mixed himself an extra-big drink. I knew Dad was really off-kilter when he forgot to offer Mom a drink and me a Coke.

Dad dropped into his favorite chair, took a gulp of his drink, and said. "It was a one-sided war zone in Westtown last night. The Klan, who think they are God's Christian solders to protect the white race, are a bunch of cowardly savages, They wreaked havoc last night."

Mom asked Dad, "Who was out there with you, Andy?"

"The police and fire departments, and the mayor. They're assessing the damage and mayhem. Some fires are still burning, so the fire department is working to control them. I observed and made notes for my article and editorial. Alabama State Troopers and Alabama attorney general, Ralph Black, showed up in the early afternoon. They tried to look busy, but I think they came just so they could say they did their jobs. I tried to interview Ralph. He brushed me aside by saying, 'It's not an appropriate day for an interview, Andy. Maybe later.' Shit, he's such a coward. I know there won't be a later because he doesn't want to go on the record."

"Andy, watch your language, please."

"Lillis, if you had seen what I saw today, you'd be cussing like a sailor." Dad paused, and took another swig from his glass. "I'm sorry, Honey. I didn't mean that. Today has been the worst day of my life. What useless evil destruction and carnage."

I couldn't keep quiet any longer and said, "Dad, I know Marvin is probably dead. *I can't believe I said that out loud.* I know Mr. Douglas and Dr. Marshall are dead. Did you know they weren't brothers? Old man Zach told the Klan they weren't. He said they were queers. I don't know what that means. Marvin seemed to know, but he didn't explain it to me."

Dad hesitated, staring at the ice rattling in his glass, so Mom answered, "Steve, Dad and I have known for some years they weren't brothers. I think a few others in Delphi knew, but we kept their secret quiet, because we respected and liked them so much."

I shook my head, still confused. "What does *queers* mean, Mom."

Mom stood and walked around the room. I was sure she knew what the word meant. Mom was real smart, but maybe she didn't want to tell me.

She finally sat down and said, "Some men prefer to be with other men.... It's not that they don't enjoy the company of women, they prefer to live with a man rather than a woman.... Do you understand?"

I thought back to the first time Mom and Dad talked to me about the birds and the bees and sex and babies. They were nervous, and I kinda enjoyed it, but this was much harder, and I said what was on my mind, "I guess Mr. Douglas and Dr. Marshall were queers." I lowered my head, feeling ashamed for having said it, so I put my hands in my lap and then I gazed up at them, hoping the bad feeling would go away.

"Steve, look at me," Dad said.

"Yes, sir," I said, tears running down my cheeks.

"Moses and Joshua were two of your best friends. Don't let one word get between you and that feeling. They were fine men. They liked you. No, they loved you. You must hold on to the feeling and know that Zach and the Klan will meet their justice, if not in this life, when they meet their Maker."

Dad lifted me up and hugged me. I didn't want to let go, and I kept crying until all my tears were gone. I did feel a little better.

"You okay now, Steve?" Dad asked when he put me down.

Although I still felt a little shaky, I nodded, and had to ask, "Yes, sir, but why did they move to Delphi? Wouldn't they have been safer in Birmingham or somewhere up North?"

"Birmingham's not the paragon of tolerance, Steve. In fact, Bull Connor, the Public Safety Commissioner, keeps the city anything but safe for Negroes. And a couple of years ago, a newly-built home of a Negro was bombed and destroyed, probably by the Klan. Fortunately, no one was hurt or killed. Maybe Moses and Douglas would have been safer up North, but I can't say for sure. The North's not exactly the paragon of tolerance either."

Paragon of tolerance, I thought, *must be Dad's new favorite phrase.* "Gosh, Dad, I didn't know all that, but why did Moses and Joshua move to Delphi?"

"Oops, I skipped over your question the first time you asked it, but I can answer it now. I went to their house years ago to interview them for the newspaper. I wanted to do a human-interest piece about why they moved to Delphi. They were clearly upset, so I told them the article would just be about the value of their work in the community as a doctor and a librarian. They were still upset, so I told them that the article would state that they were brothers. They asked me to drop the idea of any article. I still remember what Joshua said, "Andy, the least said and written about us publicly the better. We appreciate your friendship and trust you, so I will tell you why we moved to Delphi."

Dad paused as if unsure what to say, "It's complicated. I'll try to keep it short. They were living in Atlanta. Joshua had his medical practice in their home. Moses worked in the only Negro Library in the city. One of Joshua's male patients was mad about his treatment and the cost. He started a rumor in the Negro community that they weren't brothers. The backlash from Negroes got so bad, they decided to move. Joshua had an aunt who lived in Westtown, and she told him how nice Delphi was and that the whites were also nice. They moved soon thereafter, but sadly the aunt died six months after they settled in Delphi. That is the story, son. It's best we leave it in the ground when Joshua and Moses are buried."

"Oh yeah, I didn't think about that. When will they be buried?"

Dad looked at Mom as he always does when I ask him a tough question. She nodded to him. "There are no dates yet for the funerals and burials. When we know, you can go with us. I'm sure it will be a moving ceremony and bring people to tears. I'm going to have another drink. I'll get you and Mom one too."

Dad gave Mom her drink and I got a Coke, took a sip and asked, "Dad, how many people were killed?"

"Ah, my son who always has more questions. I've heard numbers as high as twenty or so. I won't know for sure until the assessments are complete."

"Why didn't police and firemen come to Westtown last night?"

Dad rubbed his forehead and pushed his head back as if he were trying to squeeze a thought out. "Tough question to answer, son. I'm fairly sure some police and volunteer firemen are Klansmen. The awful irony of the situation is that some of the volunteers were probably Klan members who started the fires. If I'm right, they chose Klan duty last night instead of performing their sworn public duties."

"Marvin said the same thing last night, but he added that men from the paper mill were probably in the Klan. Marvin knows a lot about this town."

"I know. Marvin's probably right on all three counts."

"Mr. Graves was there last night, Dad. He wore a red hood instead of a white one, and he was called the Grand Turk. I also saw Jimmy Jackson."

Dad gazed at me as if he thought I had seen ghosts. "I'll be damn, I saw them today working on putting out fires. Those hypocritical sons of bitches. No, that's not right, their murdering bastards. And you actually saw them last night, right?" Dad asked.

"I didn't see their faces because they never took their hoods off. But it was them for sure." I told Mom and Dad everything from the time I left home last night until I got home, and to make sure they understood how awful it was, I repeated the worst parts by saying, "Marvin and I watched as Mr. Graves pulled out a pistol and shot Mr. Douglas and Dr. Marshall in the legs. Then he instructed a few Klansmen to throw them back in their burning house. The Klan laughed and shot their guns in the air, and then went whooping to

Mr. Douglas' warehouse and torched it. When Marvin and I tried to get back home, three Klansmen, led by Jimmy Jackson, happened to see us. They threatened to kill us both, but Marvin talked them out of killing me. Jimmy told me to run home, and Marvin demanded I run and wouldn't take no for an answer. I looked back as I was running. I saw them shooting at Marvin as he staggered and fell to the ground. One of the Klansmen saw me. He lifted his rifle. I thought he was going to kill me, but then he pointed the rifle down."

When I stopped talking, Mom cried and Dad stomped his feet in anger, but I had to say, "Dad, Marvin and some of my other friends live in Westtown. Are they dead or alive?"

Dad turned to Mom for reassurance. When she nodded, he said, "Nancy and Billy are all right, Steve. I saw them helping their neighbors who had suffered fire damage and maybe a death. It grieves my soul, son, to have to tell you that Marvin is dead."

I stood up, rigid as a pole. "I know. I was there. But Dad what did you see?"

"Are you sure you want to know?" Dad asked.

Although I stated to quiver, I said, "Yes."

Dad looked at Mom again, and she nodded again, so he said, "His body was found on the side of the road near his house. He had been shot three times in the back. His parents picked his body out of the bushes and carried him home. Miss Mable cleaned his hands and face before they took him to the mortuary owned by Nancy's father."

My quiver became a quake as I fully realized what Marvin had done. He had taken those three bullets for me. I rocked back and forth, trying not to fall, but then I let loose, "Goddamn it! My best friend died for me. I'm a coward. I ran away. Fuck the Klan. Fuck 'em all. I can't stand …"

I collapsed on the floor, twitching, hollering and crying. I wished I would die. I hated myself for being alive.

22

Seven Days of Funerals

May 28—June 3, 1949

I HAD BEEN TO ONE FUNERAL IN MY LIFE. An older man who worked for Dad had passed away when I was seven. His service was held at our Presbyterian church. I'm ashamed to say it, but although the service was serious, I was bored. The minister said a lot of good words and other people did also, including Dad. We sang a few boring songs. At the cemetery, when his casket was lowered in the ground, I could only wonder, *Is he going to heaven or hell?*

The next seven days seemed like a constant stream of funerals. I'm sure Nancy's father, the mortician, was busy as were the preachers.

Dad told me the official murder count was twenty-five, and he had to attend all the funerals because he was determined to write and publish an obituary for each person murdered in Westtown. Dad also said, "Steve, I'll go to all the funerals even if I can't write the obituaries because most of the murdered people were my friends."

Mom and Dad let me go to two funerals. The first funeral was Marvin's on Monday, and I was in for a big surprise.

I quickly realized that a Negro funeral was nothing like a white one. I mean, instead of being bored, from the moment I walked into the Westtown Baptist Church it was anything but boring. The choir sang beautiful Negro gospels, songs with voices that seemed to be singing to God. The preacher said good things about Marvin in a loud voice, as the people were always waving their arms and shouting things like "Amen," and "Halleluiah" and "Praise the Lord." I couldn't help thinking, *Why don't Presbyterian worship like this? People would enjoy going to church and they'd come more often.*

I whispered to Dad, "Why does everybody seem so happy even when they're crying?"

Dad cupped his hand around my ear and said, "Negroes like to celebrate a person's life with joy, and at the same time they cry and mourn the person's passing."

I didn't stop there and asked, "Why don't Presbyterian worship like this? We would enjoy it and come to services more often."

Dad cupped my ear again. "Son, Presbyterians' name is absolute piety, and their game is stoicism. We Scots are not a joyful crowd."

I had to cough to hide my urge to laugh. *Where does Dad get those ideas. It almost sounds like a poem.*

Don't get me wrong, that funeral wasn't easy for me. In the church, Marvin's casket was open, and people were lined up to pay their respects. As I passed him I wondered if he was watching the whole ceremony. If he knew I slipped the white library's copy of *Journey to the Center of the Earth* under his shoulder, he would have laughed. I couldn't believe it when Marvin's mother said, "Steve, thank you for coming. Marvin loved you." I thought. *How can Miss Mabel be nice to me when I'm the one responsible for Marvin's death?"*

It was even harder for me at the graveyard. When Marvin's casket was lowered into the ground and dirt was shoveled into the hole, I started sobbing and my knees suddenly buckled, but Dad grabbed me and held me upright until my legs felt stronger. As we drove home after the service, I was worried how I would handle the funeral of Mr. Douglas and Dr. Marshall the next day.

On Tuesday, the church was crowded. There were more white people there than had been at Marvin's funeral. However, the singing and preaching and amening were quieter.

As I looked around, I saw Nancy in the choir. *Darn*, I thought, *I'm pretty sure she wasn't there yesterday*. I started thinking about what I should say if I saw her today. *Just keep your cool, Steve, and don't say anything stupid*. But truth is, her face was calm but I could see tears glittering on her cheeks most of the time. I hardly took my eyes off of her the entire service. After the service ended, I was glad the caskets weren't open. I tried not to imagine what their bodies looked like. I was better at the cemetery, even when their caskets were lowered into graves side by side. I did cry. *But why am I so calm? I gotta think on that.*

When the service ended, people didn't leave immediately. They kept gathering with friends and talking quietly. I heard one elderly Negro woman say, "Two of the finest men I ever knew. How we gonna get along without them? Joshua doctored to our bodies and Moses to our minds." I wanted to run up to the lady and hug her, but I didn't. Then I saw my grade school friend, Terry Burton.

"Hey, Terry," I said, "did you know Dr. Marshall and Mr. Douglas?"

"Hey, Steve. Not really, but my Mom and Dad knew them and wanted to pay their respects."

"Mr. Douglas did Shakespeare plays in Westtown. I went there to see *The Tempest*," I said, knowing I was bragging.

Terry looked bug-eyed, saying, "You were there with all those colored people?"

I grinned. "Yes, but my Mom and Dad were with me, and there were a lot of other white people."

"You're a real ding-a-ling, Steve."

I was going to respond to Terry's insult when Nancy walked up. "Hey, Steve. Nice to see you."

Terry's jaw dropped wide open. Nancy noticed and said, "Hi, I'm Nancy. Are you Steve's friend?"

"Yes…uh, we'll be freshmen in high school in September." He glanced around as if he were worried somebody might notice him talking to Nancy.

Nancy, as smooth as ever, said, "Did y'all enjoy the service. I thought it was done well."

Terry, still looking around, said, "Yes….Sorry, I gotta go."

Nancy and I were quiet as Terry walked toward his parents. When he was far enough away, we giggled, then Nancy said, "Do you think he's mad, Steve."

"No, but he's confused. He's probably giving his Mom and Dad an earful."

"Yeah," she said. Smiling, she added, "I'll try not to confuse anyone else."

Nervous, I blurted, "Say, I bet your Daddy's been busy." *Why did I say that?*

Her smile turned to one of sadness. "Too many funerals going on, Steve."

"I'm sorry. I shouldn't have said that."

"It's okay. What you and Marvin tried to do that awful night was heroic. I know you and Marvin were good friends. You must miss him a lot."

"Yes, I do. But Nancy, I'm not heroic. My friend was killed, and I ran away. I'm a coward."

She touched my arm gently and was about to say something when Dad walked up. "Hi, Nancy. How are you doing?""

She took her hand off my arm and said, "Hi, Mr. Thompson. Considering all that's happened in Westtown, I'm doing fine."

"I understand, Nancy. It's been an awful time. Sorry, Steve, we've got to go home now. I have to write more obituaries."

"Okay Dad. I'll be right there."

Nancy said, "Steve, before you go, I have to tell you that my parents have decided to move to Atlanta. Dad's already found a job there and a house for us. Mom and I are going there later today and a moving van will arrive tomorrow with our all our belongings. I hope you're not disappointed."

I stammered, "But...but...why didn't you tell me?"

"I'm sorry. Everything is moving so fast, I didn't have time. Mom and Dad made all the decisions in a flash. I wish they had asked me. You know how kids are treated."

"Yeah, I know. Kids are always the last to find out about anything."

She handed me a piece of paper and said, "This is our new address. We don't have a new phone number yet. I have your number. Maybe you can come to Atlanta for a visit."

"I'll try, but I don't even have a driver's license." I said, hoping I could do it.

"I don't have one either. Maybe you could come on a Greyhound or Trailways Bus. I see Mom. I have to go." She reached over and touched me again. I wanted to kiss her, but didn't.

She waved goodbye, but it was really more like a gentle wave as she moved her fingers up and down slowly.

She's perfect, I thought.

That night after the funerals, I lay in bed, thinking about Nancy. *God I'm going to miss her.*

But I had no way of knowing what might happen after Marvin and Moses Douglas and Joshua Marshall were murdered. Maybe, just maybe, Mr. Graves and Jimmy and the other Klansmen will be arrested for murder.

After I fell asleep, I had a dream about Nancy, and we were dancing under the stars. I woke up in the morning and smiled because I remembered the dream.

23

Steve's Birthday Redux

Friday—June 17, 1949

YESTERDAY WAS MY BIRTHDAY. I turned fourteen, and I couldn't have cared less. Mom and Dad wanted to take me to dinner at the nicest restaurant in Delphi. Crowds really bugged me. Most people had heard what Marvin and I did that night. Everybody calls it the Night of Terror now.

Mom kept insisting we go. She thought it would take my mind off recent events. I knew they were trying to make me feel better, so I finally agreed to go. All in all, it was a pleasant evening. The food was excellent, and while people would turn their heads and look at me and smile, no one came to our table to talk. When we left the restaurant, a lot of people applauded. I liked that because it reminded me of Moses' plays and Nancy.

Saturday morning I thanked Mom and Dad again for the birthday dinner.

Mom seemed pleased. "I'm glad you enjoyed it, Steve. Dad liked it as much as you did. It's going to be a long, hot summer before you start high school in September. What are you going to do today?"

"Not much. Maybe I'll go to the library and say hello to Miss Kathryn. She's always fun to talk to."

"Well, whatever you do, stay close to home. Dad said he'd come home for lunch at noon. Try to be here."

I went to the library at eleven o'clock. It was still quieter downtown than normal. I guess people figured it was best to stay home after the Night of Terror. If it wasn't for Miss Kathryn, I'd have no other reason to be here.

"Hey, Miss Kathryn," I said. She was arranging books on a ladder to the top shelf.

"Hey, Steve. Help me get down."

I helped her down, and she said, "Thanks. Have you heard the news?"

I hoped it wasn't more bad news. "Uh, no, ma'am."

"Jimmy Jackson and two other guys have been arrested."

My mouth was wide open, and I struggled to say, "You're kidding?"

"Nope. Heard it from a reliable source, but that's all I know. I'm sure it'll be public knowledge soon."

I felt tongue-tied but managed to mutter, "Wow. Excuse me, I gotta go home."

Dad came into the house and shouted, "Have I got some news."

I called out to him, feeling like I was bringing tidings of great joy. *Gosh*, I thought, *where did that come from*. "Jimmy Jackson and two other guys have been arrested."

Dad laughed. "Steve, I guess I'll have to call you our junior detective."

Mom chimed in, "Y'all wash your hands and come eat lunch before we talk business."

She had fixed us grilled cheese sandwiches and a small salad. We washed it down with sweet tea."

I told Dad that I heard about Jimmy Jackson from Miss Kathryn. I couldn't wait to hear what Dad had to say. He took a big gulp of tea and launched into his story.

"My goodness," he said, "you two are all ears. Here we go with a little background."

Dad was playing his usual game of explaining things with a mix of drama and humor. *God only knows where this is going.*

"Last week, Governor Folsom got involved and demanded that someone had to be brought to justice for the murders at Westtown. I'll bet his attorney general was not a happy man. Big Jim Folsom is a tall man and usually gets what he wants. He's the first Alabama governor who has offered some help to the Negros, and he doesn't give a tinker's damn about what others think about it. Well, maybe come next election day, he might wiggle a little."

Tinker's damn, note to self, look it up.

Mom groaned. "Come on, Andy. Get to the point."

"I will, dear, in my own good time. I want Steve to understand what's going on. For a change, justice is moving swiftly on this one. Jackson and the other two, don't know their names yet, have been indicted by a Grand Jury, and they were arraigned in a Montgomery courtroom and charged with first degree murder. A Montgomery judge ruled that the three men couldn't get a fair trial in Delphi."

"Why not, Dad?" I asked.

"I have to assume the judge was convinced by the defense lawyer that a Delphi jury would find the three guilty because the jurors would want to protect Delphi's reputation as being progressive. Before you ask, I agree it doesn't make sense. I think almost any jury in Alabama would find the three men innocent."

"I was really steaming, waving my arms around, and shouted, "That ain't fair. I want to testify. I gotta do it for Marvin." *Uh oh, Mom and Dad are looking at each other.*

"Well, son, we'll have to talk about that. Being a witness is serious stuff and can be tough. You'd be a witness for the prosecution. The prosecution lawyer would ask questions first, and will likely ask you to describe what you and Marvin saw and heard that night. The defense lawyer would ask you a few questions to soften you up, and then wham, he hits you with a question like, 'Did you actually see the faces of any of the men?' That's when it gets nasty and nastier. I don't want you to get hurt."

I got my hackles up and said, "Dad, they can't hurt me. They can't hit me. They can't kill me." I realized I was shouting again.

Mom waved at Dad before he said anything, and she said, "Steve, it's not physical hurt we're talking about. It's emotional hurt. You're already hurt deeply by Marvin's death. Don't take on more of a burden."

"Mom, it's also for Joshua and Moses. I gotta do it for all three of them."

"I understand," Mom said, "let's all think about this for a while. It's not every day that a fourteen-year-old boy testifies in a murder trial."

"Mom's right, Steve. I'll find out who the prosecution's lawyer is and talk to him. Since it's the weekend, I'll make the call on Monday. Can you hold steady?"

I stopped yelling. "Yes, but I really want to do it."

"Right, I get it. Now Lillis, I bet you have a good dessert for us."

Part IV
Transitions—1949

"Urge him with truth to frame his fair replies;
And sure he will; for wisdom never lies."

Homer—*The Odyssey*

24

Andy's Dilemma

Monday—June 20, 1949

I SAT AT THE BREAKFAST TABLE STARING AT DAD, and asked, "Well, when are you going to make the call?"

Mom grabbed my hand and said, "Steve, don't insult your father like that. He's got a lot on his mind."

I wanted to say, *Me too*, but I bowed my head toward Dad and said, "Sorry, Dad. I'm just antsy."

"I know. As soon as we finish breakfast, I'll call Ralph Black, the Alabama attorney general, to find out if he or someone else will be the prosecution's attorney, and then I'll go to Montgomery to discuss the upcoming trial with anyone that will talk to me."

Dad went into his home office and closed the door. I winked at Mom and moved in front of the office door, but I couldn't hear much. Their voices sounded like mumbo jumbo. Then all of a sudden I heard an angry voice from the phone blurt out, "Goddamn it, Andy, it's Edward Macey. He and Folsom are both nigger lovers." Dad replied, "Thanks," and hung up. I assumed the angry voice was Mr. Black. I scooted back to my chair at the breakfast table. Mom smiled. I'm sure she knew I was listening, but she said nothing.

Dad came back to the breakfast table. "I talked to Ralph Black. He said Governor Folsom insisted he assign Edward Macey as prosecuting attorney. Ralph said a nasty thing about Governor Folsom and Edward Macey. I won't repeat what he said. I'm just glad Ralph is not the prosecuting attorney for the trial. He would have made sure that Jimmy Jackson and the other two got off scot-free. I'll get my things, and then head to Montgomery. Can't promise what will happen, but I'll give it my all."

I jumped up and hugged Dad and said I was sorry I acted so badly, and then I thought, *Steve, you're a nut case. Note to nut case. Look up scot-free.*

25

Andy to Montgomery

Monday—June 20, 1949

As Andy drove toward Montgomery, he wasn't sure what to expect. Edward Macey's office was in a building adjacent to the courthouse where the trial would be held. He found Macey's office number and entered even though he didn't have an appointment.

An attractive young lady with red hair sat behind a desk and said, "Good morning, sir, how can I help you? I'm Mr. Macey's secretary."

He smiled as he was always partial to red headed ladies. "My name's Andy Thompson. I'd like to see Mr. Macey."

"Do you have an appointment, Mr. Thompson?"

"No, ma'am, I was hoping he might be available."

"Please have a seat. I'll ask Mr. Macey if he will see you."

Macey came out of his office. "Mr. Thompson, what a pleasure to finally meet you. I see you've met my new secretary. Ruth is a bright, lovely young lady. She's also studying to be a paralegal. I've heard so much about you and your fine newspaper in Delphi, the *Delphi Delta News*, right?"

"Yes, but most people today call it the *Delphi News*."

"I like it either way. Please come in my office and take a seat. What can I do for you?"

"If you have a few minutes, Mr. Macey, I'd like to discuss the upcoming trial of Jimmy Jackson and the two other men."

"Sure, I'll talk about anything that the laws of Alabama allow. By the way the other two men's names are pure southern: Bubba Smith and Willie Warden. Speaking of names, how about first names for you and me? Call me Ed, Andy. I've heard a lot about your son's bravery in Westtown. You must be proud of him."

"I am, Ed, but Steve would say he was a coward the Night of Terror, which is the name most people in Delphi use."

Andy paused and thought about how to approach Ed with his next question. "Ed, no disrespect intended, I must ask you where you stand as the prosecution's lead attorney. To be more blunt, where do you stand on the race issue? Do you think a white jury will convict a white man for murdering a Negro?"

"Fair questions, Andy. It's my job to make sure the jury brings in a guilty verdict. At their arraignment the three defendants were charged with murder in the first degree. As to the makeup of the jury, we, the prosecution, will do our damnedest to get a mixed jury. Of course, the defense will try to minimize the number of Negros on the jury. However, I'm sure you remember another famous Alabama trial, or trials really, popularly called the Scottsboro trials. The U.S. Supreme Court ruled unanimously in 1935 that Alabama had consistently excluded Negros from being on juries and ordered the State to forthwith stop excluding them. I know ours is still not a perfect system. The county voter registration office plays games all the time to deny a Negro person a voter certificate. But the local branch of the NAACP is strong and aggressive. The president of the branch is Mr. E. D. Nixon and the secretary is Mrs. Rosa Parks. I know them, and I'm sure they will help as much as they can. That said, it will be tough, but we'll do our best to get a balanced jury." Macey paused for a moment, "And Andy, while I grew in Alabama surrounded by segregation and racism, I've always tried to be color blind, especially in the courtroom."

Andy nodded. "Sounds good."

"It's more than *sounds,* Andy. I'm going to tell you something that's off the record. You can't take notes now and you can't print anything in your newspaper about what I tell you. I'll let you know when the item is announced publicly. Yes?"

Andy wanted to shout *yes*, but he said calmly, "I'm all ears and as long as necessary, my pens and notebooks are in my valise and the *Delphi Delta News* presses will not be running."

Ed laughed heartily for a moment and then said, "I think we're going to get on well, Andy. I can't decide whether your response is a metaphor or just fact. Doesn't matter. As is known, Governor Folsom wants to see justice done for the atrocities committed in Westtown. He pushed the grand jury hard, he pushed the attorney general hard, he's pushing me hard, and he's pushing the legislative committee that is responsible for assigning a judge to the case to pick his choice. Folsom's man is Frank Johnson. He..."

Andy butted in, "Never heard of him."

"I'm not surprised. Most people haven't. Get this, he's a Republican, a rare breed in Alabama. I hear that Folsom likes him because he shares many of Folsom's opinions on how Negroes in Alabama should be treated with dignity. If that proves to be the case in this trial, we may have a sympathetic judge or at least a fair one."

"Interesting," Andy said, "but what if the legislative committee doesn't choose Folsom's choice?"

"Have you ever met Folsom?"

"A couple of times. He's huge."

"Yep, six feet, eight inches tall, and *there's the rub*. I suspect Folsom is selectively meeting with legislative committee members whom he feels are on the fence. When he talks to each of them, only a few are tall enough to get anywhere close to his face. They have to crane their necks back to speak directly to him. Or if he decides to lean over them and hover like a bird of prey, most just relent to escape from him. Oh, I'm sure Big Jim Folsom will see to it that his man is chosen. In fact, I think I'll call Folsom and see if he can put some heat on the voter registration office to make sure we get Negro names on our jury selection list."

Andy got up and walked around the room, and then said, "Ed, It's known only too well that Folsom had been charged once a few years ago for sexual impropriety. He settled the case out of court, but the terms of the agreement were never made public. Could that be a problem?"

"Andy, I can assure you that Folsom wants to see the three defendants found guilty."

Andy scratched his ear and tried to look aghast. "Wow, I feel super and I know I'll get a good night's sleep."

Ed laughed. "I'm glad you feel better and that *all's well that ends well.*"

"Ed thanks for the second allusion to Shakespeare. Have you seen many of Shakespeare's plays?"

"Yes, quite a few," Ed said. "In fact I attended one of Moses Douglas' plays in his Westtown theater several years ago. I liked it very much."

"I'm glad you liked it, Ed. Moses Douglas was a wonderful man and friend."

Ed nodded. "Andy, please tell me why you're really here. I suspect it has to do with your son."

"You are prescient, Ed. But to put it simply, Steve would like to testify for the prosecution. He saw and heard things during the Night of Terror that were so awful I'm afraid it's shattered his soul and his faith in mankind in ways hard to imagine."

"I'm sorry to hear that" Ed said and added, "Andy, please tell me what Steve..."

Ed's secretary came into the room. "Mr. Macey, there are two lawyers in the conference room who have an appointment with you now."

"Thanks, Ruth. Please tell the gentlemen that something important has just come up, and apologize for me, but we'll have to reschedule the gentlemen."

"Yes, sir."

"Now Andy, please tell me what you can about Steve's Night of Terror."

Andy explained everything that Steve had told him and what he observed when he went to Westtown the morning after the Klan atrocities. Andy closed by paraphrasing Steve's last comment yesterday, "I have to testify for Marvin and Joshua and Moses. I gotta do it for all three of them." Andy felt wasted, he's body sagging.

"Andy, no one, especially a kid, should have to experience that. Perhaps if Steve testifies, it will help him deal with the horrors of that night. As you know, Andy, you can't testify about what you just told me. The court would consider it hearsay. Can you bring Steve here as soon as possible? I'll move things around on my calendar whenever you can come. I'm going to focus all my attention on this case. I must talk to Steve and determine whether or not he's truly up to testifying."

"Steve will be delighted. He wants to testify, and I'm sure he'll do whatever you think is necessary."

Ed stood and shook Andy's hand. "I think we're through for today. I'll await your phone call."

"You'll hear from me shortly. See you soon." Andy left Ed's office and drove back to Delphi, thinking about his talk with Macey.

I was in my room reading a book when I heard Dad say, "Lillis, I'm home."

I bounded downstairs and shouted, "Dad, how did it go?"

"Hey, Steve. Let me get a drink. Lillis, I'll get you one and a Coke for Steve. Let's sit at the dinner table and I'll tell you everything."

Mom and I sat down at the table, and I said, "Dad, I'm all ears."

Dad laughed. "That's a phrase I used with Mr. Macey. Like father, like son."

I laughed too, and then Dad said, "Okay, Mr. Macey and I discussed a lot of things and this will take a while. There are two things I can't tell you. A judge has been assigned to the trial, and Mr. Macey told me in confidence and off the record who it was. I can't violate that confidence. Mr. Macey and I also had a brief discussion about Governor Folsom, but it's not pertinent to this trial."

I started squirming. "Dad, is the judge good or bad for this trial?"

"Steve, I can't answer that. This is a good lesson for you to learn. If you agree to hear something in confidence, you must abide by that agreement in all aspects. Mr. Macey will tell me when the judge's name has been officially released, and then I'm free to discuss who it is."

"Thanks, Dad. This legal stuff is pretty complicated. I wish I could be a fly on the wall and hear..."

Mom interrupted me. "Steve, let Dad tell us what he can."

"Yes, ma'am."

"Here goes," Dad said, and he continued talking for thirty or forty minutes. He had to backpedal several times, explaining that he wanted to be sure things were in the proper sequence and context. He concluded by saying, "Th-Th-Th-That's all folks."

Mom and I laughed in unison as we were used to his silly attempt to mimic Porky Pig. Dad did this often when he was talking about something difficult. I guess he wanted to end on a happy note.

I couldn't wait to ask, "Dad, when can we meet with Mr. Macey?"

"Soon. I assure you that Mr. Macey wants to talk to you. He needs to judge if you're fit to testify, or if you'll wilt on the witness stand."

Steve grinned ear-to-ear. "Wow, Dad, I'm ready to testify at any time."

"Steve, don't get the cart before the horse. Although it's late afternoon, I need to tend to newspaper business to make sure things are running smoothly, and I'll check my calendar for days we can meet with Mr. Macey. I should know tomorrow morning what looks good. I know you're antsy, but try to relax. And don't forget that the path forward is fraught with legal difficulties. We must be prepared to deal with each one as it comes up."

"Yes, sir, I sure will." And then I thought: *Look up the meaning of fraught. Then it hit me, thought and fraught rhyme and each has seven letters. I love words.*

Dad broke my thought chain, saying, "Lillis, can you cook up some grub now, so I can go to the newspaper office soon?"

Mom said, "I reckon I can rustle up some grub for you two cowboys. Go wash your hands like nice cow hands."

Dad and I looked at each other and laughed. Mom never, ever talked like that.

26

Back to Montgomery

Tuesday—June 21, 1949

DAD JOINED MOM AND ME at the breakfast table. Of course, I hoped he was going to say that we could go see Mr. Macey today. *I know, I'm antsy.*

Dad smiled at me. I smiled back but didn't say anything. I had learned when to keep my mouth shut, at least I thought I had.

"Good morning all," Dad said. "I trust you both had a good night's sleep." *His way of teasing.* "Any questions?"

Mom and I didn't respond.

"My, my," Dad said, "has a cat got both of your tongues?"

Neither Mom nor I spoke.

Dad appeared perplexed. "Am I a victim of a conspiracy?"

Wearing her most patient face, Mom said, "Perhaps, we're waiting for you to tell us something important?"

"Aha, the cabal of silence is over. It may interest you that I am prepared to call Edward Macey this morning about arranging a meeting with him. And, by the way, I have enjoyed the brief period of silence you both performed so well, especially you Steve. Let's have breakfast, and then Steve you and Mom can join me in my office while I call Mr. Macey."

When we finished eating, we went into Dad's office. He said, "Let's get started. Lillis you sit to the right of me and Steve to the left. I call him Ed, but of course, Steve, you address him as Mr. Macey. I'll dial his number now."

"Good morning, Mr. Macey's office. How can I help you?"

"Good morning, Ruth. This is Andy Thompson. I'd like to speak to Mr. Macey."

"Of course, sir, I'll put you right through."

"Andy, good to hear from you so soon. How is your family doing?"

"Ed, they're fine. Steve is sitting beside me as is my wife Lillis. I think they will be able to hear you. Is that all right with you?"

"Sure, Andy, unless you and I have something to discuss that is confidential. If that happens, you'll have to ask Steve and Lillis to leave the room."

"Ed, Steve and Lillis are nodding yes."

"Fine. Andy, speaking of confidential, Judge Frank Johnson has been formally assigned to our case, so you can write and talk about him as much as you wish. Good morning, Lillis. Good morning, Steve."

Dad held his phone close to each of us and I said, "Good morning, Mr. Macey." Mom added, "Good morning, Ed."

"Hi again," Mr. Macey said. "Andy when can you and Steve come to Montgomery? I'm available today."

I held two thumbs up.

"Ed, Steve just held up two thumbs, so we'll leave Delphi shortly. See you soon."

"Good. Well then, I'll see you two later today. I'll say goodbye."

Dad and I hit the road, and it normally took less than an hour to get to Montgomery. I didn't feel antsy, but I was sure excited. I felt like I was going to meet the Wizard of Oz. Dad and I seemed to go out of our way to talk about anything other than the upcoming trial and my part in it, if Mr. Macey agreed. Dad also said I should pay attention to what I saw and heard. He said it was important to be familiar with everything that around us.

After Dad parked, he pointed out the courthouse where the trial would take place. Mr. Macey's office was in a tall building adjacent to the courthouse. When we entered Mr. Macey's office, I saw a beautiful redheaded lady.

Dad said, "Ruth, please meet my son, Steve Thompson."

"It's a pleasure to meet you, Miss Ruth."

She laughed and said, "Steve, please call me Ruth. Miss Ruth makes me sound old. Mr. Macey is waiting for you in a conference room that adjoins his office. Let me show you."

Ruth took us into Mr. Macey's office first. I had never seen such a fine office. All the wood was dark brown and highly polished. The three chairs facing Mr. Macey's desk were also dark brown. But the chair's cushions stood out. All three had scenes of animals on them, a deer, an elk, and a soaring eagle, in colorful woven patterns. All the walls had light brown book cases containing lots of big books. I assumed they were for legal rules and cases.

Ruth opened another door and we entered the conference room. *This place is a maze.* The conference room was larger than the office and had a huge oblong-shaped, light brown table with ten chairs around it. The chairs weren't as ornate as the office chairs. So much for my first attempts to pay attention to everything. I thought, *This ain't gonna be easy.*

Three men and one woman in the conference room stood up. One said, "Welcome, Steve, I'm Ed Macey."

"Hello, Mr. Macey," I replied.

"Andy and Steve, let me introduce Sam Lancaster and Clark Hughes. Sam will be one of the attorneys working with me on this case. Clark recently graduated from the University of Alabama law school. He will be observing all the proceedings in this case, and I suspect he'll come up with several good ideas. Mrs. Kelly is a court stenographer. Please have a seat. There's a pot of hot coffee and Danish rolls on the side table and a few sodas in the small refrigerator. Help yourselves."

I got a Danish and a lemonade. I wondered why no one was talking. It seemed eerie.

Dad spoke up. "Ed, I told Steve to call you Mr. Macey. Since Steve has a lot on his mind now, can he call all adults by their first names?"

"Andy, it's okay with me except for Mrs. Kelly who is our senior stenographer." He looked at everyone and they nodded.

I was glad Dad asked the question, but he forgot the golden rule for kids in Alabama. We called adult ladies Miss, like Miss Kathryn, the Delphi Library librarian. Marvin called my mother Miss Lillis, and I called his mother Miss Mabel. Adult men were called Dr. or Mr., like Marvin called my father Mr. Andy. I called Marvin's father Mr. Jake. And *dadgummit*, that's what I'll do. Oh, I flubbed that golden rule sometimes, but here goes.

Mr. Ed said, "Well, Steve, we have a number of things to do today. Let me outline what we plan. First, I want you to tell us what happened the night of May 25, 1949, in Westtown. Second, we'll ask you questions about what you said. Third, we'll do a wrap up and discuss next steps. Andy, while Steve has to carry the ball, you can chime in at any time with a question or comment. Steve, you ready to go to work?"

I tried to be calm. "Yes, sir, Mr. Ed."

Dad and Mr. Ed stared at me and then smiled. I figured they must have got it. Hell, they were southern boys once.

"Your Dad told me about your ordeal the Night of Terror. One of our legal problems is that your Dad can't tell the court what you told your Dad. That's called hearsay. You have to testify and tell the court and jury what you experienced that night."

I spoke up and said, "Mr. Ed, I want to testify. I have to do it for Marvin and Moses and Joshua."

"Steve, I admire your honesty and your sense of duty to your friends."

"It's more than duty, sir. I can't make them come back to life. I am obligated to do this for them. I hope you understand."

Mr. Ed looked around at everyone in the room and smiled. "Steve, I'm not smiling to make fun of anyone. I have worked with youngsters like you in many courtrooms, however I have never worked with a kid so well spoken and determined. But I want to be up front with you. This trial will be one with more ups and downs than you can imagine. The lead attorney for the defense is Peter Hastings. He specializes in defending members of the Ku Klux Klan. In fact, people call him the Klan Lawyer. As if that isn't enough, he has never lost a criminal trial featuring a Klan member. Juries always find his clients not guilty. So, Steve, that's the difficult journey we have ahead. Do you understand?"

"Yes, sir. It's kinda like Sisyphus having to roll the rock uphill, and then when he gets near the top, the rock rolls back downhill, and he has to start all over again for eternity. I guess we'll have to continue making the defense roll that rock up and down until they run out of steam."

Mr. Ed smiled again. "So, you know Greek mythology, Steve?"

"Yes, sir. Well sorta. I read a lot and I checked *Bullfinch's Mythology* out of the Delphi Library. The librarian recommended it. She's a nice lady. The book was interesting. I didn't wade through it all, but I did read the Sisyphus story. My mother also read me most of Homer's *The Odyssey*, and she explained a lot of things about it, but it was tough slogging for me."

"My goodness, Steve....I think we better get started. Our three newest attorneys will join us shortly. Their fist names are Garth, Oscar, and Ben. They will listen and not ask questions. Ah, here they come. Have a seat, gentlemen. You're just in time. Now, Steve, please tell us everything, and I mean everything, that happened the Night of Terror. Mrs. Kelly will use her steno machine to type what you say in a strange code. Later, she will transcribe what you said into English. We need to have a record of what you said. If you need to take a break, just say so. I know this may be hard to do. Please take your time."

"Yes, sir." From there, I lost track of time. I just kept talking. I had to take several breaks. One to go to the bathroom and three when I teared up talking about Marvin and Moses and Joshua. Dad was always there to hand me a dry handkerchief. When I was finished, I just stopped talking.

"Thank you, Steve. We know that wasn't easy. It's almost eleven. Who wants to eat?"

My hand shot up first and everybody followed, except Mrs. Kelly.

"You sure you don't want to eat, Mrs. Kelly?" Mr. Ed asked.

"I will eat, Mr. Macey. I brought my lunch, and I'll also transcribe what Steve said, so you have a paper copy soon."

"Thank you , Mrs. Kelly. Ruth, you still here?"

"Yes, sir." Ruth said. She had been sitting in a corner where you couldn't see her.

"Ruth, please call Martin's Restaurant and make reservations for nine. I hope you will join us."

"I'll call them right now, and I will join you."

She picked up a phone in the conference room, and zap, we had the reservations.

"Okay, let's get going. My treat, but no shop talk," Mr. Ed said. "Martin's gets crowded at lunchtime. I can drive. My car is in the basement garage of this building. We can squeeze six into it. It's not far. Garth, Oscar, and Ben, you'll have to drive one of your cars. *Tallyho!*"

Mr. Ed led the way, and I was off on another adventure. I had heard of Martin's, but I had never been there. Note to self, *What's shop talk mean.*

We had a blast at Martin's. Great southern food. Most people told jokes and some talked football too much. Football's okay, but basketball was my game.

I thought Mr. Ed told the best joke when he said, "A rabbi, a Hindu, and a lawyer are in a car that breaks down in the countryside one evening. They walk to a nearby farm and the farmer tells them it's too late for a tow truck but he has only two extra beds and one of them will have to sleep in the barn. The Hindu says, 'I'm humble, I'll sleep in the barn.' But minutes later he returns and knocks on the door and says, 'There is a cow in the barn. It's against my beliefs to sleep in the same building as a cow.' So the rabbi says, 'It's okay, I'll sleep in the barn.' But soon, he is back knocking on the door as well, saying, 'There is a pig in the barn, and I cannot shelter in a building with a pig.' So the lawyer is forced to sleep in the barn. Shortly, there is another knock on the door and the farmer sighs and answers the door. It's the pig and the cow.' "

Dad and I couldn't stop laughing, but the others didn't laugh long while Mr. Sam only yawned. I supposed they had heard the joke before. *Sore heads.*

Ruth, who sat next to lucky me, whispered in my ear, "I bet Ed and Clark and Sam start talking football. I don't give a fig for football, but it always happens at social events. It usually gets nasty. Ed and Clark are Alabama grads and Sam is an Auburn grad." Even I knew that shouting *War Eagle* and *Roll Tide* was like mixing oil and water. I had to work hard not to laugh when Ruth used the phrase *fig for football.* I thought, *That's a nice alliteration. I wish I could stop pausing so much and stick to the point.*

Well, as Ruth predicted it sure did get nasty. Mr. Ed said, "Sam, have you gotten over the pasting the War Eagles suffered last December. I think the score was 55 to 0. Am I right?"

Mr. Sam glared at Mr. Ed and said nothing. Then Mr. Clark piled on and said, "Don't worry, Sam, I think Alabama will show some mercy next season and beat Auburn only 45 to 0. Roll Tide!"

Mr. Sam jumped up and said, "Excuse me, I have to go piss on Alabama." As he walked toward the rest room, I thought his inference was clear.

I had no idea how this was going to end when Mr. Ed stood and headed toward the rest room. Shortly, Mr. Ed and Mr. Sam came back, smiling at each other and arm in arm. Mr. Ed said, "Clark and I owe Sam a huge apology. We abandoned one principle that is essential for all of us to remember. We are not Alabama versus Auburn, we are a team of prosecutors who are obligated to search for the truth in criminal cases. We must not forgot that principle. Now, enjoy yourselves. We'll have to leave soon."

I liked the ending. I knew I was showing off when I said to Ruth, "Well, that was a *lollapalooza*, what did you think?"

Ruth laughed and said, "Steve, if you mean the football fiasco, all's well that ends well, but where did you get that word? Did you make it up?"

"Nope. It's like a doozy or the cat's meow."

"You've quite a vocabulary, Steve. Now, I've got a question for you. Do you have a girlfriend?"

"No ma'am."

"Steve, don't call me ma'am. I'm only twenty-two years old, and I don't believe you. Do you have a girlfriend?"

"You caught me with a broadside. I did have a girlfriend. She and her family moved to Atlanta recently. I miss her."

"Well, I'm told long distance romances are hard to maintain. Perhaps you should think about looking for..."

At that moment, Dad sat down in an empty chair next to Ruth, and said, "What have you two youngster been talking about?"

Ruth responded, "Anything but football. The upcoming trial and the lawyers were hot topics. Don't ask, we know it was shop talk."

Dad said, "My, my." So now I understood what shop talk meant. I can take that item off my note-to-self list.

Mr. Ed broke our conversation by saying, "Okay troops, let's roll. We have work to do.

Well, I wondered why they wanted to question me. I've told them everything I know. *Get over it, Steve. You'll find out soon enough.*

Sure enough, after everyone was settled in the conference room, Mr. Ed said, "Steve, questions time. I know you've already told us about the Night of Terror, but now we want to do a practice run as if you were in the witness chair at the trial. We'll try to keep this short. First, as the prosecuting attorney, I'll ask you questions. Then Sam, as the defense attorney, will ask you questions. Mrs. Kelly will not record the session, but she will take notes. Do you understand?"

"Yes, sir. You're Alabama, the prosecution. Mr. Sam is Auburn, the defense. I guess you're testing me to see if I'll be a good witness."

Everybody laughed. Mr. Sam said, "Bingo, on both counts, and yes, Steve, that's the way it is. Some people become quite rattled in the witness chair, especially when cross-examined by a defense attorney."

Mr. Ed started asking questions. "Steve, I'll start with questions I find most important. We want you to keep your answers as short as possible. If I think more information is necessary, I'll ask another question. So, to begin, why are you sure it was Jimmy Jackson's voice the Night of Terror?"

"First time I heard his voice was when he shouted at Marvin on our float for the Delphi Mardi Gras parade on March 1, 1949. Jimmy shouted at Marvin something like, 'Hey, colored boy. You no god-damn American pilot. You better watch yourself.' "

"How did you know for sure in was Jimmy Jackson?"

"Well, I didn't at first. But Fred Watson, who works for my Dad, was driving the tractor pulling our float. He saw and heard it all. He stopped the tractor, and yelled, 'Jimmy, get the hell outta here. We don't cotton to your kind.' Jimmy shouted back, 'Fred, ya a white piece of nigger-loving shit.' " I looked over at Mrs. Kelly. She was writing something down. Maybe Fred Watson's name?

"Hold on, Steve, don't say that Fred Watson worked for your Dad. Perhaps the defense will let it slide although it's unlikely. We never know when we might gain some purchase on the defense."

"Huh, I don't get it. You want to buy the defense?"

"My goodness," said Mr. Ed, "I finally used a word our bright, potential witness doesn't understand. Steve, this use of purchase means *to take hold*."

Everybody laughed. I blushed.

"Back to work. Steve, when did you learn what Jimmy's last name was?"

"Dad mentioned it when we got home after the parade."

"When was your next encounter with Jimmy Jackson?"

"Last month, I attended a rehearsal of a play produced by Mr. Moses at his theater in Westtown. It was Shakespeare's *Romeo and Juliet*. The rehearsal started at two o'clock and ended about five. Then I ran home and when I approached the town square, I saw five white guys. I recognized Jimmy and two of the other guys who hassled Marvin during the Mardi Gras parade. Jimmy saw me and yelled, 'Hey, pipsqueak, I know you. You tell that colored boy that I'm gonna whup his ass and maybe worse next time I see him, you hear?' "

"Was that literally what Jimmy said?"

"Yes, I can't get those two sentences out of my mind. Jimmy did say a few things I can't remember, but he's never said anything nice."

"Steve, all you needed to say was that first sentence."

"Yes, sir."

"When was your next encounter with Jimmy."

"This is the tough one and last one. On the Night of Terror, my parents told me to stay home. I disobeyed them and slipped out of the house about ten o'clock and headed toward Westtown. I had to warn Marvin. It was dark, no moonlight. But before I tell you, I gotta tell you about Mr. Graves who works at the mill and likes Shakespeare, he..."

Mr. Ed cut me off. "Steve, Mr. Graves has not been charged with a crime. I didn't want to slow you down when you told your story before our lunch break. Let's stick to Jimmy."

Mr. Sam said, "Ed, let Steve tell what he knows. This might be useful later."

Mr. Ed didn't look happy, but he said, "Okay, Steve, continue where I cut you off."

"Yes, sir. Well, I was near old man Zach's haunted house when I heard guns firing and men talking. I hid in the bushes across the street from the haunted house. A group of Klansmen stopped there too. All of the Klansmen wore hoods, but only one wore a red hood. I heard him say, 'Let's torch this old house.' I thought I had heard that voice before but I couldn't place it. The voice changed his mind, and another Klansman said something like, 'Graves, let's get old man Zack.' That's when it hit me. Mr. Graves was the voice. The Klansmen called him the Grand Turk. At the rehearsal last May during a break, he sat down by me, and we chatted about the play. When he got up to leave, he said something like, 'Steve, some advice. In the future, stay away from here. Things are not as they appear…I have to be going.' I didn't understand the meaning. Dad said it was a veiled threat."

I stopped talking and stood and said, "I have to go to the bathroom."

Mr. Ed said, "Let's all take a break. Clark, please show Steve to the men's room." As we walked out of the conference room, I heard Mr. Ed say, "You were right, Sam. This will be useful."

When Mr. Clark and I came into the conference room, Mr. Ed asked, "Steve, are you ready to continue."

"Yes, sir, but I have to tell you more about Mr. Graves and the Klan before I get to Jimmy. Marvin and I observed something so awful that it's hard to talk about it."

"Steve, I understand."

Am I getting myself in another pickle, I wondered? When I told my story earlier today, I had to decide how to portray Moses and Joshua. As I thought it through, I decided I wouldn't describe them as queers as Zach had convinced the Klan they were. I figured as long as I said nothing about that weird word, I wasn't lying. "After Mr. Graves and the other Klan members left, I found Marvin at his house. I told him the Klan were headed toward the house of Moses and Joshua. Then I told Marvin what Jimmy had said, and he said he didn't care about Jimmy. I couldn't believe how brave Marvin was. I was scared to death. Then Marvin said, 'Steve, we gotta go to Moses' and Joshua's house right now. Follow me. Stay low. Jump in the bushes if you hear anything coming.' "

I had also decided to keep Nancy's name out of my story. I don't know why but I smiled and thought, *She's not a major actress in this play.*

"I followed Marvin as he led me through an alley and some paths. We heard gunshots and yelling and saw smoke from a fire. Marvin pointed to something ahead and said, 'We call that Westtown Mountain. We'll crawl up it, so we can see their house.' We crawled to the top and we saw things that I still have nightmares about. The house was burning. Then we saw Joshua and Moses come out of the house, their hands up. The Klan started beating them and yelling things like 'String 'em up,' and, 'Cut off their peckers.' Mr. Graves, the Grand Turk with the red hood, stepped up and pushed several men aside and shot Joshua and Moses in both legs. Then he ordered four men to throw Moses and Joshua into the burning house. Other men fired their guns in the air and cheered. The Klan mounted their horses and rode in the direction of the warehouse. We crawled to another spot and watched the Klan burn the warehouse down. I was crying with my head on Marvin's shoulder. He patted my head and said, 'Steve, we have to get outta here before the Klan heads back to Delphi.' "

I stopped talking and looked at everyone in the conference room. I was crying. Dad handed me a handkerchief. I dabbed my eyes. The room was silent. Mr. Clark and Ruth were also dabbing their eyes. Then I had another crazy thought, *Misery loves company.* I felt better and said, "I'm ready to tell you the last part when Marvin and I encountered Jimmy Jackson."

Mr. Ed said, "Steve are you sure? Maybe we should take another break."

"No, sir, I'd like to finish."

Mr. Ed looked at Dad. He nodded his head. Mr. Ed motioned at me to continue.

"I asked Marvin where we were going. He said, 'I'm going home. You get your white ass home.' Right then we heard horses running and we jumped in the bushes close to Marvin's house. One of the riders must have seen us and yelled at us to come out. Marvin went out first. I followed him and saw four riders in white hoods. I was sure the rider who told us to come out was Jimmy. He said, 'Fellas, we got here, the nigger-boy Marvin who thinks he's an American pilot, and we got his pipsqueak friend Steve.' One of the others said we should be hanged. I was so sure the first voice was Jimmy Jackson that I spoke up, 'Jimmy, we ain't done you no harm. Leave us alone.' Jimmy made his horse rear up and told me to mind my manners or it would be my last words. Marvin stepped in front of me and said, 'Mr. Jackson, I'm the one you're mad at. Leave Steve out of this.' Jimmy said, 'Ain't that nice. Tell you what, I'll be nice too. Steve, you run home now like a good little boy.' Trying to act brave, I said, 'I'm not going anywhere without Marvin.' Jimmy fired his rifle in the air, and said, 'You better run Steve, or I'm gonna kill you. I'll fire my rifle three more times. If you ain't running home by then, you're done.' Marvin pushed me in the direction I had to go and said, 'Run. You get going, Steve, these guys aren't kidding.' "

"I need to pause, Mr. Ed. The toughest part is coming."

"Take all the time you need, Steve."

After I had composed myself, I said, "Thanks, I'm okay. All three Klansmen fired the first shot. I looked at Marvin. He shoved me toward home again, and said, 'Run, Steve! Run!' All three Klansmen fired the second shot. I stood still. Marvin shoved me again, and cried out, 'For Christ's sake, Steve, run like hell!' I started running when all three Klansmen laughed and fired the third shot into the air. I heard Jimmy call one of the Klansmen *Bubba*. I looked back and heard Jimmy Jackson say to Marvin, 'Okay, nigger, let's see how fast you can run.' Then I heard Marvin yell for the last time, 'Keep running, Steve. Don't stop.' While I was running, gun shots seemed to come from everywhere. I looked back and saw the men shooting at Marvin. He staggered and fell. One of the Klansmen saw me, lifted his rifle and then lowered it. He didn't shoot at me. I turned and ran fast, feeling like the coward I was, but I kept repeating in my head and sometimes out loud, 'Keep running, Steve,' until I got home."

I stopped and said, "That's it." I didn't know why, but I wasn't crying.

Mr. Ed sighed and said, "Thanks, Steve. I have to tell you that you are not a coward. To repeat myself, I know how hard this is for you to have to keep retelling your story."

"Yes, sir, but since Marvin and Joshua and Moses were killed, I have to keep telling the story."

"Right," Mr. Ed said. "Are you ready to be cross-examined by Sam. He'll keep it short."

"Yes, sir. I know this is going to be difficult."

Mr. Sam said, "Steve, I won't ask you any questions about Mr. Graves. What you said he did is terrible, but we'll deal with that later. Now, try to imagine that I am Mr. Hastings, the lead defense attorney, and that you are in the witness chair being cross-examined by him. First question. How can you be so sure it was Jimmy Jackson?"

"I recognized his voice and he called me Steve."

"Did Jimmy ever take off his mask?"

"No, sir. None of them did."

"Did you recognize Bubba's voice?"

"No, sir, I only heard his voice once."

"There are several young men in the Delphi area called Jimmy. In fact, we know of three that work at the Delphi paper mill. Of course, since your Dad is the owner and publisher of the *Delphi Delta News*, your family is well-known in Delphi. Perhaps one of the other Jimmy's knows your name. Do you think this is possible?"

"No, sir, I don't know anyone else named Jimmy."

"Steve, it so happens that young Jimmy Jackson's father is also called Jimmy, so they likely have similar voices. Perhaps, the elder Jimmy was the person you encountered on the Night of Terror. Do you know the elder Jimmy?"

"No, sir, I don't. But I don't think the elder Jimmy could have known all the things Jimmy and I said that night. Too much for the old man to remember."

"Steve, since you don't know the elder Jimmy, how can you claim to know anything about his memory retention abilities."

"I can't, but I know the voice I heard on May twenty-fifth was the young Jimmy. Maybe there's a test where I can prove it."

"Perhaps, there is. But you claim to have seen the murder. Did you?"

"Yes, sir."

"Who killed Marvin?"

"I don't know for sure. It could have been one of the three, two of the three, or all three."

"So, they were all masked and you can't identify the killer. I submit, therefore, that you are an unreliable witness."

Mr. Ed spoke up, "That's enough, Sam. It was a good cross. Steve, you did well, and what I really like is how your story is so consistent telling to telling. You can't imagine how mixed up a witness' story can become. Let's take a brief break and do a wrap."

Some got a soda or coffee and stood around talking. Before I went to go to the bathroom, Dad said I did well.

Mr. Ed called the meeting back to order and asked for comments to two questions, "Is Steve a reliable witness? Will he melt on the witness stand under cross-examination?"

I raised my hand. "Yes, Steve?"

"Mr. Sam, is Jimmy's father really named Jimmy?"

Mr. Sam looked surprised and said, "No, Steve. He was invented to see how you would respond. In fact, we determined that Jimmy's father died three years ago."

"Thank you."

"Okay," Mr. Ed said, "I want answers to my two questions. Sam, you go first since Steve exposed your mousetrap."

"Yep, I've been exposed. A big YES to the first question, and a big NO to the second question."

Mr. Ed said, "Perhaps, we can end the Q&A right now. Does anyone disagree with Sam's answers?"

No one said anything. Most just nodded. Mr. Ed said, "Then it's a wrap."

Mr. Clark stood and said, "Ed, I'd like to make a suggestion. Steve's comment about a voice test reminds me of a speech I heard at the University of Alabama in my last year of law school. Alastair McDonald, a medical doctor at the University of Alabama Medical School in Birmingham has studied voice recognition for years and is now one of its noted specialist. In fact, he has also become a noted expert witness at criminal trials and others. I can try and contact him if you wish."

I wanted to yell, YES, but I kept my mouth shut.

Mr. Ed immediately said, "Fascinating, Clark. Yes, please call him and see if we can meet either here or in Birmingham. And now the wrap is over. Any more questions?"

Dad spoke up. "Ed, has a murder weapon been found?"

"No, Andy. I wish it had. The Delphi County coroner found three bullets in Marvin's body. The bullets do not match the bullet type used in the only rifle found in Jimmy's possessions. We found no weapons in the possession of the other two. That said, while it would be helpful if the murder weapons were found, it's not legally necessary to find it to get a conviction. Andy and Steve, there's another thing you need to know. The defense, prosecution, and the court will likely call for depositions from Steve and our other witnesses. Each side must provide the other side their prospective witness list in advance of the trial. One last chance, any more questions?"

"Uh, Ed, could I say something," Ben said.

"Sure, but keep it brief."

"Ed, when Steve was telling his story about his first meeting with Jimmy Jackson, I think we have a problem. Steve didn't know Jimmy Jackson, and he mentioned that it was Fred Watson who recognized Jimmy the night of the murders. My questions is: How did Fred know it was Jimmy? He must have met him earlier. I suggest we add Fred to our witness list in hopes that Fred can explain it. We sure don't want the defense to catch that."

"Damn, Ben, you're absolutely right. Does anyone disagree with Ben's analysis?"

Nobody responded.

"Good. Ben, you get in touch with Fred Watson and see if he can give you a rational description of how he met Jimmy. If so, we can be sure it's noted in a deposition. Now, by the powers vested in me by no one, I declare this meeting adjourned." Mr. Ed banged his hand on the table as if he had a gavel.

Everyone gathered around and shook hands and chatted. After that, Dad and I left for home. We were ready for one of Mom's great meals.

27

Dr. Alastair McDonald

Wednesday—June 22, 1949

CLARK WAS IN HIS OFFICE WONDERING about how to contact Dr. McDonald when Ruth came in and said, "Hey, Clark, I found a University of Alabama Medical School phone directory in our office files. She handed it to Clark, opening it to a page and pointing, "Here's a phone number for Dr. McDonald. I hope it works."

Clark was single, twenty-four years old, and found Ruth quite attractive. He replied, "Thank you, Ruth. Please stay if you have time. Who knows how this is going to turn out?"

"Here goes," Clark said.

"Hello."

"Am I speaking to Dr. Alastair McDonald?"

"Yes, who do I have the pleasure of speaking to?" Clark held a thumb up to Ruth. She nodded.

"Dr. McDonald, my name is Clark Hughes. I'm a lawyer in the Montgomery offices of Edward Macey, Esq. Two years ago, I heard your lecture about the work you do as an expert witness on voice recognition. It was fascinating. Do you have time to discuss it now?"

"Yes, but no more than five minutes."

"Thanks. Did you hear or read about the Night of Terror inflicted on Negroes by the Ku Klux Klan in Delphi on May twenty-fifth?"

"Yes, I'm afraid I did. It's another tragic plight on the social character of our state. I assume you may have need of my services for, as you call it, the Night of Terror?"

"Yes, sir. Mr. Macey is the lead attorney on the trial of three Klansmen for murder. It starts in a few weeks." Clark briefly described

Steve and what he claimed to have seen and heard concerning Jimmy Jackson.

"Interesting, Clark. Who is the presiding judge in this case?"

"Frank Johnson."

"I've heard of Frank. I'm told he's a fine jurist. So where do we go from here?"

"Sir, we'd like to meet with you in either Birmingham or Montgomery as soon as possible to discuss in detail what you do and how you do it."

"Clark, it so happens I will be in Montgomery on Friday for a luncheon. I could meet with you after that, but I have one stipulation. Judge Johnson and the lead prosecution and defense attorneys must be at the meeting."

"Dr. McDonald, I'll do what I can to make it happen, and then I'll call you and let you know where we are."

"I'll await your call, Clark. If I'm not available tell the person who answers the phone your message and they will get it to me wherever I am. I have to go now."

Clark held two thumbs up, as did Ruth, and they smiled at each other. Clark knew the way forward was a tough task. Judges and lead attorneys were hard to corner. They all usually had several balls in the air at once.

Clark knew he was smitten, but said simply, "Well, Ruth, we better get to work. Any ideas?"

Clark listened carefully for Ruth's response. "Well, I reckon Mr. Hughes that we've got Ed and Dr. McDonald in the bag, so which one of us should try to corral Hastings and Judge Johnson? Let me opine that Hastings wouldn't dare not come when he's told what the meeting is about because he's likely to object to voice recognition that involves his clients. Of course, Ed is obligated by law to reveal his potential witness list to Hastings, as Hastings is to us. Now, Judge Johnson certainly has an obligation to come. He's the presiding judge. If he needs a little arm twisting, I bet Ed can get Governor Folsom to provide some elbow grease. All problems solved."

Clark laughed, playing her game, saying, "Well, *kiss my britches*, I think you've described a winner, Ruth. But seriously, we need to talk to Ed."

"I'll get us an appointment right now."

Clark described to Ed the conversation with Dr. McDonald, including the stipulations to meet on Friday. But he yielded to Ruth to explain the plan. She went over it carefully with Ed, not daring to play with words as she had with Clark.

Being the newest member of the firm, Clark was concerned about what Ed might think. Had he stepped out of bounds by working with Ruth?

He was relieved to hear Ed say, "You both have done a great job. You make a good team."

"Thank you, sir," Clark said, "but you must know that Ruth came up with the plan, not me." Clark grinned at Ruth. Knowing he was a bit too eager, he liked her even more.

"Ruth," Ed said, "now I'm sure you were the right person for our agency. I also know you're the highest rated person in your paralegal class. Don't ask me how I know. That's my little secret. And I will now follow your plan with one adjustment. I will personally call Peter Hastings and Judge Johnson. I'll also call Governor Folsom and tell him what's going on. I'll let you know if we have a problem."

28

Judge Frank Johnson

Friday—June 24, 1949

JUDGE JOHNSON WAS PLEASED TO HAVE HEARD that all the necessary participants would be available on Friday afternoon, and that Dr. McDonald would be at Judge Johnson's offices by two o'clock, or there abouts.

Judge Johnson sat in his conference room, expecting Peter Hastings and Edward Macey to be in his offices at one o'clock, well before Dr. McDonald would arrive.

Judge Johnson's law clerk showed Edward Macey to the judge's chamber at exactly one o'clock. Judge Johnson stood and said, "Welcome, Mr. Macey. Please take a seat at the table." Turning to his assistant, he said, "Tony, please get me the dossier that's open on my desk. It's a mess, so organize it for me and take your time." Tony scurried off like a rabbit.

Twenty minutes passed before Tony returned with the dossier and Peter Hastings, who said, "Your Honor, I'm sorry I'm late. I was talking to one of my clients, Jimmy Jackson."

Johnson was sure Hastings was playing head games with him but decided to let it go for now. "Fine, Mr. Hastings, please take a seat."

"Gentlemen," said Judge Johnson, "we are here today to meet with an expert witness that the prosecution hopes to use in this case. His name is Dr. Alastair McDonald. I have prepared a dossier on him. It is most impressive. I'll provide both counselors with a copy, but first, I haven't received any witness list notifications from either the prosecution or defense. I'm sure you have plans to do depositions or enter exhibits with there chain of custody. And don't forget disclosures. I don't like surprises. Please get started because the tentative trial date is July twenty-seventh." The judge handed both counselors a copy of the dossier.

While Hastings and Macey were poring over the dossier, Tony came into the conference room with Dr. McDonald.

Everyone stood and Judge Johnson said, "Welcome, Dr. McDonald."

"Thank you. I came a little early. Is that all right?"

Johnson looked at Hastings, and said, "Not at all. I like a person who is early. Let me introduce Peter Hastings, the chief counsel for the defense, and Edward Macey, the chief counsel for the prosecution. The prosecution may ask Dr. McDonald to be an expert witness. Would you like to make a few comments, Dr. McDonald?"

"Yes. Before we talk about the technical details of what I do, I want to make it clear that I will be considering whether or not I want to be an expert witness in this case. Is that clear?"

"Fair enough, Dr. McDonald. I prepared a dossier on your background and credentials, which is interesting reading. I talked to a few judges and lawyers you've worked with, and they all speak highly of you. I suggest we proceed as follows: Dr. MacDonald will start by explaining the technical details of his voice recognition process. Then Mr. Macey and Mr. Hastings will ask questions and make comments. I will also do the same. Now, before we start, we'll take a brief break, so we can have a snack and a drink and chat with each about anything except this case. Tony, please have the snacks and drinks brought in, and no alcohol."

Everyone booed and laughed, as did Judge Johnson. The judge knew this would be a good ice breaker but also knew that moments like this seldom changed many minds. Johnson watched Macey and Hastings carefully as they chatted, for he knew each man was quietly studying each other trying to find a clue that might give them an edge at the trial. When the chatter died down, Judge Johnson smiled and called the meeting back to order.

Once everyone was in their seats and settling down, Judge Johnson looked around the room, waiting for the idle chit-chat to stop. "Gentlemen, Dr. McDonald has the floor."

Dr. McDonald stood. "To start, I'd like to explain the brief history of voice recognition. It's brief because the first device to replace personal human conversations with a one-on-one device was Alexander Graham Bell's invention of the telephone in 1876. However, another engineer named Elisha Gray claimed to have invented a similar device earlier. That dispute aside, why is this history important? Let me explain with an example. Suppose Peter had a friend name Frank and called him on the phone. But when Frank's phone was answered, Peter didn't recognize his friend's voice, so Peter said, 'I must have the wrong number.' The voice responds, 'You have the right number. My name is Edward. I'll get Peter.' As a voice recognition—."

Frank, Peter, and Edward laughed, knowing they were the butt of McDonald's joke.

McDonald smiled at them, continuing, "As a voice recognition expert, I wonder how likely Peter is to recognize Edward's voice if he should answer Frank's phone again. Current theory and experts have concluded that it is highly unlikely. As convoluted as this example is, it's at the heart of my voice recognition test. Now I'm sure all of you would like to know how my test works, but I can't tell you for several reasons."

Hastings straightened his back and spoke up. "I'll object to Dr. McDonald as an expert witness without knowing more about his test."

Judge Johnson said, "Mr. Hastings, you'll have your chance for questions and comments, but I do take your point. Please continue, Dr. McDonald."

"Thank you. When I've work with different courts, the issue of my test is always the sticky wicket. It's not that my test is private or has a legal patent, the very essence of the test if revealed would give the prosecution and defense the opportunity to prepare their witnesses and strategies in a way that might make the test moot. My test does not favor either the prosecution or defense. In fact, I would prefer that I worked at the pleasure of the court...that is the presiding judge. Even though I was contacted by the prosecution, if I agree to be an expert witness, my test will be unbiased. The test on the subject witness will be done in a soundproof room in my Birmingham office. Mr. Macey, Mr. Hastings, Judge Johnson or their representatives may observe the test through a one-way window but will not be able to hear what is happening in the room. The person being tested won't be able to see the observers or hear them speak."

Turning to Judge Johnson, McDonald asked, "Your Honor, are my comments clear and understood?"

"Quite clear, Doctor. Please continue."

"Thank you. One last point and then I'll sit down. As I'm sure you all know, the person who is likely to take the test is a fourteen-year-old boy named Steve Thompson. Young people are always a risk as a witness. I've seen them start crying when experiencing a tough cross-examination, although many do hold up admirably. Which is Steve? I can't say, but my test requires patience, stamina, and insight to perform correctly. The test is scored in a way that requires analysis as to final meaning. I guess this is where I say I yield the floor back to Judge Johnson."

"Thank you, Dr. McDonald for the excellent summary of the work you do." Judge Johnson knew he was handling the discussions as if they were in a courtroom, but since these men were used to that environment, he thought it appropriate. The judge said, "Mr. Macey, you have the floor"

"Thank you, Your Honor. Dr. McDonald, if I understand you correctly, you're saying or implying that most witnesses fail your test. I assume that means that they fail to identify the voice in question. Is that correct?"

"Yes, to a point. Perhaps I wasn't clear in my last comments. The test scores are scaled, so *fail* is too strong a word for how most perform the test. Failure, to me, means a person who was unable to complete any part of the test correctly."

"That being the case, how do think Steve Thompson would do on the test?"

"Steve would be a new case, and therefore, I wouldn't want to prejudge the outcome."

"However, in a sense, you want to hedge your bets."

McDonald laughed and said, "If you want to use that metaphor, I don't object. But I would remind you that current theory would predict that Steve could not recognize the voice in a difficult test."

"I see," said Macey, "I'd like everyone here today to know that Steve and his parents have agreed that he will be a witness. That's all, Judge Johnson."

"Are you ready, Mr. Hastings?"

"Your Honor, could we have a fifteen minute break? I'm expecting important papers to arrive soon."

"Of course, I think we all need to get up and walk around a bit. Tony, please check the lobby and bring Mr. Hastings his papers as soon as they get here."

Exactly fifteen minutes later, Tony burst into the conference room and handed Mr. Hastings his papers.

Judge Johnson grinned and said, "Quite a dramatic entrance, Tony. Thank you. Now, gentlemen, the meeting is called to order. Mr. Hastings, do you want to discuss your papers?"

"Yes, Your Honor, I've had a few of my associates calling Alabama judges and others who may have worked with or knew of Dr. McDonald. I'd like their comments added to your dossier."

"Mr Hastings, I wrote the dossier so I could somewhat familiarize myself with Dr. McDonald. If you read the dossier carefully, you'll see names from judges and lawyers as far flung as New York and California. But you should consider it a paper, to use your word, that you and Mr. Macey can use as you see fit. It's like all the papers that lawyers prepare to help them plan trial strategy. Also, if I add the names and comments of the people you contacted, I would have to afford Mr. Macey the same opportunity. Would you like to add names Mr. Macey?"

"Absolutely not, Your Honor."

"Sorry, Mr. Hastings, the rules of fair play apply here. So, counselors, please submit your witness list and subpoenas to each other and the court as soon as possible. The clock is ticking. Am I clear?"

Mr. Hastings rubbed his eye as if something was in it, or perhaps it was his annoyance with the judge. "Yes, Your Honor."

"Mr. Macey?"

"Yes, Your Honor."

"Thank you. Mr. Hastings are you ready to question Dr. McDonald?"

Hastings did not respond to the judge. "Dr. McDonald, just a few questions. You've been quite circumspect about the details of your voice recognition test. Why?"

"If you require me to describe the precise details of my test's construction and application, we may as well stop right now. The test would be useless, and I would decline to serve as an expert witness in this case."

Hastings appeared to squirm, but continued, "Dr. McDonald, I'm not suggesting you need to tell us everything about the test, but I have to be confident it will be fair and not favor either party. Can you assure me that it does?"

"I will tell you this. The test can be conducted in several different ways depending on the case at hand. Generally, the test is graded on five levels: 0%, 20%, 40% and 100%, that is the subject failed every aspect of the test at 0% or the subject completed every aspect of the test at 100%. I also want to make a few comments about being an expert witness. That person has proven by their education, knowledge, and accomplishments to be an expert in their field. For example, psychologists, bankers, engineers, and doctors have been expert witnesses. I'm sure no one in this room, including myself, has more than an inkling of how these experts perform their work. Finally, my understanding is that an expert witness does not have to be approved by all parties in a case,"

Hastings still looked unconvinced. He said, "Dr. McDonald, a fascinating reply to my question. I think you would like to be involved in this case. Am I right?"

Dr. McDonald appeared weary. "Yes. But, as I said before, I will not prejudge the outcome of any case I take."

"I see. One last question. How many people have scored 100% on your test?"

"None, but scores of 80% are common. Of course, it's up to the counselors to convince the jury to vote on their behalf."

Everyone in the conference room, including Tony, sat up in their chairs and appeared startled.

Judge Johnson finally said, "Is that all, Mr. Hastings?"

Hastings appeared to savor the moment. "Yes, Your Honor."

"Gentlemen, we'll take a ten minute break, and then do a wrap.

As the men sat down at the conference table, they were still digesting what had just happened, as it had appeared that Hastings had won the day.

Judge Johnson opened the meeting by saying, "Gentlemen, since the primary purpose of this meeting was to meet Dr. McDonald and to learn more about his voice recognition test, it appears we have come some way in that regard. Our discussion has certainly had its twist and turns. Without repeating the prior discussions, I'd like each of you to state your position on accepting him as an expert witness. Mr. Hastings, please go first."

"Your Honor, I feel like I've been treated as the bad boy in the class. I will accept the doctor only if Steve Thompson's test results are 100%."

"Thank you, Mr. Hastings. Mr Macey, you are next."

"The prosecution accepts Dr. McDonald as our expert witness with no conditions attached."

"Thank you, Mr. Macey. Dr. McDonald, any comments?"

"Your Honor, I called a friend in Delphi yesterday. He speaks very highly of Steve and his parents. He asked that I not reveal his name. I suspect he's concerned about backlash from some people in Delphi. He did recommend a name I can reveal. It's the chief librarian at the Delphi Library, Kathryn Davis. I called her and she couldn't stop talking about Steve and his achievements. I'd sensed those qualities about him based on what Mr. Macey and others have said. So, yes, I would like to be the expert witness, if for no other reason than Steve deserves his day in the witness chair for what he has done."

"Thank you, Dr. McDonald, and the court accepts you. Mr. Hastings, perhaps like your English forebearers at said battle, I don't consider you the bad boy in this group. In fact, you are doing your job as the defense's chief counselor very well. I respect that. Of course, in the courtroom, you must defend your clients as you see fit, including objections to the expert witness. However, if you wish, the court will accept you as agreeing to Dr. McDonald as an expert witness, even with your 100% condition. Do you agree, Mr. Hastings?"

Mr. Hastings smiled at the judge and said, "Yes."

"Thank you. I'll have the court clerk see that the agreement gets into the Court's records. Any more comments?"

No one spoke, and the judge said, "Hearing none, the meeting is concluded. Hopefully, I'll see you in the courtroom on July twenty-seventh."

29

Prosecution Preparations

Monday—June 27, 1949

ED MACEY CAME TO WORK EARLY. He leaned back and put his feet on the desk, thinking about the tasks that had to be completed quickly, before the trial started—exactly one month from today. After several minutes of pondering, he opened the office door and asked Ruth into his office. "Please have a seat. I want to compliment you again for how well you worked with Clark. Now we have quite a lot to do in the next few days."

"Thank you, sir. What would you like me to do?"

"Gather Clark, Sam, and the junior attorneys in the conference ASAP."

"Yes, sir, will do." She started to go but turned back, her face showing worry. "If you don't mind, I'd like to tell you a concen I have about the trial."

Ed smiled and felt certain she would introduce something pertinent to the case. "Yes, what's your concern?"

"Sir, I may be out of line, but I think Mr. Hastings will early in his cross-examination of Steve ask him, 'Steve, how does the court know for sure you were in Westtown on the night of May 25, 1949? Did anyone other than Marvin see you in Westtown?' Sir, if no one else saw Steve, we might be in a big pickle."

Ed rubbed his cheek, knowing he had also thought of this possibility. He decided not to mention this to Ruth and said, "An excellent point. At the meeting, let's see what concerns the attorneys have, including the new boys, the three stoogies." Ed laughed at his own joke.

Ruth winced and said, "I assume you mean Garth, Oscar, and Ben."

"Yes. Sorry, Ruth, attorneys are notorious for ribbing one another. Some call me *The Hatchet Man*. It's all in good fun."

"Yes, sir. Anything else before I find the attorneys?"

"Nope, please round them up."

Ed, Clark, Sam, and the three new attorneys sat around the conference room table. Ruth sat next to Ed to take notes on assignments and other decisions.

Eyeing everyone at the table, Ed said, "Gentlemen and Ruth, we need to be sure we have all our bases covered before the trial. Like we did last week, we must always look for holes in our preparation. Ben has talked to Fred Watson and found his explanation quite plausible. Clark and Oscar will take care of subpoenas. Sam and Ben will work on our depositions. Garth and I will work on the defense's depositions. Again, I want all of us to constantly think about this question: What are we missing? Let's start. Sam, you go first."

"Ed, Ben and I have been keeping an eye on the defense witness list that has been disclosed to us, and looking for as much information about these people as possible. A new name, Rodger Dalton, has just popped up. The only thing we've found so far is that he is a registered voter in the county. We'll keep at it."

"Good, Sam. Clark you're next."

Clark, paused, as if he were perplexed. He said, "I started working on subpoenas yesterday. I'll show them to Oscar after the meeting. I can't think of anything else right now."

Ed listened to the other responses, finding them all wanting except Sam's. "Gentlemen, you all need to screw on your brains tighter. Let me give you an example. Ruth asked me a simple question just before this meeting: Do we have a response if Mr Hastings should ask Steve if he can prove he was in Westtown the Night of Terror?"

Ed had never seen his five attorneys so quiet and downtrodden. He knew he had to bolster their spirits. "Listen, we are a team and we will persevere in moments like this. I'm not trying to put Ruth on a pedestal. In fact, I glanced at Ruth when I mentioned her question.

She was blushing with her head down. Let's all consider this a learning experience. Does anybody know a good joke?"

Clark spoke, "I thank Ruth for the question. She's a smart cookie."

When everybody laughed, including Ruth, Ed said, "Well, *cookie* qualifies as a joke. But tell you what we're going to do. Ruth, please see if you can get Mr. Thompson or Steve on the phone. If you make contact, we can use this new fangled speaker so everyone in the room can hear what they say."

Ruth called the Thompson residence from the conference room, and in short order had Mr. Thompson and Steve on the phone. She handed the phone to Ed, and then hooked up the new *fangled* speaker.

Ed took the phone and said, "Good morning, Andy and Steve. It's Ed Macey. Can you hear me okay?"

"Loud and clear, Ed," Andy said.

"Andy and Steve, we are using a new fangled speaker in our conference room, so everyone here can hear what you say. I have with me Sam, Clark, Ruth, Oscar, Garth, and Ben, all of whom you have met."

"Ed, since we can only hear you, we'd like to say hello to everyone," Andy said. Steve added, "This is Steve. Hello everyone."

"Andy and Steve, we're calling this morning because of a question Ruth asked this morning. What if Mr. Hastings asked Steve in the witness chair if he could prove he was at Westtown the night of May 25, 1949? Another way to put it is: Andy, did either you or Steve see anyone that might have recognized Steve, other than Marvin and the hooded Klan members?"

"Ed, let me and Steve talk about it for a bit. We'll talk in our living room and be back soon."

"That's fine. We'll be waiting."

After about five minutes, the group heard Andy say, "I think we have an answer. I'll let Steve explain it."

"Hi, Mr. Ed," Steve said. "After Dad and I talked things through, I realized who could prove I was there. I don't know why I didn't remember when you interviewed me."

Ed interrupted Steve, "Don't beat yourself up over this, Steve. Many witnesses forget important details, especially in a case as complicated as this. Take your time. We aren't in a hurry."

"Yes, sir, Mr. Ed. Last Tuesday, I told you about going to Marvin's house when the two of us left to check if Moses and Joshua were okay. What I forgot to say was that Marvin's mother, Mrs. Mabel Gibbs, heard us and came into the room where we were. Marvin thought his parents were sleeping. Miss Mabel asked what we were up to. When Marvin told her, she told him to stay home because he might be killed. Then she asked me why I wasn't home like she had told me to do yesterday. Marvin defied his mother and pulled me out the back door and slammed it shut right in front of his mother. I think everything else I have told you is correct."

Ed sat quietly in his chair, as did the others in the conference room. As he observed Ruth wiping away tears, he finally said, "Thank you, Steve, you're a brave lad."

"No, sir, I'm a coward. Marvin was the brave lad."

"Well, let that be for the moment. I'm glad Marvin's mother saw you that night. The question is: Will she agree to testify at the trial? Any comments Steve or Andy?"

"Ed," Andy said, "as a Negro woman, Mrs. Gibbs would likely be in the cross-hairs of the Klan in Delphi and beyond. And to put her on the witness stand, it's hard to imagine the racist questions Mr. Hastings might ask her. Could the woman stand the barrage of questions without crumbling before our eyes as she relives Marvin's last day?"

"Mr. Ed," Steve said, "I love Miss Mabel. I don't want to see her get hurt, and I agree with Dad."

Ed knew Andy and Steve's concerns were valid. Tapping his pencil on the table, he thought over how to respond to them. Thinking as he answered them, he said, "You Thompson boys are quite a pair. I know you're both aware of how important the voice recognition test is. Dr. Alastair McDonald is our expert witness who will conduct the test. I also have a new idea to propose. Andy and Steve, can you visit Mrs. Gibbs at her house and ask her to be a witness on our behalf?"

"Ed, Steve and I need to talk alone. We'll be back shortly."

In less than two minutes, Andy said, "As you called us, the two Thompson boys will do it as soon as possible. Hopefully today or tomorrow."

Before Ed could respond, Clark said, "Ed, I'd like to help. Perhaps Mrs. Gibbs might have some legal questions."

"Good idea, but no subpoena yet, Clark. What do you think Andy and Steve?"

"Sure," Andy said, "I agree and Steve is nodding yes. We'll try to give Clark a heads up on the time of any meeting an hour before it takes place."

Ed was beaming since today was going better than he could have imagined. "Well, we've made some progress. Before we finish, do any of my staff have a question or a comment? Hearing none, I declare this meeting over, so Andy, Steve, and Clark can get to work setting up a meeting with Mrs. Gibbs."

30

Defense Preparations

Monday—June 27, 1949

Peter Hastings was ready to conclude a meeting with his staff. They were making trial preparations and he asked once again, "Gentlemen, any additional comments or questions?"

Hastings' number two attorney, Carter, said, "Peter, I added Rodger Dalton to the witness list. I'm sure the prosecution will depose him. He's got a checkered past. How do you think he'll handle cross-examination?"

"Carter, Rodger is a good friend, and I'm sure he'll do fine."

"Hate to be pushy, but what if the deposition reveals that Rodger is your friend?"

"Carter, let go of it. I'll take care of Rodger. Now, you and I have to go to the jail and keep our defendants in line."

A jailer led Hastings and Carter to a private room where they could talk to the three defendants alone. The room was standard jail gray with one door and one small window just below the ceiling. Another jailer led Jimmy Jackson, Bubba Smith, and Willie Warden into the room. As the jailers left, one said, "Mr. Hastings, if you need anything, knock on the door."

Hastings said, "Thanks. Good morning, gentlemen. Please be seated. Are the jailers treating you all right?"

Jimmy Jackson leaned back in his chair and grinned. "I reckon we can't complain. A couple of jailers even said they know we won't be found guilty because you're the best damn lawyer in Alabama."

"Well, that's reassuring, Jimmy. But what we have to discuss today are the ways to make sure that happens."

"What kinda things?" Jimmy asked.

Hastings smiled, having come to learn that Jimmy was the absolute leader of this three guy pack. "We're in a critical period of our preparations for the trial."

"I thought everything was ready. You said we wouldn't be found guilty." Jimmy said.

Hastings was getting annoyed. "Jimmy, a wise man always plans for things that can go amiss."

Willie elbowed Jimmy in the ribs. "Let Mr. Hastings tell us what his plans are."

Jimmy stared at Willie as if he had committed a sin, but said nothing.

"Thank you, Willie," Hastings said. "Let's look to literature as an example of what I'd like you three to be and how I'd like you to act. Have any of you heard of a book titled *The Three Musketeers*?"

The three defendants looked at each other with dismay.

Bubba said, "Mr. Hastings, we ain't very good students."

"That's not important. I know you're good guys because you believe in the Klan way. I'll explain why the book is important. It was written by a Frenchman many years ago, and his three main characters were part of an elite group of swordsmen who could fight better than any other group. And they were like you three, they fought the oppressors of the day, so they could help those who needed it. Their slogan was *All for one, and one for all*. That's how I want you three to think of yourselves. Do you think you can do that?"

"I reckon so, Mr. Hastings," Jimmy said. "I like knowing how the three French guys acted, but who was considered the leader?"

Hastings shook his head. "Jimmy, if you must know, it was a guy named Athos."

"Then I'm Athos," Jimmy said.

"Okay, but keep in mind *All for one, and one for all*. Willie, what do you think?"

Willie shrugged. "I reckon I've always considered Jimmy our leader. I ain't gonna call him Athos, but I might call him Asshole."

Hastings and the defendants laughed.

"Bubba, what do you think?" Hastings asked.

Bubba squirmed and said, "Jimmy's okay. I don't care what he's called. But I'll tell you one thing for sure, I don't want to fry in that electric chair at Kilby Prison 'cause I didn't kill nobody."

At that moment, Hastings realized that Bubba was the weak link in the chain, and he said calmly, "Of course, you're not going to die in the electric chair. You plead not guilty as did Jimmy and Willie."

"But Mr. Hastings," Bubba said, "what if the jury finds us guilty. I really didn't kill nobody that night."

Hastings rubbed his neck as if it hurt. "Bubba, it's my job to see that the jury doesn't bring in a guilty verdict. I'll tell you straight that even though you claim you didn't kill anybody that night, you aided and abetted a crime and are, therefore, complicit in the act of murder. But Bubba that's not going to happen. We'll enter an appeal and take it all the way to the United States Supreme Court if necessary. So Bubba, please calm down and work with Jimmy and Willie and Carter and me. Remember it's *All for one, and one for all.* Do you feel any better, Bubba?"

"Yes, sir, I reckon I do."

"Good, and all of you remember that defendants are considered innocent when the trial starts. The prosecution has to convince the jury beyond a reasonable doubt that you are guilty. That's a big order for the prosecution to pull off."

Hastings and Carter, continued telling the defendants some of the details of the defense's trial strategies in hopes that the three men would calm down and trust them.

"I think that's all fellas. We'll come to see you again shortly to tell you about any further developments. Thanks for your attention and help. We know it's tough being in jail, but hopefully you'll be out of here soon."

Carter knocked on the door and told the jailers that their meeting was over. One of the jailers escorted Jimmy, Willie, and Bubba back to their cells.

As Hastings and Carter were being escorted to the jail exit, another jailer said, "I sure hope you get those three boys off, but I'm sure you will because people call you the Klan's lawyer."

"Well, thank you. Don't worry, we'll do everything we can to make that happen."

Out on the street Hastings said, "Damn it Carter, I wish I had never been labeled the Klan's lawyer. It's more of a liability than an asset. Oh well, back to the office. We've got a lot of work to do. I need to give you an additional assignment. I want you to become Bubba's buddy. Visit him often and treat him as if you were his big brother. We can't let him create a problem. He's skittish as hell right now. I'll get in touch with Rodger Dalton. He may become a more important witness because of Bubba."

31

Mrs. Gibbs' Dilemma

Monday—June 27, 1949

DAD AND I WERE WAITING FOR MR. CLARK to arrive. Dad had been able to get in touch with Miss Mabel right after Mr. Ed's meeting broke up. I sat in the living room twiddling my thumbs as I thought about everything that had just happened. I tried to be positive about the voice recognition test with Dr. McDonald, but what if I flunked it and we lost the case? And are we asking too much of Miss Mabel? She's already lost her son. While I was still worrying about everything, the door bell rang.

Dad opened the door. "Welcome, Clark. You got here faster than I thought you would."

"Never late for an important appointment, Andy."

When Clark saw me, he said, "Hey, Steve, how is the star of our show?"

I decided to tell a little white lie and said, "I'm doing fine, Mr. Clark."

"We better get going," Dad said, "I told Mrs. Gibbs we'd be there at three. I think she's anxious to see us."

As Dad drove us toward Westtown, I got a case of the willies. I hadn't been there since all the funerals in May. I hoped I wouldn't come unhinged. When we got to Miss Mabel's house, she invited us in and tapped me on the head. "Steve, I got some good fried chicken for you to eat, and you can take what you don't eat home. Your dad told me you will testify at the trial. God bless you, Steve. So, how you been doing?"

I was stunned. My head was twirling back in time when Miss Mabel had said the same thing to me about fried chicken. How can she be so kind after I was the one that led Marvin to his death? I took a deep breath and replied, "Thank you, Miss Mabel, and I be doin' fine."

"Hey, Mr. Andy. I haven't seen you in a long time."

"Time flies, Mrs. Gibbs, and thanks for meeting with us so soon."

"And you must be Mr. Clark Hughes. Welcome." Miss Mabel offered her hand and Mr. Clark shook it. I thought that she eyed him suspiciously, but maybe not. *Hell, what do I know?*

"Thank you, Mrs. Gibbs. It's a pleasure to meet you."

Miss Mabel said, "Likewise. We can all sit around the big table in the kitchen. Anybody want sweet tea?"

I raised my hand, Dad and Clark followed.

Is this going to be a tea party? I thought.

Miss Mabel served the tea, and said, "Well, Mr. Andy told me what y'all wanted to talk about. I get it you want me to be a witness at the trial of the three Klan guys who kilt my son. But, maybe Mr. Clark can explain all the legal mumbo-jumbo I don't know nothin' about."

"I'll be glad to Mrs. Gibbs. Steve worked hard to jog his memory, and he finally remembered that he's sure you were the only person who saw him in West—"

"You mean to tell me, Mr. Hughes, that none of them Klan members saw Steve?"

Mr. Clark looked distressed but tried to put on a good face. "No ma'am, I didn't mean to imply that. Of course, some Klan members saw Steve, including the three men charged with murdering Marvin."

"I'm glad you see it my way. What else is important?"

Whew, Miss Mabel and Mr. Clark are having some basketball game, taking long shots at the hoop. I think Miss Mabel is making the best shots.

Mr. Clark said, "The process to become a witness has a number of steps. A subpoena is issued, which is a legal order requiring you to testify on behalf of the prosecution. Mr. Edward Macey, the head of the prosecution team, would decide when you'd be called into the courtroom as a witness. Before you testify, you'd wait in a room with other potential witnesses. You can't talk to anyone about the—"

I could see that Miss Mabel was about to blast off, and right then she snapped, "Stop right there, Mr. Hughes. If I get your drift, I'm legally required to testify even if I don't want to."

Oh my goodness, Miss Mabel just made a slam dunk right over Mr. Clark's outstretched arm.

Mr. Clark said, "Uh, no ma'am, we would never force you to testify. We'd withdraw the subpoena."

She paused and then said, "I reckon that's okay, but I feel the evil eye is comin'. If I testify it'll go away, but if I don't, the evil eye will tell everybody I'm a bad woman."

I saw Mr. Zeke, Marvin's father, standing in the door frame of the kitchen. Miss Mabel looked up and saw him. Mr. Zeke was tall, stood erect, and looked like a boxer. *I bet he could whip everyone in the room with one hand tied behind him.*

He finally roared in a deep-throated voice, "Mabel, who are these white men? What's goin' on?"

Looks like the tea party is over.

Miss Mabel responded, "Zeke, Mr. Andy Thompson talked to me this morning after you went to work at the quarry. You know Mr. Andy. He owns the Delphi newspaper. And you know Steve. He and Marvin were good friends. The other man's named Mr. Clark Hughes. He's a lawyer that's working on the case about Marvin's killers."

Mr. Zeke nodded at Dad and me, and then said, "Mabel, sure I know Mr. Andy and Steve. I like them. Steve's a good boy. But what's the lawyer doin' here? Are we in trouble?"

Miss Mabel explained to Zeke what the lawyer wanted her to do.

After she finished, Mr. Zeke looked angry, instead he said in quiet voice, "Mabel, you must be crazy. If you're a witness, every Klan guy in Alabama will want to be the one to lynch us. You want that to happen?"

Miss Mabel stood up and said, "Zeke Gibbs, Steve Thompson is sticking his neck out for us. He's gonna testify and try to prove Jimmy Jackson and the other two get convicted. You don't believe me, you ask Steve and his daddy. Now, I'm gonna tell you what I want to do and I need your blessings, Zeke I want to testify. I ain't scared. I owe it to Marvin. Yes, he was our only living son and we all still grieving but that's no reason not to stick our necks out."

Miss Mabel sat down. For sure, she was the bravest person in the room.

Out of the corner of my eye, I saw Mr. Zeke walk slowly toward Miss Mabel. Everyone in the room was so quiet, you could hear a pin drop.

He pulled her up and hugged her, and mumbled, "Mabel, I'll help anyway I can. I love you. I miss Walter and Marvin so much. How could God take our two boys? It hurts, Mabel. It hurts so awful."

He started crying and couldn't stop.

Miss Mabel put her arms around Mr. Zeke and said, "I know, honey. God ain't never fair to colored people. But we gonna be all right. I love you, too."

Everyone was quiet and some were in tears, when Dad said, "I suggest we take a break before continuing."

We got up and started moving around, saying little.

I tugged on Dad's sleeve and asked in a quiet voice, "Who is Walter?"

"Steve, let's go outside.'"

On the front porch Dad said, "Walter was Marvin's older brother. He was three years older than Marvin. He died of a bad case of the flu when he was two years old."

"But I thought the big flu pandemic was over."

"It is, Steve. But we have flu with us every year. Some years are worse than others. Everyone was distraught when it happened."

"How come I haven't heard about it?"

"After a short period of mourning, Mabel and Zeke asked everyone to stop talking about Walter's death. We've certainly honored their request."

"Did Marvin know?"

"I'm not sure, but please don't ask Mabel or Zeke that question."

I finally understood and said, "Yes, Dad."

Before the meeting resumed, I was trying to put two and two together about other things. There were so many ups and downs today, I was still confused. After Miss Mabel and Mr. Zeke calmed down, the meeting began. Everyone was polite and nobody raised their voice. Miss Mabel asked Mr. Clark to explain again what she had to do. I could tell that Mr. Clark appeared happy to be off the hot seat. She even smiled when he told her the subpoena would be served to her by hand tomorrow. He told her more about how the process worked in the witness room. I probably missed something, but Miss Mabel didn't object. When he told her about how depositions work, and that both the prosecution and defense have the right to ask her to do a separate deposition, she got a bit testy. Mr. Clark made it clear that both the prosecution and defense would have lawyers in the room during a deposition. This satisfied her, but she made it clear that she knew that Mr. Hastings was the Klan's favorite lawyer.

Then she said, "I think that's enough. Y'all can go home. And Steve don't forget your fried chicken, and you tell your Mama hello for me."

We got home and Mr. Clark left, after thanking mother for the dinner invitation. Then Dad and I sat down with Mom for another one of her good dinners.

Dad explained the main points of the meeting, including Walter.

Mom thanked Dad, and said to me, "Steve, I'm sorry you had to hear about Walter that way, but we had to honor the Gibbs' request."

"I agree, but one thing bothers me. I know it's not as important as Walter, but it seemed strange that Mr. Zeke went from being a tough guy who thought Miss Mabel was crazy to being a nice guy who couldn't stop crying."

"Steve, as usual your inquisitive mind wants to understand things. I think I can explain Mr. Zeke's change," Dad said. "He works in a quarry north of Montgomery that contains valuable granite marble. A lot of the granite has been shipped to Washington D.C. for years and used in the construction of many of the government buildings in the city. I visited the quarry years ago and wrote an article for the newspaper. It's a tough place to work. The Negro men who worked there are supervised by white men who drive the men hard. Kinda like the paper mill near Delphi. The men have to develop a hard outer shell of toughness just to survive day to day, like Mr. Zeke probably did. And inevitably, the men take that hard shell home with them, as I suspect we saw when Mr. Zeke came home today to a big surprise. I would think most people would be surprised, if not angry."

I nodded, figuring Dad had it right. But then Mom said, "Steve, I have another thought about Mr. Zeke's behavior. Andy, I agree with what you said about Mr. Zeke's experiences in the quarry. But that doesn't explain his almost instance change. I think he was embarrassed because his male ego had met his match. Do I think he was playing a game? No, but he certainly had to regain a higher ground, and he did. And remember the agony he displayed when he talked about the loss of both Walter and Marvin. Ego aside, he was their father."

Mom stopped talking, smiled, and then said as she often does, "Well, I've got a cherry pie ready to come out of the oven. Who wants a piece?"

As I lay in bed, my mind kept spinning around about today. Mom and Dad are real smart. They both made good points, and they didn't get mad or criticize each other. I couldn't help thinking, *I wonder if I'll be like them when I get older.* I rolled over, and started crying as I thought about Walter and Marvin.

32

Depositions

Wednesday—June 29, 1949

DAD AND MOM DROVE ME TO MONTGOMERY this morning for my deposition. We knew Miss Mabel was coming for hers this afternoon. Mr. Ed had said the prosecution and defense had agreed to swap chairs midway through the process, so that both men would have a chance to be the lead deposer. Mr. Ed also called Governor Folsom and told him things were moving along well, which the governor was glad to hear.

Mr. Clark came back to Delphi yesterday to coach Miss Mabel and me separately about what to expect. Assuming Mr. Clark coached us both the same way, neither of us can talk about the trial with anyone until after it's over. We must respond to questions by listening to them carefully, thinking about an answer, and then answering in as few words as possible. Mr. Clark added that too many people want to blab on and on and they often reveal things they maybe shouldn't. He also said that both sides might not ask the tough questions at the deposition because they're keeping their chips close to the vest for courtroom cross-examinations. I figured that's a ploy to keep people on their toes.

When I went into the deposition room, Mr. Macey was already there. Mr. Hastings came in soon and closed the door. They smiled at each other, and that's all I can talk about.

Afterward, Dad knew better than to ask me how it went, but he put his arm around my shoulders and quietly said, "I'll bet you did well and don't mind keeping everything a secret."

I was amazed. It was as if Dad had read my mind. I could think of only one thing to say, "You would've been bored if you were in the room."

Dad smiled with his all knowing glance. "Yes, I'm sure I would have been." He winked, knowing what I said was BS. "C'mon, Mom's waiting for us in the cafeteria."

After we had a bite to eat, we were walking by the door to the deposition room when Miss Mabel walked by.

She smiled at me and said, "Hey, Steve."

I replied, "Hey, Miss Mabel," as she entered the room.

How can she be so cheery after last Monday?

"Time to go home, Steve," Mom said. "It's been a busy day."

We were walking to the elevator, when I noticed Mr. Clark running toward us. "I'm glad I found you before you left. I just got a call from Dr. McDonald. He wants to do his voice recognition test with Steve on Friday at one o'clock at his Birmingham office. He calls the test room his soundless chamber, whatever the hell that means. Andy, can you drive Steve there?"

My ears perked up at soundless chamber.

This could be like an Edgar Allan Poe story.

"Of course," Dad said, "and as a newspaper man, I'm always looking for good stories and everything associated with this trial is rich fodder for news. In fact, I've already published several articles about it."

Mr. Clark said, "I think I've read them all, Andy. They were good…contained no leaks of confidential information. Please keep it that way."

I could smell Dad's *woe is me* speech coming.

"Oh, woe is me that you should think I would violate basic publishing principles. Clark, have you no mercy?"

Mom and I looked at one another, knowing that this was one of Dad's favorite routines.

Mr. Clark smiled and said, "Very Shakespearean, Andy. Any more questions?"

"Yes, will anyone else be there?"

"Dr. McDonald said the prosecution and defense can have one observer each. On our side, it'll be either Ed or me. I assume Hastings will be the defense observer."

"Clark, does Steve have to do anything special to be prepared for the test?"

"Nope. He just needs to be there. Of course, we hope he aces the test."

Oops, I wished that Mr. Clark hadn't said that. I do love a mystery, but I was really worried that I'd screw it up.

"Clark, we need to go now. But don't worry, Steve and I will be in Birmingham on Friday at one o'clock sharp"

As we drove home, Mom said, "Steve you seem unusually quiet. Anything bothering you?"

I wanted to say no, but I knew Mom wouldn't take no for an answer. "I didn't like it when Mr. Clark said I had to ace the test."

"I agree," Mom said, "I though that was imprudent of Clark. You just have to ignore him. I'm sure you'll do well."

Dad chimed in, "Steve, I agree with Mom. And remember how you felt after your deposition. You didn't want to admit it, but I'm sure you did well."

"Thanks, Mom and Dad," I said. *But parents,* I thought, *just don't know how tough it is to be a kid.* I remained quiet for the rest of the ride home.

Mom broke the ice with her usual food speech when she said, "We're almost home. I can't wait to fix supper for my boys."

33

Voice Recognition Test

Friday—July 1, 1949

As Dad drove me to Birmingham for the voice recognition test, I felt like I was going to another world because I had no idea how this worked. I had never met Dr. McDonald and his soundless chamber. I had been to Birmingham a few times. Once, when I was seven or eight, I climbed the stairs to the top of the statue of Vulcan that looked over the valley below where the main part of the city was located.

Dad was lucky—he found a parking place near the University of Alabama Medical School. It was a huge building. We entered the lobby, and asked the receptionist where Dr. McDonald's office was.

"What are your names, please?"

"I'm Andy Thompson and this is my son, Steve Thompson. Dr. McDonald is expecting us."

"Thank you. I'll call his office." When the call was answered, she repeated our names, waited a minute, and said, "I'll tell them."

I tried to listen to what had been said on the other end, but I couldn't hear anything. The receptionist said, "One of Dr. McDonald's assistants is on her way down and will escort you to his offices."

Sure enough, a lady got off the elevator and walked up to us. "Good afternoon. Thanks for being here a little ahead of time. My name's Sue Wells. Please follow me."

We got on the elevator and I asked, "Miss Sue, how many stories on this building?"

"It's a mystery, Steve. Some say fourteen, others say nineteen. It's probably between those two numbers. We're going to the tenth floor."

The elevator stopped and when we got off a man was waiting, and Miss Sue said, "Mr. Thompson, meet Caleb. He will show you to the room where you will wait while the test is conducted. And Steve, follow me to where the test will be conducted."

As we walked in opposite direction, Dad looked back at me and said, "See you later, Steve. Knock 'em dead."

I started to feel like this might not be too bad. *Hell, I like all the mysterious things going on around here.*

"Here we are, Steve. Welcome to the soundless chamber, more technically it's called a soundproof room. Have a seat and I'll wait with you until Dr. McDonald joins."

Miss Sue was sweet. It's tough to size people up, especially older people. I think she was in her forties. Brunette, slightly graying hair, attractive I think. Then, just as I was about to ask her a question, the door opened and a man walked in.

"Hi Steve, I'm Dr. McDonald. Sue, thanks for taking care of Steve."

She got up and walked toward the door. "Steve, I enjoyed helping you. Don't let Dr. McDonald push you around."

Both Miss Sue and the doctor laughed. I was glad they could joke with each other.

"Welcome, Steve. How do you feel today? Are you afraid?"

"Not afraid. Curious."

"Hmm, about what?"

"I've never met you until now. I don't know a thing about what you do. Nobody has told me anything. I don't know if it will hurt or not. I feel like I've been put in a soundproof room and left alone. How long will the test take?"

"Steve, it depends on you, but it usually takes only an hour. I know you and I are going to get along fine. It's rare for me to work with someone your age that is so articulate."

"Are you going to tell me how your test works?"

"No. That would negate the results, and the court would dismiss it. It has to be accomplished by my asking direct questions to you during the test. It will not hurt even one iota. But one other very important thing, you cannot tell anyone about it, even your parents. If you do, the court would dismiss the results. Any more questions?"

"Yes, how does this room work?"

Dr. McDonald laughed. "It's quite simply. The room is heavily insulated on every surface—the four walls, the ceiling, and the floor—to keep out any surrounding noise. If you look at the back wall, you'll see a curtain." He got up and pulled the curtain open. "What you see is a one-way mirror. We can't see who is in the room behind the mirror. Anyone in that room can see us but can't hear us." He closed the curtain. "Any more question?"

"No, I guess it's time to go to work."

Ed Macey stared at the scene on the other side of the one-way glass into the soundproof room. He said to Peter Hastings, "What do you think, Peter?"

"Perhaps, this is a waste of our time. We can see them, but we can't hear them. And they're positioned in such a way that we can't see their faces."

"Right. And they can't hear us either. I suspect Dr. McDonald does everything he can to minimize the chances we can learn much."

Ed knew that Peter was annoyed, especially when he added, "Waste of time. Hell, Steve's wearing earphones. Why did McDonald even invite us?"

Ed knew Peter wouldn't like his answer, but he loved to irritate the defense, hoping they would take their eyes off the ball. "So that Dr. McDonald can say on the witness stand that both the prosecution and defense watched the test as it happened."

"Ed, are you suggesting how I do my cross-examination?"

Ed knew by that response that the needle had penetrated Peter's ego. Ed answered, "Of course not. Wow, you can see McDonald's face. He's either talking to Steve or asking a question. Can you read lips?"

Peter ignored the question. "Maybe he's asking Steve if he can identify Jimmy Jackson's voice."

Suddenly, Ed and Peter watched as Sue entered the soundproof room and pulled a curtain across the one-way glass.

Ed and Peter stood to leave just as Caleb came in and said, "Dr. McDonald thanks you for observing the test. If you please, I'll show you to the elevator."

As the elevator door closed, Ed studied Peter's face. He looked agitated. Ed suspected he was not happy at being told what to do by a Negro man.

After the test, Sue escorted me to the room where Dad was waiting.

Sue said, "Mr. Thompson, Dr. McDonald thanks you for sharing your son with us for the time it took to do the test. He wants you to know that Steve handled himself well during the test and that he is a bright young man. Now, I'll show you to the elevator."

As we rode down in the elevator, I said, "Dad, I can't tell you or anyone else about the test, and I don't even know how I did. But I gotta tell you that Dr. McDonald and his staff are very nice people and are super organized."

As Dad drove us back to Delphi, we didn't talk much. I think we were both afraid that we might say something that would affect the outcome of the trial. I was glad Mom didn't come. She had other events to attend. I'm pretty sure she would have been bored.

34

Readying for Trial

Tuesday—July 5 to Tuesday—July 26, 1949

TALK ABOUT TWIDDLING-THUMBS TIME, I had plenty on my hands before the trial started three weeks later. I read several books, including Charles Darwin's *The Voyage of the Beagle*. I liked that he was twenty-two years old when the voyage started. It's exciting but some parts sound really bad when he writes about people as being savages and barbarians. Still, Mom and Dad say you have to read books to understand the world. Maybe, I'll tackle Darwin's book, *On the Origin of Species*, next. I like science okay.

This morning, I asked Mom if I could go see Billy in Westtown. I hadn't seen him in a long time, and I didn't want him to think I was being snotty and didn't like him anymore. Mom seemed to rummage around in her brain for quite a while, before she finally said yes.

Before I set sail for Westtown, I decided to swing by the library to visit Miss Kathryn. I always liked to talk to her, and she knew a lot about books.

"Hi, Miss Kathryn," I said. "How you doing?" I added trying to act cool.

"I'm fine, Steve. How's the young star witness feeling?"

"Truthfully, I wish people didn't know that, because they always ask me about the case. I can't talk about it. If I did, I probably would not be able to testify."

"I understand your dilemma, Steve. I won't ask you any more questions about the trial. How's *The Voyage of the Beagle* going?"

"Well, Miss Kathryn, it's a good adventure story."

"Yes, it is, but it's much more. I have to say that Charles Darwin was a racist. His comments about people of color were abhorrent."

She nailed it, making my thoughts seem pretty weak, but I said, "Yes, ma'am. Do you know why he was a racist?"

"It's not too complicated. Darwin was a nineteenth-century white, British citizen who believed in the British Empire and its superiority over all it ruled and more. When he was young, he thought he would become a minister in the Church of England. They were called Anglicans. Put all that together, and you have Charles Darwin as he was."

Miss Kathryn seemed to know everything. "Do you think I should read *On the Origins of Species*?"

"Absolutely. In spite of what I just said, this is the seminal book on evolution. Darwin worked on this book for years and it was published in 1869 when he was fifty years old. It initially created quite a stir because many people believed that God created all the animals and plants."

"Well, I'll give it a shot after I finish the one I'm reading. I have to go. I'm going to see my friend Billy in Westtown."

"I know who Billy is, Steve, You tell him hello for me."

"Yes, ma'am, I will. See you later."

As I walked toward Westtown, I decided to retrace the route I ran back to my house the Night of Terror. My inner self said, *Don't do it, Steve. Too many bad memories.* But I overruled my inner self, knowing I had to do it for Marvin, Joshua, and Moses—for the trial.

My first stop was at the haunted house where Zach lived. I sat on the grass opposite his house and stared. It looked okay. It must not have burned. I thought about what he told Mr. Graves about Joshua and Moses being queers. I cried a bit because I knew this was only my first stop in my short journey. Just as I was ready to get up from the grass, I couldn't believe what I saw coming out of the house. It was Zach. He looked angry.

He said, "What you doing' here, boy. You come to torment me?"

"No, Mr. Zach. I'm Steve Thompson. I live in Delphi."

I was afraid what he might do, as he twisted from one side and to the other. He sat next to me and said, "I knows who you are. You the white boy who's gonna testify at the trial. I hope them three white boys are found guilty."

Wow, was I surprised. "Yes, sir, I'm the boy who's gonna testify."

"You see, Steve, I done something I ain't proud of. Did you know Joshua and Moses?"

"Yes, and I liked them a lot."

Zach rocked his head back and forth. "It's what I done that got them kilt. Did you know that?"

I wanted to say yes and tell him everything that Marvin and I saw, but I knew I couldn't because of the trial. "No, sir."

"Steve, how should a man deal with a sin? If I hadn't told 'em Klan guys 'bout Moses and Joshua, they might still be alive. But if I didn't tell 'em, they was gonna kilt me. I pray and weep for those men every day. What should I do, Steve?"

"I don't know, Mr. Zach. But I think you're doing the right thing now."

"Oh, thank you. I gotta go inside now. Nice talkin' to you."

I watched Zach enter the house. *What a troubled man*, I thought, *but maybe he is seeking salvation*.

I walked past Billy's house, deciding to double back to it later. Billy's family was lucky since their house wasn't burnt down.

As I approached Marvin's house, I thought about the night we got together to look for Moses and Joshua. Today, all the curtains were closed in Marvin's house. I didn't want to bother Miss Mabel, but damned if she didn't come out. "Hey, Steve. What you doin' here?"

I'll be darned, she asked me the same question that Zach had. "Hey, Miss Mabel. I'm gonna go see Billy soon."

"That's nice. I'm sure Billy misses not seeing you and Marvin. How your doin'?"

"Fine, Miss Mabel. I guess we shouldn't talk much because of the witness rules." I noticed that Miss Mabel seemed worried.

"That's right. I'm goin' back in the house. You be good."

"Yes, ma'am." I waved goodbye.

My next planned stop was Nancy's house. I realized along this part of my walk that my journey was an odyssey. I'll use odyssey, because the word speaks to me better.

Nancy's house looked nice. No damage that I could see. I was about to leave when a man came out of the house. He was of medium height with dark skin, and he smiled, saying, "Can I help you, young man?"

I liked that, thinking, *At least he didn't say, 'What you doin' here?'* "My name's Steve Thompson. I knew the family that used to live here."

"And who might that have been?" the man asked.

"The Dawson family. They moved to Atlanta after the Night of Terror."

"That's right. My name's Phil. I bought Mr. Dawson's business and his house. Did you know their daughter, Nancy?"

I tried not to wince. "Yes, sir, Mr. Phil."

"I'm told that she was quite an accomplished young actress."

"I've heard that too, Mr. Phil. Well, I've got to go. Nice to meet you."

"Likewise, Steve."

Truthfully, I was not looking forward to the rest of my odyssey, but I felt I had to do it. When I got to where Moses and Joshua's house used to be, memories started washing over me. I started crying. Their house was a pile of ashes. Nothing left. Oddly, there was one chair in front of where the house was. I sat down. I felt so mad at Mr. Graves that I yelled out, "You bastard. I hope you rot in hell."

"You talkin' to me, son?"

I looked to my left where the voice came from. I saw an old colored man and I said, "No, sir. I was yelling at someone else. I'm sorry I frightened you."

"I wasn't scared. My name's Laertes. I been watching you since you walked up. Did you know Joshua and Moses?"

I couldn't believe it. Laertes is one of the characters in Homer's *The Odyssey*. Mom read me the poem when I was younger, and she would explain the poem and characters to me. *Am I in a dream?*

"Yes, sir, I knew them well. My friend, Marvin, and I had dinner with them one night. It was elegant and entertaining. They were both real smart. I miss them."

"Is your name Steve Thompson?"

"Yes, sir,"

"I know you. I was abandoned when I was eleven years old. I wandered around as a hobo for years and kept getting in trouble with the law. One time, I ended up in Delphi and was put in jail for panhandling. I don't know how, but Moses and Joshua paid my jail fees and hired me to work for them. I did all kinds of things for them. Washed dishes, cleaned the house, did repairs. They taught me how to read and write and do sums, and they taught me vocabulary and how to speak better. I also helped out at Moses' theater productions, and I loved to watch the plays. I never liked my given name, Sambo, so they said from now on we'll call you Laertes. I was in the pantry the day you and Marvin were here. And I know what a lot of people thought about Moses and Joshua, but for me, they were saints and a godsend."

"Gosh, Mr. Laertes, that's a wonderful story. How did you survive the Night of Terror?"

"That's another story. When Moses and Joshua knew the Klan were likely to come here, they told me to leave Westtown until everything calmed down. They gave me their bank account numbers in Delphi along with the keys to their safe deposit box and a signed affidavit allowing me to use them. They also told me the name of their lawyer in Delphi, and they told me to contact him if I needed help. And I sure enough needed help! The bank initially wouldn't honor the affidavit, so the lawyer came to the bank with me and convinced them that the document was legally binding and that he would take them to court if they refused to accept it. They rolled over like a little puppy dog. I was able to buy a small cottage in Westtown and have money to live on. So, you see, I owe both my life and livelihood to Moses and Joshua."

Where do all these good people come from? I thought as I started to tear up again. "The person I yelled at was Mr. Graves. Do you know him?"

"Can't say I do. Who is he?"

I wanted to tell Mr. Laertes, but I had to say, "Oh, he's a nobody. He made me mad one time. I was steamed up."

"Everybody gets that way sometimes, Steve. I have to go. I'm meeting a lady friend for lunch."

I couldn't help kidding him a little, so I said, "Oh my goodness, a girlfriend, Mr. Laertes."

He laughed, his old weathered face stretching taut. "You mind your manners, Steve. I'll be seeing you soon."

I wanted to continue my odyssey, which now included Mr. Laertes, the real McCoy. I packed my mind with everyone I had talked to today and headed for where Moses' theater was. I knew what to expect, and I was not wrong. Feeling devastated, it had been burned to the ground, including the theater and all the books stored there for the Negro Library in Delphi. I kept waiting for someone to come, but when it didn't happen, I realized Mr. Laertes might have joined me if he hadn't had a lunch date.

I took my time walking back toward Billy's house. I wanted to see how things looked close-up. To my surprise, it looked fine.

When I got close to Billy's, I wondered if I should call for Billy to come out or just go up and knock on the door. I had never been in his house, and I hadn't met his mother. Marvin always said Billy was ashamed of it, but Marvin also said he had been inside and it wasn't too bad.

So, I walked right up to their door and knocked on it.

A nice looking Negro woman opened the door and said, "What you wants?"

"My name's Steve Thompson. I'm a friend of Billy's. Is he home."

"Oh, I know who you are. You that white boy what played with Billy and Marvin, bless his soul. Billy oughta be here soon. He's running an errand for me. Where 'bouts in Delphi do you live?"

"Just a short ways off the square. My father owns the Delphi newspaper."

"Wooee, your family big time. C'mon in and wait. My name's Sara Marsh."

"Thank you, Miss Sara." I looked around the living room and it was fine. "Miss Sara, your house is lovely."

"Thank you, Steve, but how come a white boy is so polite to a colored lady?"

"My Mom and Dad have always told me to treat all people alike. I'm good with that except for the Klan that wrecked Westtown over a month ago and killed so many people. I think—"

Just then Billy walked in and said, "Steve, what the hell are you doing here?"

"Billy, where are your manners?" Miss Sara said. "Steve's, a guest in our house."

"Sorry, Ma, I was just surprised to see him here. Hey, Steve, I didn't mean no disrespect. How you doin'?"

"Doin' fine, Billy. Haven't seen you in a long time. Everything's been topsy-turvy since the Night of Terror."

Billy said, "Ain't that the truth."

"How about we go visit the creek where you and Marvin taught me how to handle and toss a trot line?"

"Okay by me, but I don't set no trot lines anymore. Just didn't feel good to me after what happened, especially Marvin being kilt."

"Yeah, I get it. By the way I visited Miss Kathryn at the library before I came here. She remembers you and says hello."

"That's nice. Ma, we're going to the creek. Want be gone long."

"Okay." Miss Sara said, "You boys have fun and you be careful."

As we walked toward the creek, I said, "Don't you get tired of your parents always telling you to be careful? They must think we have thick skulls and don't get the message."

"You got that right. I just brush things like that aside and move on."

"You're smart. I gotta remember to do that."

"Don't be silly, Steve, you are smart and Marvin was right behind you. I don't know shit from shinola."

"I disagree. You know what shit from shinola means. It's import-ant. Oops, that didn't come out right."

We both laughed at each other, and I said, "Billy, I'm telling you point blank that you're smart. You just gotta get over the idea that your not. It's kinda like when you didn't want to have me come into your house because it wasn't as nice as Marvin's or mine. Now, I been in your house, and it's nice. It's clean and has nice furniture. Your mother takes good care of it."

"I reckon you're right. I'll try to remember what you said."

When we got to the creek, we sat on the grass and stared at the flowing water. I thought about my first time here. We had a great time. Billy was quiet, and I suspected he was thinking about that day too.

I stopped thinking about that first day I was here. I looked upstream and the creek the water was clear. I turned the other way, and a colored man stood straight up on the bank kinda elegant like, casting line from his rod and reel. I didn't recognize him. I reckoned he was about fifty years old, of medium height, with a well-trimmed gray beard.

I tapped Billy's shoulder. Who's that colored man fishing about twenty or thirty yards downstream?"

Billy spun his head around and looked. "Huh, never saw him. I didn't see him when we got here."

"Me either." I called out, "Hey, mister, how you doin'?"

He turned his head slowly and said, "I'm doing fine. It's a nice day and I'm fishing."

His voice was kinda smooth, almost hypnotic.

"What's your name, mister?" Billy asked.

"My name's not important. I am a fisherman like Jesus."

Like Jesus? Is this for real or am I just imaging it?

Billy spoke up, "Well, Jesus, have you any words for us?"

I was sure Billy was teasing the man, but he appeared to ignore Billy when he said, "I'm not Jesus, but I have been sent here to help Westtown heal. I know who you are. The white boy is Steve Thompson, and you are Billy Marsh. You both will do things that will aid the town's recovery."

Billy looked perplexed, "I already know Steve is doin' something important, but I'm not. What do I have to do?"

"Billy, that is one of the mysteries of life. You will recognize the way when it comes to you."

The fisherman reeled his line in. "I have to go now. Peace be with you." He walked toward the next bend in the creek and disappeared into the trees. Billy and I jumped up and ran after him, but we were unable to find him. It seemed like he had been a dream.

As we walked back toward Billy's house, he said, "Steve, I feel like I'm goin' crazy. What the hell am I supposed to do? Marvin's dead. You're testifying at the trial of Marvin's murderers. You daddy's probably writing stories about the trial."

"I don't know, Billy. I guess, like the fisherman said, you will find the way. Maybe, it'll have to do with Marvin."

Before I said goodbye, I said, "Billy, come over to my house anytime you want to do something or just talk about things." Billy appeared to be pondering things.

Now, I had one last stop to make. I slowly walked to the place where Marvin and I had our encounter with Jimmy Jackson. I looked around and everything was calm. But I could hear Jimmy Jackson's voice and the rifle shots that killed Marvin. On the road where I had started running, and had briefly looked back, I could see Marvin falling as the bullets hit him. Like Billy, I wondered what I should do now. I sat down, fully expecting someone to show up and help or give me guidance. After thirty minutes, it came to me, I'm the only one that can deal with these moments, and I must succeed in what I have been assigned to do, and that is to testify.

I stood and started walking along the route I ran that night to save my sorry ass.

The next morning, Wednesday, I did a couple of errands for Mom. When I returned home and opened our door, I heard Mom's voice and the other one sounded like Billy. I put the packages down and went to the kitchen. There was Mom and Billy having a serious conversation.

To get even with Billy, I said, "Billy, what the hell are you doin' here?"

Billy and I laughed. Mom appeared confused when she said, "Billy was explaining something important to me. I have a hair appointment soon."

Now, my curiosity was off the charts. "What's so important, Billy?"

"Steve, you won't believe this, I had a dream last night."

I said, sarcastically, "Well, I hope it didn't scare you ."

Mom scolded me, "Steve, mind your manners." Heading for the door she said, "I have to go now"

Yes, ma'am," I responded

Instead of calling me an asshole or something like that, Billy said calmly, "My dream felt real, and I remembered it. I can't usually remember my dreams, but this one just kept floating around. In my dream, I was walking around in the Delphi Square looking at the statues. And then it hit me what I had to do to honor Marvin. Then I woke up."

"Billy, what are you gonna do?"

"I'm gonna organize a campaign to collect money for a statue of Marvin. We'll put it in the Delphi Square. If the whites won't do it, we'll find a place in Westtown, maybe where Marvin was killed. What do you think about that, Steve?"

I had never heard Bill speak with such confidence. "Billy, you just hit one out of the park. Brilliant. I'll help. I'm already thinking of things to do."

"Great. I know this is what the fisherman wanted me to do. Do you think he was real?"

"Billy, I don't care if he was real, imaginary, or is still out in the woods somewhere. I'm just happy he showed you the way in your dream."

Well, my twiddling-thumbs time became a time of the past. Billy and I went into high gear on a fund raising campaign. Dad wrote a front page story for the newspaper, and Mom and Dad talked to their friends asking for contributions.

Billy and I went door-to-door asking for donations in Westtown and Delphi, but occasionally someone was real nasty. One guy in Delphi said to us, "Get out of here. The nigger got what he deserved." We thanked him and saluted. That made him even angrier, so he slammed the door in our faces.

When I told Dad the story he said we should have just left because angry people do crazy things. Dad said that we should consider putting up the statue in Westtown where it might be less likely to be vandalized. Billy and I decided Dad was right. Dad also added that we should think about ways to honor Moses and Joshua, but we'd have to do that later.

Donations were coming in fast and furious. Billy and I were delighted, until Dad threw us another curve ball. He asked us if we had considered the cost of hiring a person who could produce a statue of Marvin. We flipped because we hadn't. Billy and I had no idea how to proceed. Dad offered to try to find a person who worked in either stone or metal.

A few days later, Dad found a guy who lived in Birmingham. Dad said the guy was intrigued by the opportunity and the story behind the need for the statue. He had recommended that the statue be in bronze and about eight feet high. He also said he would design a pedestal to place the statue on. When Dad asked him about price, he said $2,000, one-half his normal fee.

We had $1,600 in donations. We were sure we could raise $400, and hopefully more.

On July twenty-third, four days before the trial, we had $2,400, giving us $400 for unexpected consequences.

I knew I wouldn't be able to be in the courtroom when the trial began. Bummer. I would have liked to see the jury selection process, but I knew that wasn't to be. If people came to the trial as spectators, the first time they would see me was in the witness chair, testifying.

Part V
The Trial—1949

"Poise the cause in justice's equal scales, Whose beam stands sure, whose rightful cause prevails."

William Shakespeare—*Henry VI Part 2*

35

The Trial—Day 1

Wednesday—July 27, 1949

ANDY THOMPSON GOT UP EARLY that morning, ate breakfast, and left for Montgomery. Last night he had said goodbye to Lillis and Steve.

Andy knew Steve was disappointed to be missing jury selection, but he also knew Steve understood why he wasn't being allowed. He hoped to attend the trial as a newspaper reporter each day the trial was in session. He wanted to write articles for the *Delphi Delta News*, even though it would be dicey about what he could report, since Steve was a witness.

Andy got to the courtroom well before the nine o'clock start time. He wanted to present his press credentials as soon as the doors opened in hopes of getting a good seat in the press box.

He achieved his objective and nodded at other reporters as he waited for the judge to begin the trial. He placed his empty journal on the table, smiling because an empty journal marked the start of a new trial or a feature story.

Judge Frank Johnson sat on the bench at nine-ten, and welcomed the lawyers and the audience. Andy knew the defendants had plead not guilty at their arraignment several weeks earlier, and he was not surprised to hear the judge say, "Mr. Macey, have you any motions to make?"

"No, Your Honor, the prosecution has none at this time."

"Mr. Macey and Mr. Hastings, I trust you won't have any additional motions after we begin proceedings. The court frowns on that unless compelling evidence is presented. Understand?"

"Yes, Your Honor," Mr Macey said.

"Fine. Mr. Hastings, do you have any motions at this time."

"No, Your Honor, but I do have one concern."

"And what might that be?"

"Your Honor, I see that Andy Thompson is in the press box." He paused.

"Mr. Hastings, stop teasing the court. Get to the point."

"Mr. Thompson's son, Steve Thompson, is on the prosecution's witness list. That's my concern."

"Mr. Hastings, one last time. What are the specifics of your concern? Do you want to object to Mr. Thomson being in the courtroom? Do you want to subpoena him?"

Andy looked at the reporters in the press box…a few shaking their heads. He took that to mean what he thought, which was that the judge was getting weary and wanted a clear answer.

Andy journal entry. *Hastings is either non compos mentis or he doesn't care if he annoys the judge. The judge is not happy with him.*

Mr. Hastings said, "No, Your Honor, not at this time."

"I see, then let's start jury selection. Bailiff, please escort the first group of prospective jurors into the jury box and swear them in."

Andy journal entry. *18 prospective jurors. 6 Negroes, 4 women, 2 men. 12 whites, 7 men, 5 women. Numbered jurors 1 to18. Get names later.*

Andy made additional notes as the judge asked the jurors questions ensuring they met the state's requirements. Satisfied with their answers, the judge allowed the two lead attorneys to start asking the prospective jurors questions.

Mr. Hastings stood. "Your Honor, the colored man named Hector Billings is not on the voter registration rolls. May I approach the bench?"

"Yes."

Hastings pointed out the omission in the rolls to the judge who appeared to nod.

Macey stood and said, "Your Honor, I have a copy of the voter registration rolls that I received yesterday. They are dated Monday, July twenty-fifth. Hector Billings' name is on it."

"Let me see, Mr. Macey."

Macey showed his copy of the rolls to the judge.

After looking through the rolls, Judge Johnson said, "Mr. Hastings, what is the date on your rolls? Hector Billing's name is clearly on Mr. Macey's copy."

Andy could hardly hear Hastings speak as he said, "Monday, July eighteenth, Your Honor."

"That issue is resolved. Return to your tables, gentlemen."

Andy watched Hastings as he glared at a young lawyer at the defense's table.

Andy journal entry. *That young lawyer is in for a heap of trouble. Get his name. Hastings continues to skate on thin ice. Trial may last longer than expected.*

Judge Johnson spoke, "Mr Macey, you may question the prospective jurors."

Andy watched, expecting there might be fireworks soon.

"Thank you, Your Honor," Macey said, walking up to a white man in the jury box. "Sir, are you now or have you ever been a member of the Ku Klux Klan?"

Andy had never seen a lawyer jump out of his seat so high. He knew the fireworks had begun.

Hastings yelled, "Objection."

Judge Johnson said, "Calm down, Mr. Hastings. State the reason for your objection."

"Sir, the Ku Klux Klan is not on trial here. I want that name stricken from the record and not used again."

"Mr. Macey, any comments?"

"Thank you, Your Honor. Mr. Hastings must have a short memory. The three defendants were identified as Ku Klux Klan members at their arrangement where they were read the charges, and plead not guilty. The police report on what happened in Westtown on May 25, 1949, was replete with the words Ku Klux Klan. Further, the state's analysis of the night of May 25, 1949, mentions Ku Klux Klan numerous times."

"Mr. Hastings, any additional comments?"

"Only that if you overrule my objection, I would like to put the court on notice that I will appeal the case."

"So noted, Mr. Hastings, and I do hereby overrule your objection. The prospective juror may answer Mr. Macey's question."

Andy thought the prospective juror looked confused, as did others in the audience. He suspected many in the courtroom were not used to legal terminology and wrangling.

Macey walked up to the same white man in the jury box. "Sir, to be sure we're clear, I'll repeat the question I asked you earlier. Are you now or have you ever been a member of the Ku Klux Klan?"

Andy was surprised when the man paused. "No, sir, I've never been associated with the Klan."

Mr. Macey asked, "Is that the Scottish word clan - c - l - a - n, or Klan like in Ku Klux Klan?"

The juror appeared confused and paused again and said, "The Ku Klux Klan with a K."

Judge Johnson interrupted and said, "Mr. Macey, that question was uncalled for. Please keep your questions to jurors direct and to the point and not encumbered with word play."

"Yes, Your Honer. My mistake. I apologize to the juror."

Andy journal entry. *Macey apologized to juror. Nice touch, might help to get the juror on his side.*

"Good. That understood, Mr. Macey, you can continue your questioning after the court takes a fifteen-minute recess. And members of the audience and the press, you may not talk to the prospective jurors. The bailiff will escort jurors to a room just off the courtroom."

During the recess, Andy chatted with reporters he knew well from other court cases. It concerned Andy, when one reporter asked, "How do you think it's going, Andy?"

Andy raised an eyebrow. "Well, if you'll tell me your headline for your next article, I might consider telling you mine. Deal?"

The reporter walked away.

When the court reconvened, Andy waited in anticipation, wondering if things would cool.

After Judge Johnson instructed Mr. Macey to continue questioning jurors, Mr. Macey asked another white man the same question about Klan participation.

Andy watched in utter amazement as Mr. Hastings leapt out of his seat, and yelled again, "Objection."

The courtroom went silent, until the judge quietly said, "Mr. Hastings, join me in my chambers. Bailiff, please ensure the audience and jurors stay in their seats and don't talk. We'll be out for a few minutes."

Andy journal entry. *10:42 a.m. into chambers. 10:46 a.m, return from chambers. 4 minutes in chambers.*

Judge Johnson sat on the bench and said, "Mr. Hastings."

"Your Honor, I withdraw my objection."

Andy heard several people in the audience gasp, as if they couldn't believe it.

At noon, Judge Johnson said, "Ladies and gentlemen, the court will take a lunch break and will reconvene at one o'clock to continue the jury selection process."

Andy jotted more comments in his journal before heading to his favorite cafe close to the courthouse. He had covered so many trials in Montgomery, the cafe felt like a second home, especially when ordering his favorite grilled catfish and hush puppies with some sweet tea. There were a few newspaper reporters in the cafe, but Andy ignored them.

After eating, he was back in his seat in the press box and opened his journal as Judge Johnson called the court to order and told Mr. Macey to proceed. Andy was curious how he would proceed to question the white men and women in the jury pool, but it was straight forward. He asked them all the same question, and all the jurors stated clearly that they were not Klan members. One white women in the pool, smiled at Mr. Macey and spelled Klan out, which drew a few laughs from the audience and even a small chuckle from the judge.

Mr. Macey started questioning the Negro jurors one by one, keeping his questions direct, as most of them appeared nervous. Then Mr. Macey said, "Your Honor, no more questions at this time."

"Thank you, Mr. Macey. Mr. Hastings, you may question the jurors."

Mr. Hastings went right up to Hector Billings and asked, "Boy, how did you pass the registration test? Can you read? Can you write?"

Before Billings answered, Judge Johnson said, "Mr. Hastings, you will address jurors by their proper name. And Mr. Billings is not a boy. Understood?"

Andy was amazed when Hastings glared at the judge and said, spitting his words out, "Yes, sir, it's Mr. Billings, not boy."

Andy journal entry. *Judge holding tight reins over Macey and Hastings. Is Hastings cooking his own goose? Fireworks! Fireworks!*

Hastings went at Mr. Billings again. "Mr. Billings, how did you prepare for the tests?"

"I studied. I read the Constitution a few times. I boned up on important people in government. Things like that."

"I see, Constitution, government, and things like that. My, my, you are a smart guy."

Judge Johnson interrupted, "Mr. Hastings, you must know that your last comment was a statement, not a question. Please just ask a question and leave the statement for your summation. Can you do that?"

"Yes, sir."

"Continue."

Hastings smiled at the judge and said, "Mr. Billings, sir, are you smart?"

"Can't say, sir. I'm just an easy going colored man trying to make it day to day."

"What are you trying to make everyday?"

"A living working odd jobs."

"Odd jobs? Do you really believe you can be color blind and render a fair judgment of the accused white men?"

Andy thought Judge Johnson was going to interrupt, but he didn't.

Billings said, "Sir, Westtown is all colored and it was colored people that were killed, so I guess most people, white and colored, think I would vote guilty, but that isn't so. The three white men are considered innocent until proven guilty. I want to hear all the evidence and witnesses before I decide. I also want—."

Hastings interrupted and said, "Your Honor, I have no more questions for this juror." Hastings returned to his table for a drink of water and walked back to jury box.

Andy journal entry. *Judge is giving some leeway for Hastings questions and behavior. Perhaps he was trying to avoid a charge of judicial prejudice by Hastings. Billings handled himself so well that Hastings cut him off.*

Andy made more entries in his journal as the questioning of jurors continued. His final entry was: *Questions and objections were batted back and forth like a tennis game, except no physical harm.*

Judge Johnson called an end to day one at three-fifteen and added the courtroom would convene at nine tomorrow morning.

36

The Trial—Days 2 & 3

Thursday & Friday—July 28 & 29, 1949

On Thursday, the entire day had been taken up questioning prospective jurors, and the questions and answers became so repetitive that Andy got bored, but he was faithful to his journal and wrote many items in it. To try and quell his boredom, he had begun to rate each witness in hopes of predicting who would finally be empaneled as a juror. Andy hoped that Hector Billings would be chosen, but he felt sure that Hastings would dismiss him preemptively. Andy appreciated that Judge Johnson kept the courtroom well in hand, especially Hastings and Macey. Several times, the judge reminded Hastings and Macey not to waste time as he wanted to wrap up jury selection tomorrow morning. Judge Johnson extended his normal closure time from three-fifteen to four-thirty to provide the lawyers as much time as he could. The last group of prospective jurors were in the box now with only three were left to be questioned. Finally, the lawyers were finished, so the judge thanked them and the jurors for their efforts. Andy felt as if the *Hallelujah Chorus* were ringing in his ears. Thursday had been a long day.

On Friday, Andy started listening to Montgomery's classical radio station as soon as he pulled out of his driveway. They were playing a selection from Bach's *The Goldberg Variations*. He listened for a short time, but his mind kept drifting back to yesterday's trial. He finally turned the radio off.

Andy arrived at the courthouse on Friday a few minutes late because he was so absorbed in thinking about Thursday's proceedings.

As he sat down in the press box, Judge Johnson convened the court at a few minutes after nine o'clock.

"Ladies and gentlemen, today is a very important day for this court. The prosecution and defense will start the process of dismissing prospective jurors with their preemptive challenges until we have twelve jurors and two alternates. The court has already granted five juror's petitions to be excused for personal reasons, The court's records will validate the reasons and decisions. Audience, do not indicate in any manner your pleasure or displeasure with a dismissal. The defense and prosecution will alternate in choosing a dismissal by stating the juror's number. Mr. Hastings, please start the process."

Andy had his journal at the ready to note the number of each dismissed juror.

Macey dismissed a juror, as did Hastings.

Andy had to write furiously to keep up with the alternating dismissals. After more than an hour, he was delighted because the pace slowed, as both lawyer had began to consult with their colleagues to consider their next choice.

An hour later, Macey addressed the court, "Your Honor, I have no more challenges. I accept the jury."

"Mr. Hastings?"

"You Honor, I agree. We have a jury."

Judge Johnson said, "Thank you both." Turning toward the jury box, he added, "And thank you jurors. You are worthy choices, and I thank you for your patience the last three days. But it is my duty to remind you of what I told you when you were first sworn in by the bailiff. You are still under that oath. You must not talk to each other about the trial until you go into the jury room to consider your verdict. You must not talk to family member or friends or witnesses or any other persons about the trial. I know this can be difficult at times, but I am confident you can do it. With that, ladies and gentlemen, the court will adjourn early today to give both sides adequate time to prepare their cases. The court will convene on Monday, August first, at nine o'clock when both sides will begin presenting their cases."

Andy wrote hastily in his journal. *Final jury composition. 2 alternates, 1 white man, 1 Negro man.12 jurors, 8 whites, 5 men, 3 women, 4 Negroes, 2 men, 2 women.*

Andy was putting his journal and a few other things in his valise when Ed Macey approached him.

"Andy, got a few minutes?"

"Sure, Ed. I was surprised at a couple of the men who survived the jury selection process."

"There are usually a few surprises. Who were your surprises?"

"I thought for sure that Hastings would dismiss Hector Billings, and I thought you would dismiss the first white man you questioned. I don't know his name."

"His name is Oliver Twist and don't laugh, that is his name. Perhaps his mother liked Charles Dickens. The last few dismissals in a case are frequently a mystery. We'll have to wait and see how the jury finds the defendants."

Andy thought Ed wanted to talk to him about Steve, so he decided to say, "Ed, you didn't want to talk to me about the mysteries of jury selection did you?"

"Nope, you saw right through me again. The trial will start in earnest on Monday. There will be opening remarks by me and Hastings, and then the judge will ask me to present the prosecution's case. Andy, I plan to call Steve into the court to be my first witness. In fact, I consider Steve my star witness. If he performs as well on Monday as he has throughout all the preparation work we've done, it will be fine. Do you think he's ready, Andy?"

"Ed, Steve has been ready since May 25, 1949."

Ed nodded. "Fine, but I do worry about things. And Andy, you'll have to have Steve here before the trial starts Monday so I can talk to him, and then he can be escorted to the witness waiting room."

"Ed, I assure you Steve is used to pressure. We'll be there bright and early next Monday."

"Thanks, Andy. I'm sure you want to get home. Please say hello to Lillis and Steve for me."

As Andy got near his home, he knew he was about to be hit by a barrage of questions from Steve and Lillis.

Sure enough, Steve ran up to him and called out, "Mom, Dad's home."

"Andy, you're home early. How did it go?"

"No questions please. Let me get comfortable and then I'll tell you what I can."

The family gathered around the kitchen table as Andy began, "It was a busy Friday morning at the old courthouse. A final jury has been selected. It seems it's a fair mix of whites and Negroes. I'm home because Judge Johnson adjourned the trial early so the lawyers would have more time to prepare for their opening statements to the jury. The trial will convene on Monday morning at nine o'clock. Soon after that the heavy duty part of the trial starts when the prosecution has to present their case first. And here's the big deal, Ed Macey wants to call Steve to the witness stand as his first witness. He's convinced—"

Steve hollered, "Holy moly, I can't wait."

Lillis asked, her face a map of concern, "Andy, is Steve ready?"

"I'm sure he is, honey. He's been ready for a long time."

"Andy, I want to go to the trial with you on Monday and every day following until it's over."

"Of course, I fully expected you would. We'll have to leave early Monday morning. Before the trial starts, Ed Macey wants to talk to Steve, and then he'll be escorted to the witness room."

"Steve, do you have any questions? I'll answer them if I can."

"No, sir. No questions. I'll take a book that I can read in the witness room."

"Good. Let's take a break. I'm going upstairs and take a short nap, and then I have to write an article for the newspaper."

Later that evening, well after of one of Lillis' excellent meals, Andy snuggled up to Lillis and whispered in her ear, "Honey, you can't tell anyone what I'm about to tell you, including Steve. Ed Macey told me he considers Steve his star witness, which implied to me that he thinks the results of the trial will hinge on Steve's performance. A heavy burden for our young son."

"Oh, Andy, my heart breaks thinking about it. He also has to have done well on Dr. McDonald's voice recognition test."

"Yes, but as far as I know, no one is aware of the results yet. Let's say a little prayer for Steve."

"Hold me tight, Andy, you say the prayer for us."

Andy paused and said, "Dear Lord, we don't call upon you very often, but we beseech you to watch over our son, Steve Thompson, as he prepares to explain in court the horrors that he has seen. Amen."

Lillis whispered, "Amen."

37

The Trial—Day 4

Monday—August 1, 1949

ANDY, LILLIS, AND STEVE, got to the courthouse at eight-fifteen. Steve had Charles Darwin's book, *On The Origin of Species*, with him. He had decided to give it a try while he was in the witness room.

As they started to enter the courthouse building, Sam Lancaster greeted them, "Good morning, Thompson family. I'm glad you're early. Steve, you're dressed well. Courts and juries always like that. I will escort you to a small office in the courthouse to meet with Ed Macey. He wants to discuss your upcoming time in the witness chair. You'll likely testify later this morning or maybe early this afternoon."

"Yes, sir. Mr. Sam, I'd like you to meet my mother, Lillis Thompson."

"Miss Lillis, delighted to meet you. Can I steal Steve away from you two now? I'll come back as soon as possible to explain the situation, likely twenty to thirty minutes."

Andy said, "Our son is in your hands, Sam."

Sam returned as he promised and said, "Steve is doing fine. He and Mr. Macey talked for about twenty minutes. He is in the witness waiting room, and I noticed he's reading quite an impressive book. Andy, I know you sit in the press box. I'd be happy to escort Miss Lillis into the courtroom and ensure she gets a good seat."

Lillis said,"Sam, that's very nice of you. I accept your offer."

When the doors were opened, the courtroom filled up quickly. The trial had obviously gotten the attention of many people.

Judge Johnson called the court to order, saying, "Good morning, ladies and gentlemen. Today, the prosecution and defense will start the process of presenting the evidence in this case. Before Mr. Macey presents the prosecution's case, we have two persons the jury needs to hear, the coroner and the police chief. We'll hear the coroner's report first. Bailiff, please escort the coroner into the courtroom."

Andy knew the coroner. He was a pudgy guy with a quick smile and a jolly laugh. Andy was also was familiar with the coroner's findings and had seen crime scene photographs of Marvin Gibbs' bullet riddled body, but he had his journal ready if something new came up. Andy was surprised when the coroner asked the judge if he could show the jury the crime scene photographs, including Marvin Gibbs' body. Hastings objected, but the judge overruled his objection. The clerk added exhibit numbers to the photos and then passed them among the jurors. Andy noted that several of the jurors teared up when looking at the photos.

Judge Johnson asked the coroner, "Sir, just exactly where was Marvin Gibbs' body found?"

"In Westtown, not far from his home. Any other questions?"

"No, sir. You may step down. Thanks for your excellent report. You are dismissed. Bailiff, please escort the Delphi Police Chief into the courtroom."

Andy found the police chief an arrogant sort. He stood tall and erect, as if always looking for a fight. Andy didn't trust the guy. In fact, he thought the guy might be somehow connected to the Klan.

When the police chief sat in the witness chair, Andy thought he looked decidedly uncomfortable.

Judge Johnson said, "Welcome Chief. I know you and the coroner work hand-in-hand on many cases. Did you happen to hear the coroner's remarks to the jury?"

"Yes, Your Honor."

"Very well. Chief, please explain to the jury the analysis you did on the weapons likely used in the murder of Marvin Gibbs."

"Yes, sir. Since we have yet to find a murder weapon or weapons, we performed a ballistics analysis on the three bullets that entered Marvin Gibbs' body from the back. Two bullets matched the caliber of a 22 rifle. The third bullet was larger as was one hole in Marvin

Gibbs' back. It matched the caliber of a 35 mm rifle. We are still searching for weapons."

"Any ideas on where they might be?"

"Your Honor, truth is they could be in a number of places. Maybe at the bottom of a lake or river. Maybe buried in the ground. Maybe given to someone not involved in this case."

"I see. Chief, thank you for testifying. You are dismissed. Mr. Macey, you may make your opening statement to the jury."

"Your Honor and members of the jury. It's nice to see you this morning. I trust you all had a good weekend. I am Edward Macey, the lead prosecutor. I will present our case for the State of Alabama. First, I will read two sentences that the jury will hear over and over during the trial." Macey paused and then spoke in a dramatic voice. "For Christ's sake, Steve, run like hell. Keep running Steve. Don't stop." Macey paused again. "Those twelve words were spoken by Marvin Gibbs, the young man murdered by the three defendants." Macey paused and pointed at the defendants. "The defendants are, left to right, Jimmy Jackson, Bubba Smith, and Willie Warden. The State of Alabama will call four witnesses: Steve Thompson, the only white person in Westtown the night of May 25, 1949, other than members of the Ku Klux Klan; Mabel Gibbs, the mother of her murdered son, Marvin Gibbs; Fred Watson, a typesetter for the *Delphi Delta News* newspaper; and Dr. Alastair McDonald, a voice recognition expert. The prosecution's witnesses' testimonies will show that the evidence in the case is factual. For these reasons, after you have heard all the evidence, at the end of the trial, we will ask you to return a guilty verdict. And one last comment, don't forget 'For Christ's sake, Steve, run like hell. Keep running Steve. Don't stop.' Thank you ladies and gentlemen of the jury."

Macey returned to the prosecution's table.

Andy journal entry. *A well done opening statement by Macey. Excellent choice of a theme by using Marvin's own words. Saw several jurors writing as Macey read the theme twice. The jurors seemed engaged.*

Judge Johnson said, "Mr. Hastings, are you ready?"

"Yes." Hastings approached the jury box and got quite close to the jurors and stared at each one for several seconds, and it appeared that the jurors were fidgeting as if uncomfortable.

Hastings finally said, "Jurors, there are only a few things you need to know, so that you will find these three fine, young men not guilty. They are innocent and we shall prove it. Remember, they are considered innocent until proven guilty. As bad as the so called Night of Terror was my three fine, young men did not commit this heinous crime. We will prove beyond a shadow of doubt that the three men are innocent."

Andy wrote in his journal. *Why is the judge letting Hastings continue? Both he and Macey are furiously writing. Maybe the judge is letting Hastings go on until he's ready to reel him in. Why isn't Macey objecting? Maybe same reason.*

Hastings continued, "There are just a few other things you must consider. Alabama has had good times and bad times, but we have always respected segregation as our way of life. Of course, most colored people know the rules and act accordingly. For those that don't follow the rules, the Ku Klux Klan carries the burden of ensuring our values are protected, especially the sanctity of white women. I challenge each juror to search their soul for what you know is right, the southern way of life, and bring in a verdict of not guilty. Thank you."

Andy looked at the jurors and the audience as Hastings walked to the defense table. The jurors appeared perplexed, as did the audience except for a few that snickered.

Andy journal entry. *A terrible opening statement by Hastings, too disjointed. If Hastings had a theme, it must be Ku Klux Klan and the southern way of life. Didn't see any jurors writing as Hastings spoke.*

Judge Johnson said, "Ladies and gentlemen, the court will recess for an early lunch. We will convene at twelve-thirty. Bailiff, please sequester the jury for their lunch. See that the witnesses in the waiting room are provided a lunch."

The court convened exactly on time. The judge hammered his gavel and said, "Mr. Macey, please proceed."

"Your Honor. I call for my first witness, Steve Thompson."

I was still waiting in the witness room, when four people came in with trays of food. A lady handed me mine, and it was fried chicken, mashed potatoes, a salad, and sweet tea. Boy, was I hungry. Mrs. Gibbs and Mr. Watson got the same meal. We had been chatting about how bored we were when Mrs. Gibbs laughed and said, "Steve, you think this fried chicken is as good as mine?"

Well, I knew the right answer to that question. "No ma'am, but this ain't too bad."

Mr. Watson grinned and added, "Mabel, I think the two are about the same."

"Why, Fred Watson, you oughta be ashamed of yourself. Steve, you see what I have to put up with from this old white man."

We all laughed and finished our lunch. Then we were chatting when the bailiff came in and said, "Steve Thompson, you've been called as the next witness."

When the bailiff escorted me into the courtroom, people gasped. I guess they expected an adult. Mr Hastings looked at me and smiled. He looked like a nice man, so I decided to do my size up thing on him. *Medium height, dark hair, age maybe thirty-five*, I thought.

I smiled at Mom and Dad as I was led toward the witness chair. The bailiff told me to keep standing.

Judge Johnson said, "Welcome, Steve Thompson. Can I call you Steve?"

"Yes, sir. It's okay. I'm a kid."

The judge smiled. "So I see. Steve, before I administer the oath, I'll ask you a few questions. Do you know how important it is to be a witness in a trial?"

"Yes, sir. It's a sacred honor to be a witness. I have to tell the truth. If I don't, I'll be guilty of perjury and will go to jail."

"Well, you've already answered my other question. I'll administer the oath. Steve, put you left hand on this Bible and raise your right hand. Steve Thompson, do you solemnly swear to the tell the truth, the whole truth, and nothing but the truth, so help you God."

"I do."

"You may sit, Steve. Mr. Macey, your witness."

"Thank you, Your Honor. Steve it's nice to see you. Are you comfortable?"

"Yes, sir."

"Steve tell the jury in you own words about yourself."

I turned toward the jury and spoke loudly, "Good morning. I'm fourteen years old, but I think most people expected an adult when I came into the courtroom."

Jurors and many in the audience laughed, but Steve continued, "I live in Delphi. I'll start high school in September. I read books a lot. You can learn a lot of stuff in books that schools don't teach you. I'm not complaining because I know teachers do as much as they can in the time they have. I like to play basketball and I like to fish. I was introduced to Shakespeare by a librarian. I guess that's enough."

"Thanks, Steve. Now, I'd like you to tell the jury in you own words what you experienced the night of May 25, 1949, in Westtown, a neighborhood next to Delphi."

I continued looking at the jury. "The night of May 25, 1949, became know as the Night of Terror. About twenty colored people were killed that night by the Ku Klux Klan."

Mr. Hastings jumped up. "Objection. It has yet to be proven that Steve knew that any colored people had been killed that night."

Gees, how can he say that, Well, I guess he's not a nice man.

Judge Johnson said, in what I thought was a calm voice, "Mr. Hastings, we cleared up that issue well before Steve was in this courtroom. I overrule your objection. Steve, you may continue."

"Thank you, Your Honor. Three of the people killed that night were my friends. Marvin Gibbs and Mr. Moses Douglas and Dr. Joshua Marshall. Mr. Moses Douglas was the librarian in Delphi's Negro Library. Dr. Joshua Marshall was the only Negro doctor in Westtown. He had his office in his home."

Mr. Macey spoke up and said, "Excuse me, Steve. I have a question. How do you know your friends were killed?"

"Because, I was there. I witnessed all of them being killed by members of the Ku Klux Klan."

The courtroom exploded. People were yelling. The jury looked confused. Had I said too much? Mr. Macey didn't appear upset. Judge

Johnson pounded his gavel, shouting, "Order in the court. If I have to ask you again, the audience will be removed from the courtroom."

The courtroom became silent and everyone slowly sat down.

"Continue, Mr. Macey," the judge said.

"Steve, please repeat the last sentence you said."

"I witnessed all of them being killed by members of the Ku Klux Klan."

"Were they all killed by one Ku Klux Klan member?"

"No, sir. Marvin and I witnessed a large group of Ku Klux Klan members kill Moses Douglas and Dr. Joshua Marshall. I witnessed three other Ku Klux Klan members kill Marvin Gibbs."

Mr. Macey said, "Your Honor, I request a ten minute break, so Steve and I can talk in private."

"Granted. Mr. Macey. I'll stay in the courtroom to oversee that no one talks about the trial. The bailiff and clerk will assist me. Mr. Macey, you and Steve can go to the counselor's private room."

Inside the room, Mr. Macey checked carefully to ensure it was private. We sat down.

"Steve, you're doing an excellent job. Your description of the three who were murdered sent the courtroom into a frenzy. I glanced at Mr. Hastings. He appeared livid. How do you feel now?"

I shrugged my shoulders. "Fine, but I didn't intend to create such a stir. Do you think the judge is mad?"

"No. He's used to interruptions when the courtroom goes a bit crazy. We need to talk about the next steps in your testimony, and this will be the hard part. I want you to tell your whole story, starting with the Mardi Gras parade when you first encountered Jimmy Jackson. Then weave the rest of the story in the sequence that things occurred, ending with Marvin telling you to run home just as he was being killed. And I want you to emphasize Marvin's words I've told you about. 'For Christ's sake, Steve, run like hell. Keep running Steve. Don't stop.' Think you can handle that?"

"Yes, sir. I've told the story many times. It's kinda like learning your lines for a stage play. But when I get to the part where Mr. Bob Graves comes in, should I mention him?"

"Steve, I know how much you want to mention Bob Graves, and I understand why. You can if there's a way to mention him without implying he was at Westtown that night. If not, we'll deal with him later."

"Yes, sir, there is a way. I can weave him into the part where I watched a rehearsal of one of Mr. Douglas' plays."

"Okay, but if you do stumble during the telling, I'll speak and ask you a question to help you get your bearings. Let's go back to the courtroom. We've got two minutes to go."

When we entered the courtroom, all heads turned our way.

Judge Johnson said, "Ladies and gentlemen, the court is back in session. Mr. Macey, you may continue."

"Thank you, Your Honor. Steve, I'd like you to tell the jury your entire story that is related to the Night of Terror."

"Yes, sir. My story starts well before May 25, 1949. For years, Delphi had sponsored a Mardi Gras parade with floats with white people, but Negroes also had their floats. As far as I know, there were never any serious problems. Oh, a few people got drunk and made fools of themselves. The date of this year's parade was March 1, 1949. Three of my buddies—Jack, Marvin, and Billy—and me built a float for the parade. We titled it *In Honor of the Berlin Airlift Pilots*. That night was when I had my first encounter with Jimmy Jackson, one of the defendants in this case."

I saw the jurors turn their heads and stare at the defendant.

"While the parade was in progress, three guys came near our float. They had on red pullover shirts with the letters 'KKK' on them and red hats. One of them yelled at Marvin, 'Hey, colored boy, you ain't no goddamn American pilot. Ya bettah watch yourself.' Then one of my father's employees, Fred Watson, said, 'Jimmy, you get the hell outta here. We don't cotton to your kind.' That's the first time I heard Jimmy's first name. Jimmy responded 'Ya a white piece of nigger-loving shit, Fred.' As several parade organizers escorted Jimmy and his two friends well off the parade route, Jimmy yelled back at Marvin, 'Boy, I'm gonna keep my eye on you.' That was my first encounter with Jimmy Jackson."

I asked, "Your Honor, can I have a drink of water?" The judge nodded at the bailiff, and he brought me a glass of water."

Ready to go again, I said, "My second encounter with Jimmy Jackson occurred on May 23, 1949. I went to see a rehearsal of *Romeo and Juliet*, one of Moses Douglas' play productions. He had a small theater in a warehouse in Westtown. He introduced Mr. Bob Graves and me to the cast as guests. Mr. Graves and I even had a short talk about the play. After I left the rehearsal, I ran home. As I ran by the town square, I saw five white guys. One of them was Jimmy Jackson. All five were dressed normally, no KKK stuff. Jimmy saw me and yelled something like, 'Hey, pipsqueak, I know you. You tell that colored boy I saw at Mardi Gras that I'm gonna whup his ass and maybe worse next time I see him, you hear?' I'll tell you about the third time I saw Jimmy Jackson later."

I then started telling the rest of my story to the court as it unfolded that night. I told it in the sequence things happened. I was doing okay until I got to the part where Mr. Moses Douglas and Dr. Joshua Marshall were killed. Right then, I couldn't hold back crying a little. The bailiff handed me a tissue. After I regained my composure, I told about crying on Marvin's shoulder. I knew I had to tell the jury about the third time I saw Jimmy Jackson, but I had to do more than think about it.

"Thank you," I said to the bailiff and turning toward the jury I continued, "My third encounter with Jimmy Jackson was the worse. Marvin had told me that I had to go home. He said the streets were still full of the Ku Klux Klan. He led me through back alleys and said if we heard anyone coming, we should jump behind some bushes. We were near Marvin's home when we heard horses. We jumped in some bushes but too late. Someone made his horse rear up in front of us and yelled, 'Git out here. We know you're in there. Move it or we'll start shooting, or maybe, we'll burn you out.' Marvin got up and walked toward the men. I followed him. There were three riders in white hoods. The same voice that told us to come out, said, 'Fellas, lookie what we got here. The nigger-boy Marvin who thinks he's an American pilot. And his nigger-loving friend Steve, who ain't worth a piece of shit. He ain't nothing but a pipsqueak. What you think we oughta do to them, fellas?' Another voice said, 'I reckon we outta go easy on the white boy.' That's when I realized the first voice was Jimmy Jackson, so I spoke up, 'Jimmy, we ain't done you no harm. Leave us alone.' Jimmy said, 'Mind your manners, Steve. You speak again, and it'll be your last words.' Marvin stepped in front of me and said, 'Mr. Jackson, I'm the one you're mad at. Leave Steve out of this.' Then Jimmy said, 'Now Marvin wants to be brave so he can save his friend. Ain't that nice. I can be nice too. Steve, if I killed a white boy whose daddy owned the newspaper, I'd be in the electric chair at Kilby Prison in a flash. You run home now like a good little boy.' I tried to act brave and said, 'I ain't going nowhere without Marvin.' Marvin pushed me in the direction I had to go and said, 'You get going, Steve. These guys aren't kidding.' Jimmy fired his rifle in the air and said, 'You better do as Marvin suggested, or I'm gonna change my mind about killing your white ass. All three of us will fire our rifles three more times. If you ain't running home by then, you're done.' They fired the first shot."

I had to pause and blow my nose. I apologized to the court and continued, "I looked at Marvin. He shoved me toward home again, and said, 'Run. Steve, Run.' They fired the second shot. I stood still. Marvin shoved me again, and cried out, 'For Christ's sake, Steve, run like hell.' When they fired the third shot, I started running. The Klan guys were laughing and firing their rifles in the air. I looked back and heard Jimmy Jackson say to Marvin, 'Okay, nigger, let's see how fast you can run.' Then I heard Marvin yell for the last time, 'Keep running, Steve. Don't stop.' I ran as shots seemed to come from everywhere. I looked back and saw the men shooting at Marvin. As Marvin staggered, one of the men saw me and pointed his rifle at me, but he didn't shoot me. I turned away and feeling like the coward I was, I ran as fast as I could, and I kept repeating in my head, and sometimes out loud, 'Keep running, Steve,' until I got home. The lights were on in our house. I opened the front door, and Dad was standing there, with Mom behind him. Dad said, 'Steve, where the hell have you been?' I stumbled in babbling like a baby. The story of the evening came out of me like rushing water tumbling over rocks. When I stopped talking, I collapsed on the floor. I wasn't even sure what I said, but I cried inconsolably, and my body started to shake as if I had epilepsy. I think I heard Mom say, 'I'll call Dr. Thatcher.'"

I stopped talking and started crying, trying to hold my head up. I stared at the jurors, but they looked blurry.

The courtroom was quiet. Mr. Macey tapped me on the shoulder and said, "Well done, Steve. Your Honor, I have no further questions for this brave, young man."

Judge Johnson said, "Steve you may step down from the witness chair. The court will now be in recess until nine o'clock tomorrow morning.

Very few people had left the courtroom. Mom and Dad accompanied me as we walked toward the door. Some people stood and nodded at me. One old lady whispered, "Bless you Steve. You are a hero." I wanted to say to her, but didn't, "No, ma'am, I'm not a hero. Marvin Gibbs is a hero."

After we left the courthouse, Dad said, "I've got an idea. Maybe we can get a hotel room in Montgomery tonight instead of driving back and forth to Delphi. And, if we're lucky, we can have a fine dinner, and then see a movie."

I was delighted because it was a new adventure, dinner in a restaurant and maybe a movie. Dad more than satisfied my desires, when he took us to an early dinner at the hotel's restaurant which was quite upscale. At the end of dinner, Dad said, "I have three tickets for the seven o'clock movie, *Twelve O'Clock High*. Who's interested?"

Mom and I couldn't say yes fast enough. After the movie was over, I said, "Dad, I loved the film. General Savage was sure a tough cookie. What did you think?"

"Well, I reckon you're right, but I thought Colonel Gately held the ending together."

Mom just smiled and yawned. Once we were back in the hotel room, she said, "Okay, my two pilots, into bed immediately. We have another long day in court tomorrow."

38

The Trial—Day 5

Tuesday—August 2, 1949

TUESDAY MORNING, we finished our breakfast at the Montgomery hotel. We arrived early at the courthouse and went through much the same drill we had done with Sam Lancaster the day before. As Mr. Sam started to escort me to the witness room, Dad called out, "Steve, we'll see you in the courtroom soon."

Lillis tugged on Andy's coat sleeve. "Honey, Steve's been awfully quiet this morning. I think something's bothering him."

Andy hadn't noticed anything, but replied, "Oh, I'm sure he'll do fine. Hes been ready for this a long time."

"Yeah, maybe," Lillis said.

Andy knew full well that Lillis wasn't convinced.

Judge Johnson entered the courtroom at nine, hoping there would be no problems with the proceedings because of this heated trial. He said, "The court is in session. Mr. Hastings, do you wish to cross-examine Steve Thompson?"

"Your Honor, at this time, I request that you grant the defense a short deferral whereby we can cross-examine Steve Thompson after the prosecution presents their other witnesses."

The request created a buzz in the courtroom as the prosecution's lawyers conversed.

Judge Johnson said, "Quite an unusual request, Mr. Hastings. Comments, Mr. Macey?"

"Your Honor, the prosecution accepts Mr. Hastings request with exceptions. The defense must conduct cross-examinations of prosecution witnesses Mabel Gibbs and Fred Watson and then Steve Thompson. After which the prosecution will present its last witness, Dr. Alastair McDonald. At which time Mr. Hastings can cross-examine Dr. McDonald."

Judge Johnson said, "Mr. Hastings do you agree to the prosecutions exceptions?"

The defense's lawyers huddled around each other in an intense conversation.

Mr. Hastings finally stood and said, "Your Honor, the defense accepts the prosecution's exceptions."

Andy journal entry. *I hope all these legal gymnastic don't confuse the jury. Certainly the audience appears confused.*

Judge Johnson looked at both parties and said, "Mr. Hastings and Mr. Macey, I hereby grant the defense's request with the exceptions requested by the prosecution. Mr. Macey, you may continue presenting your case."

"Thank you, Your Honor. The prosecution calls for our next witness, Mrs. Mabel Gibbs."

After Mrs. Gibbs was sworn in and seated, Mr. Macey said, "Mrs. Gibbs, I'm sure everyone in this courtroom joins me in offering you and Mr. Gibbs our sincerest condolences for the tragic murder of your son, Marvin Gibbs."

"Thank you, sir."

"Mrs. Gibbs, please tell the court and jury in your own words what happened the Night of Terror when Steve Thompson came to your house."

Mrs. Gibbs said, gripping a handkerchief, "Yes, sir. It's pretty simple. Steve came to our house looking for Marvin. Of course, the Klan was poking around here too. Anyway, Marvin must have let Steve in the house. I came into the room where they were, and I asked the boys what they were doing. Marvin told me they had to go and find Moses Douglas and Dr. Joshua Marshall, two fine gentlemen. I told Marvin to stay right here in our house or he might get kilt. I also told Steve he had to get home to his house like I told him to do last night when he first came looking for Marvin. Then Marvin said we gotta do this, pulling Steve out the backdoor and closing the door in my face."

Mrs. Gibbs paused and then said, "Next thing I knowed was that my baby boy's body was laying on the road near our home, kilt by the Klan." Mrs. Gibbs broke down then, sobbing as she tried to wipe her eyes with the handkerchief.

Andy wrote in his journal. *I could see that most of the women in the courtroom were wiping tears and all the women in the jury were. Wonder how Hastings will handle the cross?*

Mr. Macey held Mrs. Gibbs hand and said, "No more question, Your Honor."

"Mr. Hastings, do you want to cross-examine Mrs. Gibbs?"

"Yes, Your Honor, just a few questions."

"Please proceed."

Mr. Hastings said, "Mrs. Gibbs, I want to add my personal condolences to the tragic loss of your son."

Mrs. Gibbs had regained her composure and nodded. But she continued to stare at Mr. Hastings, as if she wished he'd drop dead.

"Mrs. Gibbs, I have a couple of questions, just to clarify my understanding of your testimony. You said that Marvin disobeyed you when he and Steve left the house without your permission. Is that right?"

"I told Marvin to stay here in our house. If your words mean the same thing, I agree."

Mr. Hastings said, "Yes, I think we agree. Mrs. Gibbs, did Marvin disobey you often and what was his demeanor as a kid?"

"Huh, what you saying? I don't know the word demeanor. It don't sound nice."

The courtroom chuckled. Judge Johnson pounded the gavel once and everyone was quiet.

"I'm just trying to clarify a few things, Mrs. Gibbs."

"Well, I'll tell you this. My boy didn't disobey me much. I ain't saying he never did. You find me a boy what never disobeyed his parents, he gotta be an angel."

There were more chuckles, but Judge Johnson ignored it this time as a defense lawyer motioned Hastings to come to the defense table. The lawyer whispered something in his ear.

Hastings walked to the witness box and said, "I have no more question, Your Honor."

Andy wrote in his journal: *How could Hastings have not seen that he had lost out to Mrs. Gibbs?*

Judge Johnson said, "Mrs. Gibbs, You can step down. You can choose to sit in the courtroom if you wish."

"I will stay, Your Honor. Thank you."

Lillis offered Mrs. Gibbs an empty seat next to her. She sat down and smiled at Lillis.

"Mr. Macey, you may call for your next witness."

After Mr. Macey called for Fred Watson, and he was sworn in, Mr. Macey said, "Mr. Watson, welcome. I'd like to get right to the reason why you're here. Please tell the jury in your own words about your encounter with Jimmy Jackson at the Delphi Mardi Gras the night of March 1, 1949."

"Yes, sir. I live in Delphi with my wife. I work for Mr. Andy Thompson at the *Delphi Delta News* newspaper as a typesetter and do other odd jobs for the newspaper. I've worked there for ten years. I didn't know Jimmy Jackson until I had a casual meeting with him on the town square about two years ago. I saw him strutting there on the town square. I smiled at him and said, 'You like yourself, don't you?' He smiled back at me and said, 'Yes, sir. I'm Jimmy Jackson. What's your name old man?' I said, 'Fred Watson. Nice talking. I have to go.' Now, back to the Mardi Gras parade on March 1, 1949, Mr. Thompson asked me to drive the tractor that hauled the float that Steve and three of his buddies had built. I was happy to do it because I like those kids. Marvin Gibbs was one of the boys. It broke my heart to hear he had been murdered. Anyway, everything was going fine until I heard someone yelling behind me. I turned and saw three guys in Ku Klux Klan garb and red hats. I caught a few words that one of the guys was yelling at Marvin. Something like 'Ya watch yourself.' The guy then gave Marvin the finger, and that's when I recognized Jimmy Jackson. I stopped the tractor and said, 'Jimmy, you get the hell outta here. We don't cotton to your kind.' Jimmy responded, 'Ya a white piece of nigger-loving shit, Fred.' When the three men were being escorted off the parade route, Jimmy yelled back at Marvin, 'Boy, I'm gonna keep my eye on you.' That's all, I guess."

Mr. Macey said, "Thank you, Mr. Watson. One question. How well did you know Jimmy Jackson?"

"Not well at all. We weren't friends. I never talked to him again after the Mardi Gras parade."

"Thank you. Your Honor, I'm through questioning this witness."

"Very well," Judge Johnson said. "Mr. Hastings, you may start your cross-examination if you wish."

Mr. Hastings walked up to Mr. Watson and said, "Mr. Watson, do you think Jimmy Jackson killed Marvin Gibbs?"

"I don't know, sir. I wasn't near the crime scene. I live in the north part of Delphi. All I heard was a lot of gun shots. Later I saw some fires."

"Why are you so biased against Jimmy Jackson?"

"If I understand your question, I'm not biased against Jimmy. I'm just a working man who wants to tell the truth."

"My, my, Mr. Watson, you're quite a sanctimonious man, aren't you?"

"Sir, I don't know what that word means."

Judge Johnson said, "Mr Hastings, either explain to Mr. Watson what sanctimonious means or ask him another question."

"Yes, Your Honor. Mr. Watson, are you a nigger-loving shit?"

The courtroom went silent.

"Objection, Your Honor," Mr. Macey shouted.

Judge Johnson said, "Counselors, approach the bench."

Mr. Macey went to the bench while Mr. Hastings appeared to be shuffling.

In a quiet voice, Judge Johnson said, "Mr. Hastings, are you trying to incite a riot in my courtroom?"

"No, sir, I just call a spade a spade. Everybody uses the word nigger, even niggers use it."

"Surely, you must worry about what the Negros on the jury will think?"

"No, sir, I don't care. I'm sure at least one white juror will see things my way."

"Hmm...You're treading on thin ice, Mr. Hastings."

"Why are you biased against me, Judge Johnson?"

Judge Johnson smiled. "Comments, Mr. Macey?"

"Your Honor, I still would like a ruling on my objection, but before you do, I request a ten minute recess to confer with my attorneys."

"Granted. Court is in recess for ten minutes."

Sam Lancaster and Clark Hughes followed Ed Macey **to the counselor's** private room. "Fellas," Ed said, "I don't know if you could hear what Hastings said to the judge, but I thought he all but admitted that there is a white mole on the jury. Even if he doesn't know, I don't want either of you to come back into the courtroom when I have to. Sam, I want you to stay in the courtroom building and nose around the records room and see what they have on all the accepted white jurors including the alternates. Check if the names they used as jurors are in public records or not. The judge allowed juror's names to be public, so any mismatches should be explored further and other things like that. Send a copy of the juror's names to Clark ASAP. Clark, you go to our offices and get Oliver, Ben, and Garth to start poring over any records they can find. Both of you come back to the courtroom as soon as you have some meaningful news. I have to get back to the courtroom before the judge decides to spank me."

As Mr. Macey walked into the courtroom, Judge Johnson noted that two of Macey's lawyers weren't with him. Moving on, Judge Johnson said, "Ladies and gentlemen, the court is back in session. Mr. Macey, I rule that your objection is sustained. Mr. Watson, you don't have to answer Mr. Hastings' last question. Mr. Hastings, do you have any more questions for Mr. Watson?"

"No, Your Honor," Hastings said.

"Mr. Hastings, are you ready to cross-examine Steve Thompson?

Before Hastings could respond, Judge Johnson watched as Sam and Clark came into the courtroom and handed some papers to Macey who read the papers quickly, and then glanced at the jurors.

Judge Johnson felt upset and said, "Mr. Macey, what's going on? I see that your two lost lambs have returned."

Mr. Macey said, "Your Honor, may I approach the bench."

"Absolutely, and you also join us Mr. Hastings."

Macey, speaking in a quiet voice, said, "Your Honor, I'm sorry to disrupt the proceedings, but we have just discovered some unknown facts that are pertinent to a fair trial. The two lost lambs you referred to are Sam Lancaster and Clark Hughes."

Judge Johnson nodded at Sam and Clark. "Mr. Macey, what might those facts be?"

"That a juror lied under oath during the selection process, but was selected as one of the trial's twelve jurors."

"Gentlemen, let's move into my chambers."

Looking at the full courtroom, Judge Johnson said, "Ladies and gentlemen, we'll recess for lunch now. Court will convene at one o'clock. Bailiff, please see the jurors and witnesses are handled properly."

Gathered around a table in the judge's chambers, Judge Johnson said, "So, Mr. Macey, what evidence do you have to support your allegation."

"Your Honor, Sam Lancaster and Clark Hughes were out of the courtroom reviewing available documents about the jurors. Sam focused on the court's record room. Clark went to our offices nearby and directed a search of locally available records on the jurors. They—"

Mr. Hastings interrupted, "You Honor, this is rubbish. We knew nothing about the prosecuting team's inquires. In addition, their actions are grounds for a new trial or a dismissal of the charges against my clients."

Judge Johnson interlocked his fingers and pushed his hands outward as if exercising. "Mr. Hastings, let's slow down. As to a new trial or dismissal, I don't need a reminder from you at this time about the law. Mr. Macey, if the prosecution has violated any legal requirements or your new evidence is wanting, I'll deal with the prosecution as required by law. Now, Mr. Macey, let's see the substance of your findings."

"Your Honor, we have two documents. The first one shows all the names and numbers of the sitting jurors at this time, including the two alternates This was obtained from court records. This second document was obtained at the Montgomery County voter registration office. We checked to see if all the sitting jurors are on it. All were, except juror number eleven, Mr. Wilbur Freeman. Both of the documents have been signed by the person who helped us in each office, and they've both been notarized," Mr. Macey said, handing the documents to Judge Johnson who began reading them carefully.

"Mr. Macey, how did you get all of this done so quickly? And how is it Wilbur Freeman got on the jury if he wasn't on the county voter rolls?"

"Sam and Clark are good lawyers, Your Honor, and honestly, they had some good luck. To your second question, we don't know. I can only speculate on the reason, but it's a fact that he wasn't on the county voter rolls. Perhaps someone bribed a person that works in the voter registration office to post Freeman's name on the rolls while prospective jurors were being vetted."

Mr. Hastings leapt out of his chair, "These documents haven't been subjected to a chain of custody review."

Judge Johnson scratched his head. "Mr. Hastings, be careful, I'm worried that your acrobatics may result in an injury. As to the chain of custody, we are experiencing the start of that process right now. Excuse me, I'll be right back."

Judge Johnson went into the empty courtroom and found the bailiff. "Hi, Jimmy, do you know why I don't call you by your first name?"

"That's easy, Your Honor, it's the same name as one of the defendants, and I appreciate that you don't."

"Good. I have something you need to do. Go to the jury room and escort juror number eleven, Wilbur Freeman, to my chambers."

"Yes, sir, right away. I know who he is."

Soon after Judge Johnson was back in his chambers, the bailiff came in and said, "Your Honor, this is juror number eleven, Mr. Wilbur Freeman."

"Thank you, bailiff." As the bailiff closed the door, Judge Johnson turned back to the attorneys, "Gentlemen, meet Wilbur Freeman."

Wilbur Freeman appeared visibly frightened. He was a small man, very skinny, and thinning gray hair. "Please, Mr. Freeman, sit down next to the gentleman to my right, Do you have any idea why we want to talk to you?"

"No, sir, Your Honor, I just sit quietly in the jury box listening to everyone. It's interesting."

"Mr. Freeman, we have strong evidence in hand that proves that Wilbur Freeman is not you real name. What is your real name? But before you answer, remember that you might go to jail for lying to the court."

Mr. Freeman looked like he was in a chicken coop about to be decapitated for dinner. He said, "Uh...My real name is Baxter Defoe. I didn't want to do it, but I was backed into a corner."

"How so, Mr. Defoe?"

"Your Honor, I've done time in prison for a robbing a small store in Montgomery. I'm on parole now, but I violated it. I've laid low since…that is until he found me."

"Are you a member of the Ku Klux Klan?"

"I was, but I haven't participated in the Klan since I got out of prison."

Judge Johnson thought for a moment how to phrase his next question and having decided, said, "Mr. Defoe, what's the name of the person who found you?"

"Your Honor, do I have to answer that question? I'm afraid for my life." Mr. Defoe appeared to be sweating.

"Mr. Defoe, if you answer, we will provide you some protection. If not, I will have the bailiff turn you over to the deputy sheriff who will put you in jail awaiting further action."

Mr. Defoe still looked caged, but finally he said, "His name is Bob Graves. I don't know how he found me, but he said if I didn't cooperate with him, he would turn me into the authorities for my parole violation. He added that if I cooperated with him and voted not guilty in the trial, he would pay me $500."

Mr. Macey spoke up, "Your Honor, if you recall, Steve Thompson testified in court yesterday that he met Bob Graves at a rehearsal of *Romeo and Juliet* at Moses Douglas' theater in Westtown. Since Bob

Graves has not been indicted for a crime related to May 25, 1949, we choose not to pursue it any further. Obviously, we made a mistake."

"Yes, I recall Steve's testimony yesterday. The matter of Bob Graves will be pursued later. Mr. Defoe, if you are correct, it appears that Bob Graves not only threatened you, but also bribed you. Mr. Defoe, is it also possible that Bob Graves bribed someone in the voter registration office?"

"I reckon it's possible, Your Honor, but I don't know."

"Mr. Hastings, did you know that Mr. Defoe was not a bona fide juror?"

Mr. Hastings looked like he was about to perform one of his acrobatic moves, but instead he said, "Absolutely not, Your Honor. I never saw or heard of either Wilbur Freeman or Baxter Defoe until I saw him in the jury box."

"Well, gentlemen, here's how the court will proceed. When the court reconvenes, our first action will be to replace juror number eleven with alternate number one. Since the alternates were sworn in with the original jurors, the trial will continue. Any objections?"

"Hearing none, let's move into the courtroom as it's nearly one o'clock."

I was getting antsy in the witness waiting room. The lunch they gave us was okay. At one o'clock the bailiff finally came to get me. When I entered the courtroom, no one gasped. I figured that was good. But there were several gasps, including mine, when we all realized a new juror was in the jury box, a Negro man.

I had a flashback moment to the day when Billy and I went to the creek. As Billy and I sat by the creek talking, we saw a fisherman who looked like the new juror. I couldn't believe it. He was medium height, kinda elegant. Maybe fifty years old. Trimmed gray beard. *How can this be? Now this is weird.*

Judge Johnson, said, "Juror number eleven, as the newest member of the jury panel of twelve, you are still under oath as are all the jurors. Sir, do you understand?"

The juror stood and said, in a clear and articulate voice, "I do, Your Honor."

Judge Johnson said, "Thank you, juror. Steve you may sit down. You are still under oath. Are you ready?"

"Yes, sir." I wanted to say, *You bet I am.*

"Your witness, Mr. Hastings."

Mr. Hastings smiled at me as if he liked me, and said, "Hello, Steve, nice to see you. Are you enjoying being a witness?"

"Well, sir, enjoy is not the word I'd use, but I'm glad to be in the courtroom. It's my duty."

"I like that, Steve. Yes, we all have a duty in the courtroom to tell the truth. Are you telling the truth, Steve?"

I think, *Mr. Hastings' nuts.* "Yes, sir, I am."

"Do you, dream, Steve?"

What's he getting at? I thought. "Yes, sir, I suppose everyone does."

"What do you dream about?"

"Sir, that's a tough to answer, but I guess I dream about a lot of things. Steve thought, *What's going on?* "Sir, they're all over the map. Some are funny, some are about girls, some are about sports, and some seem like horror stories."

Mr. Hastings smiled at me. "Steve, do you think your dreams are very imaginative?"

Mr. Macey stood. "Objection, Your Honor. Speculation. Mr. Hastings is asking Steve to answer an absurd question, because how can anyone know for sure how imaginative their dreams are."

"Sustained. Mr. Hastings, please rephrase your question or drop the subject."

"I'll move on, Your Honor. Steve, do you have many friends in Westtown?"

"Well, there's Marvin, Moses Douglas, and Joshua Marshall, all of whom are dead. Then there's Billy who was also a good friend of Marvin's. Then, of course, there's Mrs. Gibbs, a wonderful lady. That's about it, I guess. I might have forgotten a few."

"Quite a list. Were they all colored?"

I think I know where he's going, I thought. "Yes, sir, they all lived in Westtown."

"So I imagined. Do you have many white friends?"

"*Ah*, I thought, *here comes the trap.* "Yes, sir, quite a few. I went to elementary school in Delphi where I had many white kids and adults as friends. Too many to remember. I can write a list of their names if you want me to."

"Well, Steve, since all white people have many white friends and very few colored friends, is it safe to safe to say you're a nigger lover?"

The courtroom went silent until Judge Johnson, said, "Mr. Hastings, approach the bar."

Yep, that was the trap, I thought. Mr. Hastings took his time walking up to the bar. I couldn't hear what they talked about, but when Mr. Hastings came back, he looked mad.

Then he said to the judge, "Your Honor, I have no more questions for this witness."

Judge Johnson said to me, "Steve, you may step down, and you may stay in the courtroom if you wish."

I sat in an open seat behind Mom, but then a nice man seated next to Mom offered to switch seats with me, and I immediately swapped with him.

Judge Johnson looked stoic and said, "Mr. Macey, you may call your next witness."

Mr. Macey called out for Dr. Alastair McDonald. I almost freaked out. This was the big one. I thought back to the day when I took the voice recognition test in Dr. McDonald's soundproof room. I kinda enjoyed it but had no idea how I did. I'll find out today.

After Dr. McDonald was sworn in, Mr. Macey said, "Dr. McDonald, please tell the court your credentials to have become a renowned expert on voice recognition."

As he started listing his credentials, my head felt like it would explode. I lost track of the number, but they were all impressive.

Mr. Macey then asked, "Dr. McDonald, how many voice recognition test have you administered?"

"Nine hundred and fifty. I maintain accurate records."

"When did you administer your test to Steve Thompson?"

"On July 1, 1949, at one o'clock.."

"How did you deal with a fourteen-year-old boy?"

Dr. McDonald smiled and said, "Mr. Macey, perhaps you should rephrase your question to something like, 'How did a fourteen-year-old boy deal with an aging doctor?' Steve was most inquisitive when he came into the soundproof room. I explained everything to him about the room, but he never asked how the test was to be conducted, which I found amazing. Everyone wants to know how the test is done."

"Dr. McDonald, I think it's time to ask the question everyone in the courtroom has been waiting to hear. Dr. McDonald, how did Steve Thompson do on the voice recognition test?"

"Mr. Macey, Steve Thompson passed the test."

I wanted to yell but sat quietly, while many in the audience simply gasped.

The judge let the noise subside, then said, "Mr. Macey, I will ask the next question. Dr. McDonald, at the meeting in my chambers on June 24, 1949, Mr. Macey, Mr. Hastings, and I met you for the first time to consider you as an expert witness. Do you remember the meeting?"

"Absolutely, Your Honor."

Wow, I thought, t*his is getting interesting.*

Judge Johnson said, "Dr. McDonald, after a lengthy discussion about you and your test, all parties in the room accepted you as a court expert witness. That included myself, Mr. Hastings, Mr. Macey, and you with one important stipulation, Steve had to score 100% on the test. You just testified that he passed. Did Steve's score meet the 100% stipulation?"

It's too quiet, I thought, *I can't stand it.*

Dr. McDonald, looking at Mr. Macey and Mr. Hastings, and said, "Judge Johnson, Steve Thompson scored 100%."

Mr. Hastings jumped up before anyone could react and said, "Objection, Your Honor. I reserve the right to withdraw my agreement to the stipulation."

At least Mr. Hastings has put the kibash on any loud audience behavior, I thought.

Judge Johnson appeared angry, but he said evenly, "Mr. Hastings, you demanded the 100% stipulation, and then agreed to it with all the others. The agreement has been in the court's records for over a month. Of course, you'll get your chance to cross-examine Dr. McDonald. Your objection is overruled."

I saw the judge peek at his watch. Then he said, "Ladies and gentlemen, the court will be in recess until tomorrow morning at nine o'clock when Mr. Hastings can start his cross-examination of Dr. McDonald if he wishes."

When Mom and Dad decided we'd drive home, Mom started humming. That always meant she had a new recipe in mind for dinner. We didn't have to arrive early the next because I was no longer on the hot seat.

39

The Trial—Day 6

Wednesday—August 3, 1949

WE GOT TO THE COURTHOUSE in time to get our seats. I had *On The Origin of Species* in the witness waiting room. I must confess I didn't read it all. A lot of it was pretty turgid—*New word for me, I love it.*—and hard to understand. I'll give it another chance later.

Judge Johnson called the court to order and said, "Bailiff, please escort the jury into the jury box."

"We're ready to begin proceedings. Mr. Hastings, you may cross-examine Dr. McDonald."

I couldn't wait, and I hoped it wouldn't become a bummer. *Steve,* I told myself, *don't use silly words.*

After Dr. McDonald was settled in the witness chair, Mr. Hastings asked, "Sir, are you getting tired of being an expert witness in this trial?"

"No."

"That's good, for I have some questions. Do you really think Steve Thompson correctly identified Jimmy Jackson in your voice test?"

"Yes."

"Sir, how can it be that a fourteen-year-old boy could score 100% on your test when no one else has?"

"I don't know?"

"You don't know? How can that be? Please be more specific."

"The simple answer is that it's a mystery. More specifically, the brain is a complex organ, and there is much that we don't understand about it. Why was Albert Einstein able to conceive of the theory of relativity? Why was Shakespeare able to write such incredible plays and poems? Why was a young Mozart such an accomplished musician and composer? All we know is that some people are born with insights that most of us don't have. As to Steve, perhaps he has some insights that are special. I really don't know."

"Well, Dr. McDonald, that was all very interesting, but I still don't trust your test results because you refuse to talk about them. So, how does your test work? And don't forgot, you swore to tell the truth."

"Mr. Hastings, when asked that question by you and others, I declined to be specific. Revealing the process to anyone associated with the court, including Steve, would give an unfair advantage to them, thus invalidating the test."

"I understand, Dr. McDonald, please explain the test."

I opened my notebook in preparation for taking notes.

"Mr. Hastings, all of you will have to visualize what I'm explaining. Perhaps, if the court has an easel with a large blank pad of paper on it, I could draw some figures."

Judge Johnson said, "We have something like that. Bailiff, please bring us an easel and paper. Any objections, counselors?"

Both counselors said no. As the bailiff set up the easel, I readied my notepad.

Dr. McDonald began drawing on the big sheet of paper, "To start with the test is made up of five empty rows. Each row has five empty cells. Questions?"

The counselors said no for the second time. Then the judge asked the jurors if they understood the figures. They all answered yes. *Wow*, I thought, *this is more than interesting. It's sensational.*

"Next, in the soundproof room in my office, my assistant and I recorded the voices of five young, male individuals one at a time. We asked each of them to memorize a short sentence of six to eight words. One of the voices is Jimmy Jackson's. We had them say the sentence about eight times, and then we picked the best one to serve our need. We didn't alter the voices in any manner. Questions?"

Mr. Hastings looked itchy and said, "So, Dr. McDonald, are you and your assistant the only ones who choose the final voices."

"Yes, and as I am the expert witness, I'll repeat under oath that we play no favorites."

"How can I trust you, Dr. McDonald?"

Mr. Macey stood. "Objection, Your Honor. Dr. McDonald has answered all the question with patience and under oath. The jury will make the final judgment after Mr. Hastings' final remarks."

"Objection sustained. Mr. Hastings, move along, please."

"Yes, Your Honor, I'll move along as fast as I can. Dr. McDonald, what else do you have to tell us about your test?"

"Mr. Hastings, I'm sorry you don't trust me, but moving along, there are a few more steps in the test. After all five of the voices are recorded, we numbered them 1 to 5. The number 3 was assigned to Jimmy Jackson. Let me draw them."

In addition to writing notes in my notepad, I started drawing the five rows with five cells in each row, so I was ready to put the numbers 1 to 5 in each in cell as Dr. McDonald wrote them for the jurors to see.

Dr. McDonald said, "I'll start by writing the numbers 1 to 5 in the cells in the first row. Note that the numbers read, left to right, in sequence as 1 to 5. In the second row, the numbers are, left to right, 3, 2, 5, 4, 1, and all 5 numbers are present but in a different order. In the third row, the numbers are, left to right, 5, 1, 4, 2, 1. As you can see, the number 3 is missing, and replaced by a second number 1. In the fourth row, the numbers are, left to right, 4, 2, 1, 5, 3, and all 5 numbers are present but in a different order. In the fifth row, the numbers are, left to right, 2, 4, 5, 1, 5. As you can see, the number 3 is missing, and replaced by a second number 5. I know this may appear complicated at first blush but I think things will be clearer after I describe the last step in the test."

Mr. Macey, stood and said, "Your Honor, I request that Dr. McDonald's drawing be accepted as an exhibit."

Judge Johnson said, "Objections?" He paused for a few seconds and then said, "Hearing none, so ordered. The clerk will number this exhibit."

I finished my drawing and held it up to admire it.

I was glad I had my ruler, so I could make the drawing look neat. *I'm a neat freak. My mother thinks I'm a mess.* Dr. McDonald was doing great. Whenever he could, he looked at the jurors when he spoke, and they appeared to be watching him intently.

1	2	3	4	5
3	2	5	4	1
5	1	4	2	1
4	2	1	5	3
2	4	5	1	5

"As I was saying, the last steps will take us to the conclusion of the test. My assistant and I made five separate recordings of the five voices for each of the five rows. For example, the first row had voices number 1, 2, 3, 4, 5. The last four rows were recorded in the same manner using the voice numbers you can see on the drawing. With those things completed, we were ready for Steve to take the test. A reminder, he knew absolutely nothing about the prior steps. We provided Steve headphones that fit comfortably around each ear. We then told him that we had five recorded voices, including Jimmy Jackson, that he would listen to five separate times. We told him he could ask for one replay of each row if he wished. Then we told him we'd ask him to identify Jimmy's voice in each row, and my assistant and I would write down his answers. That concluded the test. What proved to be amazing was that the two rows which did not have Jimmy's voice, Steve said, and I quote, 'Jimmy's voice is not in that row.' You might properly ask how Steve was able—"

Mr. Hastings interrupted and said, “Thank you for the explanation, Dr. McDonald. Your Honor, I have no further questions for this witness.”

Judge Johnson said, “I’ll allow Dr. McDonald to finish his last statement, and then he can be excused.”

I don’t know why, but Mr. Hastings turned and looked at me in a snarky manner. *He’s not happy.*

“Briefly, Your Honor, the reason Steve was able to detect that Jimmy’s voice was not in two rows when others who had taken the same test had not been able to is imprecise. What many psychologist have observed is that most people performing a test want to please the teacher or professor, if you will. Even if the person taking the test doesn’t know the answer, they will offer an answer. Perhaps, Steve had prepared himself so well mentally for the test that he was able to ignore pleasing me. All I can say for sure about Steve’s ability is that his brain and memory works in ways we don’t fully understand. I’m finished, Your Honor.”

“Thank you, Dr. McDonald, you may step down from the witness box.”

I wish they would stop making me sound like Superman. It embarrasses me.

Mr. Hastings appeared to be seething when Judge Johnson asked him, “Mr Hastings, since Dr. McDonald was the prosecution’s last witness, are you ready to present the defense’s case?”

“Yes, Your Honor. I have a witness who just came forward to us. We haven’t had time to depose him or to mention him to the prosecution. He has come forth on his own volition and has information pertinent to this case.”

“Mr. Macey, comments?”

“Your Honor, in the interest of fair play and the truth, we do not object to the new witness.”

“Mr. Hastings, please proceed.”

“You Honor, the defense calls for Bertrand Holloway. He is in the courtroom since he isn’t on the official witness list.”

After the bailiff led Mr. Holloway to the witness box, the judge asked him a few questions and gave him the oath. Then I sized him up.

He was a scraggly looking old man, maybe sixty-years-old, wearing workman's coveralls. He had gray hair and an unkempt gray beard.

Mr. Hastings strode to the witness box and said, "Mr. Holloway, let me start by asking you a few questions. Where do you live?"

"Acorn, Alabama. It's up in the north part of the state."

"What county and how far up north?"

"Acorn County. It's pretty fer up north, almost to the state line. I reckon Huntsville is 'bout thirty miles north of Acorn."

"Pray tell," said Mr. Hastings, "and I hear Acorn's a nice, small town. Am I right?"

"Oh, yes sir, we are a nice town with 'bout fifteen hundred nice people and we all get along and treat everybody the same."

"What is it that moved you to offer to be a witness in a trial so far from your home?"

"Well, sir, that's a bit of a story."

"Mr. Holloway, please tell us your story in your own words."

"Yes, sir, be pleased to do so. Well, you see I used to work as a mechanic at a car repair shop in Acorn. I'm retired now and after my wife died six months ago, bless her soul, I was alone with nothin' to do. I was talkin' to one of my buddies and he said he liked to go to the Huntsville courthouse and watch trials. He said you get to laugh and cry, and sometimes you'd learn somethin'. Well, dang if he wasn't right. I've been goin' fer 'bout four months. You wanna hear more, Mr. Hastings?"

"Well, I reckon I do, Mr. Holloway. What trial or trials motivated you to contact one of my lawyers?"

"Yes, sir, that's the last part of my story. A few weeks ago I went to a trial, and I couldn't believe what I heard. It wasn't a criminal case, it was a tort case. I learned 'bout tort by goin' to trials. Anyhow, two partners had sued each other and both claimed the other had stolen company money. I didn't write the partners names down. I'll just call them Bob and Bill. Bob said he had overheard a conversation between Bill and a man named Freddy Flowers. You see, I knowed all this because it came up in the trial. The second day, I was at the trial, this expert witness named Dr. Alastair McDonald was there. He was an expert on somethin' called a voice recognition test. It was crazy. I didn't understand much but he claimed the test proved that Bob had not recognize Freddy Flowers' voice in the test. So, Bill would have won the case, except the partners came to an agreement before the trial went to the jury for a decision. What a nutty trial. I think I got it right."

"Mr. Holloway, what a story, but I still don't get why you came to us. Can you tell me that?"

"Yes, sir, I'm sorry. I knowed I'm kinda slow, but I ain't dumb. I've been takin' the *Birmingham News* for years. After your trial started, I read articles in the paper, and when I saw McDonald's name, I decided to call your lawyer. I've always supported the underdogs, and I feel kinda partial for the defense."

"I see, Mr. Holloway. Your Honor, I'd like to talk to my lawyers at the defense table. I'll be right back."

I watched the defense table carefully with my ears perked up. Of course I couldn't hear what they said, but all the lawyers appeared intense.

"Your Honor, I have no more questions for this witness."

"Fine. Mr Macey, do you wish to cross-examine the witness."

"Yes, Your Honor." Macey paused, twirling a pencil in his hand as he approached the witness, saying, "Mr. Holloway, that was quite a story you told. Sir, do you know what a sundown town means?"

"I'm not sure."

"Well, I'll tell you what it means. It's a town that orders all Negros to leave town by sundown. In fact, some sundown towns order all Negros to be out of town almost all the time. Is Acorn a sundown town?"

I saw Mr. Holloway starting to squirm.

"Can't rightly say. I mean, maybe a few people do that. Not me."

"Mr. Holloway, in you testimony you said and I quote from the transcript, 'Oh, yes sir, we a nice town with 'bout fifteen hundred nice people and we all get along and treat everybody the same.' Do you remember saying that."

"Well, I reckon I do."

"Acorn has always been a notorious sundown town. You could be charged for perjury by this court, Mr. Holloway. Are you or have you ever been a member of the Ku Klux Klan?"

"It's a secret society, so I can't answer that question. I—"

Judge Johnson said, "Mr. Holloway, you must answer the question or the consequences could be serious."

"I was for a while, but I haven't been to a meeting in years."

Mr. Macey said, "Mr. Holloway, the trials you visited in Huntsville, were the courtrooms all white people or a mix of whites and Negros?"

Mr. Holloway appeared to be lost. "All white."

I think I know what Mr, Hastings strategy is, I thought. *He's relying on Mr. Macey to do his dirty work, rather than admit to the court the witness is impeachable.*

Mr. Macey asked, "Have your ever been in a courtroom with a mix of whites and Negros."

"No."

"Mr. Holloway, do you recognize the name Bob Graves?"

Mr. Holloway squirmed even more. I was starting to feel sorry for the old man.

"No."

"Your Honor, I have finished with my cross-examination of this witness."

"Mr. Hastings, do you have more witnesses to call?"

"No, Your Honor, not at this time."

"Mr. Holloway, you are dismissed. Bailiff, please keep the witness in the courtroom. I want to talk to him in my chambers after we adjourn.

Mr. Macey stood and said, "Your Honor, we deposed a defense witness named Rodger Dalton. He was added to the defense's list of witnesses quite late. Will we get a chance to cross-examine him?"

"Mr. Macey, you know full well that the defense can decide not to call a witness if they wish. Any comment, Mr. Hastings?"

"Only that your ruling is correct, Your Honor."

Gee whiz, I thought, *what's going on now? Maybe Mr. Hastings decided that Rodger Dalton might get tangled up during his cross-examination witness as did Mr. Holloway.*

Judge Johnson said, "Counselors, please be ready to present your closing statements to the jury tomorrow morning. Ladies and gentlemen, court is adjourned. We'll convene tomorrow at nine o'clock."

Dad and Mom decided to drive home rather than spend the night in Montgomery. That was fine with me. I couldn't wait for another of Mom's fine dinners along with a piece of pie.

40

The Trial—Day 7

Thursday—August 4, 1949

I WAS STILL PONDERING WHY MR. HASTINGS seemed to roll over like a pussy cat yesterday. The best I could come up with was that he let Mr. Macey do the dirty work on Mr. Holloway. I decided I had to go to the higher authorities that I trusted, my Mom and Dad.

"Dad, do you think Mr. Hastings fared very well yesterday?"

Dad laughed, keeping his eyes on the road as he drove us back to Montgomery.

"No, Hastings had a terrible day. I'm pretty sure he and his staff were delighted when Holloway came forward, but I dare say that he and his staff failed to vet Holloway carefully, and woe be to the young lawyer who first answered Holloway's phone call. However, Steve, I detect that you have an opinion."

While I was thinking about what to say, Mom chimed in and said, "Well, I'll tell you what I think. Hastings is a coward and so used to winning all his cases defending the Klan, he took his eyes off the ball and failed to understand that Judge Johnson and Mr. Macey were unlike any of the prior judges and prosecutors he had faced."

Dad said, "Mom got the last word and she nailed it. Here we are. Let's hustle, We don't want to be late. I think the jury will get the case today."

Judge Johnson sat down on the bench saying, "Ladies and gentlemen, the court is in session. Mr. Macey, please present your closing statement to the jurors."

Mr. Macey maintained a comfortable distance from the jurors. "Good morning, I want to thank you all for your patience and attention throughout this trial. The evidence in this trial proves beyond a shadow of doubt that the three defendants are guilty. Let's review the evidence that proves the guilt of these defendants. At the beginning of the trial, the coroner testified that the body of Marvin Gibbs was found near his parents' home, and he showed you, the jurors, photos of Marvin's mutilated body. Next the Delphi police chief testified that, while no murder weapon had been found, ballistic analyses had shown that Marvin had been shot three times in the back, twice by a .22 rifle and once by a .35 mm rifle, which did the most damage to Marvin's body. Thus, the coroner and police chief substantiated three facts. One, the location of Marvin's body, and two, no murder weapon had been found, and three, the type of bullets that killed Marvin."

Mr. Macey paused and stepped a little bit closer to the jury box. I wondered what he was doing when he said, "Jurors, the defense will likely try to convince you that since no murder weapon has been found, you must bring in a not guilty verdict. That is factually incorrect. The law does not require a murder weapon in a criminal trial. The jury may decide that the evidence overwhelming supports a guilty verdict. I'm sure Judge Johnson will repeat that fact to you later."

Mr. Macey paused again. I guess he wanted to give the jurors a chance to think about what he was saying. "We will now consider the testimonies of the prosecution's witnesses. Mrs. Mabel Gibbs, Marvin's mother, testified that Steve Thompson was indeed in Westtown the night of May 25, 1949, also known as the Night of Terror. Mrs. Gibbs bravely testified to offset the defense's contention that Steve might not have been there. Fred Watson participated in the annual Delphi Mardi Gras parade on March 1, 1949. Fred testified about his encounter with Jimmy Jackson, one of the defendants in this case. Fred validated that Jimmy is a member of the Klan and the threats he made to Marvin Gibbs and the vile words he yelled at Fred. Fred's testimony was also necessary because it provides a bridge to Steve Thompson's testimony concerning Jimmy Jackson. As well, ladies and gentlemen of the jury, Dr. Alastair McDonald, the voice recognition expert witness, testified in detail about the voice test he performed on Steve Thompson. When Dr. McDonald announced that Steve had not only passed his test and identified Jimmy Jackson's voice, he clearly stated that Steve is the first person to have received a score of 100% on the test. So, we finally come to Steve Thompson as a witness. His testimony about his experiences on May 25, 1949, was so compelling and heartrending it was hard not to cry at some point. Steve described his eyewitness accounts of the deaths of three of his friends, Moses Douglas, Dr. Joshua Marshall, and Marvin Gibbs. Jurors, these stepping stones in the prosecution's case from the testimonies of our witnesses tie together a web of the facts and the truth. Before I close, please remember Marvin's last words when he died, 'For Christ's sake, Steve, run like hell. Keep running Steve. Don't stop.' Ladies and gentlemen of the jury, I ask that you return a guilty verdict for all three defendants. Thank you."

After a pause that allowed Mr. Macey to return to the prosecutor's table, Judge Johnson said, "Mr. Hastings, please present your closing statement to the jurors."

Mr. Hastings strutted toward the jurors as if he didn't have a care in the work.

That's a bad attitude to project, and now he's cozying up close to the jurors, almost in their faces.

"Well, ladies and gentlemen of the jury, that was quite a performance Mr. Macey put on for you, bringing tears to your eyes and having the temerity to tell you what I might say or do. If you don't know what temerity means, it means audacity. Then he said he wove a web around the testimonies of his witnesses to prove his case. Well, all he proved was more like a Rube Goldberg idea, which doesn't prove anything."

Yikes, he's saying things to the jury that I don't even understand. I looked at the jury and most of them were looking at each other as if they didn't get it either.

Mr. Hastings continued, "What I can tell you is that the defendants are not guilty. I don't know who killed Marvin Gibbs, but I can tell you it wasn't any of the defendants. And all this hullabaloo about the Klan is just a smoke screen to muddy the truth. But what isn't muddy is the fact that a murder weapon hasn't been found. The prosecution says it doesn't matter. I say it does, and now, I know you will do your duty as God-fearing Christian people and bring a verdict of not guilty for the three young men, Jimmy Jackson, Bubba Smith, and Willie Warden. And remember, it's always about our southern way of life, protecting our white women and properly taking care of scoundrels, and you know what I mean. Thank you."

The courtroom went quiet. I had never heard so much mumbo jumbo from a lawyer.

Judge Johnson finally broke the silence. "Mr. Macey, you're allowed a rebuttal if you wish."

"I certainly do, Your Honor." Turning to the jury, he said plainly, "Ladies and gentlemen of the jury, I have never heard such a closing statement as Mr. Hastings just made. It's filled with many things that have no bearing on this trial, including his last comment which was pure Ku Klux Klan ideology. As to the rest of his comments, he didn't offer any evidence or witness testimonies to substantiate his comments. Our legal system is based on the principle that proven evidence is the foundation of a fair trial. As to the need of a murder weapon, I will repeat that the law does not require it. Thank you."

Judge Johnson said, "The court will take a fifteen minute recess."

Mom and Dad and I remained in our seats. I had a bunch of questions to ask them, but I knew it would be inappropriate to ask them now. Mom handed me her unfinished crossword puzzle, and I finished it but for a few words.

When Judge Johnson came back into the court, he announced, "The court is back in session. Members of the jury, I will now read my instructions to you. A copy of my instructions will be provided to you when you begin your deliberations. Several things need to be repeated. The defendants in this trial are assumed to be innocent until they have been proven guilty. The burden of proof lies with the prosecution who must prove that the evidence in this trial is so clear and convincing that the defendants are guilty. As to the point of no murder weapon having been found, you, the jury, may bring in a guilty verdict if you decide the preponderance of evidence is clear and convincing. Your function in this trial is to reach a unanimous verdict that is based solely on the evidence. No statement or ruling or remark that I made during the course of the trial was intended to indicate my opinion as to what the facts are. You as jurors will consider the evidence and determine the facts in this case. To reach a verdict of guilty or not guilty, the jury must be unanimous or we will have a hung jury situation to deal with."

The judge paused and took a sip of water. "You, the jury, will determine the credibility of the witnesses and the weight of the evidence. You may consider the appearance and manner of the witnesses on the stand, their intelligence, their opportunity for knowing the truth and for having observed the things about which they testified, their interest in the outcome of the case, their bias, and, any prior inconsistent statements, or whether they have knowingly testified untruthfully as to any material fact in the case. You should not arbitrarily disregard believable testimony of a witness. However, after you have considered all the evidence in the case, you may accept or discard all or part of the testimony of a witness as you think proper. Use your common sense in considering the evidence, and trust that you may draw reasonable inferences from that evidence; but in doing so, you should not indulge in guesswork or speculation. From consideration of these things, you should determine which witnesses are more believable and weigh their testimonies accordingly."

The judge paused and took another sip of water. *Gees, he must like water a lot.* "You may not discuss the case with anyone or remain within hearing of anyone who is discussing it. There will be occasional recesses during the deliberations. During the recesses, you may not discuss the case with fellow jurors nor go to the scene or make any independent investigation or receive any information about the case from radio or the newspapers. You must discuss the case only in the jury room when all members of the jury are present. When you start your deliberations, you will first select a jury foreman or forewoman. I will provide you the necessary forms on which to enter your verdict. Jurors, you are free to ask the court for clarifications and other materials pertinent to the case while in deliberation. Write your questions on a piece of paper and the bailiff will bring it to me for consideration. I thank you as you perform a duty that is the bedrock of our legal system. That concludes my instructions to the jury. Bailiff, please escort the jurors to the jury deliberation room."

Judge Johnson waited until the jury was out of the courtroom, and then said, "Ladies and gentlemen, the jury will deliberate everyday, exclusive of weekends. When the jury reaches a verdict, they will be sequestered in hotel rooms until the defendants and the counselors are settled in the courtroom. Then the jury will be brought back to the courtroom and their verdict will be announced. Audience members and reporters will be responsible to find a way to hopefully be informed. With that, ladies and gentlemen, the court is adjourned."

41

The Trial—Day 8

Friday—August 5, 1949

DAD AND MOM DECIDED TO STAY in Montgomery overnight because the jury's deliberations could end at any time. Hotel space was tight, so we had to stay in a motel on the outskirts of town. The motel recommended a nice restaurant. After we ate, Dad said we had to go to bed early because he wanted to get up early the next morning to see what was up with the jury.

Mom woke me Friday morning. We had a quick breakfast and got to the courthouse at seven o'clock. It was the start of another hot, humid day, so we found a nice place to sit under some oak trees in a nearby park.

Mom and I read our books. Dad paced a lot, and every thirty minutes or so, he walked around to see if there was any news. Nothing happened until about ten o'clock.

Dad came running toward us and yelled, "The jury has reached a verdict. Let's get in line."

Well, that wasn't that easy. When we lined up at door, someone came out of the courtroom and told us it would be at least thirty or forty minutes before the counselors and the court's staff members were ready. We did get into the courthouse, where it was cooler.

I asked Dad, "Is it a good sign for our side that the jury has reached a decision so soon?"

"Could be, but it still could go either way. I know the waiting is frustrating."

Finally, as if the Red Sea had parted, the doors opened and in we went. Mom and I sat together, and Dad sat at the reporter's table.

Judge Johnson entered at eleven o'clock sharp and said, "The court is in session." He pounded his gavel, "Ladies and gentlemen, I will not tolerate any outbursts when the verdict is announced. The courtroom will be emptied if necessary. Bailiff, please escort the jurors into the jury box."

I felt both hot and cold as the jurors sat down in the jury box. They all looked so serious that I had no idea what those looks meant. I looked around the room and most people looked serious too. I thought, *Yes, this must be serious business.*

Judge Johnson asked the jury, "Jurors, have you reached a verdict?"

The Negro man who was the alternate that replaced the dismissed juror stood and said, "Your Honor, I am the jury Foreman, and yes, we have reached a verdict."

My God, that man, I'll call him the mystery juror, is also the Foreman. Weird upon weird.

Judge Johnson said, "The court clerk will accept the verdict from the Foreman and read it."

The court clerk opened the envelope with the verdict, and she read it carefully to herself, and then announced, "Your Honor, the jury finds all three defendants guilty of all charges in the indictment."

The courtroom remained quiet as the judge had ordered. I wanted to yell out, *Justice has been achieved*, but of course I didn't.

Mr. Hastings stood and said, "Your Honor, I request the jury be polled, and I request the three defendants be polled separately."

"Thank you, Mr. Hastings. I will poll the jury. Juror number one, how do you find defendant, Jimmy Jackson?"

"Guilty for first degree murder, Your Honor."

"Juror number two, how do you find defendant, Jimmy Jackson?"

"Guilty for first degree murder, Your Honor."

And so it went through all twelve jurors for Jimmy Jackson, and then Bubba Smith and Willie Warden. *My God, Moses would have loved this. It's like one of his Shakespeare plays.*

Judge Johnson said to two sheriff deputies, "Deputies, please take the defendants back to jail. The court is now adjourned. The court will convene on Monday at nine o'clock to consider the sentences of the defendants."

Audience members, attorneys, and the jurors started walking around in the courtroom talking about the outcome. I tried to find the mystery juror to thank him, but he had left the courtroom. *If this is the man Billy and I saw at the creek*, I thought, *he must come and go as he pleases.*

42

The Trial—Day 9

Monday—August 8, 1949

BECAUSE IT WAS FRIDAY, we decided to go home after the jury rendered their verdicts. It was nice to be home for the weekend, but I could hardly wait to get back to the courtroom to watch Judge Johnson sentence Jimmy, Willie, and Bubba. I figured that must be one the hardest things a judge has to do in a criminal trial.

Monday morning we got up early. Mom fixed us a nice breakfast, and we got to the Montgomery at eight o'clock. The heat wave was still with us. As we walked from the parking garage to the front of the courthouse, I was startled by what a saw. There were two large groups of people on and around the courthouse. Some in the two groups talked to each other, but a lot of people yelled at each other. I noticed guys in Klan wear just like Jimmy Jackson wore to the Delphi Mardi Gras parade, red pullover shirts with the letters "KKK" inscribed on them. They wore red hats, with the Blood Drop Cross symbols prominent at the front.

"Dad," I said, "what's going on?"

"Steve, I was afraid something like this might happen. The trial has been surprisingly free of trouble so far. But it looks like the true Alabama South is now rearing its ugly head. I'm worried some in the crowd might recognize you. Let's see if we can enter the building."

Just as Dad reached to open the courthouse door, someone called out, "Hey, that's Steve Thompson, the hero in this case." Then another person yelled, "He ain't no goddamn hero. He's a traitor and a nigger lover!"

Dad swiftly opened the door and the bailiff and two deputy sheriffs pulled us in. The bailiff said, "Mr. Thompson, Mrs. Thompson, and Steve, welcome. Don't worry we have things under control in the courtroom. Follow me."

He led us through a narrow corridor. At the end of the passageway, we walked up a staircase to a door that led into the judge's chambers. *Wow, this is neat.*

Judge Johnson rose from his desk and thanked the bailiff. He then shook Dad's hand, "Well, Thompson family, I'm sorry we had to be so secretive, but I'm not surprised the Klan is making its presence known. Ed Macey called Governor Folsom, and he said he is ready to call for national guard troops if necessary. At this time, it is more of a shouting contest between the Klan and those who support the verdict. But I worry that when the sentences for first-degree murder are announced more trouble will flare up."

The judge looked at his watch and said, "Mr. Thompson, where did you park your car?"

"In the parking garage close to the courthouse."

"Good. The courtroom doors will open soon. Let's enter now. Bailiff, please stand near where the Thompsons sit to protect them and ask the two deputy sheriffs to assist you. Bailiff, one more assignment. When the trial adjourns today, escort the Thompsons out the same way you brought them here. Then take them down to the court parking lot under this building and find a safe way to escort them to their car. I'm particularly worried about Steve. Please keep a close eye on him."

"Ladies and gentlemen, the court is now in session. A reminder, the court will not tolerate any inappropriate behavior throughout today's proceedings. Any person who creates a problem will be escorted out by deputy sheriffs. Today's proceedings will be about sentencing. The court is obligated to sentence the three defendants as the jury's verdict specified all three defendants are guilty of first-degree murder. The defendants, of course, have the right to appeal their case to a higher court, which can order the case retried or tossed out, or the higher court can rule that the appeal is without merit and the case will stand as decided. Prior to announcing a sentence, each defendant has the right to address the court if they wish."

Judge Johnson paused and carefully scanned everyone in the courtroom. "Audience, please allow the defendants to address the court without interruptions. It is both a courtesy and a requirement of you as spectators at this trail. Mr. Jimmy Jackson, would you like to address the court?"

Jimmy stood very slowly and said, "Your Honor, I know what you're gonna do to me. And I know nothing I say is gonna change it. But I still insist I'm not guilty and that pipsqueak, Steve, will get what he deserves someday. That's all I gotta say." Jimmy sat down.

Judge Johnson said, "Thank you, Mr. Jackson. Mr. Willie Warden, would you like to address the court?"

Willie stood and held his head high and said, "Your Honor, I agree with everything Jimmy said. And I ain't guilty." Willie sat down.

"Thank you Mr. Warden. Mr. Bubba Smith, would you like to address the court?"

Bubba stood and stared at the judge and the audience. He was shaking so badly that I thought he might cry.

"Uh…uh…Your Honor, I, I didn't kill nobody. I swear I only shot my rifle in the sky. I didn't shoot at nobody. I don't want to die. I'm not guilty of killing nobody. And I know where the rifles are hidden. I can show you." Bubba stayed standing and said nothing else, his eyes damp and his hands held out as if begging.

Judge Johnson said, "Unfortunately, Mr. Smith, my choices are limited. The location of the rifles is no longer important, and the fact that you were there when Mr. Marvin Gibbs was killed makes you an accessory to the crime. Finally, you were found guilty for first-degree murder by the jury. There's nothing more to be said, Mr. Smith."

I leaned over and whispered in Dad's ear, "I believe Bubba, Dad."

Dad whispered, "I'm inclined to believe him also. But the judge has made the situation clear."

Judge Johnson said, "Mr. Jackson, please stand. Alabama state law requires that I sentence you to be executed in Kilby Prison. The date for your execution will be set after all the appeals on your behalf have been exhausted."

Jimmy didn't bother to look at the judge. He just sat down.

Judge Johnson proceeded, "Mr. Warden, please stand. Alabama state law requires that I sentence you to be executed in Kilby Prison. The date for your execution will be set after all the appeals on your behalf have been exhausted."

Willie did look at the judge. Then he sat down.

Judge Johnson said, "Mr. Smith, please stand. Alabama state law requires that I sentence you to be executed in Kilby Prison. The date for your execution will be set after all the appeals on your behalf have been exhausted."

Bubba had to hold himself up using a chair for support. Then he fell down on the floor, and Mr. Hastings had to help him get up and sit down. I really felt sorry for him.

Judge Johnson said, "I'd like to say to the three defendants that I wish you well and may God have mercy on you souls."

Someone in back of the courtroom yelled, "Judge, you're the one that's gonna need God's mercy, you son of a bitch!"

Judge Johnson responded calmly but loudly, "Deputy sheriffs, please escort this man out of the courtroom."

I turned to watch as the deputy sheriffs approached the man. He wore Klan gear similar to what Jimmy had worn at the Delphi Mardi Gras parade. After the man was out of the courtroom, Judge Johnson said, "Deputies, please escort the three defendants back to the jail. A date will be set soon to transport them to Kilby Prison. Ladies and gentlemen this court is now adjourned."

The bailiff started escorting us to our car as he was instructed by the judge. As he led us toward the best route to our car, I could hear a lot of yelling still going on, and I got one quick look at what I thought were Alabama State Troopers or National Guardsmen or both.

As the bailiff helped us into our car, I asked, "Mr. Bailiff, what's your name?"

He smiled and said, "Jimmy." We all had a good laugh.

I said, "Thank you, Mr. Jimmy for all your help. We might not be alive if it wasn't for you."

He said, Thank you, Steve, and God bless you and your family."

Our drive home was uneventful. As Dad was driving home I said, "Mom and Dad, at first I was delighted that all three men were found guilty and sentenced to die. But now, I feel empty. Is that crazy or what?"

Mom said, "Steve, I think it's entirely normal. It's how I feel now, especially for Bubba Smith."

"Yeah, me too, Mom. I know I testified that one of the men lowered his gun and choose not to shoot me, but I can't honestly say which guy it was. My bet now is that it was Bubba Smith."

Dad chimed in, "Well, my two favorite people, I agree with your analysis. What say we just cruise home quietly and dream about the dinner Mom will fix us."

"I'm exhausted after the trial today," Mom said, "but I'll do the best I can."

"Dad, I have an idea. You and I can fix dinner tonight."

Mom laughed. "Now I feel better. I'll just sip a glass of wine and watch you two chefs do your thing."

"Lillis, what's an apron?" Dad asked.

We couldn't stop laughing. Later, Dad's joke became part of family lore.

43

At Home

Tuesday—August 9, 1949

IT WAS REALLY GOOD TO BE BACK HOME and to know that we didn't have to go back to the courtroom again. But I still felt bad about Jimmy, Willie, and Bubba. I mean I understood they had done bad things, but the good book tells us we have to forgive people in hopes that they can be redeemed. Perhaps I was wrong but that's the way I felt.

Dad went to the newspaper's office very early this morning. Poor Dad had been burning the wick at both ends with days at the trial, as well as his newspaper responsibilities.

Dad got home at nine o'clock and went into his office and closed the door. Mom joined him later, and the door remained closed. I figured they were up to something, and this something was me.

Mom opened the office door and called out, "Steve, please come into Dad's office and join us. We've got Dr. McDonald on the phone."

Dad said, "Sorry we were in the office alone for so long. You probably wondered what we were doing."

I couldn't help being sarcastic and said, "Well, yes!"

Dad ignored my crass comment and said, "Dr. McDonald's on the phone from his University of Alabama Medical School office where you took his voice recognition test. He has one of those new speaker phones like the one Ed Macey used in one of our conversations with him. He can hear what we all say, but we have to cluster around our phone to hear him. Dr. McDonald, we're all here, including Steve."

"Good Morning, Steve. Nice to hear your voice. Can you hear me?"

"Yes, sir, it's nice to talk to you."

"That's good. I was remiss in not talking to you after the trial. All I can do is to thank you now for being such a good witness, not only on my voice recognition test, but on everything else you did as a witness. Now tell your Mom and Dad to call me Al, and I would guess you would want to call me Dr. Al."

"Yes, sir, Dr. Al." I look quizzically at my parents. *What is going on?*

"Al, this is Andy. I need to explain to Steve why we called you. Steve, Mom and I are worried about your safety after all the things that happened and all the Klan's shenanigans. We were trying to decide where you would be safe, both as a place to live and go to high school. We decided to call Al and he said he had some ideas. Over to you, Al."

"Thanks, Andy. Steve, I know it's hard at your age to become uprooted from your Delphi home and friends, but I think your parent's concerns are well founded. I live in Mountain Brook, an nice residential area close to Birmingham, and my house has a large unused bedroom with its own bathroom, and I would be honored to let you use it at no cost. I also have a full time employee who takes care of the house and grounds. He's a very nice fellow, and he could drive you to school and pick you up. In fact, we are the only two that have lived in the house since my wife passed away four years ago. All my children are adults and live elsewhere, so I'm sure you would liven up the house." Dr. Al paused a moment, "Andy, I need to ask you a personal financial question related to Steve's education. Would you and Lillis like Steve to go to a private high school or a public one?"

Dad said, "Well, Al, we're not rolling in dough. A small town newspaper owner and editor doth not much money make. I'm sure private school's tuition rates are quite expensive. Is there a good public high school near where you live?"

Dr. Al said, "In fact, there's a good one quite close to my house, Mountain Brook High School."

Mom said, "I'm glad to hear that. We're not poor, but we're certainly not rich or even close to it. Steve would have been attending

Delphi High School if the Night of Terror had not occurred. Steve, how do you feel about this?"

"Mom, the last thing I want is to be a burden on you and Dad for my schooling. And I trust Dr. Al since he likes the school."

Dr. Al said, "I know the Mountain Brook High School principal, Weldon Williams, quite well. I would be happy to call Weldon and discuss enrollment. Summer's a good time to approach him. What do you all think?"

Mom spoke first, "Al, that's an interesting and generous offer. Could the three of us drive to Birmingham and see your house and meet your employee, and if possible, visit the school and meet Weldon Williams?"

"Lillis, of course you can. I would've been surprised if you hadn't asked. Fortunately, I have a light schedule today. I'll call Weldon after we conclude our conversation."

"Al, it's Andy. I have a question. What is the political bent of Weldon?"

"Good question, He is definitely liberal. I'm sure you know, Birmingham has more than its fair share of racists. Start with Bull Connor, the so-called Public Safety Commissioner, who has his hands on the police department and is associated with local Klan groups. Weldon and I have discussed the race issues in Birmingham several times. Of course, we haven't been able to solve the problem."

Well, I'm used to all that stuff. Sounds like Delphi. I hope I get to ask a few questions.

"Thanks, Al, that's helpful. I also have a request. When you talk to Weldon, I know you'll have to explain Steve's background to him. My request is that you forego all the trial stuff or at least keep it to a minimum. Our objective is Steve's safety. Can we primarily focus on Steve's scholastic accomplishments?"

"I understand, Andy, and I agree with you. I think Weldon will cooperate, and I will give Steve a strong recommendation."

Dad said, "Good, that's all I can ask. I bet Steve is chomping at the bit to ask questions."

"Dr. Al, thank you for all your suggestions," I said. "I like you very much. Mom and Dad think I want to stay in Delphi, but I'm smart enough to understand the situation. In fact, I like to read all kinds of books for knowledge. I'm not afraid of a new adventure, and I can't wait to visit your house and the school. I have one question. Does the school have a basketball team?"

Everybody laughed, and Dr. Al said, "Yes, they do, Steve. In fact, they have a well-rounded sports program. They also have a theater and a teacher who produces plays, just like your friend Moses Douglas produced Shakespeare's plays."

"Wow, I like all that. Thanks."

Dr. Al said, "Okay. It's time for me to get going. I'll try to get in touch with Weldon shortly. Goodbye."

We sat quietly for a time, each in their own thoughts. Mom broke the ice, saying, "What a nice man. Ah, let's see, grill cheese sandwiches, a nice salad, and sweet tea. Anybody interested?"

Dad and I stood, saluted Mom, and said in unison, "Yes, ma'am, Chief Cook."

While we were eating lunch, Mom said, "Steve, I was surprised when you agreed to Al's suggestions so quickly."

"Mom, I meant it, but of course I'll miss some of my friends, especially Billy."

And Dad added, "Don't forget if this works out, we'll visit you as often as possible. And you can come to Delphi if we think it's safe when you have long breaks, like Thanksgiving, Christmas, and Spring Break. Lillis, thanks for the great lunch. I'm going to write my editorial for the newspaper in my home office. I've got a hunch that we are going to hear from Al sooner, rather than later."

I helped Mom clean the kitchen, and then I sat in the living room and started reading an Agatha Christie novel, *Murder on the Orient Express*. Miss Kathryn, said some people turn up their noses at her books. I like them. Good stories.

I had been reading for thirty minutes when Dad called out, "Lillis and Steve, Al is on the line in my office."

Mom and I got there in a flash.

Dad said, "Al, Lillis and Steve are here."

"I'm glad you're all together," Dr. Al said. "I got in touch with Weldon just in time. He's leaving for a vacation off Mobile Bay the day after tomorrow. Can you can drive to Birmingham tomorrow? He'd love to meet you all and show you around the school."

Dad looked at Mom and me and we nodded. "Al, we'll make it happen. When would you like us to arrive at your house?"

"How about ten o'clock? You can meet my house manager, Marvin Lloyd, and we can show you around the house."

My God, another Marvin. That's got to be a good sign.

"We'll be there. What's your address?"

"3044 Canterbury Road. There's a big sign with the house number on it. Marvin and I will be on the lookout for you. I have to go now. See you tomorrow. Goodbye."

Dad said, "Okay, gang, I suggest we leave at seven o'clock tomorrow morning. That should give us ample time to get there. We don't want to be late."

Mom said, "I'll fix us a good dinner tonight and a light breakfast in the morning. And Steve, bring a book to read."

"I always do, Mom. I'm reading Agatha Christie's novel, *Murder on the Orient Express*. It's a page turner."

44

Birmingham

Wednesday—August 10, 1949

As Dad drove us to Birmingham, he said, "Al's place is harder to find than I thought it would be."

The house came into view, and I blurted out, "Wow! It's like a mansion. It's kinda like what Judy Garland said in *The Wizard of Oz*, 'Toto, I've got a feeling we're not in Delphi anymore.'"

Dad and Mom laughed, and then we saw a Negro man standing on the front porch with Dr. Al. It was like a dream come true because I was sure the man was Marvin.

He opened our car doors and said, "Good morning and welcome. My name is Marvin Lloyd. I work for Al."

Dr. Al said, "I add my welcome. Do you have any bags or things we can help you with?"

Mom replied, "No thank you, Al. We didn't plan to stay overnight. What a beautiful house you have."

"Thank you, but Marvin is responsible for the maintenance and upkeep of the house and gardens, and as you can see, he does an excellent job. There is one rule we have here, we use first names, and we ask our visitors to do the same, and Steve I wish you'd stop calling me Dr. Al. Can you do that?"

I was still awed by Marvin. He was a stately man, about six-feet tall, well dressed, and maybe in his fifties. His hair was graying and he had a well-trimmed beard. I finally said, "Yes, Al, I'll try."

As Al led us into his house, Marvin walked beside me and said, "I followed your trial by reading *The Birmingham News* reports. They had an article every day of the trial. You did a great job, and I'm honored to have the same first name as your friend who was murdered by the Klan. Al told me that we must keep the trial low profile because of your safety needs."

"Thanks, Marvin, but I wish everyone would stop coddling me."

Al called out to Marvin and me as we were lagging behind, "Come on you two. We've got a tour to do."

Marvin and I laughed, saying in unison, "Yes, sir."

Marvin and Al showed us the downstairs first. All the rooms were larger than any I had ever seen. There was a long entry way with a living room to the right and a dining room to the left. Farther along there was a den and a library and then a game room. The floors were all polished wood with some oriental rugs scattered about to provide some color.

Dad, and especially Mom, asked a lot of questions about the furnishings, and the paintings on the wall. Al said that most of the paintings came from Europe, and the furniture was built in North Carolina.

I couldn't wait to see the bedroom that Al said I could use, and finally, we went upstairs.

Al said, "Steve, there are six bedrooms upstairs. I use one, Marvin uses one, and the others are empty. Marvin, please show Steve the bedroom that we think is perfect for him. I'll show Lillis and Andy the other empty bedrooms."

Marvin said, "Steve , follow me. I hope you like it."

The bedroom was on the back, right hand corner side of the house. It had windows on the sides with great views of the backyard gardens. There was a large size bed that I could wallow around in to my heart's content. There was a table on the other side of the room where I could do my homework or play games. But best of all, the room had several large bookcases where I could start my own library.

"Marvin, how the hell am I going to use this much space?"

"Steve, I'll leave that to your devices. But I think you'll find that any empty space in your bedroom will soon be overflowing. Now, let me show you the private bathroom."

When Marvin opened the bathroom door, I was agog. It was a palatial room of ivory tiles with a bathtub and walk in shower and a toilet with another toilet looking device. I had no idea what that one was for.

Al and Mom and Dad walked in, and I said, “Can you believe this bedroom and bath? If I live here, I’ll feel like a grand potentate.”

Al said, “Steve, a grand potentate you will not become. Marvin and I live together as friends, and so will you.”

“Sorry, Al. I was just trying to be funny.”

“I know and funny you can be. But we need to be at the school at noon. Marvin and I have already fixed lunch. Let’s eat, and then go to the school.”

At lunch, Dad said, “Al, I know public schools are essentially free, but do you think there’ll a be a problem with the fact that Steve would be a transferee from Delphi High School?”

“I doubt it. Kids transfer to new schools constantly, but you need to ask Weldon that question. We better get going to the high school. It’s not far.”

As we got into the car, I noticed Marvin was not going with us, so I said, “Come on, Marvin, get in the car.”

“I can’t go to a white school, Steve, unless I’m the janitor or take care of the toilets or something like that. You know how it is around here.”

I nodded and thought, *Now I have to leave Marvin behind again. Will it ever end?*

“Hello Weldon, it’s good to see you,” said Al. “Let me introduce the Thompsons. This is Lillis and Andy, the parents. And this is Steve, the fourteen-year-old bright kid I told you about.”

Mr. Weldon said, “Welcome to Mountain Brook High School Lillis, Andy, and Steve. I’m sure Steve will be able to enroll in our high school. Al raves about what your son has achieved. And Steve, I know of Al’s voice recognition test, and the fact that you are the first person to have scored 100% on the test is incredible. Al didn’t tell me this, I read about it in *The Birmingham News*.”

Oops, it seems everyone has read that newspaper, I thought.

“Thank you, Mr. Weldon. But I want to be treated like all the students in the school, not like I’m special.”

"Good for you and don't worry, we try to treat all students equally. Well…I have to admit that star football players receive a lot of attention."

"I don't play football. But I do like basketball. I read a lot of books and have started to read Shakespeare."

"Those are excellent choices and we have them all. Now, I'd like to show you around the campus and the facilities. Follow me, please."

Mr. Weldon stopped in front of the main two-story building. "You can see that the school is quite new. Soon after World War Two, Mountain Brook's city fathers and the school board started planning for the new high school. Prior to that, there were only elementary schools here and high school age kids had to go to other high schools in the area, mostly Birmingham. I thought it was a miracle that the city was able to build this new facility in a little over two years. We opened the school for the first time in late August, 1948. So Steve, you'll start here in our second year, which means that your freshman class will be a bit larger than the upcoming sophomore class, and larger again than the upcoming junior and senior classes."

Mr. Weldon then showed us some of the class rooms, the library, the gymnasium, the theater, the track, and the football and baseball fields. I was super impressed. Delphi High School was nice, but nothing like this.

I said, "Mom and Dad, I'd like to go to school here."

Dad nodded at Mom and she said, "Mr. Weldon, of course we'd like for Steve to have been able to attend school in Delphi. That not being possible under the current circumstances, we'd like to enroll Steve here. What do we have to do?"

"If you have time now, we can go in my office and fill out a few forms. It won't take long. You'll need to send me copies of Steve's elementary report cards and any of his other accomplishments that you think are important. You can mail all of that to me. I'll give you my business card. Al, you and Steve will have to cool your heels while we work on the forms."

We sat on a bench in front of the school. "Well, Steve, it seems that the die is cast, and you will be living with Marvin and me for four years."

"I can't wait. When can I move in?"

"Your Mom and Dad will have to decide that. Since school starts in a few weeks, it'll have to be soon."

Ten minutes later, Mom and Dad and Mr. Weldon came out of his office. Mr. Weldon said, "The deed is done, Steve. You are officially enrolled in Mountain Brook High School."

It surprised me how fast my four years at Mountain Brook High School passed. Al and Marvin were always there for me. I got a good education although a few guys at the school knew the trial story and gave me a hard time. But I handled that myself. I hate to admit it, but I had to fight one of the guys and I won, so the rest backed off. I still dream about Joshua Marshall and Moses Douglas and Marvin Gibbs, and the terrible ways their lives ended.

Dr. McDonald became a very good friend. Al, as he preferred to be called, even let me work in his office on his voice recognition program in the summer if I wasn't home with Mom and Dad.

Marvin Lloyd was my friend throughout my high school years. Marvin was always available to drive me wherever I needed to go and wait for me—until I got a car when I was seventeen. Marvin Lloyd and I had many discussions about racism and equality.

Marvin Lloyd reminded me of Marvin Gibbs, both very smart and always there for me, but even today I still dream about how I let them down.

Part VI
Forgiveness—2001

"That you were once unkind befriends me now,
And for that sorrow, which I then did feel,
Needs must I under my transgression bow,
Unless my nerves were brass or hammered steel."

William Shakespeare—*Sonnet 120*

45

The Delphi Cabin

Wednesday—March 14, 2001

STEVE WIPED THE TEARS from his eyes and cheeks. He realized that he had another dream about how he was always letting Marvin Lloyd and Marvin Gibbs down. The sun was setting at the cabin, and he looked up at Nick who was blinking because his eyes were moist. Nick said nothing.

Steve let out a deep sigh, "That's about it. What was it that guy said when he testified to Congress about his participation in the Iran-Contra mess in the '80s? Oh, I remember. It was Oliver North and he said something like, 'I'll tell it all. The good, the bad, and the ugly.' Christ, why did I think of that. Sounds like I'm making fun of everything I just told you."

Nick nodded, and said. "Maybe. But I now understand what Marvin Gibbs's statue in the Delphi Square means to you. And maybe you do need a bit of humor to help you relax. Steve, I knew you were deeply troubled by something, but I never imagined what happened to you was this awful. And it's equally disturbing to think that you were only fourteen years old when it happened, and you've lived with it since. Christ, Steve! You were so brave to stand up to the Klan. Those guys are beyond brutal! I have a suggestion. Let's have a drink and fix dinner. I propose we don't talk about what you told me, but let's engage in idle talk. It's my turn to choose a comparison. The Rodgers and Hammerstein musical *South Pacific* is one of my favorites, and one of its songs is titled *Happy Talk*. So, tonight only happy talk is allowed. Capeesh?"

Nick had elicited a smile from Steve, and he said, "Yes, your honor. I'll have a Scotch and soda."

"I'll have one too, I'll mix." Nick went into the kitchen and came out with the drinks, saying, "Professor, your drink."

"Thank you, kind sir. Are we doing happy talk or silly talk?"

"Either way works for me," Nick said, "but I want to break the rule. I'd like to ask you a question."

"I guess rules are made to be broken, but I'll let you know if it's verboten."

"Okay. Before you started telling me your story, you used the phrase 'a murder of crows.' Where the hell does that come from?"

Steve laughed so hard it hurt, but it made him feel good. "Is that all? I grant you a one-time dispensation because I love this question. I could make this a long story, but I'll keep it short. *A murder of crows* can be traced back to Middle Age folktales of the 15th century. Later people considered the term poetic, like a gaggle of geese or a piddling of ducks. But I prefer the one when people believed crows were an omen of death, and it seems appropriate after what I experienced."

"Nice delivery, Professor. Here's to *a murder of crows.*"

They tapped glasses, took a swig, and laughed. "Chicken tonight, and I'll cook it on the grill," Steve offered. "I've got some great barbecue sauce to use. You can do rice and a salad."

"Let's go to work, Chef," Nick said.

Steve punched Nick lightly on the arm, and said, "Thanks for the promotion. Chef doesn't weigh as much as professor."

They enjoyed a good meal with a bottle of red wine and stuck to the happy talk rule, although Steve could tell Nick was itching to ask more questions. At ten o'clock, they both agreed it was time to hit the sack.

Feeling tired, Steve was ready to hit the hay, and he wondered what dreams would haunt him tonight.

46

The Next Morning

Thursday—March 15, 2001

STEVE AWOKE THE NEXT MORNING, rolled over and wiped his sweaty brow. He heard noises coming from the kitchen. It had to be Nick making a pot of coffee. He washed, got dressed, and joined Nick."Good morning, early bird. Not only coffee brewing, I smell bacon."

"Your olfactory system is working well," Nick said, "You look okay. Did you sleep well?"

"Not really. I had a dream about Joshua, Moses, and Marvin. At least no ravens or crows appeared, but it is the Ides of March when Julius Caesar was assassinated. Damn, it seems I'll experience these dreams until I die."

Nick shook his head. "That's a morbid view of life. What happened in the dream?"

He wished Nick would let it be, but said, "So now you want to analyze my dreams?"

"Don't be defensive, Steve. We've come this far, let's not stop now. I want to help."

Steve poured himself a cup of coffee, and sat at the kitchen table. "You're right. The dream started on a high note at an elegant dinner party hosted by Joshua and Moses for Marvin and me. Of course, it wasn't exactly like the one in my story, but it was pleasant with talk of music, Shakespeare, and a lot of jokes. But things turned when their house caught on fire. Marvin and I ran out and watched it burn. Then we ran and Marvin kept shouting, 'Keep running, Steve. Don't stop.' I ran until I felt exhausted and the dream ended. Thank God. I couldn't wait for it to end. Have you ever experienced that?"

Steve thought Nick groaned before he said, "Yes, we all have ghost and goblins that haunt us, but I've never had consistent nightmares like you have."

"That's good. I wouldn't wish mine on anyone." Steve paused, hoping to change the subject, and said, "What's for breakfast?"

"Ah, good sir, scrambled eggs with bacon and toast, and all the jam you can slather on it."

While they ate breakfast, Nick said, "Steve, I'd like to ask you some questions about your story. I'm not going to challenge you, but I hope to better understand the aftermath of your Night of Terror. Is that okay?"

Steve snickered and said quietly, "Night of Terror. I guess that's what it was…my Night of Terror." He cleared his throat and spoke up, "It is the cowish terror of his spirit that dares not undertake; he'll not feel wrongs which tie him to an answer."

Nick grinned, and said, "Clever. Was that Shakespeare?"

"Who else at moments like this but the English language's greatest playwright and poet. It's from *King Lear*."

"How the hell do you remember that so easily?"

"I played Lear in a recent production, and although it was Lear's daughter, Goneril, who said those lines, an actor in a play gets to know other players' lines. Don't worry. Cleverness aside, I'll try to answer your questions."

They sat on the east porch where the sun was slowly rising on a beautiful morning. If only Steve's thoughts matched the day, he would have felt content. Yet his mind was a whirlpool, spinning out ideas, thoughts, and dreams, and a fear of what might come.

Trying to be funny in hopes of steadying himself, he said, "Monsieur Inquisitor, please go easy on your humble servant."

"Calm down, Steve. Remember, we're just two friends talking. What happened after you witnessed Marvin being killed and then you ran home and collapsed? How did you deal with things? Did you feel better or worse?"

"Before we get into that, I want to tell you how it came to past that Marvin Gibbs' statue is in the town square of Delphi. After the trial was over, the Klan really got their dander up, vandalizing the first two statues that went up in Westtown. Out of funds, Billy and I had to stop the project before someone got killed, but we never planned on giving up entirely. It wasn't until 1992 that Westtown and Delphi residents voted to merge the two towns into one. Now Westtown is formally a part of Delphi. Billy and I approached the new city council, which now had both Black and white members, and after we told them we would help pay for a large part of the costs of the statue, they readily agreed, and thus the statue has been on the town square ever since, which seems to prove that some progress has taken place in Alabama. Billy chose to live in Delphi. He married a lovely young lady he met in high school and they had three fine boys. Unfortunately, Billy died of pancreatic cancer two years after Marvin's statue was installed. I miss him dearly, and everything he did was for Marvin, not himself." Steve wiped tears from his eyes.

"Steve I grieve for Billy with you, yet I think it's an inspirational story. I can tell he was an important person in your life, My hunch is that there are many stories to come."

"Perhaps. I guess it's time to answer your questions. After I stopped cussing like a sailor and flopping on the floor like a fish out of water, Mom had Dr. Thatcher give me another sedative, so I could calm down and sleep. I felt better the next morning, but Mom insisted on taking me to see Dr. Thatcher. He was a nice, old man, but of course, at fourteen, most men looked old. He asked me a lot of questions, mostly about how I felt. He advised me to expect good days and bad days, especially because of the traumatic events I witnessed. While much of what he said went over my head, he was partially right, but as time went by, the bad days outnumbered the good. Is that clear?"

"Yes," Nick said. "I'm certainly not a psychiatrist, but I think today's psychiatrists would say you were and are vacillating between denial, anger, and guilt, and have yet to come to grips with acceptance."

Steve felt sorry for Nick, who was trying hard to help him understand things he knew only too well. "Nick, I don't disagree with you, but over the years, I've seen a number of shrinks. Their diagnoses and suggestions have a hollow ring of familiarity. Honest to God, I did try. I wish—"

Nick cut him off. "Steve, I'm sorry I pushed you so hard on the psychiatrist thing. Let's move on. You encountered so many interesting characters, good and bad, and some involved in the trial and some not. Perhaps you should write a book about your traumatic experiences. The story has aspects of a Shakespearean tragedy, which is right up your alley."

Steve laughed. "Which one: *King Lear, Othello, Antony and Cleopatra, Hamlet, Romeo and Juliet, Richard III, Macbeth,* and so on? Well, I'll tell you right now, it ain't gonna happen."

Nick shrugged and said, "I get it. Well, the first character I'd like to know more about is the man you called the mystery juror, and you also compared him to the stranger fishing on the creek when you and Billy saw him. Did you ever find out who he was or what he did?"

"Good choice, Nick. I was able to find his name in the jury records in the court. His name was Harold Wright. He was a professor at Tuskegee Institute west of Montgomery. You know, the place where the Tuskegee Airmen were trained to become Black pilots in World War Two at the Tuskegee Army Air Field. Wright taught English literature, and offered the students a special seminar on the works of Edgar Allan Poe, whom I really like. I never met Wright personally, but it seems it was his wont to use summer breaks and some sabbaticals to travel around Alabama looking for opportunities to encourage change. I also checked the Montgomery County voter registration office, and learned that Wright was somehow able to register even though he lived in Macon County. He was obviously a very resourceful man, and I'm sure he was able to guide the other jurors to a unanimous verdict. It's still a mystery to me if Wright was the man Billy and I saw on the creek, but I don't believe all mysteries are meant to be solved. Harold Wright died in 1980. Nick, if I ever wanted to write a book about that terrible night, it would be a biography of Harold Wright."

"A biography sounds right. What about Peter Hastings, the lead defense lawyer who was thought to be a wizard in keeping Ku Klux

Klan members out of jail. He certainly failed his clients in your trial. How do you square that? Did you ever talk to him after the trial?"

"Hastings was a piece of work. It seems every time he tried to control the narrative, he ended up on the short end of the stick, and toward the end of the trial, he seemed to give up entirely, like when he chose not to call Rodger Dalton as a witness. But he filed appeals right up the legal chain until a new governor was sworn in. The new governor replaced Jim Folsom in January 1951 and six months later he pardoned all three men. I couldn't believe it, but the more I realized what a naive kid I was the one who didn't understand Alabama politics at all. Dad helped me sort it out. I did talk to Hastings once, well after the trial. It was a chance encounter. I was in Montgomery acting in a play at the Alabama Shakespeare Festival. It was 1986, and I was playing the part of Iago in *Othello*. At fifty years old, I was surprised I got the role, but the director said he always thought Iago was better played as an older man against Othello and Desdemona. During rehearsals, we had a free day, and I went to lunch at Martin's where Ed Macey had taken his team in 1949. I was sitting alone at a table for two when a man older than me walked up and said, 'You're Steve Thompson, aren't you?'"

"I looked up and said, 'Yes, who are you?'"

"He smiled. 'Peter Hastings. May I join you?'"

"Initially, I didn't know what to say or do. Should I hit him, hug him, shake his hand, or what? Of course, I said, 'Please sit down, Mr. Hastings.'"

"Then I realized he was in the same quandary as I was, because he finally said, 'It's just Pete, Steve. How are you doing?'"

"I'm doing fine, Pete. Do you realize it's been thirty-six years since we last saw each other. How are you doing?"

"Fine for an old man. I was as surprised to see you today, as I'm sure you were to see me, but perhaps it was meant to be. I was so upset at the trial outcome that I didn't want to speak to you. I'd like to set the record straight today. I lost that trial because of my hubris, Steve. I thought I could prance into the courtroom and play the court the way I was used to doing. But because of a no-nonsense judge, an excellent prosecutor, and you, I lost. You were the most effective witness I've ever seen in a courtroom, and the fact that you were only fourteen years old makes that even more remarkable, and then you topped it off with your perfect score on the voice test. I was astonished as was everyone in the courtroom."

I felt the usual pangs in my stomach as Pete praised me.

"Pete, thanks for the accolades, but I wish people didn't see me that way. Even today, the events of that night and the trial haunt me. I have frequent nightmares that even the devil incarnate couldn't imagine. Enough of my issues, are you still practicing law?'"

"I'm sure you mean to ask, am I still the Klan lawyer? No, I've always hated that handle. I did keep my promise to Jimmy, Willie, and Bubba and filled appeals til the cows came home and the new governor pardoned them. Shortly thereafter, I stopped taking cases involving the Klan. The Klan bigwigs were not too happy, but they left me alone."

"Pete had changed so radically that I still didn't understand why. I was about to ask him when another man walked up to the table. He nodded to me, then said, 'Pete, we have to go now for your appointment.' Pete said, 'Okay. I guess this is goodbye, Steve. I'm so glad we had this chance encounter. I wish we could talk some more.' He got up slowly, and his friend held his arm and helped him walk. I hadn't noticed before, but he walked with a decided limp. I saw another man say something to Pete, and then he walked up to my table and said, 'Hi, Steve, my name's Gabriel. May I sit down?' I said, 'Of course.' Gabriel said, 'I want to thank for sharing time with Pete. He has told us so much about you, and you can't imagine how much he admires you. I don't know what you two talked about, but Pete has changed. Some years ago, he had what we Southerners call a *Come to Jesus* moment. He joined a Unitarian church in Montgomery and spent hours with the church's minister discussing religion. Whatever Pete and the minister discussed, its had a profound impact on his life and beliefs. I must go now, but one more thing, Pete has terminal cancer, but he chooses not to continue with medical treatments. He will die soon, but he's at peace with himself and his God. And God bless you, Steve.' I sat still for a while, dabbing the tears in my eyes, and left the restaurant."

"Nick, I don't know what, but I know something major had occurred. Any ideas?"

"Yes, but first, what happened to Mr. Graves."

"Well, this one is a short and sordid tale. I later learned that Judge Frank Johnson issued a warrant for his arrest just after the trial. However, because it wasn't served before he apparently skipped Alabama and went to God know where, he has never been prosecuted. It was rumored that he was killed in New York City over a bad gambling debt. End of that sad tale."

"Hmmm, so that's one fish that got away. Steve, my idea is that I see a pattern in many of your stories. I'll try my best to fit the pieces together. We can ignore Graves. He's a moral misfit. In addition to the people you've already told me about, let's consider the day that you went to Westtown to retrace your steps during the Night of Terror. You called it an odyssey. Your first stop was at old man Zach's house. He was obviously seeking salvation, and you provided him the support he needed. Your second stop was Nancy's old house. I don't know the significance of that yet, but I'm pretty sure it's important. Your third stop was with Laertes who was your link back to Moses and Joshua. Your fourth stop was at Sara Marsh's house. She's Billy's mother, whom you had never met. Billy was always reluctant to invite you into his house because he thought it wasn't nice enough. And yet, you and Billy have helped each other in so many ways over the years, including Marvin's statute on the town square. There's one last thing I'd say. After Jimmy, Willie, and Bubba were sentenced to death by Judge Johnson, you said you were delighted all three men were found guilty and sentenced to die. But then you said you felt empty, and you wondered if you were crazy or something. I guess that's all."

"Wow, Nick, that's quite a list. How the hell did you remember all that. It's spot on."

"I'm a good listener, Steve, and I took a lot of notes. Don't forget, as a stock broker, I always had to keep good notes. But I have another idea. Before we delve into what I think all this means to you, let's go to Delphi and visit Marvin's statue. I feel much closer to him now. Anyone who would sacrifice his body to save another person is truly a hero. Then I'll treat you to an early dinner downtown. Then we can talk about my thoughts."

"I accept your offer, kind sir, and I can't wait to hear your psychoanalysis of my fragile self."

"I do have a question. Did Moses Douglas and Dr. Joshua Marshall finally get any recognition in Delphi as Marvin Gibbs did?"

Steve actually smiled, saying, "Oops, sorry to have overlooked that and sorry I've been telling the stories in such a scattered way."

"Forget *scattered*, Steve. It all works."

"Okay. After the success with the city council with Marvin's statue, Billy and I approached the city council again. Since the old white and Black libraries had become one several years ago, we suggested that the Delphi Public Library be renamed the Moses Douglas Public Library. Then we suggested that the one integrated medical clinic in Delphi be renamed the Dr. Joshua Marshall Medical Clinic. There were several meetings of the city council and a couple of old fogies were being holdouts. But lo and behold, a motion was finally passed."

Steve smiled again at Nick. "After the jury had been selected on day two of the trial in Montgomery, Dad felt as if the *Hallelujah Chorus* were ringing in his ears. Dad could be a funny man often."

"Steve, I'm glad you still have a sense humor. I'm also glad that Moses and Joshua were finally honored. Since I have no more questions, I think it's time to get back to young Steve's story."

47

Reconciliations

Friday—March 16, 2001

Steve and Nick sat on a bench facing Marvin's statue and looked quietly for quite a while as if they were meditating.

Steve broke the silence. "Nick, I want to thank you for what you said and felt about Marvin. I think of him almost every day and night. During the day, it's usually pleasant thoughts, but at night…well, you know what haunts me."

Nick listened carefully, and then he noticed an older guy staring at them, "Steve, look at that fellow over there. Do you recognize him?"

Steve stared back at the guy for a moment. "I can't believe it, I'm sure it's Jimmy Jackson. Nick, why do all these people from my past keep coming forward?"

"Maybe you should ask him."

Steve was unsure but called out, "Jimmy, Jimmy Jackson."

Jimmy took a couple of steps toward them. "I don't mean you any harm, but are you sure you want to talk to me?"

Steve decided to soften his words and the moment. "Yeah, let's try. Besides we're both so old now, we can't really harm each other. I'm sixty-five. I put you at about seventy-three. C'mon over and talk to us."

Jimmy moved slowly and sat on the bench next to Steve. "You're close, I'm seventy-four. Who's your friend?"

"Jimmy, meet Nick McAdams."

"Pleased to meet you, Nick McAdams. Are you a Scotsman like Dr. Alastair McDonald who did the voice test that Steve aced?"

"And pleased to meet you, Jimmy Jackson. My Dad is a Scotsman and Mom is a Black woman. I guess you call that mixed-blood in the South,"

"Well, Nick, I have to set you straight on that. Most people down here just use Black and white. I learned years ago that all people have the same blood, but there are different blood types. It's likely that my blood type is the same as either you or Steve."

Steve was surprised to hear Jimmy talk about blood types.

He listened as Jimmy continued, "Steve, I gotta tell you something. I know it doesn't bring Marvin back, but I'm really sorry for what I did. Willie and I shot Marvin. I'm pretty sure Bubba didn't shoot him. That's all I can say."

"Jimmy," Steve said "that must have been hard for you to admit. How are Willie and Bubba doing?"

"After we were pardoned, Willie and Bubba started working at the paper mill. Willie led a good life and died in 1986. Bubba was never right again. Four years after the pardons, he committed suicide."

"I'm sorry to hear that. I could tell at the sentencing that Bubba was struggling. What did you do after the pardons?"

"You're not gonna believe this, but after working at the mill for three years, I decided to go a junior college in Montgomery and study to be a medical technician. That's where I learned about blood types. I also learned how to take people's blood pressure, and give shots… oops, wrong word."

All three men laughed.

"Anyhow, I also do a lot of other things for the doctors and nurses. But I gotta tell you that I'm not a saint. I've had dreams about what we did to Marvin. I still have some Klan friends, but I don't go to meetings. I just pay them no mind. I reckon I gotta go now. It was nice to see you Steve and to meet you Nick."

The men shook hands, and Jimmy walked across the square the way he came and was soon out of sight.

Steve turned to Nick. "Why do people keep coming to me? What do they want of me?"

"Steve, it's not what they want of you, but what they want to give you. Now, let's go have that early dinner."

They got back to the cabin at six, and Steve wondered why Nick was being so circumspect about what had transpired the last two days.

"Steve let me fix you a drink and then we'll sit on the west facing porch and discuss what I'm thinking. What would you like to drink?"

"I'll have what you have, Nick." Steve wanted to say, *"It's about time,"* but he let it go.

"A Scotch and soda, my good man. Here's to better times."

They clinked glasses, and Nick said, "Steve, I'm sorry I've kept you waiting, but I needed to think carefully about the events of the last two days before I could talk to you about them. Is that okay?"

"I wish I had a better reply at hand, but let's go."

"Steve, I see no need to detail the events again. You know them all better than me. But if we consider Billy Marsh, Howard Wright—the mystery man, old man Zach, Laertes, Peter Hastings, and Jimmy Jackson, I find they all represent a common thread. In different ways, they are all seeking your forgiveness."

"Nick, I can't fathom that because I was the reason Marvin died, and everyone says my testimony led to Jimmy, Willie, and Bubba being sentenced to death."

"You're a stubborn one, Steve Thompson. You weren't the reason Marvin died. You tried everything a fourteen-year-old boy could think of to save him. But in this one example, Marvin saved your life when he said, 'Run, Steve, run.' That was Marvin's way of absolving you of any guilt. As to Jimmy, the jury provided the verdict, not you. Jimmy's visit was obvious. Between every sentence he said today, you could hear his plea for forgiveness, as have most of the others." Nick stopped talking.

"What would you have me do, almighty psychoanalyst?" Steve asked.

"First, don't patronize me, Steve. It's not becoming of you. The real question you have to deal with is why do you refuse to forgive yourself when others clearly guilty of crimes against Blacks sought your forgiveness. Did you want them to get on their hands and knees and beg forgiveness?"

Steve slowly rocked back and forth. Nick watched carefully, forever unable to forget what was about to happen. Steve started crying inconsolably and rested his head on Nick's shoulder as he had done on Marvin's shoulder on the night Joshua and Moses were burned to death.

After a while, Steve started to calm down. Still red-eyed, he said "Nick, how could I have been so stupid not to see these things."

"Try to remember a Shakespeare quote for this moment. I'll go first, *To thine own self be true.* What do you think?"

"Good, it's *Hamlet*. I'll respond with another *Hamlet* quote. *We favor what we are, but know not what we can be.*"

"I understand your feelings a little better now. You easily beat my quote."

"Nick, I can't thank you enough for your help. So let me ask you this. Do you think I should try and contact Hastings and Jackson and thank them for their help?"

"I would advise against it. I think you were gracious enough with both men. Don't overplay your hand or they may think your acting high and mighty."

"I get your point. Nick, I don't know where things with me might go next, but I'm feeling sure things can only get better. Let me get you another drink, and I'll grab some nuts and chips to munch on."

Steve brought the drinks and goodies out, and the two men talked in idle chit-chat for awhile.

Steve said, "Nick, what time is your flight tomorrow?"

"Three-thirty in the afternoon."

"That's good. I have one thing we have to do in the morning, so the timing is good. I've got one phone call to make now, and then I'm hitting the sack."

Nick said, "I'm pooped too. I'm going to bed now. This has been a trying two days. Goodnight, Steve."

48

Redemption

Saturday—March 17, 2001

STEVE OPENED HIS EYES SLOWLY. He looked at his bedside clock, it was 8:30 in the morning. He couldn't believe he had slept soundly all night. He heard Nick in the kitchen humming and rattling pots and pans around. He laid his head back on the pillow and tried to piece together his thoughts and dreams. He remembered a pleasant dream where Marvin and Billy took him to a creek and taught him how to set a trot line, but that was it, no terrible thoughts. He got out of bed and took his time washing up and getting dressed. It was almost nine o'clock when he went into the kitchen. "Good morning, Nick."

"Well, bless my soul, you look spick and span and ready to eat. Did you sleep well?"

"Nick, are you sure you're not Merlin the magician or a voodoo doctor who waved a magic wand over my body. I've haven't slept this well in a long time, and I don't remember any bad dreams."

"That's great, but I assure you I'm no magician. However, I have a thought about the word 'Nevermore' that you have referred to several times. As I understand Poe's poem, he uses the word a number of times, but he bends the meaning from a helpful one to a difficult one that ultimately drives the poem's narrator insane. Perhaps you have been bending toward the wrong meaning."

"Could be, Nick. Nice analysis. It may not be absolutely correct, but I like the thought of bending it as you suggest."

"Well, let's don't dwell on it anymore, but enjoy the moment. Sit down, hot coffee, pancakes with maple syrup and bacon coming up."

They ate so heartily that any conversation was mostly absent, until Nick said, "Steve, I'm gonna miss you and this incredible experience as soon as I have to get on the airplane in Montgomery, but don't worry, I'll call you often to see how you're doing."

"I don't doubt you will, and I appreciate all your help. We do have to make a stop soon, but I will get you to the airport on time. I'll do the dishes now. You best pack your bags because we won't come back to the cabin after our next stop."

"I'll be ready," Nick said, "but I am intrigued to know what the next stop is all about."

"Cool your jets, Nick, as the kids say."

After they left the cabin, Steve showed Nick the house where he grew up and the offices of his father's newspaper, the *Delphi Delta News* which now had a new owner.

Steve started driving west and said, "Nick we're headed toward Old Westtown. That's what the locals now call it, even though Westtown is now officially a part of Delphi. Tradition has carried part of the day. Around this corner is where Nancy lived when she was a kid. The house we're headed to is just around the next corner."

"That's a good looking house," Nick said. "Who lives there?"

"Let's find out." Steve pulled over, walked with Nick up to the house and knocked.

An attractive white woman opened the door and said, "Hi, Dad. And this must be Nick."

Steve hugged Alice and said, "Nick, this is my daughter, Alice Thompson Mosley. She lives in Durham, North Carolina, where she teaches courses in Childhood Education at Duke. My son, Daniel Thompson, couldn't be here today. He's a United Airlines pilot and is on duty. He tried to swap his schedule, but no go. He's really sorry he couldn't be here."

Alice said, "Nick, now that Dad has filled you in on his family tree, it's a pleasure to meet you. I've heard a lot about you. I know my mother Barbara, Dad's ex-wife, would have loved to be here, but sadly, she died three years ago."

"I was sorry to hear about Barbara's death. All those years ago when Steve was married to your mother, I knew your mother Barbara well. She was a nice lady."

"Thank you. Let's go in the living room. Nick, let me introduce my step-mother and actress, Nancy Dawson Thompson."

Nancy embraced Nick, as if he were her long lost son, "You are a sight for sore eyes, Nick. I've wanted to meet you for a long time, but you know-who kept putting me off."

Nick stepped back, really seeing her for the first time, and realizing how beautiful she was, "Nancy, more than once, I've told Steve that I thought you had more to do with his life story than he was willing to reveal. I think that gives you and me the privilege to call him what he is, a rascal."

Nancy burst into laughter as did everyone else. Just then, a young brown-skinned boy walked in carrying a small bag of groceries.

Nancy said, "Thank you son. Come…I want to introduce you to our Dad's friend, Nick McAdams."

The boy said, "Pleased to meet you, Mr. McAdams. My name's Marvin Thompson. I'm named after Marvin Gibbs. He and my father were good friends. A statue of Marvin is on the Delphi square."

Nick responded, "I've seen his statue on the square several times, and I know what happened to him in 1949. Of course, your Dad knows it even better because he was there and witnessed everything. I have to sit down. I feel a bit off kilter after what I've learned the last few minutes. Marvin, please sit beside me."

Marvin did not hesitate to sit beside Nick. Family members gathered around as if in a worship circle. Nick said, "Thank you, Now I do feel that indeed the circle is unbroken." Nick paused and looked at everyone, all of whom appeared as if they didn't understand him or were worried about him. So he said, "Where can a guy get something to eat and drink around here?"

Nancy, taking his cue, said in a deep southern accent, "Well, I reckon, Yankee, you done come to the right place. We gonna spread out so much southern food and hooch that it's gonna knock your socks off. Team Thompson, let's git to work."

And work they did and when Nick tried to help, they shooed him away and told him he was a guest. It wasn't just a snack, but a complete meal. The younger folks sat at one table, and the older folks sat at another. The talk was loud and mostly funny.

As the meal came to end, Nancy said, "I want everyone on clean up duty, and that includes you Steve Thompson. Nick and I are gonna rest and have a little chat."

She took Nick by the hand and led him into another room. "Nick, I don't know what to think of things right now. When Steve took you to the cabin, he was his usual nervous and neurotic self. I've lived with his belief that he was responsible for all the evil deeds that happened on the Night of Terror. Many of us have tried to dissuade him from that belief to no avail. Yet, when you and he came in today, I realized Steve was a changed person. Why? Nick, the only explanation must be your influence."

"Nancy before I answer your question, I have one for you. How did you and Steve finally get together after all these years?"

Nancy giggled like a little girl, "Nick, in many ways it's a wonder we ever did. When my family left Westtown for Atlanta in 1949, I asked Steve to come see me if he could. I gave him my new address. Of course, as a silly young girl, I thought he would come right away, but he didn't. Then, in the summer of 1957, just before he started at Duke in September, guess who showed up in Atlanta, Steve Thompson. He stayed with my family for four days and we talked a lot. We both agreed it wasn't time to contemplate anything right away. We also agreed that we loved each other but had to wait before doing anything serious. I was studying acting at an Atlanta integrated acting school, and Steve was off to Duke for advanced degrees. Life moved on and in 1975 we unexpectedly met again at a summer stock festival in Montgomery, of all places. The play was *Romeo and Juliet*. I was Juliet and Steve was Romeo. Why the director let two older people play those youthful roles was beyond us, but we had a good time and were well received. Steve and I decided then to get married, and that we would elope. While the mores in Alabama were a bit better than they were when we were kids, there were still significant barriers for biracial couples. We skedaddled out of Alabama and were married by a justice of the peace in Durham where, because of Duke, the town was pretty liberal. And twelve years later Marvin was born." Nancy stared at Nick with a wry smile. "Balls in your court, Nick."

"Nancy, that was quite a story. So the childhood sweet hearts finally earned their just desserts. But I'm still confused. Why do you think Steve didn't tell me about your marriage?"

"Nick, even though Durham was liberal, we decided it best to tell only close family members and very good friends. It was his choice not to tell you. You'll have to ask him."

"I think I'll let that slide. Okay, my turn to tell you another story."

Nick proceeded to tell Nancy what had happened the last few days at the cabin. He summarized most events but was quite explicit about yesterday events.

Nick wrapped up his tale by saying, "In the last few moments of Steve's redemption and understanding of the meaning of all his encounters with people from his present and past were when he rocked slowly back and forth and started crying inconsolably. He rested his head on my shoulder as he had done on Marvin's shoulder on the night Joshua and Moses were burned to death. When Steve calmed down, he wondered how he could have overlooked those obvious, if subtle, healing connections with those who needed to feel his forgiveness."

Nancy began to weep. She said, "Nick, you are a blessing. I think only you and I can truly understand Steve. You are the son of a biracial family. Steve and I are the same kind of family, with a son named Marvin. Nick, do you think I'm being silly?"

He wrapped her hand in his. "Absolutely not, Nancy. I'm sure you remember this, but Steve told me the story about how you two met. It's fascinating. You met one afternoon in Moses Douglas' Negro Library, and while you corrected his definition of 'star-crossed lovers' in Shakespeare's *Romeo and Juliet*, perhaps his first thought that star-crossed lovers were blessed by the stars foresaw somehow what your lives would come to mean to each other."

Nancy was still wiping her tears, and said, "Nick McAdams, you're a miracle worker. What a delightful and creative way to look at things. In this case, I think Mr. Douglas would agree with you. Now before I start crying again, it's time we joined our families."

"Right," Nick said, "and I have one last suggestion. Steve has definitely improved. But I think the less we mention this the better. He'll probably still endure bad moments, but hopefully now he can deal with those moments with more insight."

Nancy was smiling and laughing. She said, "At your command, miracle worker."

Nick took Nancy's arm and led her back to the living room. Everyone stared at them as if they had been gone a long time.

Alice finally spoke, "I guess you two have been talking about us all."

Nick laughed and said, "No, Alice, only you."

Steve said, "Nick's a jokester. It's not you. It was me. Everybody come closer and sit down. I need to tell you a short story." Once they had all settled in, Steve began. "As I'm sure most of you know, I've had my up and downs since May 25, 1949. Even though many of you insisted I was not responsible, I was convinced I was responsible for the deaths of three good friends that night. I've also had such bad dreams. Some feature a raven who seems to caw 'Nevermore.' Many of you probably thought I was crazy. Well, I'm here to tell you today that I am not crazy. I have two people to thank for helping me, Nancy and Nick. Nancy has constantly helped me, and the last few days, Nick has led me to redemption. I don't want to get sappy and tied up in anything like a religious conversation about redemption, but I assure you I do feel redeemed. That's about it."

Nick leaned over and said to Nancy, "I guess that solves our concerns."

She kissed him on the cheek.

Obituary

Delphi, Alabama, March 18, 2022.

Steve Andrew Thompson, born on June 16, 1936, passed away quietly in his sleep at his home in Durham, North Carolina, on March 17, 2022, at age 86. His loving wife Nancy Dawson Thompson was by his bedside as he departed this earthly world, as were his three children Alice Thompson Mosley, Daniel Thompson, and Marvin Thompson.

Steve's parents were Delphi residents Andrew and Lillis Thompson. Andrew was the owner and editor of the *Delphi Delta News* for many years.

Steve led an exemplary life with many significant accomplishments. In 1949 the Ku Klux Klan rampaged Westtown, the Black community adjacent to Delphi, and killed twenty-five Black residents and burned down many homes in the Black community. Steve, while trying to help several of his Black friends, witnessed the murders of his friends Marvin Gibbs, Moses Douglas, and Dr. Joshua Marshall. Fourteen-year-old Steve testified at the trial of the three defendants found guilty of murder in the first degree. Several prominent Alabama historians have called the trial one of the most significant trials in the State's history, adding that but for Steve's courage and testimony, it is likely the defendants would have been acquitted.

Steve graduated with honors from Mountain Brook High School in Birmingham, Alabama. In 1957 he earned a BA, with honors, in English literature, from Dartmouth College. At Duke University he earned with honors a Master's degree and PhD in English literature with an emphasis on the works of William Shakespeare. At Duke he became a renowned professor of English literature having written books on English literature and Shakespeare, of which several have become highly acclaimed. He also enjoyed acting and appeared on many stages, especially summer stock festivals throughout the South, and occasionally performed with his wife, professional actress Nancy Dawson Thompson.

The *Delphi Delta News* asked one of Steve's grade school friends, Terry Burton, what was so unique about Steve. He replied, "Everything. He was smarter, read books all the time, and knew things I never would have dreamed of. But most important were his thoughts on race and equality. Even as a kid, he was way ahead of the times."

The *News* also reached out to Steve's friend, Nick McAdams, who lives in Philadelphia, Pennsylvania, and asked him what Shakespeare lines he thought Steve would like read at his memorial service. Nick responded, "There's so many, it's hard to choose. But if I'm asked to speak at the service in Durham, I would end my comments with a quotation from *Hamlet* when Horatio says: *Now cracks a noble heart. Good night, sweet prince, and flights of angels sing thee to thy rest.*"

A memorial service will be held in Durham, North Carolina, on April 2, 2022, at 11:00 a.m. at the First Presbyterian Church.

In lieu of flowers, the family requests donations to the Southern Poverty Law Center and the Equal Justice Initiative, both of which are in Montgomery, Alabama.

Obituaries also appeared in a number of newspapers including the *Montgomery Advertiser*, the *Mobile Press-Register*, the *Birmingham News*, the *Washington Post*, the Durham *Herald-Sun*, and the *New York Times*.

Notes

Nevermore is fiction and seeks to present a fresh narrative about Alabama in 1949. However, the author realizes several horrible events have outcomes that are unlikely.

This book bends the curve toward justice by using three names that most readers will recognize, as well as one name that many readers may not recognize.

- James (Big Jim) Folsom was the governor of Alabama, having served from 1947 to 1951, and again from 1955 to1959. Folsom was among the first southern governors to advocate a moderate position on integration and improvement of civil rights for African Americans. In his Christmas message on December 25, 1949, he said, "As long as the Negroes are held down by deprivation and lack of opportunity, the other poor people will be held down alongside them."
- E. D. Nixon was the President of Montgomery's branch of the National Association for the Advancement of Colored People (NAACP). Mr. Nixon, by profession, was a member of the Brotherhood of Sleeping Car Porters and was a Porter himself.
- Rosa Parks was the secretary of the local branch of the NAACP. On December 1, 1955, Mrs. Parks refused to give up her seat on a Montgomery bus to a white passenger. And thus, the Montgomery bus boycott began and Martin Luther King Jr. joined the effort and came to be the spokesperson for the Civil Rights Revolution until he was assassinated on April 4, 1968.
- Frank Minis Johnson Jr. certainly takes center stage in *Nevermore*. Johnson was born in Alabama in 1918 and was raised and educated in the state. He was a lifelong Republican, while Alabama was predominately Democratic in 1949. In 1955, President Dwight

Eisenhower appointed Johnson to be a Judge of the United States for the Middle District of Alabama, and he moved up the legal ladder to become a Senior Judge of the United States Court of Appeals for the Eleventh Circuit. In 1999, he died in his home in Montgomery. The many honors and accolades that Johnson received cannot be listed here. Following are a few decisions that will give you a better understanding of the man and why he was the perfect judge to oversee the trial scenes in *Nevermore*.

1. In 1956, Johnson ordered the racial integration of the public transportation system of the city of Montgomery, Alabama.
2. In 1961, Johnson ordered the Ku Klux Klan and Montgomery police to stop the beating and harassment of Freedom Riders attempting to integrate interstate bus travel.
3. In 1961 and 1962, Johnson ordered the desegregation of bus depots, such as the Montgomery Greyhound station and the Montgomery Regional Airport.
4. In March 1965, Johnson ruled that activists had the right to undertake the Selma to Montgomery march as a means to petition the government overturning Governor George Wallace's prohibition of the march as contrary to public safety.
5. Judge Johnson received death threats and ostracism for his role in advancing Civil Rights and was protected by federal marshals for nearly two decades.

Waights Taylor Jr.'s View of The Anatomy of Nevermore

What is a story? Is it fact or fiction or both? Most authors, including myself, struggle with these questions before creating their next book. The basic tenet of a book's anatomy is simple. It consist of three parts: the beginning, the middle, and the end.

Nevermore is a work of fiction and meets the basic tenet of a book. However, it needs a thorough explanation of its roots. Authors frequently source material that is based on their background and upbring.

I will take readers on a journey through an expanded anatomy of *Nevermore* in hopes of enhancing a readers understanding of the book's essence.

I was born in Birmingham, Alabama, in1937. Steve Thompson, the main character in the book, was born in Delphi, Alabama, in 1936. So, one could assume that Steve's character is somewhat based on me.

I was born into a family that had liberal principles. My grandparents and parents imbued in me their principles and beliefs. It must be said that most southern liberals were nothing like a New York City liberal.

My father, Waights Sr., had a profound impact on me in my early years, especially those in Livingston, Alabama, from 1949 through 1953. One Christmas Dad gave me an anthology of Edger Allan Poe's stories and poems. I devoured Poe's works as did young Steve. My mother, Rose, was equally supportive and had a good friend named Lillis. Dad was quite erudite in all things Shakespearean.

In 1949, my family moved to Livingstone where my father became the publisher and editor of the weekly newspaper *Our Southern Home*.

Livingstone is 117 miles southwest from Birmingham. It was a new experience for me, as I had never lived in such a small town. The town had a population of about 3,000, included the student population at Livingstone State Teachers College, which years later became the University of West Alabama. Livingston and *Nevermore's* fictitious town of Delphi could be considered sister towns. It is 106 miles between the two towns on a west to east latitude.

When my family moved to Livingston in 1949, I became friends with two black boys, Willie Jr. and Yank, who taught me things about hunting and fishing that I knew nothing about. One of the things they taught me was how to set a trot line. *Nevermore s* Steve became friends with Marvin and Billy who also taught Steve how to to set a trot line.

Of course, no story set in Alabama mostly in 1949 is complete that does not include the Ku Klux Klan. My father was a devout southern Democrat who wrote editorials for *Our Southern Home* decrying the formation of the Dixiecrat Party led by Strom Thurman. He also wrote editorials that took the Ku Klux Klan to task. The Klan threated to burn a cross in front of our house which was one block off the town square. Fortunately, it never came to pass, although I did witness a Klan cross burning in the square. When the Klan was active in the area, people hunkered down in their homes or wherever they lived, especially Black people.

I'll summarize for readers in a simple side-by-side table the important parallels between my personal story and Steve's story.

Waights' Story	Steve's Story
Waights Jr.	Steve
Waights Sr.	Andy
Rose	Lillis
Our Southern Home	*Delphi Delta News*
Livingston	Delphi
Willie Jr.	Marvin
Yank	Billy
Ku Klux Klan	Ku Klux Klan

Readers, I hope this journey through the anatomy of *Nevermore* has or will enhance your understanding of the book, Of course, it must be said that the characters in my story and Steve's story are certainly not equal. Each character, either real or fictional, has virtues and flaws.

Judge Johnson's instructions to the jury were taken, with slight modifications, from readily available trial transcripts on the Internet.

As to the book itself, the primary part is told in the middle of the book. This is the part where Steve and Marvin encounter, in just one chapter, the atrocities that the Ku Klux Klan committed on the Night of Terror. In the book, subsequent chapters on the trial resolve some of the issues but not all. I think it's important to tell stories about southern mores, especially involving the Ku Klux Klan and other hate groups. Many might say they know all about those issues and have heard enough. I would retort, since these events occurred in the past and continue to occur today: What are you doing about it?

Waights Taylor Jr. Santa Rosa, CA, April 2023

Acknowledgments

Thanks to writers and friends who read and commented on all or parts of the manuscript: Armando García-Dávila, Arnold Levine, Liz Martin, Mark Tate, and Terry Rowan.

Thanks to Ida Rae Egli and Necia Liles who edited the manuscript several times with keen eyes for my errors in content, grammar, and punctuation mistakes.

About the Author

Waights Taylor Jr. has written seven books, starting with two non-fiction books: *Alfons Mucha's Slav Epic: An Artist's History of the Slavic People* (2008), and the award-winning *Our Southern Home: Scottsboro to Montgomery to Birmingham—The Transformation of the South in the Twentieth Century* (2011).

A murder mystery trilogy followed, featuring private detectives Joe McGrath and Sam Rucker: the award-winning *Kiss of Salvation* (2014), *Touch of Redemption* (2016), and, concluding the trilogy, the award winning *Heed the Apocalypse* (2017).

A young adult novel followed, *Henry Tuttle: The Boy Who Ran to Glory* (2019).

Taylor's latest book, *Nevermore,* was published in 2023.

He lives in Santa Rosa, California, with his wife, Elizabeth Martin, surrounded by five wonderful children and seven terrific grandchildren.